LIGHT AT THE RAT POND

LIGHT AT THE RAT POND

Richard Newberry

WESTBOW
PRESS
A DIVISION OF THOMAS NELSON
& ZONDERVAN

Copyright © 2014 Richard Newberry.

All rights reserved. No part of this book may be used or reproduced by any means, graphic, electronic, or mechanical, including photocopying, recording, taping or by any information storage retrieval system without the written permission of the publisher except in the case of brief quotations embodied in critical articles and reviews.

WestBow Press books may be ordered through booksellers or by contacting:

WestBow Press
A Division of Thomas Nelson & Zondervan
1663 Liberty Drive
Bloomington, IN 47403
www.westbowpress.com
1 (866) 928-1240

Because of the dynamic nature of the Internet, any web addresses or links contained in this book may have changed since publication and may no longer be valid. The views expressed in this work are solely those of the author and do not necessarily reflect the views of the publisher, and the publisher hereby disclaims any responsibility for them.

Any people depicted in stock imagery provided by Thinkstock are models, and such images are being used for illustrative purposes only. Certain stock imagery © Thinkstock.

ISBN: 978-1-4908-5953-8 (sc)
ISBN: 978-1-4908-5954-5 (hc)
ISBN: 978-1-4908-5952-1 (e)

Library of Congress Control Number: 2014920135

Printed in the United States of America.

WestBow Press rev. date: 11/05/14

To Nan,
A pure-quill believer, encourager,
loving wife and friend.
Square dinkham.

PROLOGUE

He waited. He watched. He wished he didn't - sometimes.

He wondered why he must struggle. Hadn't he done good? Yes. Hadn't he done bad? Much. He knew good was right and bad was wrong, so why did he struggle with it? He felt good when he did right. And when he did bad . . . well, sometimes it felt so very good.

One thing he knew for certain, if he had a magic lamp with a genie inside who would grant only one wish, he wouldn't wish for riches or fame or power. No, he would wish away The Bad he liked to do. But he often lied to himself.

He waited and watched, not knowing what he would do. But that was a lie.

CHAPTER 1

Before the time of Will, the Icks had already endured the cancellation of Johnny Quest in 1968, which made us furious fourth graders, so we swore off cartoons forever.

"It ain't fair," Stink had said.

Kenny, sullen and peeved, added, "They take off all the good ones."

Tex, Dwight and I nodded agreement.

"We don't need their crumby cartoons," I said.

Defiance gleamed in the eyes of my fellow Icks. There was a collective, "Yeah!"

"I'd rather be outside anyway," said Dwight. "Cruisin'."

Kenny stood a little taller. "Pure quill, Dwight."

"Racing!" Tex exclaimed.

"Double pure quill," said Stink.

The Icks were outdoor dogs. Neither the hottest summer day or coldest winter one kept us inside - unless parents, against their saner judgment, made us stay inside.

In 1970, the year Will arrived, the ongoing war in Vietnam haunted me almost as much as Cus Lappin did. I told my mom, "I don't want to fight in the jungle. I'm no sissy (in our 1970 Ick world a sissy was a very bad thing), but I don't like jungle fighting."

Mom, sipping her coffee, raised a brow, said, "You have experience fighting in the jungle?"

"No - you know what I mean. It'd be hard to see in the jungle. I could see the enemy better in a desert. Wouldn't be as easy to sneak up on me."

"Try not to fret about it, Jack. You're only ten."

"Almost eleven." Though getting older put me closer to the draft and inevitable jungle warfare, it also put me closer to big-time freedom. And I didn't want Mom to forget her promise of allowing me to ride on the hard road when I turned eleven.

She frowned, then brightened. "You know, you're right. I almost forgot how old you are. Where's my mind? I guess it would be best for you to enlist now, rather than wait to get drafted. *I* certainly don't want the neighbors thinking *my* son is a sissy, do you?" She smiled big, blinked rapidly as she

1

widened her green eyes. She gave me the doofus look whenever I talked or acted like one. My mom's quirky, sometimes sarcastic, humor was a wonderful part of Katherine Hobbs.

"I'll drive you to town right after lunch. I need to pick up some shelf paper at Kresge anyway."

I grinned.

She held my hand, looked in my eyes. "Quit worrying about Vietnam, Jack Andrew Hobbs. It will be over before you're out of grade school."

I trusted Mom's words, for she was wise enough to know when to speak the plain truth as she knew it. I know she protected me from some things, but her straightforward approach to matters, her willingness to meet controversy, worked best. "You think so?"

"Cross my heart, hope to die, stick a needle in my eye." She knew how to zap my anxiety. She then added, "Of course by the time you're eligible for the draft we'll probably be fighting in a desert somewhere. So you'll be fine."

"Mom!"

She smiled.

"Don't forget you said when I'm eleven I get to ride on the hard road."

"Do you think I'm slipping into senility?"

"I don't know. What is it?"

She tilted her head and laughed.

We lived in east central Illinois outside the city limits of Doverville, a town of fifty thousand people in 1970. My dad, Andrew Hobbs, was killed in 1961 by Floyd Lappin; I was two. Dad's life insurance provided for most of our household expenses, but Mom still had to, and liked to, work. She taught piano, which wasn't work to her, and had a steady flow of students. She also filled in at Son-Ray Dry Cleaners, which was a short walk across Route 150, whenever Melba Flowers's pain was too much.

In 1970 America still made things; that's why the Corben family moved north to Doverville from Oxley, Arkansas in May, and that's when I met their oldest son Will. Thus began the time of Will.

Before summer's end in 1970 the Corbens and many of us in our neighborhood would have our worlds changed forever.

CHAPTER 2

Stink led early as usual, his mouse-like face and blue eyes pinched with intensity, but Tex stood up from her white banana seat and pedaled faster, determination surging through her blue jugular vein as she closed the gap on Stink. I was stuck racing in the dangerous middle of the pack. Dwight was close on my tail; I could hear the rattle from his empty radio cage on his handlebars. Kenny, as usual, brought up the rear of the pack from the onset of the race. This was a five lapper, and because they were bigger kids, Dwight and Kenny were more competitive in our longer races.

"Hey!" Stink shouted.

Tex had bumped his rear tire with her front tire. "Outta my way, little boy." Bumping Stink's tire nudged him to the outside enough for Tex to slip past him on the inside. "Wooo hooo!" she exclaimed, leaning forward through the handlebars and not looking back.

"That's cheatin'," Stink declared as he darted back to the inside, almost crashing into me.

Ten legs churned fast on the oval track's straights, and five sneakers scuffed dirt on each corner. Brakes, according to the Icks' unpublished code, were forbidden during Rat Pond races. Only sissies were cowardly enough to feel the need to stop impending injury by using their brakes.

Before the time of Will, and even before the time of the Icks, the Rat Pond had been a place of adventure for kids. An ancient, narrow dirt path had been pounded into the black soiled hillside by years of soles and bike tires. The path started just off the alley above, then sliced a dark, steep trail through varying verdant growth for about twenty feet until it reached the pond's floor. But it was the Icks who widened the path and built the race track. We cleared, dug and scraped the fertile black soil and eventually wore an oval racing area into the center of the Rat Pond. Heavy rains meant mud, and a little mud was good for cool crashes, but too much ruined a good thing. Dwight, the Icks' biggest and brightest brain, designed a drain system using discarded plastic pipe we had found. The Icks buried the pipe and excess water filtered through it and dumped into the murky pond east of the track. Dwight's smarts kept us racing.

Today's event was the annual School's Out Race; a chase for victory to begin our summer.

Richard Newberry

Two laps to go in the five lapper. I stood and pumped my legs, drew closer to Tex's rear tire as I secured my spot in second place. But it was Tex who had first said, "Second means you're just the first to lose."

Dwight's radio cage rattled behind me. He churned his big legs and tried to pass me on the outside; his milk-chocolate hands were clenched tight around the black grips covering the chrome handlebars. Out of nowhere, Stink shot to the inside of me, and once again I occupied the dangerous middle.

A shaft of morning light broke through the Rat Pond's shadows, flicking a quick spot light on Dwight's ample face, where I glimpsed a grin. "Got us a Jack sandwich, Stink!"

"Not for long!" I shouted, shooting out from between them. "See you suckers!"

But I had committed a grave error. I was racing way too fast to make the next turn. Imminent crash seconds ahead! Then I heard it. I would not admit to having heard it, or let any of the Icks think the voice had originated from within me. I convinced myself the source of the voice came from a nefarious creature lurking somewhere outside the track. The voice absolutely did not come from any internal sense of mine that said, *You might get hurt here.* And I knew it wasn't from me because the voice - sounding extremely sissified - said, *Use your brakes!*

I threw down my left sneaker, knowing and not lying to myself that without using my bike's brakes doom awaited.

I heard Stink exclaim, "Summer's first wreck coming!"

When my sneaker hit the earth it wasn't the usual smooth connection to make a good turn. My shoe hit, my leg jolted up and down, I had zero influence on the handlebars, and the bike wobbled wildly out of control. I veered across the track, miraculously avoided Dwight and Stink, then slammed to a stop against the rough bark of a cottonwood, which we called Iron Tree.

"Wow," said Kenny, racing by.

On a nice May morning as this one was, it would not have been unusual for one or more of the hobos who found refuge at the Rat Pond to be lazing about near Iron Tree. Normally the hobos stayed west of the track in a thick-brushed section of the Rat Pond we called Hoboland. But every once in a while, Hobo Hairy or Eyeballs relaxed in the soft dirt and decades of decaying leaves that surrounded the large cottonwood. But if they were alert enough to hear the first sound of our bikes approaching the Rat Pond, they moved like ghosts to prevent detection. Thankfully, no hobos rested by the tree that day in May.

With his omnipresent gregarious smile and contagious north Arkansas drawl, Will hollered, "Nice crash there, Yank!"

I waved like I meant to crash my bike into an unrelenting tree.

Will's smile broadened as he wagged his head.

Light at the Rat Pond

I looked for serious bike damage; nothing except twisted handlebars, which I straightened and would tighten when I got back to the garage. I walked my bike to where Will stood and watched the last two laps with him. Watching and not racing was like Christmas without presents.

Tex increased the shadowy daylight between her bike and Dwight's. By height, Kenny had almost caught up to her; yet in May of 1970 Tex still stood tallest among the Icks.

"Go, Tex!" Will encouraged.

Her straight blonde hair waved at the racers behind her, and her determined blue eyes would never look back. Her clenched jaw said what the Icks already knew: Sandra "Tex" Wonderlin did not like to lose. And in five-lap races, she rarely did.

I watched Will watch the race. A glint of sunlight glistened off the crucifix hanging from his neck. His rapt brown eyes followed every racer, and he appeared to be deriving prodigious joy from just watching the Icks have fun. That reinforced what I thought I already knew from the first time we met: Will Corben was pure quill (genuine, the real deal). He genuinely liked people, wanted the best for them.

"One more lap!" he said to the racers, then turned to me, smiling. "I can't wait to race with y'all."

I smiled back. My eyes were drawn to Jesus, hanging on the cross, tiny specks of red were visible on His hands, side and feet. The Savior rested just above Will's heart. "Same here."

Tex let out a "wooo hooo" as the race neared its end with her securely in the lead in the annual School's Out Race.

It never required hindsight for the Icks to appreciate the area we named - before the time of Will - the Rat Pond. It was a crude, basically oval bowl the approximate length and breadth of an oversized high school football field; decades of untended growth surrounded it. A sentinel of small trees like mulberries, and tall trees like the cottonwood we named Iron Tree, horseweed and goosefoot, thorny briars, tangled brush and patches of gold-tipped prairie grass created a natural coliseum, sequestering the Rat Pond from the rest of the world in varying shades of green.

The area was bordered on the south by a frontage road, Bates Drive, then Route 150. To the north was an alley, the N & W Railroad tracks, then Warren Avenue, and the neighborhoods on the north side of the tracks where Kenny, Will and Dwight lived. Just west of the Rat Pond the N & W had its switchyard, and to the east a strip of houses and small businesses dotted Bates Drive, and in that strip was where Tex and I lived; Stink lived farther east, south of Route 150.

Richard Newberry

He only grumbled about his "longer than everybody else's" bike ride when the Icks' plans included something he wasn't keen about, but that was rare.

When you swooped down the path to the Rat Pond floor you discovered three, almost equal parts: our race track in the middle, a jungle-looking area to the west we named Hoboland, and on the east side was the actual dark, murky water from which came part of the name Rat Pond.

Will clapped and said, "Way to go, Tex!" as we watched her win.

I was, and I'm sure the other Icks were, taken aback by Will's cheering. Before the time of Will we didn't cheer for the victor. We all wanted to win, and didn't feel up to congratulating the person who had just beaten us, especially right after the race. Sore losers, maybe. But we also never had an audience before.

"Wooo hooo." Tex raised tufts of dust as she slid-stopped in front of Will and me. "First again," she said.

Dwight, Stink and Kenny coasted in behind her, dejected, but heads up. Losing to Sandra "Tex" Wonderlin bore no shame.

She clicked her tongue, wagged her head. "I was hoping for some competition, boys. Guess you like eating my dust."

Disgruntled, Stink said, "I had it till you crawled up my back tire." He looked to me. "You saw it, Jack. It wasn't a fair bump."

I shrugged. "Didn't really see it happen."

Tex punched my arm. "Because you were busy kissing old Iron Tree."

Stink continued. "I know bumpin' is part of racin', but it wasn't a fair bump. Not square dinkham. No way."

All the Icks had a little sweat going, but Kenny's too-big forehead flowed like Niagara Falls. "Man, I can't cut dirt in these short races." A year older than us because he flunked first grade, Kenny now rode the elementary school rails with the rest of us, except Dwight, who had to go to city school.

Dwight said to Kenny, "Our bigger bodies do better in the ten and fifteen lappers."

"Hey!" said Tex. "I'm taller than both of you."

I said, "I don't think he's talking about their height."

"I'm almost taller than you," Kenny said to Tex, wiping the flow of sweat from his bountiful forehead. His mom making him wear a crew cut and not letting him grow bangs seemed egregious.

"Okay - boys." She shifted her blue eyes sideways to take in the last race's losers. "We'll do a ten lapper next."

Kenny nodded slowly, fixed his mouth in a pinched determination. "You got it." We had all just passed fifth grade, but poor Kenny probably should have been held back again. Sometimes stupid and inevitably hurtful things are done

Light at the Rat Pond

in the name of pride and a wayward notion of misguided human fairness. "Let's line up," he said.

Kenny Hook's intellectual ability, to be kind, was stunted; yet his loyalty could not be bribed, pried, beaten or driven out of him. The Icks admired his relentless fealty, particularly Dwight, who once told me, "I'll take that over book smarts any day. A lot of smart people are pretty stupid." Dwight occasionally took up for Kenny when needed, but didn't make it a habit, for Dwight knew, to make it in the world, Kenny would have to fight and work to make his own way. And Kenny surprised us at times when he randomly lobbed bits of wisdom and knowledge at us.

"Hold up, Kenny," said Dwight. "I need a second before we start again."

"You tired already?" I asked.

He smiled at me. "Well, I did race the *whole* five laps, Jack."

The Icks chuckled. Tex said, "First race, first wreck."

I mocked a smile back at her.

"I'm not tired," said Dwight. "But I gotta excuse myself." We watched him head for cover near Hoboland.

All the Icks wore sneakers from our previous year's gym class, and all but Dwight wore blue jeans. The semi-uniformity in play gear broke down after that. The Icks, except for Will and Dwight, wore T-shirts all summer long. I never saw Will, outside of gym class, wear anything other than short-sleeved button-downs. Dwight, on the other hand, defined haute couture. His "groovy-smooth" attire shouted at us in a fashion voice of bold and lavish polyester knits. He was the first (and only) kid I knew to be proud of wearing stripes with plaids. The penchant for Dwight's "groovy-smooth" dress began at the beginning of third grade, and it made me uneasy, but since he was my best friend, I developed a certain clothing tolerance.

"Hurry up," Tex said. "I'm ready to whip you boys again."

Will, in his pleasant southern parlance, said, "That was a good race, y'all. Fun to watch."

I checked my handlebars again, then said to Will, "It's gonna be more fun when you're racing with us."

"Pure quill," said Kenny.

I nodded. "We'll have your racer ready by tonight."

"Thanks for all you're doin', Yank. Fixing me a bike and all."

Will migrated north bike less. To the Icks, it was an atrocity. Tex once said, "If you don't have a bike, why have legs?"

Kenny, looking at Will with a sadness that exemplified our feelings for the plight of the bike less, said, "I'd rather be brum and so sick I puke out my nose than not have a bike."

7

Richard Newberry

Solemn nods from the Icks.

In the 1970 world of the Icks our bikes defined who we were, what we aspired to become. A doofus or sissy kept their bike as it came from the store, but maybe added lights or - make us puke - streamers. Riding with the Icks demanded bikes that were pure quill and unique to the rider.

Dwight ambled back from the brush as Tex said to Will, "It's not right you not having a bike." Her tone indicated he had been denied basic rights, like liberty and the pursuit of happiness, or food and shelter. "But Jack's got you a cool one almost ready."

Will grinned, nodded.

I built, repaired and restored each bike the Icks raced and cruised. What customizing was beyond my ability I took to Texal Wonderlin's machine shop, Tex's dad. Texal wouldn't do it for me, but allowed me to use his tools and guidance to complete projects.

I said to Will, "Next we've got to find the stuff to build you a cruiser."

"I think one bike will be okay."

The Icks scoffed at the idea.

Dwight, settling atop his banana seat, said, "You need a racer and a cruiser. A racer says one thing, Will, but your cruiser says who you are."

"Square dinkham," said Kenny.

Stink still had a fuss to ride and didn't want to get off yet. "I would've won if she didn't bump -"

Tex screamed.

CHAPTER 3

Katherine Hobbs sat in her sun-filled kitchen and enjoyed the last few sips of black coffee before she got busy again. Jack was already out the door and on his bike; she probably wouldn't see or hear from him until lunchtime. School had just let out for the summer, yet unlike some parents, Kate appreciated having her son home. She smiled over the coffee cup as she thought maybe she'd be less appreciative if, like Melba Flowers, she had three children home for the summer.

The smile faded as a familiar taunt crept inside her, trying to spoil the peaceful morning. A formidable enemy attacked when unexpected, and this familiar mocking had insidiously good timing. Instinctively, Kate touched her gold wedding band with her thumb and forefinger. Over the years the ring had become a talisman to her when she was accosted by the Creeping Taunt. It helped sometimes; sometimes it didn't.

She closed her eyes, said, "I will not listen to you today." She thought about Jack's birthday, playing the piano, friends like Melba and Nadine, learning to hang and finish drywall - good things. Kate thwarted the enemy's derision. "I know you'll be back. But not today, Buster."

Her green eyes drifted to the kitchen's large window where a cool breeze soughed through the screen she and Jack had put in last evening. She listened to the wavering songs of robins carrying on their spring business, and heard the whine of tires on Route 150 as cars and trucks headed in to and out of Doverville. Kate sipped the coffee cup dry, looked at the kitchen's worn linoleum, paneled walls, old cabinets and ugly, pea-green Formica counters. She wagged her head as she had many times before at the person who had chosen such a color.

She said to the kitchen, "You are next on my list."

Tragedy was the Great Revealer. Months after Andrew was murdered, Kate began to learn things about herself she never would have believed. Some weaknesses were magnified and she continued to work on improving them, but strengths she didn't know she possessed also were revealed. One of the biggest things she was learning was that most individual limitations were self-imposed.

For instance, Kate, without any formal or informal apprenticeship, had taught herself carpentry, and she and Jack were in the process of remodeling their home a room at a time. Texal Wonderlin - his wife Nadine was one of

Richard Newberry

Kate's best friends - owned and operated a neighborhood machine shop and knew a thing or two about using his hands to earn a good living. He once told Kate, "You've turned yourself into a pretty decent carpenter." The statement carried heavy weight because Texal was meticulous and short with praise; he didn't say things he didn't mean.

So boosted by rare praise from her neighbor, Kate and Jack were learning how to install floors, drywall, some plumbing and general repairs. Texal cautioned her about plumbing, "You might want to hire a plumber for certain jobs," and warned, practically threatened, her away from electricity without someone to be hands-on with her. "I know you could learn it, Kate. Not a doubt in my mind. But you mess up with electricity, it's not like ill-fitted plumbing that gets a leak. No, ma'am. Electricity will kill you dead." Texal, therefore, availed himself whenever it involved wiring at the Hobbs' home.

A year earlier, when Jack was only nine, Texal told her, "We both know Jack is handy - no he's more than that. The boy has a gift. Gets it from Andy I suppose. Yep, he does. And he's catching on quick. He'll know how to do it all by the time he's eleven or twelve."

Jack, like his father, had amazing talent with his hands and tools. She wanted a little credit because of her ability to play piano, but Jack would never be a pianist. The detached garage behind their house was the hangout for the Icks when they weren't pedaling to adventure. The garage also housed Andrew's collection of tools, and his son used them deftly. Jack fixed the Icks' bikes, changed oil in Kate's car, did the tune-ups, and even replaced the car's fuel pump and starter - before he was eleven!

Eleven. Jack would be eleven in June. Hadn't she and Andrew just gushed over their baby as he slept in the white bassinet next to their bed? They couldn't, and didn't want to, take their eyes from Jack's soft, pink flesh, his tiny mouth and fingers, and his peaceful baby sleep. Each subtle, newborn movement seemed a miracle.

"Is he still breathing?" Andrew would ask, leaning closer to his son.

Kate smiled and admired her doting husband/new father. "He's fine, Andrew."

It seemed only yesterday when Andrew had encouraged Jack up and walking at ten months. The new father beamed at his son's accomplishment. Andrew stuck his thumbs in his shirt, posed as if giving a formal speech, and said, "Give a child a walker, and he will only go where it will allow him. Teach a child to walk, and he will go where he wishes."

"Great, Andrew. I can't wait to see where our ten-month-old wishes to go."

Andrew Hobbs smiled at his wife. One of the first places baby Jack walked was directly toward their sharp-edged coffee table. A stumble and thump later,

Light at the Rat Pond

Jack had a bleeding gash on his chin. Kate watched her husband comfort Jack, then calmly remove the table from the living room. She never saw that piece of furniture again.

"Eleven," Kate said, clearing the breakfast dishes to the sink. She poured the bacon grease out of the black iron skillet into an empty milk carton. Passing clouds eclipsed the sun's light that had poured through the kitchen window, casting the room into a somber shadow.

Andrew had helped potty train Jack, and then the great husband/father was gone forever. Kate absently washed the dishes as the familiar taunt tried to work its way inside. "Stop," she quietly demanded.

Now Jack was old enough to be worried about fighting in jungle warfare. She sighed. "Too fast. Too soon."

She finished the dishes, slipped into the tiny laundry room just off the kitchen and her slender fingers began routinely folding socks and T-shirts and other cottons. She thought back to a conversation she had had with her mother almost seven years ago. Kate had been standing where she stood now, folding laundry, while Irma dictated to her from the kitchen.

"Katherine, you are twenty-eight years old, and –"

"I know how old I am, Mom."

"And Jack is four now and is going to be five soon."

Kate stayed busy with the laundry, thinking, *Thank you for the obvious.*

"Andrew has been gone now for two years –"

Irma made it sound as if Kate's murdered husband had simply wandered off and not found his way home.

"– and I think it's time you became interested in finding a husband. Besides, Jack needs a man around, to be a father. And if you want to have any more children, you've got to get started . . . very soon."

Kate didn't respond; too many times she'd heard this decree.

Yet Irma added a twist to her speech when she cleared her throat and said, "I know losing Andrew was beyond what you could have imagined, a . . . living nightmare. I know when your father dropped dead at the store I sure didn't know what to do."

Irma's gold rings clinked against the porcelain cup as she took a drink of coffee. "With Maury gone I was a basket case. My mind whirled. I didn't know half the time if I was coming or going. Three children to raise," she sighed. "But time passed, and healing came. I moved on, Kate. Maury would've wanted it."

Maurice Murphy and Irma were married for almost twenty years. Happily? Kate supposed so, but what do young children really know about their parents' marriage? Kate knew her dad was an affable man who laughed easily and people seemed to genuinely like him. Everywhere they went in Doverville people

11

Richard Newberry

knew Maury. And their inclination was to return the smile he offered. Kate also knew her dad died too soon. Yet she wasn't so sure he would have wanted his widow garnering a variety of men and their company.

"Are you listening to me, Katherine?"

"Yes, Mom," she said, not turning from the laundry.

Irma cleared her throat again; a sign she was having trouble spitting out what she really wanted to say. "This isn't easy - Katherine - but I have to ask. Have you somehow been . . . soured on men?"

Kate stopped folding a T-shirt.

Irma stammered, "Is - is . . . has the trauma been - you know, uh - has it been so dramatic that you no longer like men?"

Kate turned, "What?!"

Irma stood near the kitchen table, nary a strand of her forever-auburn, wavy hair out of place, enough Maybelline to take her back ten years, and wearing a fashionable, yet immodest yellow dress. She put the coffee cup on the table. "I'm just concerned you've changed -"

"Changed?!" Kate wondered if her mom's dress was too tight and restricting the flow of blood to her brain.

Irma gathered herself, said firmly, "Just tell me, Katherine: Do you still *like* men?"

A white sock dangling from her hand, Kate rolled her eyes, wagged her head, then laughed.

"I do not think it is funny."

Kate faked a deadly serious look. "You're right, Mom. This isn't funny." Kate burst out laughing.

Irma bristled. She stood even more erect. "I am not going to be mocked by my own child."

Kate put the sock on the dryer, turned back to her offended mother. "Jack's father is dead, Mom. I know he's not out for some long walk and I'm not waiting for him to come home again. I have and am moving on. And why do you think I have to have a husband right this second?"

"I don't like your tone."

Kate just stared at her.

"You know perfectly well that raising a four-year-old isn't easy -"

"Jack's a good boy."

"I know, but he needs a man's influence, just like you could use a man in your life."

It came out before Kate could stop it. "No, Mom, I don't. It's *you* who has to have several men in your life."

Irma's eyes grew. Her mouth pinched. "What are you saying?"

Light at the Rat Pond

"Nothing. Never mind." She turned back to the laundry.

Irma didn't pursue the truth her daughter had breached, instead she said, "Jack won't be a cute little boy forever. Teenage years are out of this world, Katherine. Lord knows and so do I. So do I. Children make lasting, stupid decisions at that age."

That was an insinuation that hurt Kate. She looked back at Irma. "Thanks, Mom."

"It wasn't just you, Katherine. Don't be so sensitive. Belle and Steven had their share of poor decisions."

But theirs added together didn't equal Kate's, and Irma, subtly and not so subtly over the years, reminded Kate of that. She even had a special name for Kate's most reproachable act: the Deplorable Indiscretion.

And the Deplorable Indiscretion didn't need to be brought to Kate's remembrance. Many were the days that she punished herself because of real and supposed ramifications due to the Deplorable Indiscretion.

Irma's rings clinked against porcelain as she fidgeted with the cup. She cleared her throat, said, "So. You still like men, and you have aspirations of finding one someday?"

It had been years since Kate caused great grief to her mother with the Deplorable Indiscretion. Why not stir things up a little. She shrugged and did not answer her.

13

CHAPTER 4

Tex screamed as often as blue moons graced night skies.

She flailed at the air above her handlebars, almost tipped over with her red racer. Five other pairs of eyes tried to spot her foe.

I finally saw it and said, "Man, Tex, it's only a sweat bee."

She paused her attack to glare at me. "I don't care!" She continued the assault.

The Icks knew of nothing Tex Wonderlin feared – except bees. Any wayward bee invading her airspace was instantly attacked with intent to annihilate.

I clapped my hands, thus ending the tiny sweat bee's purported malicious existence.

"Thanks," she said.

"Still," said Stink, "I had it won until she ran right up my a-apple."

From the time of Will the Icks worked at taming our miniscule use of foul language when we were around our new friend. Curse words and phrases, therefore, were discarded for more euphemistic expressions which used fruit, vegetables, types of grain, fabrics, combinations thereof . . . or whatever popped into our young minds. I know they were less offensive to Will's ears, but I don't know if they proved as cathartic as household vulgarities.

"Quit with the sore loser, Stink," said Dwight. He toed down his kickstand and ambled across the race track toward an old box elder we named Booty Tree. The tree had a small hollow about four feet above the ground and we used the hollow to stash our oof (money) tube and other Ick assets. Dwight kept his transistor radio in it during races.

Dwight straddled his orange racer and said, "Tex's win was pure quill." He set the black and gold radio into the small cage that was mounted between his racer's handlebars. He had a similar cage mounted to his orange cruiser; Texal Wonderlin had made them. He snapped shut the cage's lid and clicked on the radio. CCR's *Up Around the Bend* was playing. "Man, I like that song, but they're gonna wear out another good one."

"They always do," said Stink.

"They" was The Big 89 WLS in Chicago.

I said, "I'm not tired of this one yet."

14

Light at the Rat Pond

Kenny swiped sweat from his forehead. "I got sick of that one about troubled bridges."

"*Bridge Over Troubled Waters*," Dwight corrected. He knew the singers, song titles and most of the words of the songs we heard. Dwight Flowers, besides being a groovy-smooth dresser, dug music.

"I hadn't heard hardly any of this music until y'all. Sounds good to me."

Tex clicked her tongue. "No bike. No music. You have been deprived."

Will just smiled.

"We gonna race, or what?" Stink asked.

Tex bumped her front tire into mine. "Speaking of racing, nice wreck out there, Jack." She tilted her head, glanced sideways at me. "Did you start to use your brakes?"

How in the world could she . . . ? I lied. "Never even thought about it."

Somehow, I think she knew the thought had briefly entered my mind. Like my mom, Tex had mysterious ways of sensing things that were hidden to most of the outside world. I later discovered it was a phenomenon generally common to the female species.

Will asked, "Why do y'all call this the Rat Pond anyway?"

"Big rats in there," answered Stink, pointing toward the water. "Big white ones."

"White ones?"

The Icks nodded and looked across the track to where the placid, murky water covered the earth. Shafts of sunlight dappled its dark surface, and like a reflection from a poor mirror feral growth around the pond could be seen on the water. At the far east end a black, rotting limb jutted up from a tree buried below the water; smack in the middle of the pond a third of a rusting burn barrel - an empty fifty-five gallon drum - mounded out of the water. The steep north bank rose twenty feet or so to meet the brush that bordered the alley. Dumpers chose the northeast corner because of access and the water was deeper there, so yesterday's treasures were more easily concealed. By 1970 dumpers were few and far between, but we occasionally scavenged the verdant north bank for discarded treasures. The junk we didn't pick up was hidden by brush and briars and material decay.

Will said, "Doesn't look very deep."

"It's not," said Dwight. "Down there where that limb sticks out is the deepest. Maybe three feet."

We didn't know the Rat Pond's original need, or who owned the property. It seemed to have been the remnant of some ancient and abandoned dig. Outside of rain runoff, its water source was a mystery. Shorty Morgan, who owned or had owned every acre of land in our world, said the property belonged to the

15

Richard Newberry

railroad. Nobody ran us off the property, or seemed concerned we were playing there; that was what mattered to us.

"Rats big as dogs," said Kenny, catching up to Stink's statement.

"Wow," said Will.

"They ain't that big," said Stink. "More like big tomcats."

"That's still big, y'all."

"Square dinkham," Kenny said.

The Icks were drawn to adventure like ladies to a newborn, but we never ventured into the pond's murky water. We poked and prodded with sticks, but that was it. In the early spring the water had a translucent quality, by May it was murky and summer's dog days brought a slimy green creeping yuck. The water never made a foul odor, but it was also never inviting.

"Look!" Tex pointed toward the south bank.

"Yep," I said.

"Don't usually see them this early in the day," said Dwight. "They usually start moving later."

Will strode across the track for a closer look. The rest of us had already seen plenty of the big rats; the awe had faded, but we joined Will for his sake of excitement.

"I see it movin' in the weeds over yonder!"

"Yep," I said.

Stink, sniffing the tips of his fingers, said, "You'll get to see it good in a second. But it'll be gone quick."

Spring storms, steady rains and life's stuff limited our use of the Rat Pond since Will arrived the first of May. This day our new friend would experience much, but not all, of the Rat Pond's mystique; he would meet Hobo Hairy and Eyeballs another day.

The big rat hesitated under the green umbrella of May apples. "What's it waitin' for?"

"Be patient," Dwight said. "I think they're a little scared of the light."

Will's brown eyes were locked onto the May apples; our eyes stayed on him. He looked older than eleven, probably because of what Tex had said about him his second day at school: "He's better looking than Elvis." She stated it as a matter of fact, no innuendo, just an observation. For in 1970, as far as I could discern, she had not yet fostered interest in boys outside of beating us in bike races and baseball. She had, however, by spring 1970, disclosed an affection for punching my arms.

Will's comeliness, wavy brown hair, and southern drawl had captured the attention of many fourth and fifth grade girls at Kickapoo Elementary School; even some of the sixth grade girls took notice of the attractive and amiable new

Light at the Rat Pond

boy from Oxley, Arkansas. Jealousy lurked behind the suspicious eyes of the boys who were getting old enough to care about such things. The Ick males seemed oblivious to whether Will looked like Elvis or Eddie Munster.

The May apples shook.

Said Stink, "Big rat on the move."

Will's eyes widened with his smile.

"Here it comes," I said.

CHAPTER 5

Scared would not do. Terrified was . . . better, but not quite enough for some. Paralyzed and tears guaranteed success. Scared wore off, terrified worked on all but the Foolish Brave, and the Foolish Brave taught him that they needed the ultimate level of fear which produced paralysis and tears. He knew who needed what level just by observing them when he warned them of the consequences of their reactions. He could fathom beyond scared, nervous eyes and terrified, quaking lips and limbs. His was a visceral discernment, a supernatural gift, he supposed, of being able to see inside the Prize, to their core. Some called it the human soul or spirit. He didn't believe the nonsense of an eternal soul or spirit of the human animal because he knew how to kill it.

It was exciting to look inside them and see who meant the most to them. Unfortunately many were predictable. The predictable, unlike the Foolish Brave, were defeated by what terrified them. And what terrified them wasn't threats of horrible consequences to be afflicted upon their mother or father or brother or sister or grandparents. Those threats scared them, but they didn't scare them into being silenced. He knew their predictive cowardice, could see it in them. Hurting their family would not bring the ultimate silence, it would not kill their soul, for their utmost concern was for themselves. They loved themselves more than anyone, above any other, and they knew it, though probably never admitted it - until squarely confronted by terror. They were easily silenced and defeated because it only involved *their* precious lives.

He would not deny his own self-love. He wasn't stupid, or a hypocrite; even the hypocritical church goers had to wrestle with the words of their beloved Jesus when He talked about loving our neighbors as ourselves. Self-love, recognized by one of fiction's most precious characters. Nobody could deny self-love's existence, it took no god-man to recognize it. Humans pretended to be altruistic and not in love with themselves, but the hypocrites lied, especially those enamored with ending their own miserable lives. No greater love has a man than for himself. That made him smile.

He told himself he wasn't a liar or a hypocrite because he sometimes loathed himself, he didn't pretend, he didn't deny the evil inside. Well, he did have to hide some things. Maybe he was, after all, just a little bit of a liar with a hint of hypocrisy. It was necessary for survival. He smiled again.

Light at the Rat Pond

The Foolish Brave. The few he had encountered intrigued him, made the bad he did more exciting, more of a challenge. They too had self-love abiding within, yet they chose others above themselves. Freakish, he thought, yet undeniable. The destruction of the Foolish Brave brought him the greatest joy. Their defeat and silence never came easily, and like any hard-to-obtain prize, when obtained, brought the greater sense of accomplishment. Just getting the Foolish Brave to the verge of paralysis and tears . . . well, what in life was better?

CHAPTER 6

Horns blasting, bells clanging, black locomotives thrusting their diesel engines, the pshhhtt! of compressed air, and steel slamming against steel resounded often from the N & W switchyard that occupied a chunk of ground west and a little north of the Rat Pond. Natives rarely heard the commotion, yet visitors always heard it. Visitors and newcomers to the neighborhood required a time of hearing adjustment because of all the train racket. Multiple pairs of rusty-colored steel rails funneled into two pairs. One pair tracked west, the other headed east toward Doverville; in Doverville the rails gradually turned north toward Chicago. Those rails paralleled our alley for more than three miles.

The sudden violent bang! and boom! of full and empty boxcars being slammed into by charging locomotives would at times arouse even the natives' hearing. It was one such sudden collision that caused Will to flinch.

The rat's pointy white nose poked out from under a May apple, followed by its scuttling, furry white body.

Will exclaimed, "There it goes!"

The rat quickly vanished in the lush undergrowth.

"Hey, y'all." He turned and faced our content faces.

"Some big rat, huh, Will?" asked Kenny.

Stink boasted, "Probably ain't that big in Arkansas."

"I got some news you might not like," said Will.

A sudden, strange look overcame Dwight's big face.

"What?" Tex asked.

"Yeah, what?" chimed Stink.

"That was no rat."

Dwight's brown eyes fell to the earth.

I said, "It wasn't? Yes it was."

"Is that the critter y'all see all the time, Yank?"

We looked at one another - except for Dwight - and nodded at Will. "Pretty much all look like that. Yeah," I said.

"Well, that ain't a rat."

Dwight closed his eyes, put a hand to his forehead, muttered, "I knew it. I knew it."

"Knew what?" I asked.

20

Light at the Rat Pond

Dwight raised his eyes as Kenny - looking like Dwight's answer would determine the entire world's fate - asked, "What do you know, Dwight?"

"That that big thing isn't a rat," Will answered, trying to spare Dwight.

It was the second blasphemous utterance Will had made in less than a minute. The Icks - except Dwight - decried Will's obvious error.

"You're not from here!"

"You're crazy, man. It was too a rat!"

"You don't know what you're talking about!"

"Yeah," Kenny added.

"Well, then," said Will, "I guess I ate rat before."

Generally speaking, Will wasn't known for bragging, teasing or melodrama, therefore Kenny's eyes widened as he asked, "You eat rats?"

"I don't think so."

A clamor persisted at the Rat Pond because of the obvious effrontery cast against the area's name sake.

Tex, with a daring, skeptical brow, asked, "What do *you* say it is, Will?"

Dwight answered instead. "It's a possum."

Except for Will, I think there was a gasp among the other Icks. Dwight couldn't hide a strange look of shame or betrayal . . . or failure. Maybe it was a coalescing of the three. Whatever it was, it was painful.

"Possum?" I said.

"Yep," said Will. He wasn't boasting, for he knew the magnitude of the situation.

"Possum," said Kenny.

Dwight nodded.

"Beans and rice!" Stink exclaimed.

"They look like rats," said Tex.

I said, "I think they're a kind of rat."

Dwight sighed. The weight of the truth was upon him. "No, they're not."

"They look just like rats," Tex said.

"They sure do," Kenny said, avoiding the truth.

"But they're not," said Dwight. "They're marsupials. Rats are rodents."

Will said, "Never heard the word marsupial till now."

Kenny was gazing to where we last saw the creature. "They sure look like rats."

"You're right," said Will. "I can see y'all thinking it's a rat."

A train horn moaned a blow, putting a note to the Icks' despondency.

Will told us about his Granny Corben cooking possum and lathering it with barbecue sauce. "I think it tastes about the same as coon."

"You eat raccoon?"

21

Richard Newberry

"It's been a while, Yank."

The somberness was broken when the Icks - except Will - burst with laughter. He eventually joined us with a genuine grin.

"Y'all are gonna have to try it sometime."

More laughter.

When the teasing and jesting subsided, I asked Dwight, "Why didn't you tell us they were possums?"

"Yeah," said Stink.

"Well, at first I wasn't real sure. Then, the more I saw - I knew. But we'd already named it the Rat Pond. I didn't want to mess it up."

Will said, "I think it's easy to get confused when something looks like something it's not. Know what I mean?"

The Icks nodded. But on that May day none of us had any idea how dangerous that confusion could be. The days ahead would reveal it.

"I'll tell you this," I said, "I don't want to change the name to the Possum Pond."

"Sounds sissy," said Tex.

"Yeah," said Stink and Kenny.

Dwight looked at the water, then surveyed the race track and Hoboland. "It's always been the Rat Pond to us."

"It's a good name, y'all. And I'll bet there's rats in there."

"Gotta be," I said, feeling a bit of vindication. "Gotta be." Nods all around. A name change would not be forthcoming.

The sound of a slide-stop and bike chain rattling against its guard took our attention to the alley above us where a rider loomed. He was at the entrance to the Rat Pond, poised to shoot down the trodden hill. The bike was probably stolen.

Dwight clicked off the radio in the middle of Rare Earth's *Get Ready*. Looking up, I said, "Oh, crud."

No confusion existed about who or what was Cus Lappin. He looked like and was pure-quill wicked-mean.

22

CHAPTER 7

He rode alone.

Most kids mean enough to cut dirt alongside Cus Lappin were serving time in Doverville Detention Center - a facility Cus also served in from time to time. He stood on the pedals and coasted down the hill, slid-stopped in front of us. His dust fell on our sneakers.

"The big bad Icks," he said, swiping long, dirty, brown hair away from his eyes. "Retard. Blackie. Weasel. Barbie. Hobbs." I was not offended at the lack of a nickname. "The sissies are all here."

Animals and insects sensed the presence of a malevolent creature as birds hushed singing, buzzing bees vanished from the air and the creeping and crawling things hid.

Stink cracked, "Out on parole, Cus?"

Together we feared him not. But like a cunning wolf, Cus was patient, and would wait for the sheep to be scattered from the flock, then attack.

"Shut up, Weasel, unless you want me to pound your face - again." His threatening eyes were hazel, and his left one was slightly lazy, so when he shifted his glare toward Will, only his right eye followed. "Who's the pretty boy?"

Will stepped forward before we could warn him and extended his hand to Cus. "I'm Will Cor-"

WHAP! Cus growled, "Keep that thing away from me, Pretty Boy, or I'll cut it off next time."

Will withdrew his reddening hand, said, "Sorry, I just wanted -"

"I don't want nothin' from you, Pretty Boy." He cocked and tilted his head, said, "You look like a sissy. You a big sissy, Pretty Boy?"

I pulled Will back to the flock, and Tex said, "Jealous he's so good looking, Louse?"

Word was out that several of the Lappin clan kids had been or were infected by various parasites such as hookworms and head lice. Only Tex had the audacity to give that nickname to Cus, one that he really didn't seem to mind because he thought she meant he was a despicable person, which he never pretended not to be, but Cus did not yet know the way Tex intended Louse. It was Kenny who discovered louse was the singular of lice.

23

Richard Newberry

The closest thing Cus had to a smile he showed to Tex. "You gotta crush on Pretty Boy, Barbie?"

"Same as you, Louse," she said.

His smile became a sneer. "One of these days I'm gonna show you a bad hurt, Barbie."

Dwight said, "Always good to see you, Cus. Your charm makes us all feel a little better."

Filthy follicles draped his lazy eye, therefore Dwight got Cus's one-eyed glare. "You think so, Blackie? Huh? You think so? 'Cause I got somethin' you might not like to see. Got it right here." He pulled it out from the right hip pocket of his worn and dirty jeans. It clicked, then flipped out a shiny steel blade about six inches long. "Right here," he said, grinning maliciously as he brandished his new weapon.

"Where'd you get a switchblade?" I asked.

"Probably from his mom for his birthday," Stink said.

"You wanna be the first blood donor, Weasel?" He closed the blade and stuffed the knife in his back pocket.

While the Rat Pond served as a slice of heaven to the Icks, Cus's presence proved, like Vietnam, hell was real.

Kenny inched forward. "We don't want you here, Lappin."

"Ain't that too bad, Retard." Cus lifted a thick leg over the bike frame and let it fall to the dirt. He wasn't a big kid, like Dwight or Kenny, or tall like Tex, but he was stout and thick muscled. He reminded me of a fleshly Rock'Em Sock'Em Robot.

Cus mocked a lunge at Kenny, but he didn't budge. "I don't care what you want, Retard. I go where I want and when I want."

If Kenny Hooks had any measure of Lappin's meanness, it would've been - without the switchblade - a good fight. Kenny was a tall twelve, and big, Dwight's weight but not chubby. Yet his latent power had little foundation because of Kenny's gentle nature. It could take him all day to get truly rankled about an injustice, but if you messed with an Ick, it took only seconds for Kenny Hooks to be ready to fight. "I'm not afraid of you, Lappin."

Cus whipped out the pearl-handled switchblade and flipped out the blade.

Will gasped, Stink like me, stood frozen, Tex subtly moved away, Dwight postured to be ready to help Kenny, and Kenny's eyes widened but he stood his ground.

"You want this, Retard?" He jabbed the knife at Kenny. "Huh? Huh?"

Poignant history connected me to Cus Lappin. In 1970 I didn't know how Cus's uncle, Floyd, had murdered my dad; Mom hadn't given me details.

Light at the Rat Pond

Standing on our race track at the Rat Pond, my eyes fixed on the switchblade, I wondered if Floyd had stabbed him.

Because Will was new to our world, particularly Cus's part in it, I didn't know if he was as scared as he looked, or, like the inveterate Icks, he wasn't so much scared stiff, just temporarily shocked by the switchblade Cus wielded. The Icks weren't foolishly fearless, we respected, and at times feared, possible dangers, but when it came to having the potential of Cus showing up anywhere in our world - the Icks had contingency plans.

Dwight reflected how our shock was giving way to a preparedness when he calmly said, "You need to cool it, Cus. We dig your new weapon. It's pretty scary. But we're done bein' scared by it."

He swung the blade until it pointed at Dwight. "When I stick this in your fat black gut you'll be scared."

The Lappin clan lived a few miles east of our neighborhood, north of the tracks, inside the city limits, on Star Street. Impoverished homes dotted Star; six of the families living on the street were Lappins. Dwight knew Cus from city school, where Cus - to the ecstasy and safety of the faculty - seldom attended. And the Icks were grateful he seldom visited our world; yet, his infamous visits were memorable.

Tex had completely slipped from the scene, which garnered boldness in the Icks standing before Cus and his switchblade.

"Come on, man, just cool it," I said.

"Why don't you make me, Hobbs?"

A junkyard plighted the north end of Star Street, and Mom said they couldn't use guard dogs because they couldn't find any dogs as mean or meaner than Cus and his cousins.

Tex returned from her mission to Booty Tree, where she had gathered our weapons. Her rolled up red T-shirt bulged with them.

A gradual moment of genius had made its way to Kenny's brain. "We don't make trash like you, Lappin. We burn it."

"You're a retard, Hooks." Keeping the switchblade pointed at me, he asked, "What's in your shirt, Barbie?"

Tex held out her shirt as the Icks approached her and plucked weapons from it.

Tex brought rocks to a knife fight.

CHAPTER 8

When Cus was coasting down Rat Pond's hill, Kate was taking a break from household chores and sitting down on a dark, rich-brown mahogany bench that stood in front of her Acrosonic piano. The beautiful, dark mahogany upright fit perfectly in the small and bright remodeled parlor; its sound was very melodious to her well-trained ear. It had come from Murph's Music - her father's store - as a present to Kate when she turned eight. She glanced at the wall clock; she had twenty minutes until her first student arrived. Her nimble fingers got busy with Mozart's rambunctious *Rondo Alla Turca*, one of Kate's favorites.

Maury Murphy, more than once, had said to his daughter, "Katherine the Great!" And then his face beamed with his innate, infectious, genuine smile as he added, "No other man's daughter better strikes with caress the keys to beautiful music." His smile would fade but joy remained. Once, he said, "Katey, in one year you play as if you have had ten years of stringent tutelage from Mozart himself."

Maury wasn't as stingy giving out compliments as Texal Wonderlin, but when it involved musical talent, he, with his natural compassion, strictly critiqued all those he instructed.

On a Friday evening after the last student had left the store, Maury and Kate sat side by side on a piano bench and played a duet of *Rondo Alla Turca*. When they finished, Maury turned to Kate and said, "You have far surpassed my ability, and my ability to take you further. But I have a friend who can take you to glorious heights."

Those words saddened Kate. "I want you to teach me, Dad."

Maury hugged her, kissed the top of her head, smelled a hint of strawberry shampoo in Kate's straight auburn hair, and said, "You are gifted, Katey. And you know my words don't come only from a proud father. In all my years of music I've been privileged to sit beside two pianists I would call prodigies. One was my father."

"Grandpa Murphy?"

Maury nodded.

"I wish I could have known him longer." Benjamin Murphy died when Kate was three. She remembered her dad's smile and grandpa's being the same; and Grandpa Murphy always smelled like peppermint. "He was a nice man."

26

Light at the Rat Pond

"Yes he was. And I know today God Himself is blessed by the gift He gave to my father." Maury's green eyes briefly glazed over as he thought of his father. Snapping back to this world, he asked, "Do you know who is the other prodigy?"

Kate's thin legs fidgeted under her yellow sundress. She blushed and looked down as she meekly said, "Me?"

Maury beamed again, nodded. "And listen to your father now. Humbleness is a rare and most precious thing. Something to be practiced everyday of our lives, for it benefits all that surround us. You have a fair share of it, Katey. But never be ashamed or apologize or embarrassed by your God-given talents. They are there to benefit our fellow man, and if our fellow man is jealous - and some will be - that is their character flaw, not yours. Confidence is often misconstrued and vilified by those who lack the desire to make something of their lives. But talent combined with confidence is a fulfilling life. It leads to success in many things, and it is most useful when humbleness is embraced."

Kate loved her parents, but her mother chose to keep an emotional distance. Irma never related to her children - except for maybe Kate's older brother Steven - as well as Maury did. Their father listened and responded to his children, played with them, laughed with them. Maury knew how to be a respected father who expected obedience, yet made the important position of father a fun and engaging one. Irma was always . . .just a parent. She loved, it seemed, more out of duty, as if she could never break out of the consuming role of rigid parent. Not to say Irma never had fun, she had fun, just not much with her children. Kate felt guilty at times because she always loved her dad more than her mom.

"So, Katey, I exercise my humbleness by recognizing you need a more superior teacher than I to take you to those glorious heights."

"But I like practicing and playing with you, Dad."

Maury smiled. "And we will continue doing both, Katey dear. Maybe more than ever before."

Kate's saddened heart rebounded to a familiar joy she was accustomed to when with her father.

"Did you think dear old dad was just going to abandon you? Banish any such thoughts. Besides, the time will come when you'll not be as eager to be stuck side by side with your dear old dad."

"That will never happen."

"Ah. The not-so-wise words of a pre-teen girl." Maury positioned his fingers above the keys. "Oh, I know you'll always love me, Kate. But someday I'll have to make room for other boys." He winked.

Kate blushed again.

Richard Newberry

"But not for a while yet. So you're stuck with dear old dad for a long time." His fingers dangled above the ivories. "I'm ready."

Kate grinned. "Swing," she said, and they started thumping out a favorite swing tune.

Kate was thirteen in the summer of 1948, and one morning she was opening the music store with her dad when Maury, store keys still in his hand, crumpled to the tiled floor from a massive heart attack and died in front of his daughter. Kate never was the same girl.

She didn't realize she wasn't playing the rollicking Mozart tune any longer; she had transitioned to a somber piece she had written in college. The parlor clock showed ten more minutes before her student arrived.

Not the same girl. She quit playing the piano for a year, and it was the worst year of her young life. The hurt in her heart led to an anger that invited a bitter attitude which brought along a year's worth of ugly rebellion. She often clashed with Irma, her favorite target, but even her sister Belle and brother Steven were targets of her unresolved anger. The Murphys never were regular church attendees, and when Maury died, their attendance dropped dramatically. Kate had no more than a surface understanding of church and God, and things religious, yet she had always felt a fondness for God because of the way her dad spoke of Him. At Maury's death, privately and eventually publicly, she denounced the existence of God. She would not and could not believe in, let alone trust in, a heartless deity. Irma further entrenched Kate's sedition four months after her dad's death when her mom brought home a man Kate had never met; they both smelled of alcohol as they slipped to the back of the house where her mom slept. For days, Kate's emotions oscillated between anger and rage. She seethed at her mom, and swore someday she would punish Irma.

On a rainy Saturday morning months later, Kate, weary from anger's oppression and sick from a self-imposed wretchedness, sat down in front of Dad's present to her, the Acrosonic. It had been a year since she last caressed the keys, last expressed a joy or melancholy or any emotion through the steel and copper strings. Solace, the kind given by a loving and listening friend, began to fill her as she played Beethoven's *Moonlight Sonata*. Alone in the house, her fingers floating in rhythm as if she'd never missed a day, Kate's trickle of tears became weeping, but she played on through the familiar heart sickness, wanting to forsake the loathsome misery that had oppressed her for a year. She closed her moist eyes and played Beethoven with her old familiar friend, and solace washed over her, beginning to cleanse her soul, her mind, her heart.

Kate now, in her own parlor twenty some years later, on the same Acrosonic, played *Moonlight Sonata* and reminisced about her father, who she still dearly missed. She felt closer to him at the piano, almost able to feel him on the

Light at the Rat Pond

mahogany bench beside her. She had mastered the piano and it remained a true friend; at times they traveled together on the notes to places outside of time and space, to a world of their creation, and to this world's past. And like life, sometimes those places were sad and wistful, but mostly they were places of happiness and joy.

Her dad now was a good memory. Yes, she missed him, but understood tragedy was part of life. She didn't like or embrace tragedy, she had had her share and still ignored - if He existed - God because of those tragedies. Her relationship with Irma had mended as far as it ever would, and they got along better after her mom moved to Florida in 1965. Kate vividly remembered the first night Irma brought home a "friend" and they spent the night in Irma's bedroom, and she would never forget her urge to punish her mom for it. Kate, in 1970, still wrestled with that guilt. The urge to punish had not subsided by the time she was sixteen, and that's when the Deplorable Indiscretion happened.

Kate heard a car in the driveway, looked at the clock, thought *hmmm. Little early.* She stood and went to the window, pushed back the curtain to see a dark sedan quickly backing out of the drive, then linger in the street.

A shiver cut through her. She couldn't see the driver, but she recognized the car: a brown Ford.

Kate whipped the curtain closed. The car's tires squealed as it raced away. It had to be the same car that had been following and watching her. The Ford first came to her attention when she noticed it the last two times she bought groceries at the IGA. Could be an employee, she had thought, but then saw the same car parked at her bank, the post office and in the same parking lot behind Kresge. Coincidence?

"You're just being paranoid," she told the curtain before peeking out the window. A Sunbeam Bread truck rushed by on the frontage road as she looked for any sign of the Ford.

But she really didn't think she was "just being paranoid". No. She had started to believe there was menacing intent within the dark Ford. The Creeping Taunt tried to pry its way in, but Kate said "no" as she touched her gold wedding band.

She worried that her stalker had come from her haunting past, and was connected to the Deplorable Indiscretion.

CHAPTER 9

The long-haired Rock'Em Sock'Em Robot warned, "Better not throw one of those."

Tex said, "Don't worry. It'll be more than one."

"Square dinkham," said Kenny. The Icks were ready for a stoning if necessary, save for Will. He did not pluck a rock from Tex's shirt.

"I'd like to see you try and hit me, Barbie. You probably can't hit -"

A small rock zipped past Cus's head, briefly stunning the brute.

"I missed on purpose, Louse."

Tex wasn't lying - or bragging. She could shatter discarded liquor and beer bottles from staggering distances, and had a missile-launching arm in centerfield; she pegged would-be scorers at home plate as routinely as the earth spun to the sun.

Cus's sneer returned. "You're lucky you missed."

Dwight said, "No, Cus, you're the lucky one."

"You need to cut dirt out of here," I said, rolling the rocks in my hands.

Cus shot us a deadly one-eyed glare.

"Yeah," said Kenny. His right hand was loaded and cocked.

Cus folded the blade into its pearl handle, slipped the switchblade into his hip pocket and picked up whomever's bike it was out of the dirt and climbed on. He cracked a mean smile as he turned the handlebars toward the hill. "I'll see you on the tracks sometime. But you won't see me till it's too late." Without any run at all, Cus pedaled up the Rat Pond's hill, demonstrating his powerful legs.

Once he was out of sight we filled Tex's shirt with rocks and she reloaded the hole in Booty Tree.

"That was somethin', y'all. I gotta say, I was scared of that guy."

Dwight said, "The Hell's Angels would be scared of that guy."

"Y'all stood up to him pretty good."

I climbed on my black racer. "We're sort of used to him. But he's got us before. Ask Stink."

Stink, getting on his blue racer, nodded. "He caught me by myself. And he's right. I didn't see him coming. Snuck up on me, knocked me off my bike, punched me in the head twice like it was a chore his mom gave him. Then he just rode away."

Light at the Rat Pond

"You gotta be kidding me?"

"He's not, Will." Tex was pedaling her red racer around the track. "That's why the Icks stick together. And when we're not together, be watching."

"Is he around all the time?"

"No," she said. "We don't see him much."

"Once is enough," said Will, smiling.

"Pure quill," said Kenny.

Dwight straddled his orange racer and clicked on the transistor. Ray Stevens was singing *Everything is Beautiful*.

Stink said, "Why did he even have to be born? I wish he'd die."

Dwight, with a broad smile, asked, "You don't like Ray Stevens? What's the cat ever done to you?"

"You know who I mean!"

"Couldn't be lucky enough to have a world without Louse Lappin," said Tex.

Dwight said, "I don't think Death wants to hang out with him."

"You're right," I said. "Wouldn't be fair to Death."

Said Will, "I reckon we've all got a dose of mean in us, but that kid's got an extra big dose."

"I'd say he's got enough mean to be the biggest mean dealer in Doverville," I said.

"Square dinkham," said Kenny.

"What do y'all think's wrong with him?"

Stink, circling the track with Tex, said, "It'd be easier to say what's right with him: nothing."

I said, "He's just plain mean, Will."

"Got the mean gene," said Dwight. His brown eyes drifted toward Hoboland and fixed on the wild growth. I wondered if he started thinking about his brother Nicky. Dwight and Cus had things in common besides going to city school. They both had family in prison, both were from impoverished homes. Dwight's dad was dead, Cus's was usually in jail; both kids could have chosen similar paths in life, but Dwight was determined to overcome big and small obstacles and seek excellence. Cus wasn't.

"Got the mean gene," Kenny repeated.

Will said, "I'm wondering if anybody's ever told Cus about Jesus."

There was spontaneous laughter among the other Icks.

I caught myself. "Sorry, Will. We're not making fun of you. It's just that . . .you got us with that one."

Before the time of Will, talk of Jesus saving Cus would have never been uttered from the lips of an Ick. Frankly, talk of Jesus or God rarely breached

Richard Newberry

our conversation. And to hear Cus's name mentioned in a sentence with Jesus made me only think of Cus ending up in hell.

Said Tex, "I don't think Louse wants to hear about Jesus."

"Why not?"

Stink said, "Didn't you just meet the living nightmare?"

"I respect your faith, Will," said Dwight. Melba Flowers got her family up on Sundays and off to church frequently. Her poor health limited her attendance, but she led the way if the pain wasn't too severe. Dwight seemed to learn a thing or two at church, yet was not, as far as I could discern, a true believer. "But that cat ain't worth gettin' a knife in the gut."

I nodded.

"Got to do scary things for God sometimes, Dwight."

Dwight shrugged.

"Not stupid things," I said.

"'Cast not your pearls before swine'."

Dwight, Will and I turned to look at the giver of that wisdom, who was sitting on the white seat of his gold racer. He frowned, then flushed with chagrin before gathering himself and offering a half-grin. Kenny looked at Will for support.

Will smiled, said, "You might be right."

"What the heck does he mean?" I asked.

"It's something Jesus told his disciples," answered Will.

I asked Kenny, "You even know what it means?"

"I think so. Maybe. I'm not sure."

Kenny was an enigma. His reading and writing skills, at best, were equivalent to an average second grader, his thoughts sometimes lagged by minutes regarding an ongoing topic of conversation, his math skills were awful, but his ability to remember certain things outstripped the amazing ability of many mothers and wives. He collected words and phrases like other kids collected Hot Wheels. Pure quill, square dinkham, brum, oof tube . . . all words Kenny Hooks introduced to us; some of the obscure words came from a book his aunt gave him for a birthday. We were called the Icks because of him. One Saturday in 1968, while we were cruising the alley, we were debating on a name for our bike gang.

"Hell's Angels," said Stink.

Tex argued for "Glory Stompers".

"Black Panthers," said Dwight. Four white faces glanced at Dwight before dismissing his idea.

"No," I said. "We need something. . .new. Our own. Something. . .what did you call it, Kenny?"

Light at the Rat Pond

"Pure quill?"

"Yeah. Pure quill. Genuine."

Kenny, at the back of the pack, said, "How 'bout one like that . . . you know . . ."

We didn't.

"Sort of like, but not really like, that one gang. Aw, you guys know. Something like . . . the Icks."

We almost crashed laughing. But that Saturday morning in 1968 we became the Icks.

I could tell Will was contemplating Kenny's "pearls before swine" comment. "Might be wise words, Kenny. I should pray on it, that's for sure."

Kenny smiled and shrugged.

Tex and Stink were flirting with a race. Tex called out, "What are you guys doing over there? Let's race or do something."

Stink slid-stopped. "Let's do a bakery run!"

"Yeah," agreed Tex.

"Okay," said Kenny.

Will asked, "What's a bakery run?"

"I don't think you'll like it," said Dwight.

CHAPTER 10

Bakery runs differed from going to the bakery as going shopping differed from shoplifting, and bakery runs were born out of the Icks' insatiable appetite for daring and adventure. Most of our adventurous desires led to an expected thrill and limited bodily harm, and the police would not be involved, nor would they care. A tiny segment of our daring desires would have grabbed the attention of those called to protect and serve. Either way, innocent adventures or less noble activities, knowledge of these happenings would have unnerved caring parents.

Tex, with skill and nerve, stood alone atop our daring mountain, followed by Stink who had daring but not Tex's skill; I had moderate skill but less daring, Kenny and Dwight shared in our daring but rarely instigated it. We didn't yet know Will's daring capacity, it seemed low, but we later witnessed something spectacular from our new friend. And without challenges and thrills and daring and excitement the Icks might as well have resigned to the putridly boring existence of sissies.

We were influenced early and often by our mentor, and the greatest daredevil of all time, Evel Knievel. Our part of the world had three strong television broadcast signals: CBS, NBC and, thankfully, ABC. ABC broadcasted *The Wide World of Sports*, and the Icks were glued to the screen whenever our hero was ready to risk it all. On reruns, we had witnessed Evel's horrific crash at the fountain at Caesar's Palace in 1967, but his crashes did not enervate our resolve to emulate acts of daring. In April of 1970 Evel set a record by jumping eighteen cars, then a month later he jumped thirteen Pepsi trucks, which ended in a bad crash, but in June of 1970 the Icks were primed for a record attempt by our greatest daredevil. Tex, who practically worshipped Mr. Knievel, was carefully working out the details of her next thrilling jump. Dwight, for his engineering prowess, and I for my mechanical skills, were being consulted almost daily, and she made us take an oath of secrecy to build anticipation. The jump attempt was scheduled for the middle of June.

Will looked to me. "What's a bakery run, Yank?"

"It's something we do for fun." A feeling unfamiliar to a bakery run began to sneak into me as I started to explain. Usually I just felt some nervous excitement before a bakery run, but telling Will evoked a twinge of . . . shame. "But Dwight's right. You won't like it. You should just wait outside."

34

Light at the Rat Pond

"I like fun," said Will.

"Well," I said, looking for words to palliate the fun we were about to perpetrate. "It's a different kind of fun. You'll see. I'll tell you more when we get to the bakery."

Will nodded as Dwight slipped me a wary smile.

"We gotta get some oof," said Stink.

Oof - money - would be used as cover in the upcoming adventure. "Can I get it, Dwight?" asked Kenny. Dwight was the Icks' current treasurer, therefore responsible for our collective assets.

"Sure."

Kenny strode across the track to Booty Tree and took out our oof tube. The oof tube was a twelve inch section of yellow bike frame I'd cut off a parts-only bike. I sanded the ends smooth and slipped a pair of black handle grips over each end; it's where we stashed our dimes, nickels and pennies. "How much?" Kenny asked.

"Enough for three," said Stink.

When Kenny started toward us, I remembered back to another adventure we perpetrated that involved a Sunbeam Bakery truck. Kenny was at the center of it, and lucky to be alive.

35

CHAPTER 11

It was a typical humid summer afternoon in 1968. We were kneeling in the grass under the cover of the Wonderlins' cherry tree; I could smell fresh-cut grass from the lawn next to us. We were perched ten yards from the frontage road and hidden from traffic in either direction.

Stink, smiling, looked at Kenny. "You are gonna be the grooviest cat yet."

Kenny gripped the rope tighter, gave us his best groovy-cat, not-scared face.

The first civilized structure east of the Rat Pond's wild growth was a Sunbeam Bread outlet. Blue and white bread trucks with a golden-haired girl plastered on their sides hustled away from the outlet's docks in the wee morning hours, and returned in the afternoon and evening. The brilliant plan that had us perched under the cherry tree involved a returning bread truck.

"Man, this is gonna be neat," said Mikey.

The Icks nodded.

Mikey never became an Ick. He was the nephew of Van and Lilly Gordon, and he visited our world a few times beginning in 1967. He had some coolness, our age, but he just wasn't around enough. Dwight and Tex called him "Big Mike" because he was smallish, like Stink. He didn't say much and had timid tendencies, but the Icks liked him. I always sensed he felt protected when he was with us. I supposed he was bullied quite often. That summer day in 1968 was the last time we saw Mikey.

Tex said to Kenny, "You remember what to do?"

Kenny, sweat popping out on his too-big forehead, nodded. Maybe he was just beginning to realize the danger, but the Icks weren't fretting because we knew it would be fun but not dangerous to Kenny.

Our brilliance that led us to the cherry tree in the summer of 1968 hatched the day Kenny brought a nice thick rope from home to add to the fun of playing cowboys and Indians. We quickly discovered it made a great lasso. After roping ourselves many times, we dared Kenny to try and lasso a bread truck. He grabbed the dare with bravado. "I'll do it!"

So two days later, we hid in the Wonderlins' front yard, waiting for the bread truck that Kenny could lasso. "Can I try for a car?" he asked.

"No," said Stink.

36

Light at the Rat Pond

We hid our grins from Kenny. We knew he'd never be able to lasso a huge bread truck; there wasn't nearly enough rope. The attempt was what we were dying to see.

"Why not, Stink?"

"'Cause if you lasso a car, how are you gonna know where it's gonna stop?"

"He's right," said Tex.

"If you get a Sunbeam truck," Dwight said, "we know it'll stop at the bakery." Because of his penchant for defending Kenny, it took coaxing to get Dwight in on the roping plan. And since Dwight knew the impossibility, he agreed. Besides, pulling pranks on fellow Icks was an approved practice, for we knew that pranks helped build some kind of character within us.

Kenny, almost a minute later, nodded slowly, said, "Good thinking."

Absolutely.

East and westbound cars rolled past us on the frontage road, most of them obeying a non-posted lower speed limit.

"What should I do after I lasso it?"

We fought back grins, and there wasn't a pure-quill, Ick-made answer for the impossible.

"Just ride it out till you get to the bakery," said Stink. "Then sneak away."

Said Tex, "We'll meet you in the alley."

Sweat now streaked Kenny's forehead. He nodded, said, "Right. Okay. Good plan."

I saw a big box coming from the east on the frontage road. "Hey! I think one's coming."

Dwight craned his thick neck. "Yep."

Stink said, "Get ready."

"I'm ready," said Kenny. He checked his loop.

Mikey looked at Kenny with wide blue eyes. Mikey had not been privy to the Icks' plan to prank their fellow Ick, but I had thought he recognized the impossibility of it. Yet Mikey looked at Kenny as if Kenny were Hoss Cartwright in the flesh, ready to perform a brave act.

We nudged Kenny forward, positioning him for a clear shot at the truck. The rest of us scooted to positions where we could get a good view of the spectacle. We primarily wanted to see the driver's expression and Kenny's face.

I said, "Everybody stay down until I say now."

I checked the road. Nothing from the west and no vehicles behind the bread truck. It would be perfect.

"Get ready," I said, hearing the rattle of empty bread racks from inside the approaching truck. My excitement was at its zenith. "Now!"

Richard Newberry

Kenny sprung up, stepped toward the road and the bread truck, twirling his lasso.

We stayed back, letting our grins overwhelm our faces. Kenny had an earnest expectation of roping the blue behemoth, and we couldn't wait to see the look on the driver's face. This would be hilarious.

It happened at thirty-five miles per hour.

The driver never looked at the boy with a big forehead standing by the frontage road and twirling his rope. A disgruntlement among the Icks and Mikey quickly passed for in the next second Kenny let the rope fly - and it looped over the truck's big chrome mirror!

In a frozen moment of time our friend turned to us wearing a big dumb grin of accomplishment. The moment was snapped when Kenny realized the rope was flying out of his hands, and when the end of his rope was reached - he didn't let it go. His tall gangly body was yanked off the Wonderlins' Kentucky bluegrass and hurtled toward the passing bread truck and waiting pavement. Miraculously, he stayed on his feet for a few yards, but didn't let go of the rope.

We were standing and shouting, "Let go! Let go of the rope!"

Kenny fell on the pavement and somehow landed on his butt instead of his face. He bounced a couple of times on the concrete surface before surrendering the rope. His only injury was a deeply bruised buttock.

Now Kenny returned from Booty Tree with the oof. "Got it," he said, holding out his hand to show us the coins. "Hey, Will, you gonna do a bakery run with us?"

"I don't know yet 'cause I don't know for sure what it is."

"What we do is go into the bakery -"

I interrupted, "Hey - uh, Kenny, why don't you tell Will about the time you roped a Sunbeam truck."

Kenny grinned, still able to feel the glory of that moment, and whenever it was mentioned, like this time, he instinctively reached for his buttock, also a feeling he hadn't forgotten. "Yeah, Jack; that was cool, wasn't it?"

"One of the coolest things an Ick ever did."

"Square dinkham," said Dwight.

So Kenny started giving Will a demonstrative replay of the truck roping, which gave me more time to figure out how I'd explain to Will about our "different kind of fun".

CHAPTER 12

People had known about the place, but it had been forgotten, so now it was a perfect place. At times, like a junkie, he craved to be in the hidden place, surrounded by cozy shadows, where he was free to indulge in his favorite intoxicant; free to entertain the ideas that seemingly came from nowhere and found his fecund mind where the ideas blossomed into stark fantasies. A fertile and vivid imagination, to him, was both a gift and a curse: a gift he was born with, a curse to his prey.

He turned the knife in his hand, intrigued by how the stainless steel blade captured what little light surrounded it and reflected its razor-sharp menace. No better accomplice could he ask for to help carry out his deeds. A silent cohort, which secured the silence he needed to further his deeds, to capture his Prize. The mere brandishing of his cohort enhanced the fear, moved it to terror, which would lead to paralysis and tears. He had given the weapon an appropriate name: The Silencer.

And even the Foolish Brave froze at the first glimpse of The Silencer.

CHAPTER 13

"Let's cut dirt," said Tex.

"Bakery run!" Stink exclaimed, racing Tex up the hill.

Dwight, a Three Dog Night song coming from his transistor, backed up with Kenny to get a run at the hill; Dwight led the way and Kenny followed. Bike-less Will had been a passenger on my handlebars, so we walked up.

Halfway up the hill Will pointed to the brush just west of our track. "Y'all got a name for that thicket yonder?"

"We call it Hoboland."

"Real hobos go in there?"

I smiled. "Well, we think they're real hobos, but maybe you'll find out they're really traveling preachers. Then we'll have to change it to Preacher Land."

Will smiled back. "I reckon I've never seen a real hobo."

"You will - and they don't look like possums."

The Icks were waiting on the alley. Tex said, "Come on you two."

At the top of the hill I leaned my head west, in the direction of the switchyard, said, "Let's go get a cold one first," stalling the inevitable bakery run.

Five bikes raced on the alley's hard-packed surface toward the oasis at the switchyard. The alley's complexion and terrain varied over the stretch of east and west miles we rode on it. It had a chipped-rock base that the county road department every two years coated with an oil emulsion to keep down dust. A fresh spray of oil created a mess for bike riding, so until I turned eleven and could ride the hard road, we were forced off of our bikes for a day after an oiling.

Because, occasionally, heavy trucks from the railroad rolled on it, the alley was smoothest near the switchyard, which made Will's ride between the bars more comfortable. Very few cars used the alley, and except for around Sid's Tavern, the farther east we rode on it the rougher the surface became. Houses no longer dotted the old road on the far east end; spindly trees, radical brush and prairie grass consumed the alley on either side the farther east we rode. Cline's Oil Company was the only thing that interrupted that primitive stretch of the alley.

The chrome-topped drinking fountain at the switchyard's office was the same kind we had at Kickapoo Elementary School, only the railroaders' water

40

Light at the Rat Pond

was cold enough to burn our throats. The Icks had discovered the icy oasis on a hot July day after some fierce Rat Pond races. The brakemen and engineers and other workers saw us often riding the alley and playing along the tracks, so when we asked them if they had a pop machine in their office we were invited to indulge in the coldest, free refreshment an Ick could want. Thereafter we would slip in and out of the yard office with our thirsts quenched.

"Mercy goodness," said Will after his two big slurps. "That's cold!"

"Best there is," said Kenny.

Our ins and outs at the yard office did not come without the temptation to linger, for in the confines of the office area, which also housed school-sized lockers on both sides of a small dining area, the Icks encountered something rare to most of us. Save for Tex and Stink, the Icks didn't have air conditioning at home. The yard office air rivaled its water.

Back out in the heat and humidity of the early June day, Dwight and Tex were laughing while Stink pretended not to care.

I asked, "What did we miss?"

"Stink sniffed a roly poly up his nose," said Dwight, still laughing. "And it came out his mouth!"

The sincere concern in Will's voice when he asked, "Why'd you do that, Stink?" caused hysterical laughter.

Catching her breath, Tex said, "It's what he does. If you haven't noticed, he's a sniffer. Likes to smell different stuff."

Kenny asked, "What did it smell like?"

"Nothing," said Stink.

Stink's given name was Jerry, but the Icks upon observing the sniffing habit quickly dubbed him "Stink", and Jerry never minded. His parents owned a successful floral business across Route 150 on the south frontage road, two miles east of my house. Evidently, according to Stink, the floral environment bred sniffers. His paternal grandfather, who started the business, was a sniffer, as was Stink's father; his mother did not pick up the habit, but a younger sister did.

"Taste good?" I asked.

"Like an M & M."

"Really?"

"Really, Kenny. Want to try one?"

Kenny cast his green eyes to the gravel at his feet before he sought out Dwight. "Aw, Stink, you're lyin'."

A black N & W locomotive roared its diesel engine to life and yanked a string of freight cars into motion with a sudden rippling bang, which startled the pigeons feeding on spilled grain near the steel rails. They, along with their

41

Richard Newberry

cohorts perched on power lines above us, took to flight with the muted clapping of variegated wings.

Tex hit her pedals first. "Bakery run."

No more delaying the inevitable.

We headed east on the alley. I usually felt pure excitement mixed with a twinge of trepidation as I prepared for what we were about to do. Now anxiety mixed with a twinge of shame as I carried Will toward the bakery. I still craved the excitement, but didn't want to trouble my burgeoning relationship with my new friend. I was the one who first approached Will at Kickapoo during recess, and I liked him immediately. Frankly, it was hard not to like the smiling boy from Oxley, Arkansas, unless you were jealous of his good looks. A genuineness in the form of kindness, trust and innocence permeated Will Corben. He was different, in a strange but good way, from the kids I knew. Nevertheless, I still craved the excitement of a bakery run.

We parked our bikes at the rear of the L-shaped bakery. The bakery's graveled parking lot started just off the alley and ran the length of the white-block building's west side. An eight-foot-high chain link fence surrounded the parking lot, but over the years a gap was created in the fence nearest the alley; a gap the Icks could easily slip through. On most of our trips to the bakery we procured the day-old baked goods in an honest manner. Bakery runs were not so honest.

Dwight clicked off his radio.

"Who's buying besides me?" Kenny asked.

"I will," I said quickly. Kenny handed me some oof. I looked at Tex. "You want some, just in case?"

"Let Stink have it this time."

It was set. Kenny and I would be the fronts, the *honest* distracters.

I looked at Dwight, who was sitting on his white banana seat, then to Will who stood beside him. I hesitated.

"What are we waiting for?" Tex asked.

I said to Will, "You wait here with Dwight. Okay?"

"Why don't we all go, Yank?"

"You can go," said Stink. He looked at me and said, "We all had our first time." Stink knew this wasn't something Will would want to do.

"I've been to a bakery before, y'all."

Tex said, "Probably not like this."

"Just wait here with Dwight," I said.

Dwight came out with it. "Jack knows you won't dig it, Will. They're gonna heist some cakes while they're in there."

CHAPTER 14

We called it a "heist" because it sounded cool and less egregious than stealing.

"Why heist them? Y'all have money."

"Because it's exciting. Fun," said Tex.

"Yeah," said Kenny.

Said Stink to me, "Let's let him try. He'll find out how cool it is."

"I don't want to try it, Stink, it's wrong. Stealing's wrong." He looked at Dwight. "Ain't that right?"

Tex said, "Dwight isn't against fun or a heist. He's heisted a couple of times. He just gets too much attention when he goes in there."

Kenny scrunched his face in a display of quandary. "They sure do keep an eye on you in there. Wonder why?"

Dwight shrugged at Kenny, but he knew why. The only time the Icks even considered Dwight's different skin color was when other people called attention to it.

"Jack," said Will, "you don't see the wrong in this?"

I didn't know exactly how the other Icks felt about it when they were trying to go to sleep at night, but I knew it was wrong, and it troubled me at times. I didn't want to hurt Mom, and it would hurt her if I got caught. Most of our adventures were just fun, exciting and dangerous in degrees, but this one at times haunted me with a measurable amount of shame. I did my best to shield against the shame by telling myself there was very little harm done by swiping day-old cherry pies, banana flips and assorted cakes. Still, my conscience spoke loudest in the quiet times.

Will said, "Jack?"

"Uh . . ." This wasn't a quiet time; this was a time when the world crowded out the voice of conscience. "Yeah - uh - it's cool. Like Tex said, it's some excitement."

Will didn't mask his disappointment as he said, "I'm not doin' this, y'all."

"We know," said Stink. "Just wait with Dwight."

"No. I'm not stickin' around for this. It's wrong." He walked away, heading toward the alley.

"Hold on, Will," I said. He turned. "It's only old cakes and stuff they're just gonna throw out if they don't sell 'em."

Richard Newberry

"Jack, what's the difference between stealing and somebody like Cus?"

"Big difference."

"Yeah," said Tex.

Kenny agreed. "Yeah. We're not like Lappin, Will."

"Let him go," said Stink. "We don't need a sissy riding with the Icks anyway. He's gonna ruin all the cool stuff."

"He ain't a sissy, Stink," I said.

"Maybe I am, Jack, if not stealing is being sissy. I reckon I'm a big one. I'll see you later."

I asked, "You're coming over later and helping me finish your bike, right?"

He glanced back, said, "I'll be there," and started walking.

Not out of Will's hearing, Tex said, "He's going to mess up our fun."

"He's a goody two shoes," said Stink, once Will was out of sight. "He's probably gonna go tell on us. We gotta ditch that sissy."

My mind and heart were engaged in an extreme, multi-roped battle of tug of war. I shot a look at Stink. "He ain't a sissy," and said to Tex, "We had fun racing with him there, right?"

Tex flipped her blonde bangs to the side. "You know what I mean, Jack. We like to do stuff that's exciting and dangerous. Some of it he won't like."

"So he can just not do those things."

She asked, "And he's going to be an Ick?"

"No sissies in the Icks!"

I felt my face flush. "Stink, if you call him a sis-"

"Listen up!" Dwight jumped in. "I know we gotta little problem here. We're gonna have to try to figure it out. But what that cat just did was first-chop, pure quill. Don't you guys get that?"

"He's not first-chop or pure quill. He's just scared."

"No, Stink," said Dwight. "You're wrong. He's not even in Scared's neighborhood, man. Think about it. He's the new kid, right? He's trying to make new friends, right?"

"We've been nice to him," said Tex.

Kenny said, "I like Will."

A car we didn't recognize drove by us on the alley. Probably one of Sid's early customers.

Dwight continued. "We know Will is different from us. One of the first things he asked me was what I thought about Jesus. The only time I've had that question asked is at church or from my mother and grandmother. How many kids you know just up and ask that question? I'll bet he's asked you all that."

We all, some reluctantly, nodded.

"So what's the big deal about that?" Stink asked.

44

Light at the Rat Pond

Dwight said, "Kenny and I have to go to church. We know about Jesus and some Bible stuff, don't we Kenny?"

Kenny appeared to not know where Dwight was going with this, thus he sounded unsure. "I know a little, Dwight."

Stink scuffed at the gravel. "What's that got to do with it?"

"When has Kenny or I asked any of you guys what you thought about Jesus?"

"Never," I said.

Dwight nodded.

"So?" said Tex.

"So," said Dwight, "Will Corben is a genuine believer, man. He talks and acts and lives what he preaches. It would be easy for him to not say anything, to mess it up with us. He's new. He could just go along with us, try to fit in . . . make an impression."

Dwight wasn't looking at us anymore. His eyes were thinking, moving in reflection. And from what I knew about my best friend, his big brown eyes were revealing admiration for Will. "But no, that cat stands up to us for what he believes in. That's a bold move for a new kid, and you gotta dig bold, pure-quill people, man." His eyes came back to us. "That's why I said what he just did was first-chop, pure quill."

A little silence fell on us before a smile came on me. I looked at all the Icks except Dwight, because he wasn't there. "You guys remember Mr. Hammond's science class when he was teaching again about us coming from monkeys and apes?"

Tex cracked a small smile, looked at Dwight. "Will raised his hand and asked Hammond what he thought of the Bible. And Hammond says," - imitating his voice - "'This isn't the time to discuss something like the Bible'. But Will says," - imitating Will - "'Well, sir, I reckon you can think what you want but I don't believe this monkey business.'" Tex's smile grew as she pushed back her bangs.

"It was cool," I said.

"Yeah," said Kenny.

Dwight nodded.

"Will's an Ick," I declared.

Stink said, "We'll see."

Tex asked, "Are we doing a heist?"

Four pairs of eyes looked at me. I scuffed at the gravel, looked down. "I don't know."

"I do," said Stink, slipping inside the fence.

"Me, too," said Tex, following Stink.

Kenny's eyes remained on mine, and I deferred to Dwight's, which revealed nothing in their placidity. His choice had been made for him.

"Well . . . crud," I said, and slipped through the fence with Kenny behind me.

45

CHAPTER 15

The piano lesson ended while the Icks were slipping inside the fence. A minute after the student's mother backed out of Kate's driveway Kate's phone rang; she knew who was calling. "Hello?"

Nadine: "I am not looking forward to taking Sandra to find a dress tonight. You would think I was asking her to parade naked on Main Street. I told you my cousin Julie's getting married, didn't I?"

"Yes."

"So I have to get that girl a dress. She isn't going to the church dressed like a hobo. By the way, there's this new guy racing - car 32 - who's better looking than Richard Petty. I swear. Tall, lean, dark hair. Kinda has a dark brooding look about him with some gorgeous blue eyes. I saw him near the stands so I had to follow him back to the pits for a closer look. I tell you, Murph, if I wasn't married . . ."

"But you are."

"Yes, darn it, I am. You should go to the races with us next Sunday. I'll make it so you two meet. His name's Johnny Quick - how about that for a name? Don't get me started on all the innuendos I could come up with for that good looking man. Anyway, you've only been with us once to the races. It - he - would be a good reason for you to go again. I think he's a big fan of piano music - and piano players."

"And you know that because . . .?"

"I asked him."

"You asked him?"

"Sure did. Why not? I think it might be some kind of sign. He's not as good looking as Steve McQueen, but he's on Steve's block."

Nadine Wonderlin lived a robust life and made her stories and thoughts known by an energetic, loquacious tongue. The full-figured blonde passed her tomboy, daredevil genes directly to Sandra. Texal Wonderlin's relaxed, easy-going nature somewhat mitigated Nadine's ebullience, anchoring his wife so she didn't spin off of the planet.

"So what do you think, Murph? If you don't nab him, I might."

Kate smiled. "Right. You might - never in a million years."

"But after a million . . . you never know."

46

Light at the Rat Pond

Kate laughed. "You're full of wind, Nadine. I don't know anyone who loves their husband more than you love Texal."

"Have to. Contractual obligation."

"Stop it."

Nadine laughed, then said, "But seriously, you need to consider going with us next Sunday."

"I'll think about it."

"Kate Hobbs, that's what we say to our kids when the answer is most likely no."

Kate smiled. "Speaking of races, between you and my mother, I don't know which one is going to finish first at setting me up with a man."

"My selections are all lean prime beef, Murphy." Nadine stopped to take a drag from her unfiltered Kool. "How is Mama Murphy anyway?"

"She called two nights ago and said she was doing fine, very fine. That tells me she's obviously having fun with her own selection of lean prime beef."

"I so envy her."

"Yeah, right. But she was pleasant enough. I've told you before we get along much better since she moved to Florida. And she of course wanted to know if I had a man in my life yet."

"Tell her I'm trying."

"I did."

"At the rate you're going Jack's gonna have a date before you do. And get this, I think finally Sandra is starting to notice boys – just a little. At least I think that's what that was about."

"What what was about?"

"I caught her in our bedroom the other day sampling a little of my Chanel. You should have seen her face," Nadine laughed. "I don't think it was from getting caught either. I think it was from what the perfume implied."

"You know, eleven is about the age I remember starting to take notice of boys."

"You remember your first crush?"

"Kenneth Wayne."

"Boy, that took no thought. You must still have it for him. Give me the tawdry details."

"There are none. I admired him from afar. I was too shy."

"I'm glad I have my soap operas, Murphy, because your love life is as racy as a nun's."

"Can't help it."

"That's why I'm here to help. You are too pretty and too nice to deny a good man the privilege of getting to know you. You've told me yourself you'd

Richard Newberry

like to have another baby before it's too late. How else are you going to have that chance? And let me be myself here and be insensitive: you are not getting younger, Kate."

"I know. I know."

"So I'm gonna take you to the races this Sunday so you can meet Johnny Quick, right?"

"We'll see."

"We'll see? You're hopeless, Murphy. Speaking of hopeless, what do you think of our new neighbor?"

"I haven't met him yet. I think he works thirds at the foundry."

"Yeah, he does. His name's Curt Lewsader, I call him Creepy Dude. He sulks around like some kind of spook over there. I tried to speak to him, but he just looked at me and slinked right into his house."

"Maybe he didn't hear you."

"Do you seriously think my voice doesn't project?"

"You have a point - and a . . . good voice."

"Yes I do, and that guy was just being a creep. Good thing he's not a good looking man. I might begin to wonder if I'd lost it. What I need to lose is some of my hip layers."

Kate laughed. "I think you still have it, Nadine."

"Says my friend who has the love life of a ninety-year-old nun."

They both laughed.

A bit later Nadine said, "I have to get off here and get some lunch ready. Cheryl's complaining she's about to starve to death. Wonder if the Icks would mind a four-year-old riding along? She needs to hush because my story is on in a few minutes."

Nadine's "story" was *Search For Tomorrow.*

"Before we get off I need to tell you something. It's probably nothing, but it's sort of bothering me."

"What's up?"

"Maybe I'm just being paranoid, but I think somebody's been following me."

"What's been happening?"

"Three times just recently - at K-mart and the IGA and the parking lot behind Kresge - I've noticed the same brown car parked just far enough away that I can't tell who's inside."

"What kind of car is it?"

"A Ford, I think. I don't know. So many of them look the same to me. Jack would know, but I don't want to scare him if it's nothing."

"Maybe next time you go to K-mart Texal and I should follow you and see

48

Light at the Rat Pond

if the brown car is there. Texal's pretty easy going, but he's got a subtle way of putting the fear of God in people."

"I don't want to bother you two with what is probably just my wild imagination."

"It wouldn't be a bother, Kate. And what if it's not your wild imagination?"

"I probably wouldn't have said anything about it, but just before my first lesson this morning a car pulled into the driveway then backed out and kind of lingered for just a second, like he was saying, 'I'm watching you,' then drove away."

"Think it was the same brown Ford?"

"I know it was."

CHAPTER 16

Bakery runs, or heists, had been ongoing for two years - without a single Ick being caught. We only hit the place five or six times a year, and during a heist we always had fronts making legitimate purchases. We quickly learned Dwight brought too much attention, hence his waiting in the alley. The Icks did shop at the bakery as rightful patrons throughout the year, and during those righteous trips Dwight came inside with us.

Stink opened the heavy glass door ahead of us, causing the overhead bell to clink and tinkle, and cool air rushed at us along with the smell of day-old bread and other baked goods. The retail space was small, so cover and quickness had to be paired for a successful bakery heist.

Two ladies were at the counter making purchases. I noticed the clerk was new. Not a good thing. The frumpy lady wearing her blue smock with the Sunbeam girl logo on it tapped the keys on the NCR register yet her eyes, under thick blue eye shadow that matched her smock, stayed on the entering Icks. We moseyed to the back table where goods were about to mold, and the only way a clerk had a good view of us at the cheap table was to lean over the counter and eye us. That never happened - until this day. The frumpy new clerk's suspicious eyes were still on us. Obviously, Sunbeam had hired a pro.

I furtively eyed Tex and Stink. Tex's eyes teemed with excitement, for she knew the new clerk had escalated the challenge. Normally the hardest part was getting hidden goods past the counter and out the door without them spilling out of our T-shirts.

Stink moved from the table and pretended to be interested in hot dog and hamburger buns. Kenny, unaware of our precarious situation, shuffled through the pies and grabbed a cherry one. "What are you getting, Jack?"

He used my name! Crud!

Kenny saw my expression. "What's wrong?"

Most of the clerks knew us by name, but I didn't want this new one having access to mine. I think I sounded calm when I told him, "Nothing. Just trying to decide."

Tex was smiling. "How about a Suzy Q?"

"Maybe," I said.

I glanced back at the clerk. She somehow could engage her customers

50

Light at the Rat Pond

while keeping her eyes on us. Where did they get this woman? Before anything could be stuffed under Tex's or Stink's shirt, we needed a diversion outside of our usual legitimate purchase tactic. Our tarrying only seemed to bring about tighter scrutiny from the clerk.

Kenny started for the counter with his cherry pie. I whispered to Tex, "Can't do it today."

"Yes we can."

Stink turned from his pretentious fascination with Sunbeam's bun selection. He too had the look of excitement, brought on by this wary clerk.

I glanced at them, then at Kenny, who was next in line. I looked back at Stink and Tex. "No," I whispered, just as a diversion happened.

The door's bell clinked and tinkled when an older man with a cane stepped inside the bakery. With the clerk's attention diverted for a second, Tex and Stink made their moves. I snatched up a Suzy Q and walked up behind Kenny.

"Warmin' up out there," said the old man in a loud, going-deaf voice.

The clerk smiled at him, then rang up Kenny's pie. Stink and Tex stood behind us. Those heisting never rushed out of the bakery because that might raise suspicion. The escape would come as an innocent, casual departure. Yet this clerk accelerated my heart, causing a sheen of sweat on my fingertips. I wanted Stink and Tex out of the store.

I pushed my dime across the dark Formica counter and left a sliver of sweat there. I gave her my best you-can-trust-me smile and said, "Yep, it's warm."

Kenny, Stink and Tex started for the door, and as I turned to follow them, the clerk said, "Just a minute."

My fellow Icks pushed through the door, leaving me to face her alone. I expected her to leap over the counter, restrain me, then pursue my fleeing friends.

I turned. The old man with the cane shuffled to the counter. The clerk's eyes were intently searching me, but she made no move to capture me. When a smile finally broke her face, I was perplexed.

"You're Jack Hobbs," she said, as if relieved. "I thought you looked familiar. When that tall boy called your name it got me to thinking. I couldn't let it go. You're Andrew Hobbs's son, aren't you?"

My sweaty fingers had smashed their impression into the Suzy Q I held. "Yes."

"You look like him." She began to ring up the old man's purchase. "I went to high school with your dad. He was a very nice guy, and good looking. It was a horrible thing that happened to him."

Maybe it was petty, but when people said it "happened" to my dad, it made it sound like his murder came about by chance. It didn't. It was murder.

51

Richard Newberry

"Why is it the good ones are gone too soon?"

"I don't know," I said.

"I knew your mom a little. Katherine, right?"

Only Grandma Murphy called her that, but I said, "Right."

"Please tell her Imagene Johnson - Tucker said hello. Come to think of it, I'll probably see her in here sometime. You guys must live close by."

"Yep."

She smiled as if recalling a past fondness. "You look so much like him."

I left the bakery relieved, yet my mind raced in different directions because of Imagene Tucker.

When I reached the alley the Icks' faces changed from glum to glee.

Tex punched my arm. "We thought you got caught."

"Man, Jack," said Stink, "what happened in there?"

"What happened was you guys left me behind."

"Hey, you know the deal," said Tex.

And I did. When it came to sticking up for one another outside of a bakery heist, Ick loyalty was better than gold. An Ick, or Icks, caught in a heist took the consequence without being a rat.

"I know. Square dinkham."

"That was far-out exciting, dudes!" said Stink.

"Maybe the coolest one ever," said Tex.

Kenny told me, "I'm glad you didn't get in trouble."

"Yeah. Me, too."

Dwight said, "For maybe the coolest run ever you don't seem too excited, Jack. What's up? What happened?"

"Ah, nothing really. The lady just knew my dad. Went to high school with him."

The Icks nodded, but did not prod further. At our ages, we didn't know how to talk about my dad's murder, or how to comprehend it or explain it, so we buried it. I dug it up alone a lot at night while lying in bed.

"Let's cut dirt and go eat," I said.

We rode to the Rat Pond and split the heisted sweet treats, devoured them in the shade of Booty Tree. Sugared up, we raced our bikes.

"I gotta go," said Stink. His ride home for lunch was the longest: across four lanes of Route 150 and over a mile east on the south frontage road. "I gotta do some stupid thing with my aunt later. I don't know when I'll be back."

Parents were sometimes inconsiderate in regarding *our* daily plans.

At the alley, we were greeted by the muscled-purr of a V-8 Mopar engine. A local legend was about to make an appearance across the tracks on Warren Avenue. We sat on our bikes looking west, quiet with respect and awe.

52

Light at the Rat Pond

I didn't need to announce it, we knew who was coming, but I still wanted to say it: "Rick Spencer is about to pass."

CHAPTER 17

Warren Avenue's pavement was the arterial road for the neighborhood on the north side of the tracks, where Kenny and Will lived; Spencer's muscle car rumbled east on Warren into our view.

"'68 Dodge Super Bee," I said, feeling an urge to salute.

"Orange," said Dwight, proud that his racer was also orange.

Five Ick heads, reverently silent, followed the tempered growl of Rick Spencer's beastly Dodge. Bikes and baseball ruled our world in 1970, but we had begun to yearn for the blessed hope and glorious day when we'd get our driver's license and own a car like Spencer's Super Bee. Though Tex's admiration for the Dodge was every bit as deep as the other Icks', she let it be known she would never own a car with *Bee* in its name.

When the orange deity had passed from view, Dwight said, "That is one groovy-smooth ride."

"I'm going to own a red GTO," said Tex.

"'Vet for me," said Stink. "Midnight blue with four on the floor. Hearst shifter."

Kenny looked at his racer. "I want a gold Firebird."

We had painted our racers and cruisers the colors of our dream cars.

Tex leaned close and punched my arm. "What about you?"

I noticed something odd about her, but did not dare mention anything about the whiff of perfume that had to have come from her. "You know my car."

Together, the Icks said, "Black Mustang with a 427."

"Square dinkham," I said.

Ball of Confusion was playing on Dwight's radio. He turned up the volume and moved his ample upper body to the groove of the Temptations.

We snickered.

Grinning, he said, "You cats just wish you could move like me."

I said, "Tex can - if a bee's after her." I rolled away to avoid her punch.

"I wish," said Tex, "I had your clothes, Dwight."

"Really?" asked Kenny.

"Sure. That way I could burn them so they wouldn't be around to hurt my eyes."

Still moving to the music, Dwight said, "Jealous."

Light at the Rat Pond

Said Stink, "I gotta go." He pedaled away, then stopped. "You guys wanna go strawberryin' tonight?"

"I'm finishing Will's bike. It's gonna take a while."

Tex stood and balanced on her pedals, then lifted her front tire and turned a three sixty before settling the tire back atop the alley.

Kenny admired the heck out of the stunt. "Cool."

"Thanks. Been practicing." She frowned. "I've got to go to stupid town tonight with Mom to buy a stupid dress for some stupid wedding." Tex spit. "So I'll probably be late getting back."

"You in a dress?"

"Don't make me come over there and punch you, Hobbs."

Said Kenny, "I've never seen you in a dress, Tex."

While many of the girls at Kickapoo Elementary wore dresses almost everyday, Tex Wonderlin never did. Most of the kids that went to our school were forced to wear good school clothes; blue jeans were rarely part of one's school clothes - except for Tex. She wore polyester slacks and blue jeans, and like the rest of us, corduroy in the fall and winter.

Gazing down the alley, she said, "And I hope to keep it that way, Kenny."

Maybe I misunderstood, but I thought, though barely perceptible, her words lacked vigorous conviction. I considered the earlier whiff of perfume as I stole a glance at my tall, blonde friend. Her angular features and piercing blue eyes were from her dad, but something . . .feminine was emerging from Sandra "Tex" Wonderlin. I would not be the first to tell her.

She pointed her eyes at me. "Take a picture, it lasts longer."

I think I blushed.

"Well if you two can't go," said Stink, "I -"

"I can go," said Kenny.

"Nah, that's okay. Let's wait till we can all go. It'll be more fun."

Kenny nodded.

Stink pedaled away. Tex said, "I told Dad I'd mow the yard. I'll see you guys after while." She raced to catch up with Stink.

Kenny headed west; lunch and chores waited for him.

Dwight and I slowly pedaled on the alley. "You coming over tonight?" I asked.

"Yeah. I'll be there." His radio blasted *American Woman*. "This is a good one," he said.

I absently nodded. A restlessness troubled my thoughts.

Just before we reached the back of the bakery, Dwight stopped. "Something botherin' you, Jack?"

I stopped beside him. I always wanted a brother, thought it would be the

Richard Newberry

coolest thing. Kenny, Will and Dwight had brothers; Dwight's was in prison. Dwight and I were friends, and quickly best friends, since we first met on the alley when we were in second grade. Both of our dads died before we knew them, certainly a reason for our swift, close bond. And I wondered if I could be closer to a brother than I was to Dwight. It seemed impossible.

I scuffed at the alley with my left foot.

"What's up, Jack?"

My best friend knew me better than any of the other Icks knew me. Tex did have an ostensibly supernatural instinct that transcended the male Icks' discernment, something akin to what my mom had, only not yet refined.

"I don't want you to think I'm being sissy, Dwight."

"You're not a sissy, Jack. Everybody who knows you knows that. You can be a little wishy washy at times, but that's not sissy."

"Wishy washy? Like Charlie Brown? Man. That ain't cool."

"What's up, Jack?"

I looked at the bakery, Dwight looked at it, then back to me. "Ahhh," he said. He clicked off the radio. "So that's it."

"I guess I'm being wishy washy about the bakery heist."

"Nah. That ain't wishy washy, Jack. That's you goin' at it with your conscience."

"That's different?"

"Big diff."

"I guess . . . I don't know."

"Now that's wishy washy."

I smiled.

He said, "Will's words have been planted like seeds in your brain, dude. You gotta little guilt trip growing, right?"

"Yeah. I guess."

"C'mon, *Charlie*."

"It's just that . . . you're right. I'm feeling a little guilty about stealing."

Like a good friend, Dwight listened.

"It's not the only time I've felt bad about it. Sometimes when I'm trying to go to sleep it keeps me awake. But then when I'm with the Icks it's a cool thing to do. I don't want to spoil our fun. I usually don't think this much about it. You're right, it's probably because of Will." For the first time I began to see how Will could be a sword rather than a peace-maker among the Icks. "You think Will planting seeds is bad?"

"Not necessarily. I think Will is gonna be Will no matter what or who. He's gonna make some exciting things happen around here without trying. But when it comes down to it, Jack, each one of us has to decide what we're gonna do."

56

Light at the Rat Pond

"What do you mean?"

"We've all got conscience, man, and we all have to choose who we listen to," - he pointed to his head - "up in here."

"It's not just my head. My stomach's a little messed up, too."

"Square dinkham, Jack. 'Cause the biggest player of all in this will be our hearts." He pounded his thick chest. "It's just not always the first to know."

While I pondered my best friend's words it occurred to me I had noticed but had chosen to ignore a possible division that involved Will and Dwight. My stomach churned as my mind considered what Dwight must think about me spending the night at Will's house a few nights ago. Before the time of Will, I had to beg and plead to spend the night at a friend's house, and rarely was permission granted. After Mom met Will's parents, the first time I asked to stay over at Will's, permission was instantly granted. It was never a problem for me to have a friend at our house, and Dwight had stayed several times. Will had not yet stayed at my house, and for reasons I didn't know at the time, I was never invited to stay over at Dwight's.

And was I now beginning to want to spend more time with Will, rather than Dwight? Maybe because Will was new I gravitated more toward him. Did Dwight notice? Dwight was used to the fact we all went to Kickapoo while he went to Doverville city school. But had I been unintentionally slighting my best friend? I would be on high alert for any tension regarding my friendship with both friends.

"You dig it, Jack?"

"Dig it, Dwight."

"Wanna do a bakery heist with me then?"

We both laughed.

Before we cut dirt from behind the bakery, I looked east as far as my eyes could see, until the alley became a distant thin line and met the blue sky with its wispy high clouds. All of the houses backed up to the alley had at least one burn barrel standing on their property near the alley. Some were old and rusty, others solid but faded brown from heat, and newer ones still held their original paint. All of the barrels had vent holes poked in them on the sides near the bottom.

Dwight swiped sweat from his forehead and clicked on the transistor. A commercial about a hot drag strip outside Chicago roared with revved up motors and souped up, revved up voices; the Icks always wanted to go to the "Smokin' Strip near US 30 . . .where the great ones RIDE! RIDE! RIDE!"

The first two houses after the bakery were small, asphalt-shingled bungalows that Shorty Morgan had built when he first moved up from Kentucky. In those days Route 150 and the frontage roads didn't exist; what was now our alley was part of the thoroughfare. Shorty owned the ground the state purchased to build Route 150 and the frontages.

Richard Newberry

In 1970, a young, childless couple rented the house closest to the bakery, and an old widower friend of the Morgans rented the other bungalow, his name was Dutch. Next came Shorty and Thelma Morgan's big red-brick house, then Van and Lilly Gordon's well-maintained ranch-style; they had purchased the third-acre lot from Shorty. The Wonderlin house was next, and Texal and Nadine had built a small machine shop on the narrow half acre they had bought from Shorty. Between the Wonderlins' and our house stood another small bungalow that Shorty owned; in 1970, a taciturn unfriendly sort lived there. Our house was a ranch-style like the Gordons', but Dad had built a detached garage behind our house a year before he was murdered. Our yard was spacious with trees and shrubs that made it a hide-and-seek paradise. Sid's Tavern sat just east of us, then came Harper's Field; all that property Shorty either sold or still owned.

We set feet to our pedals and rode east while *My Baby Loves Loving* played on the radio.

On the opposite side of the alley the multiple rails at the switchyard funneled into a single pair of steel tracks just east of the Rat Pond; they pointed straight to where the orange sun rose on summer mornings, then disappeared. Between the Rat Pond and Shorty Morgan's house the tracks rested on flat weed less earth. Shorty used the level earth on the north side of the alley by tilling the rich black soil every spring; his garden was huge and immaculate. Beyond Shorty's garden, untamed growth consumed and roamed the earth on both sides of the tracks; abundant prairie grass among the weeds created a natural stage for the Icks to act out our dramas of war, cowboys and Indians, hide-and-seek and other more clandestine adventures.

The earth, soon after Shorty's garden, began growing upward above the tracks on each side, eventually nestling the rusty-colored steel in an ever-deepening valley, the farther east the rails went the less play-friendly the verdant hillsides became.

The gold-tipped prairie grass was swallowed up by white-blooming ladies mantle, horse and pig weed, fox tail and thorny canes of black raspberries. While mostly uninhabitable for the Icks, birds and rabbits and bees flittered and frolicked in their ideal play land. We occasionally spotted groundhogs, chipmunks and snakes moving about in the brush.

Dwight slowed his pedaling, clicked off the radio. He said, "Man."

I said, "What's wron - crud."

Up ahead, Shorty Morgan stood with a weathered hand atop the rim of a burn barrel; with his free hand his long flexing index finger signaled us to pull over to him.

Dwight muttered, "Now what did we do?"

58

CHAPTER 18

Ambrose "Shorty" Morgan looked like a stick of Slim Jim dressed in blue bibbed overalls with a tanned, large Ping-Pong ball head, where a straw fedora usually sat atop. We never saw much of his skin, but what was exposed was perpetually weathered brown, wrinkled and rugged, and his long lanky frame belied a raw strength enmeshed in his wiry muscles from decades of long hard working days.

Dwight and I pedaled toward him, and as we passed the burn barrel of his first rental house somebody lunged at us from behind the barrel. "Boo!"

I swerved, almost crashed into Dwight.

"Gotcha all good," Will said, grinning.

We stopped. I said, "Thought you went home?"

"Nah. Just walked the tracks for a little."

"You boys get your hind ends down here!"

We whispered as we approached Shorty.

"Who's that?" Will asked.

"Thinks he's Johnny Law," said Dwight.

"Shorty Morgan," I said.

"Shorty? He's anything but short, Yank."

Dwight grumbled, "Thinks he owns everything and everybody."

I said, "I think he used to."

Shorty moved in front of the barrel, spit some nasty black tobacco out the side of his mouth without taking his beady eyes off of us. "You're burnin' daylight I ain't got time to burn, boys. Now get yourselves here!"

Dwight muttered something I couldn't understand.

Shorty's eyes strayed from us to across the alley where uniform rows of green emerged from the black earth. At the east end I could see red berries on the straw under the strawberry plants' green leaves; they were ready for harvest. Shorty flipped the chew from his mouth and stuck a Pall Mall cigarette between his lips. From a breast pocket he took out a wooden match, struck it on his boot sole, started smoking. When we got closer I noticed the chew had left a stain on the corner of his small mouth. His face, like Stink's, was small featured, but he was at least six four and he could pick up a fat watermelon with one hand.

"Hey there, Mr. Morgan." Will's way was always genuinely friendly.

Richard Newberry

Despite what happened earlier with Cus, he offered his hand. "I'm Will Corben. I live yonder across the tracks. Just moved up here."

Shorty looked at Will's hand like the boy had offered him a snotty handkerchief. Shorty's fingers stayed hooked on the straps of his overalls. "What are you doin' on my property, Corben?"

Will lowered his hand, looked back at the brown burn barrel, then to Shorty. "Just trying to scare these two. Did a good job, don't you think?"

He took a drag from the cigarette. "I think I catch you on my property again I'm gonna put some lead in your hind end."

"Sorry, sir. Didn't mean to trespass."

"Yes you did."

"Yes, sir, you're right."

"You bein' some kind of smart aleck, Corben?"

"No, sir."

I could sense Dwight wished he had our hidden Louisville Slugger to put upside Shorty's round head. I said, "He's just polite, Shorty."

He turned his slate-gray eyes on Dwight and me. His voice was a low gravelly one, "Speakin' of trespassin', I catch you or your negro buddy or any of those other heathen buddies of yours messin' around in my garden I'm gonna fill your hind ends with lead, sure as I'm standin' here."

Before the time of Will, the Icks sometimes raided Shorty's garden to gather artillery for our nocturnal clandestine activities. "It ain't us."

"Now that's a bag of moonshine, Jack Hobbs." Shorty wasn't a demonstrative speaker, more like a talking statue; only his lips moved, as if he were conserving energy for more vital tasks. "I know your mother isn't raisin' her boy up to be no liar."

He slowly shifted his eyes between Dwight and me. "I know it's you gettin' in there stealin' my strawberries and tomatoes."

"I like workin' a garden," said Will. "Maybe I could help you when it's time to weed it."

He turned to Will. "Does that look like I don't know how to weed?"

"No, sir."

"And why would you want to spend time weedin' my garden? Something wrong with you, Corben?"

Will smiled. "More than one thing I reckon, Mr. Morgan. I guess we've all got something wrong with us."

Shorty's eyes widened. "Where you from?"

"Oxley, Arkansas, sir."

Shorty had moved to the Doverville area from southern Kentucky before the Japanese bombed Pearl Harbor; most of his gravelly baritone parlance had

60

Light at the Rat Pond

succumbed to northern influence, yet a pinch of his southern roots remained in his voice. "They teach you to be disrespectful to your elders down there in Oxley, do they?"

One of the last things Will Corben would ever be was disrespectful. I said, "He's not being a smart mouth, Shorty. He's just . . . different than us."

"Different? That what you call it? I call it what it is, disrespect."

"Sorry, Mr. Morgan."

"Why would anyone want to weed another man's garden? Don't seem natural. Do you see weeds in my garden?"

We all looked at the garden.

"It's a fine looking garden, Mr. Morgan. And you're right, I don't see any weeds. But they'll come - course I don't need to tell you that."

Shorty just stared at Will.

"I just like workin' a garden, Mr. Morgan. We had a big one like this down home."

"Then have a big one up here."

"We do, sir."

Shorty crushed the Pall Mall butt under his boot as his wary small eyes regarded Will. He hooked his thumbs in the overalls' straps and said, "Peculiar boy, wantin' to weed another man's garden just for the likes of it."

"C'mon, guys," said Dwight, "let's go."

The hushed rumbling of Rick Spencer's orange Super Bee on Warren Avenue briefly stole our attention.

Shorty muttered something, then announced to us, "Just heed what I said and every last one of you stay out of my garden." He gestured north across the tracks with his bulbous head and said to Dwight, "Wouldn't be a bad thing for you to stay on your side with your own. Quicker than a pig's whisper this alley's gonna be crawlin' with you people, tell you that."

Dwight had felt the sting of Shorty's racist tongue before, and like the times before, Dwight never flinched.

Will came out with, "What do you think about Jesus, Mr. Morgan?"

Shorty glared at him.

"You know, the Christ of the New Testament. Jesus in the Bibl-"

Shorty growled, "I know who you're talkin' about, Corben," and then took God's name in vain.

"Sorry, Mr. Morgan."

Only once had I witnessed Dwight Flowers so angry his nostrils flared; that involved Cus Lappin. Now they flared again as his big brown eyeballs locked on to Shorty's beady gray eyes. I think he actually bit his tongue before he said,

61

Richard Newberry

"We gotta go now, but you have a groovy, far-out rest of the day, my brother." Dwight spit on the alley while still engaging Shorty before pedaling away.

"I ain't no brother to no negro!"

"Well, sir," said Will, "if you believe in the Bible, we are all related."

Like the saying goes, if looks could kill, Shorty smote Will Corben right there on the alley.

I said, "C'mon, Will. Let's go."

He settled in between my handlebars and we rode away from a mildly befuddled and yet very angry Shorty Morgan.

CHAPTER 19

"Smells good doesn't it, Yank?"

We weren't quite to the Gordons' house when we began to smell the soft, sweet honeysuckle that the Gordons allowed to grow on part of their white wood fence.

"Yep," I said.

"Reminds me of home."

We stopped near the Gordons' burn barrel where Dwight was waiting for us. Will squeezed out from between the handlebars and said, "Sorry about Mr. Morgan, Dwight."

"Don't apologize for him."

"He's used to it, Will."

"He is? You are?"

Dwight shrugged. "You think that's the first time I've had to listen to that old man's gibe?"

"Nah. I reckon not." Will looked back to where Shorty had been standing, said, "I know folks can be ugly as sin," then looked at Dwight. "Doesn't mean anybody should have to get used to it." He took us both in with his brown eyes when he said, "You know, we really are all related."

Dwight's chuckle grew into a big-face grin. "Man, you almost gave that old dude a heart attack telling him that."

Will grinned, said, "But it is true."

Dwight laughed and slapped his own leg.

I asked, "How do you figure we're all related?"

"Adam and Eve, Yank."

Dwight and I exchanged glances.

"Don't y'all believe in them? Or what about Noah and his kin? They're closer to us than Adam and Eve. We all came from that family."

I shrugged. "I've heard of 'em, I think. I don't know Bible stuff, Will."

"You go to church, Dwight. What do you think?"

Dwight also shrugged. "I'm not sure. To tell the truth, I don't pay much attention when I'm there."

I said, "The books and teachers at school say we evolved from monkeys and what not."

Richard Newberry

"Apes," Dwight added.

"That's a bunch of hogwash, y'all. That evolution stuff is nothin' but wild guessing by folks who don't want nothin' to do with the truth, with what the Bible says."

I said, "You seem real sure they're wrong at school."

"They are," he said, and added, "square dinkham!"

Will's first known use from Ick vocabulary grew smiles on Dwight and me.

Said Dwight, "I do not want to be related to Shorty Morgan."

"Don't blame you," said Will.

Before the time of Will, what I knew of Biblical things I could articulate in less than thirty seconds. From the time of Will, I began to learn that what Will had in him was not just knowing facts from a book, but that holy Book was somehow transforming him with an invisible power that I could only sense or see through Will.

Grinning, Dwight said, "I don't know, Will. Jack kinda looks like a monkey."

"You mean ape," I retorted, and raised my arm, taking turns scratching my pits. "Ooo, ooo, ooo!"

"See, Will!"

We laughed.

"I gotta head for home," said Will.

Dwight switched on his transistor and asked, "You wanna go to our cutover?"

"Nah. This is closer."

The Corbens lived north of the tracks directly across from the Gordons' house, and no path had been trampled into the two brushy slopes between the alley and Warren Avenue. When Will got his bike he would use the switchyard crossover - like Kenny - to go home.

Before he made it to the thicket of the weeds and briars Will turned and said, "I just remembered it's Wednesday, Yank. We've got church tonight. I don't know if I'll have time to work on the bike."

"Come over after lunch as soon as you can and we'll get it finished before you go. That way you can ride it home."

"I thought you had to help your mom this afternoon?"

"Yeah. I'll get done."

"Okay. I'll be back over as soon as I eat and do some garden work."

"See you then."

"Hey, Dwight?"

"What's up, Will?"

"Remember, there's only one kind of race."

64

Light at the Rat Pond

I thought there were at least three: five, ten and fifteen lappers.

Will said, "The human race!"

Dwight smiled and wagged his head; we started for the garage and heard a mower's motor start. Tex was mowing her yard.

Dwight kept his orange racer and cruiser at our house where they were safer, and I put them in the garage at night. His original racer was stolen from his front porch in 1967. Nothing was proven, but Dwight lived too close to the Lappin clan for them not to be suspected. Frankly, we all lived too close to the Lappin clan.

"You're comin' over later aren't you?"

"That's always my plan, Jack. But you know Mother's plans are the boss."

Melba, Dwight's mom, worked days at Son-Ray Dry Cleaners, which was situated almost straight south of our house, across Route 150. Mom filled in for her at the cleaners on the few days a year Melba was in too much pain to get out of bed. Dwight's grandmother watched Dwight and his two younger sisters while Melba worked, and Melba worked everyday except Sunday and Wednesday afternoon. Dwight always had plenty of chores.

We parked the bikes between the garage and house and walked the alley until we came to the cutover behind Sid's Tavern. Sid's had undergone renovation in '68 and the dented and scratched white aluminum siding was replaced by Masonite siding that Sid had painted red, white and blue - but not to honor our great country. In the Doverville area a sharp schism existed in its populace; a schism, for many, founded in generations of bloodlines. And owner Sidney Craddock used the schism in a brilliant marketing scheme. One side of his tavern was painted St. Louis Cardinals' red, the other side was painted in Chicago Cubs' blue; the window frames were painted white. The front entrance had the birds-on-the-bat painted on one side, and the Cub and C were on the other side. For since the rivalry was intense and generational yet generally a friendly one, Sid's experienced no more fisticuffs than would be expected on a busy, raucous tavern night when the teams played one another.

Sid hired Dwight and me in '69 to pick up trash on his white-graveled lot and burn beer and liquor boxes a couple of times a week. It took no effete cajoling to convince our moms we should be allowed to work with fire. After all, we were working with it, not playing with it. So Dwight and I earned pop and candy money, and both even stashed some away.

"For a big car, I like it," I told Dwight. Sid had also added a carport on the back of the tavern in '68. A 1969 black over blue, Chrysler Newport rested in its shade.

"I'd take it," said Dwight.

East of Sid's graveled parking lot lay Harper's Field, a flat green two acres

65

Richard Newberry

west of Richard and Shirley Harper's home. The Icks and friends were allowed to use it for pick-up baseball and football games. Harper's Field is where I first met Dwight Flowers.

Across the alley behind Sid's, an ancient path, widened by decades of bikes and foot traffic, cut down to the tracks and up the north slope. The cutover looked like an unruly dirt-brown part in the earth's otherwise green cover. On the south slope, an old mulberry tree stood next to the path's entrance.

"Those will be ripe soon," I said, pointing at the red-turning-dark mulberries.

"So will the raspberries," said Dwight. "I like them better. They don't give me the squirts like those do."

We liked the wild black raspberries more for their capital potential. Dwight and I appreciated and worked the free market system; we were rarely if ever, brum - Kenny's word meaning without money.

I said, "Mom caught a big ol' carp on mulberries last year."

Dwight nodded. "You told me. My Uncle Reggie uses 'em."

We stood and looked at the mulberry tree. Robins and sparrows fluttered in and out of the old tree's dark, green-leafed branches, picking the fruit with their nimble beaks.

Nothing was said between us, but I knew we were stalling going down the path to the tracks because Cus Lappin had promised revenge.

I said, looking toward the tree, "Maybe I should get the bat."

Dwight's eyes focused on the ground near the trunk of the mulberry where we kept the old Louisville Slugger. He then looked at me and said, "There's two things I'm wondering about, and one of them's what you're thinking."

"What's the other?"

"That car parked at Sid's. The brown one."

We had our backs to the parking lot. I started to turn but caught myself, suddenly feeling uneasy. "Yeah. It's a '66 Galaxie. Sedan."

"It's been there two days in a row, and for two days in a row whoever is sitting in it has been watching us."

CHAPTER 20

I could feel the driver's eyes on us. "Maybe we should –" The Ford started and its tires crunched on the gravel as it rolled toward us. I went straight for the bat we had hidden in the weeds. Dwight and I now faced the car, hoping to get a look at the driver. The Ford turned west on the alley; its front windows were down but the driver didn't look our way, so we only got a passing profile of the long-haired, smoking man. He turned left and headed for the frontage road.

"We're acting like a couple of sissies," said Dwight.

"He didn't even look at us when he went by." I felt a little silly holding the bat at my side.

"I know. And it wasn't Cus, that's for sure."

Cus's age remained a mystery to us, though we were certain he wasn't old enough to drive. We also were certain Cus was capable of stealing a car, or coercing a fellow miscreant family member into helping him extract revenge.

Dwight said, "We're letting our imaginations work us over."

"Yep. We are." The car had been parked at Sid's yesterday, before Cus's threat today. Still, I couldn't shake the uneasiness the brown Galaxie presented. We were not imagining today or yesterday that guy sitting in his car and watching us at the cutover.

I carried the bat down to the tracks, Cus's most likely point of attack because of all the concealing brush.

"He's not gonna make me scared all summer, Jack. That's what he likes."

"Just gotta be careful."

"I know, but I cut through here all the time, and I'm not gonna start waiting for somebody to come help me. I'll be watching out for that crazy dude."

"Carry some rocks – or keep the bat with you."

"I'll do something."

We climbed up near the brambles on the slopes to investigate the coming black raspberry crop.

"Two weeks," Dwight decided.

I concurred.

We helped our moms pick the precious fruit to make their pies, cobblers and jam; some were canned or frozen for fall and winter holidays, but Dwight and I devoted two solid weeks in hot June to profit-picking. Mom and Melba

67

Richard Newberry

had staked claims to some of the more fruitful spots, so we ventured east for profit-picking to avoid a turf war with our moms. And there were so many berry brambles rambling up and down the slopes of the tracks that even the hungry, busy birds couldn't dent a profitable harvest. Picking worms for the bait shops was a longer season, but raspberry picking was far more lucrative.

We walked the rails for a bit, then Dwight said, "Got to head out."

He started up the north path and I stopped him with, "Hey."

He looked back and down at me. "That's for horses, man."

"Funny. You want this?" I asked, holding up the bat.

"Nah. It's okay."

He started to turn and I stopped him again. "And - uh - I just . . . uh -"

He took a step down. "What's up, Jack?"

"I - uh . . . I think Will's right. I'm sorry you have to put up with that crud from people like Shorty."

"It's cool, Jack. Don't worry about me. I probably don't have to put up with it, I could get stupid and fight and all that, but I'd be being stupid and fighting more than I want to. So that kind of crud, once I get over being mad about it, makes me work harder. Makes me know it ain't gonna be easy. But, Jack, it won't stop me, even with all the crud I'm gonna be successful, I'm not gonna be poor, Jack. No way."

"I know you're smart. I think someday you'll be rich. You're already pure quill."

"Thanks, Jack. There's plenty of ignorant fools around, but there's plenty of good dudes like you and the Icks, too. See ya."

I watched my best friend go up and out of sight. Like me, he didn't remember his dad. Samuel Flowers had been killed in combat in Vietnam in 1962, a year after my dad was murdered in the A & P parking lot by Floyd Lappin, Cus's uncle. Melba Flowers worked her arthritic body as hard as she could to make ends meet. The compensation from Samuel's death provided little to ease the burden of raising four children. Melba spent money she didn't have to try and prove her oldest son Nicky's innocence, but Nicky was in prison. Samuel's mother and Dwight, along with his two younger sisters, did all they could to help Melba.

A train's horn a mile west sounded through the railroad valley as I walked up the south path; chirping gold finches had joined the rusty-breasted robins and sparrows in their pursuit of mulberries.

At the alley, relieved I didn't see the brown Ford parked again at Sid's, I looked at Harper's Field and recalled the day three years earlier when I saw a kid about my age come up to the alley from the cutover. He stopped and watched us play baseball.

Light at the Rat Pond

I was waiting to bat, and yelled, "We need another outfielder!"

The kid moseyed into the vicinity of right field and Tex threw a glove to Kenny, who tossed it to the new kid. The kid tried to hide it, but Dwight's grin was too big for the Rawlings glove to hide. I would never forget that moment.

If you could see some things coming, you'd do all you could to stop them from happening, but stopping them - unknown to you - would not be wise. Standing on the alley looking at Harper's Field on that Wednesday in June of 1970, I had no way of seeing what was coming in a few days on that flat, green acreage, or elsewhere in our little world.

But like the moment I first met Dwight, I would never forget them.

CHAPTER 21

He took a swig from the can of beer he'd wedged between his legs. A car approached from the opposite direction on the frontage road. He sucked in a long, last drag from his cigarette and flicked the smoldering butt toward the open driver's window of the passing car. A crooked grin exposed yellowing and crooked teeth as he peered at the side mirror and saw brake lights coming from the car that just passed. He accelerated and chuckled, said to himself, "Perfect shot," and took another swig of beer.

He would be glad when all of the watching was over and he could get down to executing the plan. He was careful not to get too close to be identified, but he wanted them to at least suspect somebody was watching, put a *little* fear in them. Patience for the plan, he told himself. *Learn routines. Then strike.*

He pulled onto Route 150 and drove east; his foot was heavy from the alcohol, he wanted to feel the power of the V-8 as it rolled heavy on the road.

When he heard the trumpets blast the introduction to Johnny Cash's *Ring of Fire* he twisted the radio's volume knob until Johnny's voice filled the car and spilled out of the open windows. Not quite noon and he had a good buzz going. For no other reason than he just felt like it, he rested his left arm on the door and flipped up his middle finger at the west bound vehicles while he shouted obscenities at them.

How to execute the plan was beginning to form in his mind after just a few days of watching. He might have to bring a gun in order to more effectively set the plan in motion, but he would do the *finish work* with his weapon of choice. He took his gesturing hand from the window and used it to search the floor under his seat. Ah, there it was. He pulled out the sheathed knife and set it on the passenger seat. He slid the blade from its leather cover, admired the shine of the razor-sharp steel.

Patience for the plan.

He would indulge in their fear, for he craved the fear of others.

Patience for the plan.

Better than any of the booze or drugs, he got higher and more free in the course of perpetrating these evil deeds.

Light at the Rat Pond

Patience for the plan.
To him, if was eroticism.
Patience for the plan.
Just a few more days left until the erotic execution.

CHAPTER 22

I could've eaten peanut butter and jelly sandwiches everyday for lunch, and Mom slathered on the ingredients, exactly the way I liked it. I washed down a big bite with cold milk and said, "You should sell these."

She was nibbling on an egg salad sandwich. "Not everybody could live on peanut butter and jelly, but thanks."

A whirling box fan just outside the kitchen blew air on our feet and legs. I said, "Hot in here today."

"I know. The breeze is gone."

"Maybe we should put in an air conditioner."

She sipped her ice water. "I've been thinking about it."

"I'd even pitch in some raspberry money."

"Speaking of berries, have you checked to see how they're doing?"

"Little bit ago. Two weeks, maybe."

"Don't forget we're heading into Kresge right after lunch."

"I know. How long will it take?"

"Less than an hour - unless we're stopping by the Army recruiter's office to get you enlisted. I'm worried about you being called a sissy."

"Funny. You should be on Carol Burnett."

"I'm auditioning next week. That's why you've got to get the oil changed in my car. It's a long drive."

"Flying would be a lot faster."

"Can't afford it. That reminds me, do you have what you need to work on my car?"

"Oil and filters are in the garage."

"Good. I have to be back at one thirty for my next lesson. By the way, the car seems to be making a funny noise. Have you noticed it?"

I had, but pretended I hadn't so I could hear her description of the problem. "No. What's it doing?"

"You haven't heard that . . . clunk, clunk or . . . clink-thump sound?"

"Is it more of a clunk or clink? How much thump do you hear?"

"Well, it's -," she caught me smiling. "Jack Hobbs, you are bad, mistreating your one and only mother."

"I'm sorry. Couldn't help it. I love when you try to describe a car sound."

72

Light at the Rat Pond

"You should be on Carol Burnett."

"Can we ride out there together?"

"Not in my car. It's clunking and clinking and thumping."

I laughed, she smiled.

"What's for dessert?"

"Nice try. You had enough sugar in those sandwiches."

"I'm gonna change the oil as soon as I can when we get back 'cause I got to get Will's bike done before he goes to church tonight."

While helping with the dishes, I said, "Will's been asking me to go to church with him."

"Oh?"

I tried to gauge her response. Mom always seemed . . . sensitive whenever talk turned to church or God, religious things. "Yeah. I told him I'd have to check with you."

"I see." I could not read her. We rarely discussed religious things because it wasn't part of our lives. Staying busy with the soapy dishes, she asked, "Do you want to go with him?"

I rinsed a plate and set it in the drainer. "I don't know. Maybe."

"So you're not sure?"

"I guess." My greatest motivation for wanting to go with Will and his family to church had more to do with a secret purpose rather than pleasing Will or fulfilling a religious obligation. "No, I think I'm sure I'd like to go."

"We'll see," she said, but seemed to wrestle with her answer. "Oh, I don't care if you go to church with Will, Jack. They seem to be very nice people. So if you want to go, you have my permission."

The Corben family had made a good and fast impression on my mom. Friends were welcomed to spend the night at our house almost anytime, but I had to put on quite a performance, which included begging and pleading, to convince Mom to let me stay at a friend's house. The first time I asked to stay at Will's I mentally and emotionally prepared for battle. My battle plans were never exercised because when Will and I approached her she said, "Sure."

I rinsed the last dish and said, "Thanks. I don't know when I'll go, but I'll let you know."

She smiled wide and blinked rapidly when she said, "Good thinking." Another doofus moment for me.

"I almost forgot. There was a new lady at the bakery today." As soon as I mentioned the bakery, guilt nipped at me. "She said to tell you hi."

She looked at me, waiting for the lady's name. Her smile widened and she started to blink.

"No. Wait. Her name was . . .uh – Ilene – no. . .Imagene. Imagene Tucker."

73

Richard Newberry

Her brow arched, then furrowed before leveling, and her mouth performed similar but more subtle gymnastics at the same time. The name obviously conjured acute memories. "Imagene Tucker," she repeated, more to herself than me. "Really?" Now she focused on me. "Imagene Tucker."

"Yep. I think her last name use to be Johnson."

"Really? Johnson?" She slowly nodded, said, "Hmmm."

"I take it you remember her."

"She's an old acquaintance from my high school days." At that point, nothing more was said about the new bakery lady.

Our property was one of very few that had parking off of the alley; Dad had a gravel drive put outside of the garage's east-facing overhead door when the garage was built. Mom rarely parked her '60 Impala Sport Sedan on the front drive. In 1970 I didn't appreciate the white Chevy's fine lines, wide fins and abundant chrome. It was a boat of a car to me.

Mom was backing out when I said, "We should sell this big thing and get a Mustang."

Mom shifted out of reverse and started forward. "I'd hate to get rid of this. It was our first new car."

"Why'd you guys buy a boat?"

"You mean a big car?"

"Yep."

"Well, we bought it several months after you were born because your dad worked for GM and we were going to have a - " she licked her light red lipstick, "more children, so we thought we would need a bigger car."

"I could dig having a brother or two."

She looked at me, then made the corner at Sid's, said, "I know, Jack."

Breeching religious talk set Mom in a peculiar mood, but conversation about the family we should of and could of had always started her down a path of something easy to define: sadness.

Before I could change the subject, she said, "Have I ever told you what your dad's first car was?"

"Yep. '46 Ford Coupe."

"He was proud of that car."

"It was pretty cool." I'd seen pictures of it in Mom's and Grandma Hobbs's photo albums. Watching Andrew Hobbs grow up in those albums gave me a visual nexus to learn of my dad. I was glad Mom and Grandma, from the plethora of family photos, were addicted to their Polaroids and Kodaks. But what I liked even more was Mom telling me stories about my dad. Between the photos and stories I put together a factual composite of him.

When we were passing Sid's Cub/Cardinal painted tavern, I thought about

74

Light at the Rat Pond

but didn't say anything about the suspicious brown car. Instead, I asked, "Did he know you were a Cardinal fan before you got married?"

"Of course. We Cardinal fans are proud of our winning history."

That was a *definite* gibe at our - yes, Dad loved the Cubs - Lovable Losers. "The Cubs will win this year, you'll see."

"After last season?" She laughed.

I wanted the 1969 Cubs' collapse to be erased from my memory. "We've got Banks, Beckert, Santo -"

"We have Bob Gibson."

Time to change the subject. "Tell me something else about Dad."

She turned onto Bates Drive and rolled toward Doverville. "You know that tiny scar under your chin?"

I touched it.

"You got that when you were first learning to walk."

I'd heard this story before but I gladly listened.

"We had this sharp-edged coffee table in front of the couch, and one day you were really just going to town on your feet." I saw the familiar longing and admiration in her dark green eyes. "And all of a sudden you stumbled and whacked yourself on that table." She wagged her head and slightly grimaced. "We both thought the worst, but all you had was a cut on your chin. It was a deep cut, and you bled a lot, but it wasn't your eye like we had feared." I could see relief on her face.

"And your dad, bless his heart, calmly took that table out to the garage - and I never saw it again." She smiled. "I think I did notice some of its pieces among our campfire kindling."

Mom tried to hide her emotions, but her moist eyes gave her away when she said, "I wish you could remember how much your dad loved you."

We were quiet for a while, until Mom said, "I'm thinking about going up to see Grandma and Grandpa Hobbs Friday or Saturday, what do you think?"

"Can we go tomorrow?"

"Not tomorrow."

I loved going to Grandma and Grandpa's farm. "Can I ask Will to come?"

"You're not going to ask Dwight?"

"He's been before. It'll be Will's first time."

"Okay. You can ask Will."

"Think Uncle Jim and Aunt Tracy will be there?"

"Aunt Tracy might be at the house, but Uncle Jim will probably be in the fields."

"He comes to Grandma's for lunch sometimes." And no wonder, Grandma Hobbs's - Gooch was her maiden name - Dutch lineage played well in her

Richard Newberry

kitchen. She transformed basic food groups into palate scintillating masterpieces, and when they were busy with field work, Grandma's lunches were spectacular. "We'll probably see him."

Mom said Uncle Jim and my dad looked alike, though they had different demeanors. She said Dad's relaxed way sometimes clashed with his older brother's aggressive drive, but they both had big hearts, which they inherited from their parents. Aunt Tracy, the Hobbs' middle child, had the same big heart and demeanor as Dad's.

"I hope Uncle Jim has time to take us on the tractor. He let me drive last time."

Dad decided in high school not to be a farmer. It caused, according to Mom, a bit of a rumble among the family, yet Grandpa Hobbs had watched his youngest son deftly repair tractors and combines and trucks - anything in need of repair. So with his parents' blessing and money, Dad went to the University of Illinois and got a diploma that said what his family already knew: Andrew Hobbs was a pure-quill mechanical engineer.

We parked behind Kresge, went into the air-conditioned store and Mom bought shelf paper and I bought the newest Hot Wheel. Exiting Kresge's back entrance, I asked, "Can I drive home?"

Mom fumbled in her giant purse for the keys, plucked them out and pretended to toss them my way. "Wait. Are you sixteen?"

"Almost."

"You know what that counts in?"

"Yes. Horseshoes and hand grenades - but I do get to ride the hard road in a few days."

"The hard road," she repeated. "It's called the frontage road, Jack, or Bates Drive. A real hard road usually comes when you get older. And then you'll want to get off as soon as you can."

We emerged from the store's coolness to be greeted by hazy sun and humidity. As I opened my door, I noticed it, and it startled me.

Mom started the car. "You coming?"

"Yeah," and slid inside, keeping my eyes on the car parked two rows over. Somebody sat inside the familiar, ominous Galaxie.

"What's wrong?" she asked, trying to trace my line of sight.

"Nothing. Just thinking."

"Looks like something's bothering you. Do you see something wrong?"

"No," I said, turning my eyes to her. "Just thinking."

"About what?"

"About - uh . . . if I'll have to drive this car when I first get my license."

She wagged her head and backed out of the parking space. We passed

Light at the Rat Pond

directly in front of the brown Ford and the person behind the wheel slunk down, but I noticed the person's hand resting on the open window frame had one upright finger pointed at us. Mom didn't seem to notice, and I said nothing as I furtively looked back to get a glimpse at the obscene driver. All I could tell was that it was a long-haired man.

My heart accelerated and my stomach turned uneasy. Should I tell her, or let it go to my active imagination? I had not imagined the guy's middle finger pointed at us. I chose not to say anything to Mom yet, but I would tell Dwight and the other Icks.

Had I known the very near future, I would've told Mom and the police about the dangerous guy in the brown Ford, and would've prevented a trip on a treacherous hard road.

CHAPTER 23

Tex slid-stopped her cruiser outside the overhead door, walked into the garage, said, "Hey," and punched my arm.

"Thought you had to go into town tonight?"

"Stupid dress, yeah." She studied the white bike. "Looks like you're about done. Where's Will?"

"Should be here any second." I took a wrench, ratchet and socket from Dad's Craftsman toolbox and fitted them on the bike's seat bolt and nut; I loosened the seat and handlebars, preparing them for adjustments to Will's liking.

"I see you got a back tire. It looks new."

"It is." I set the white racer's kickstand. "Couldn't find a used one."

"He bought it?"

"Nope. I did."

"Hmm. He going to pay you back?"

"Not if I have my way."

She displayed an odd smile, said, "Must be nice."

"Something wrong with that?"

She avoided my eyes. "Nothing wrong with it." Tex walked to the workbench and pulled drawers in and out with her back to me.

"I'm just trying to be nice."

"Hmm."

I shrugged, perplexed at her demeanor. Was she jealous because I planned to give Will a new tire? I'd never bought her a new tire, but I had given her other parts for her racer and cruiser. What I didn't know then was my journey into the Mysterious Land of the Befuddled, a land where I would often find myself wagging my head and muttering to myself as I tried to fathom Tex's thoughts and emotions, was just beginning.

She turned from the workbench and her expression had completely changed to a familiar and welcomed one. "The racer looks good."

"Thanks. I hope so." It occurred to me my mom had once been Tex's age, and my mom's abstruse inner workings were now far beyond my apprehension, so I noted mentally to pay attention to Tex and her moods, thinking, reactions

78

Light at the Rat Pond

and emotions to better understand the female inner workings when I got older. I later noted I couldn't understand my own notes.

Tex said, "I still wonder why he chose white? It's kind of plain."

"Yeah, wouldn't be my choice."

"Your black isn't much better."

"Black is sharp."

"Red is better."

"Because your racer and cruiser are red."

"Exactly."

"We've all got our favorite color. That's what makes us pure quill."

"Hey!" Her blue eyes brightened. "I've almost figured out my next jump."

A few weeks had passed since Tex's idol, Evel Knievel, had jumped thirteen Pepsi trucks. "You going for fourteen Sunbeam trucks?"

"I wish, but I'd need Dad's motorcycle." I could see in her face she wasn't espousing hyperbole. If Texal fancied letting his daredevil daughter borrow his motorcycle to attempt jumping bread trucks, Tex would be, with Dwight's help, designing the jump ramps.

"Anyway, can you get your hands on a good gas and oil mixture? Something that will burn, but not too fast?"

"You're gonna jump fire?"

A cagey smile spread over her fair-skinned face. "It's part of it."

"And you've already thought about using gas and oil?"

"You said before it's a good steady burn, and something you could control."

I nodded. Of course gas, oil and fire were something a ten soon-to-be-eleven-year-old boy could control. "Yeah, I did. How much are you thinking about?"

"Don't know yet. I'm still figuring it all out."

"Okay."

"I'll let you and Dwight know as soon as I get all the details down."

I nodded; excitement mingled with trepidation at the thought of her next jump.

"What's under that?" she asked.

I looked at the faded tan tarp behind the upright air compressor. "It's a surprise." I looked at her and smiled.

"Really? For who?"

"Can't say. It'd ruin the surprise."

She appeared pleased and tempted by the tarp-hidden secret. Tex and I had known each other since before starting kindergarten at Kickapoo, longer than any of the other Icks. We had always been good friends, but Dwight and I had things in common that bonded us; as a result, we shared deeper parts of our

Richard Newberry

hearts with one another. Tex, like Stink, normally shared only from the surface of their emotions and feelings.

"When is it not going to be a surprise anymore?"

"Couple of days, maybe - hey, hands off."

"Can I peek?"

"No."

"Come on, Jack."

"No."

She faked disgruntlement. "Guess I'll just have to wait like everybody else."

"Yep."

I thought about mentioning the brown Ford to her, but I dropped the idea and my mind wandered a different direction. I tried to imagine lanky, tomboy-Tex wearing a dress. I smiled.

"What, Hobbs?"

"What what?"

"You were looking at me and got this doofus grin on your face like you were thinking about something funny."

"Uh - no - I . . . uh, just -"

"Hey, y'all." Will's hard soles from his brown dress shoes clumped on the concrete floor. "Sorry I'm late, Yank." He wore a white, short-sleeved button-down and blue slacks. "Couldn't cut across the tracks, had to go to the railroad crossing. Mother promised to skin me if I messed up my church clothes."

"It's okay. I just got the seat and handlebars ready to adjust."

"Hey, Tex."

"Hey, Will."

"You look nice," he said to her.

"I do?" I think, but I couldn't prove it, Tex started to blush.

"You sure do."

Tex did have on a red blouse with some newer jeans; not her play clothes. "Gotta go to town tonight and get a stupid dress."

Will wasn't a flirt, he just couldn't help being nice. "Well, you look pretty."

She gave Will a single nod as she said, "Thank you." I, on the other hand, received from her a curt look of disapproval.

I told Will, "You'll be able to ride home. All we have to do is adjust your bars and seat."

"All right!" He climbed on for the adjustments.

"Finally," said Tex, "you're no longer bike-less."

Will grinned big.

Some serious subject matters, like religion or politics, require a tactful approach to minimize the conflict which can accompany heartfelt opinions

Light at the Rat Pond

being refuted or challenged. (That's why I cringed whenever Will flat out asked "What do you think of Jesus?" or "What do you think of the Bible?"). A subtle wading into any sensitive topic could be considered proper decorum, and a simple way of avoiding bad tempers. A truer judgment of a person's character could be discerned in the wake of a subtle approach. Tex would have none of that.

"So, Will," she said, "who are you for, Cubs or Cardinals?"

Tex's forwardness surely stunned him momentarily, for Will hesitated. I cringed, but wondered why I had never - more gracefully, of course - asked him. My pulse quickened, my stomach tightened and I stopped turning the ratchet in those seconds before Will answered.

He smiled at Tex. "Cardinal fan all my life."

I dropped the ratchet.

"Wooo hooo!" Tex pumped her fisted right arm. "Hear that, Jack? A Cardinal fan! That's three to two." She patted Will's back. "You broke the tie."

"Tie?"

I picked up the ratchet, said, "Yeah." To say my heart had been ripped out and crushed to a bloody pulp in the vise on the workbench would've been a euphemistic understatement. I could not face Will as I finished tightening his handlebars.

"What's wrong, Yank?"

I didn't answer.

Will looked at Tex, who said, "The rivalry between the Cubs and Cardinals around here is pretty . . . serious. People get in fights and stuff over it. Sid's has had a couple."

"I think all the people in Oxley are Cardinal fans," he said.

I muttered something even I couldn't understand.

Tex said, "Kenny and Jack love the losing Cubs, and me, Dwight and you are for the many-time-champion Cardinals. Three to two. You're the tie breaker."

"What about, Stink?" Will asked.

"He doesn't care," I grumbled. "Almost bad as being a Deadbirds fan."

"Jack's a little sore, Will. But he'll get over it. I gotta cut dirt and go get a stupid dress. See you guys later."

Will had the seat where he wanted it and climbed off. I started tightening the nut and still couldn't go eye to eye with him. "Can't believe you're a Cardinal fan."

"All the Corbens are. Sorry 'bout that, Yank."

Thoughtful Will was always tuned into other peoples' feelings. I looked at him, said, "Ahh, it's okay. Doesn't bother me."

Richard Newberry

"No, Yank, I mean I'm sorry you like the Cubs. That's an awful fate."

I had to smile. "Right. And you're a doofus Deadbirds fan." I started naming off all the Cubs' good players and saying this was our year and –

Will raised his hand to stop me. "We have Gibson."

Crud.

"Hey. You put a new tire on back."

"Yep."

"How much do I owe you?"

"Triple what I paid."

"My Cardinal discount?"

"That's right." I made sure the seat and handlebars were straight. "You don't owe me, Will. It's a gift."

"Really?"

"Yep."

"I can pay."

"Don't want it."

"You sure?"

"Yep."

"That's a nice thing, Yank. Thank you."

"That's what we Cub fans do."

"Ain't nothing more gracious than grace."

A train horn blasted causing Will to flinch and instinctively turn his head.

I said, "You won't notice them before long."

"That's what you keep sayin', but it's hard to believe you don't hear those big things."

"I still notice them every once in a while, but it's like they've become part of me. Sort of like a . . . heartbeat. Most of the time I don't notice it in there pounding away, but every once in a while I do."

The locomotive's engine revved and resounded down the alley. Soon the big black locomotive would roll past, its weight depressing the rails and creosoted ties as it rattled the garage's louvered windows; pulled black and brown freight cars would sway and screech as the train rumbled east.

"Take her for a spin," I said.

He footed the white racer's kickstand, pedaled the bike out of the garage onto the alley, and kept rolling until he was out of sight. I wiped the tools and put them in their place. I glanced at the old tan tarp behind the air compressor, feeling good about what was hidden there.

Will made it back to the garage at the same time the train started passing.

I raised my voice. "What do you think?"

Light at the Rat Pond

His grin said it all. "It's perfect, Jack. You're really good at fixing bikes. Thank you very much."

"You're welcome very much. You and the other Icks helped."

I had taught the Icks bike maintenance and we enjoyed keeping our racers and cruisers in tip-top shape, but nothing gratified me more than creating a new bike.

"Can't wait to race with y'all."

"Tomorrow."

"Cool."

The train rolled by, settling into a rhythmic ba-bump, ba-bump, ba-bump.

Will intently watched the passing cars. "Y'all ever try to jump on one of those?"

I saw a glint of zeal in his brown eyes. "Nah. Talked about it. Never tried it – yet."

A box car with open doors passed.

"That one looked empty."

"Probably was," I said.

"It's goin' pretty fast."

I nodded. "I know Nicky Flowers hopped a train before."

"Is that Dwight's brother?"

"Yeah. He's in prison."

Will's eyes grew. "For jumpin' a train?"

"No, not that. They say he robbed a gas station."

Melba's oldest child's criminal past discredited his adamant claims of innocence, and Nicky was sentenced to ten years, starting in August 1965. His lone alibi was shredded on the witness stand after she testified Nicky had been with her all day and night the evening Garner's Shell was robbed at gunpoint. In 1970, Melba held fast to her conviction that her son was not involved, but rather the victim of a city police department unable to make an arrest, then focusing on Nicky because of his past. He stole a bicycle when he was thirteen and broke into a neighbor's house to steal stereo equipment two years later. Both times, after light interrogations, he admitted to thieving and took his punishment; yet he vehemently denied ever touching a gun and robbing Garner's Shell.

"I didn't know that," said Will.

"Dwight hardly ever says anything about it."

"Man, that's tough on a mother. You think he did it?"

I shrugged. "I was six when it happened, and never really knew Nicky."

"Dwight think he's innocent?"

"Don't know. Like I said, he doesn't say much and I didn't meet him until second grade."

Richard Newberry

Will stared at the alley for a long moment before zeal spread again in his eyes as the train cars hurried past. "How fast you reckon it's going?"

"Fast enough I can't keep up with it on my bike."

"Guess you'd have to jump it closer to the switchyard."

"Maybe Shorty would let you stand in his garden and jump it from there."

Will turned to me and laughed. "Mr. Morgan's a gruff sort, ain't he?"

"Gruff? That's putting it mildly."

He turned again to the train, and I said, "I can't believe Will Corben is thinking about hopping a train."

"Probably against the law."

"Uh, yeah."

Still looking at the train, he said, "Reckon I shouldn't consider it then."

I recognized a struggle when it happened two feet from me, and inside Will an epic confrontation raged. The struggle wore on his countenance in an expression akin to a poor soul on the cusps of a troublesome bowel movement. I provided relief for him by changing the subject.

"What's your favorite car?"

He pried his eyes from the train. "Wha - uh - Corvette, probably."

"Stink likes Corvettes."

"What's yours?"

"Mustang."

We waved at the fellow riding the caboose; he returned the wave and smiled.

"I gotta head home."

"Yep."

"Thanks for the bike - and the new tire. It's a first-chop racer, Yank."

"I like to do it."

"I can tell. And you're good at it." He started to go but stopped. "Don't forget, you can go to church with me anytime you want."

"Okay." My other reason for going to church with Will floated to the top of my brain. "Yeah, I've been talking to Mom. She said it was okay."

Will smiled often, but this one beamed brighter than usual. "Really?"

"Really."

"Cool. How 'bout this Sunday?"

"Maybe. We'll see."

"We'll see? You sound like my mother, Yank."

Crud, I did sound like a mother. "Okay. I'll probably go."

"Cool. I'm glad, Jack." And I could tell he was.

"You wanna spend the night Friday?"

"Sure. Gotta get Mother and Father's permission, but I think it'll be okay."

Light at the Rat Pond

"Good. Maybe there'll be a scary movie on The Late Show, or Abbot and Costello."

He nodded. "See you tomorrow."

I watched him ride until he was just a thin line on the western horizon. I worked on the surprise for a half hour, then pulled down the fiberglass overhead door, rolled Dwight's orange cruiser in through the service door and locked the garage. I smiled as I recalled Will's infatuation with jumping the train.

Later, that infatuation would lead to big trouble.

CHAPTER 24

I could judge Mom's mood by her nimble fingers. She favored optimism, but occasionally reflected in melancholy tones.

"You're in early tonight," she said, her hands skillfully dancing above the Acrosonic's keys as she played a bouncy ragtime tune.

"Everybody had stuff to do."

Her talent and passion for piano, no matter her mood or the tune, almost nightly transformed our parlor into a concert hall. Mom's sister, Aunt Belle, once told me Grandpa Murphy never lacked kind words to all he met, but as a gifted musician himself he was not liberal with praising talent unless it deserved it. Aunt Belle said Grandpa considered Mom a prodigy.

Slowing to a waltz, she patted the mahogany bench and I scooted beside her; I played left hand until I stumbled over a couple of notes. Mom didn't stop. "You give up too easy. All that talent going to waste."

I had a measure of natural ability, yet the ability came without an ambition to play the piano. It disappointed her, and she was slow to get beyond it. My heart belonged to the feel and sound of a cool steel wrench or working ratchet. Mom said I should appreciate and develop both gifts.

I joined in on the waltz again; she smiled. Like the diversity between jazzy ragtime and an elegant waltz, so lived the soul of Katherine Hobbs. Her gifted hands had mastered Mozart, Chopin and the like, and tenderly soothed me in my distresses; those same hands proficiently plucked worms from the damp, dark ground, gutted and cleaned fish, and remodeled rooms in our house.

With Dad's tools, Texal Wonderlin a phone call away, and Mom's ambition, she told me, "We can do this, Jack," and we proceeded to pull up worn linoleum and rip out a sub-floor. We laid a beautiful hardwood floor, painted walls and put up new trim molding. A few weeks later we had finished the room where Mom instructed future pianists and where her talent filled our home with melodious sounds. Texal, who constantly warned Mom away from electricity and some plumbing, dubbed her the "Beast of Bates Drive", for after the parlor there became no way of stopping her ambitious remodeling plans. Mom had a creed: "If somebody else learned to do it, so can we."

We stopped playing the waltz and she said, "You stink."

"Thanks. I was playing left handed."

86

Light at the Rat Pond

"It's your body that stinks. You need to take a shower."

"Where do you want me to take it?"

"Carol Burnett is going to love you."

Our bathroom had been our second remodel project. Texal helped us with plumbing, but Mom and I did the rest. It was so nice to have a shower and not have to bathe in a tub of filth.

I padded to the living room after my shower and Mom had a bowl of vanilla ice cream swirled with chocolate topping waiting for me. Wearing mint-green cotton pajamas, she sat in a corner of the couch with her legs and feet curled under her, reading Steinbeck's *Tortilla Flats*. "We have fifteen minutes."

That meant ten minutes until I would pull the knob on our RCA console television and start watching the only two shows Mom *had* to watch, both with attractive leading men: Doctor Gannon on *Medical Center* and Steve McGarret on *Hawaii Five-O*. She and Nadine had huge crushes on the two men, but Nadine, who enjoyed attracting men from afar, would always say, "Steve McQueen is the living end." I'm not exactly sure what that meant, other than she had the ultimate hots for him.

Mom smiled at something she read.

"Is that good?"

"Steinbeck is always good. This one is funny. You should read it."

In 1970, my reading mainly consisted of baseball cards and *Hot Rod* magazines.

Mom, however, loved reading; she digested fiction and non-fiction with zeal. And reading fit in with part of her personality, the part that enjoyed solitude. Paradoxically, she was a loner who liked people. Our neighbors rarely had to ask for help because she anticipated their needs and enjoyed helping. She was an active room mother and involved with PTA. But I knew she most treasured alone times with her music and reading, or just her and I working on the house.

Halfway through my ice cream I recalled the last time we picked night crawlers for the next day's fishing.

"I don't care if you date," I whispered to her as we were on our hands and knees in the dark, shining a dimmed light at the ground.

"You don't, huh?"

"Nope." We kept our voices low.

"You think I should date more?"

"I don't know. Maybe. Sure. You don't hardly date at all."

"You sound like Grandma Murphy and Nadine."

I dropped a plucked worm into the coffee can, said, "Someday I'll be gone off to Vietnam, or moving out. I don't want you to be alone."

87

Richard Newberry

"You know, your dad was thoughtful like that." She plucked a worm and dropped it in the can. "But, Jack, don't worry about me. I'm happy, and I'll be happy when you go to Vietnam."

"What?!"

She laughed.

"Shhh," I said. "You'll be happy when I go to Vietnam?"

"Just kidding you, worry wart. What I'm saying is I don't mind being alone. Sometimes I prefer it."

"So you want me to leave?"

"When can you move out?"

We smiled and continued gathering night crawlers.

I licked my spoon and set it in the bowl. "Can Will spend the night Friday?"

"I don't know. *Can* he?"

"*May* he spend the night?"

"Sure." She closed the book, started finishing her ice cream. "His parents okay with it?"

"Should be. They let me spend the night."

"Hmmm. Hope that doesn't hurt your chances."

"Hilarious." I wanted another overnight at Will's, and began to posture for that to happen. "Think I could - may I spend another night at Will's sometime?"

"We'll see. You know I don't think overnights should be a habit."

My first sleepover since staying at Stink's house a year ago had been at the Corbens' a couple of weeks earlier. "I know." I had to maintain diplomacy. "But you like Will, right?"

"I like all your friends, Jack. That doesn't mean you need to go live with them."

Because I had earned her trust, I enjoyed the liberty of roaming the alley and the tracks, and racing at the Rat Pond. I was required to pop in at lunch to assure her I was still alive, and even when she filled in for Melba at the dry cleaners she let me roam. "The Wonderlins will keep an eye on you," and they did. The liberty to roam during the day yet not being allowed to stay all night at a friend's baffled me. I knew not to push her, yet my need for spending another night at Will's compelled me.

"So you think I can sometime?"

"I said we'll see."

I wondered how *we* would figure in the decision. Time to switch subjects. "Will asked again if I can go to church with him."

"Um hm."

"You said if I wanted to -"

88

Light at the Rat Pond

"I know. Do you want to?"

"I think so. Maybe. Yeah."

"Then I don't mind, Jack."

Robins chirped and out on Route 150 an eighteen wheeler rumbled by, daylight was fading into dusk. "Why don't we go to church?" The question exited my mouth before I could stop it.

Mom cleared her throat, her tucked-under legs fidgeted. She set her bowl down, started to touch her wedding band but stopped. "We used to go when I was your age." She uncurled her legs, rested her feet on the green carpet. The tension went out of her when she said, "I don't want to go to church, Jack."

Probably because it was just the two of us, we had a rapport and relationship unique to many child/parent relationships. She still protected me from certain things, drew lines where they needed drawn, but we, usually, were able to be open with one another, dig deeper. Yet religion had been avoided.

"Why?"

"I have my reasons, and you'll have to accept that for now. But I don't care if you go."

I nodded. "Okay." I picked up my bowl and started licking the inside.

"Uh, not proper, Jack Hobbs."

I set the bowl on the end table, rubbed my bicep.

"Your arm bothering you?"

"Nah. It's just Tex's punches are getting a little harder."

Mom curled her legs up under her again, smiled.

"You think it's funny?"

"In her way, it's romantic."

"What? Romantic - Tex?!"

"She's a growing girl, Jack."

"I know, but . . ."

"It might be her way of showing affection."

"Are you serious?"

"Does she punch other boys?"

"All the time."

"Let me rephrase that. Does she usually punch other boys in the arm like she does you?"

I'd seen her punch heads, noses and stomachs, but couldn't recall other biceps being targeted. "I don't know."

"Think about it."

My first ten years on the planet had done little to educate me or give me keen insight into the nature of females. The more I learned the less I knew. But

89

Richard Newberry

Mom's notion of Tex's motives behind her punching gave me a grand idea. "So punching like she does could be considered romantic?"

"In a way, yes."

I mulled it over. Could it be that easy?

"Okay. Go turn on the TV. I don't want to miss Doctor Gannon."

Before pulling the RCA's knob, I said, "Don't forget, only two weeks until I get to ride the hard ro- Bates Drive."

She gave me the doofus look, then said, "Shush now."

CHAPTER 25

I finished painting the engine block on my latest model, a '40 Ford pick-up, dipped the brush in thinner and cleaned the blue out of its bristles, read a *Hot Rod* magazine until my eyes were heavy, then slid under freshly-washed sheets. A comfortable breeze soughed through the screened window and ushered with it sounds of subtle whining tires out on Route 150, shrill chirping crickets and a distant mournful train horn; familiar acoustics that normally soothed my mind into deep sleep. But that night my thoughts scampered about: Will spending the night, Cus Lappin and his switchblade, going to Grandma and Grandpa Hobbs' farm, the bakery heist, Vietnam, the guy in the brown Ford, no school for three months and romantic punching.

I had begun to dismiss the notion that the guy sitting in the Ford behind Kresge was the same guy parked at Sid's. The car at Sid's seemed lighter brown and a year newer. Probably the guy at Kresge didn't like me staring at him and let me know it with a raised finger. Some people were that way.

Thinking about how wonderful life would be if Cus Lappin moved to the moon was overcome by the guilt of today's bakery heist. But the guilt gave way to dread as I recalled listening to Walter Cronkite broadcast the dreary news from Vietnam, and more gloom when I read in the Doverville Gazette the number of dead U.S. troops. I wasn't a sissy, I knew that, yet I feared fighting in a smoldering hot country where the ubiquitous jungle obscured an insidious enemy. Give me open territory to fight in so I could see my enemy coming and vanquish him. I learned later in the summer of 1970 that the enemy hid in the open, and that's what made him deadly.

The dread of Vietnam bled into my worries for Mom when I imagined them telling her of my death at the torturing hands of the Viet Cong. She would be alone. I needed to do something in advance of my deployment to that fiendish country, something to prevent her loneliness. A plan hatched in my brain. My upcoming sixth grade teacher, Mr. Gritton, was cool. He made school and learning likable, almost enjoyable; he would be a good man for Mom. The coming fall's open house at Kickapoo would be the ideal place and time to initiate my matchmaking scheme.

With at least a germinating plan for Mom's salvation by Mr. Gritton now planted in my mind, I relaxed, let my mind seek pleasant thoughts. I heard Rick

Richard Newberry

Spencer's Super Bee rumbling along Warren and it took me to the Corbens' house and Will spending the night and going to the farm and . . .Will's sister Rebecca. Another excellent plan burgeoned in my active mind; I would execute it as soon as possible.

Before I slept, a smile preceded a tingling giddiness that overcame me. What a night of great plans! I reveled in my brilliance, my last thoughts being how they knocked on and busted through the door of Genius.

CHAPTER 26

The phone rang before daylight, that usually meant Melba could not get above the pain and she needed Mom to work for her. Melba's "good days" were like most people's "feeling poor" days. When Melba couldn't go, I didn't even want to imagine her pain. About a dozen days a year Melba had to call Mom, and Mom protected Melba's job.

She came to my room an hour later, kissed my forehead and said, "I'll see you at supper. Be sure and take chances today, ride reckless, play in traffic and please don't watch what you're doing." She gave me the doofus look, which translated what she had just said into, "Be careful while I'm at work or I'll kill you when I get home."

"Okay," I said.

Mom always scheduled her first piano lessons for late morning and afternoons in case she had to reschedule; her students' parents were understanding. "The Wonderlins if you need anything."

"Yep."

"Come get me if it's an emergency." Son-Ray Dry Cleaners was a fifteen second jog across Route 150.

"Can I ride over there?"

"What if both your arms and legs were broken?"

"I'd try."

"You can't wait to ride the hard road, can you?"

I wagged my head.

She smiled. Her fair skin made her dark green eyes even more impressive. The first thing people noticed about Katherine Hobbs was her dazzling, emerald-like eyes. She wore little or no make-up because she didn't need it, but never left home without neatly painted lips and time given to her wavy, auburn hair. Mom wasn't glamorously gorgeous, yet even I knew she was beautiful.

I do not know what went on behind her eyes that morning as she looked at me, but whatever it was spoke of complex things in an array of subtle, fleeting emotions. She kissed my forehead again, said, "I love you," and slipped out of my room.

I dozed off and had a too-real dream about Kenny Hooks showing up in a plaid suit he'd borrowed from Dwight and asking me if Mom was ready for

93

Richard Newberry

their date. Kenny had ridden a gold cruiser built for two into our parlor. Mom said, "Groovy, Kenny. Let me get my lipstick on." I woke up frantic, thinking Kenny had beaten Mr. Gritton to Mom, and now my step-dad was a slow-witted twelve-year-old.

I shook off the horror and got out of bed. I found the Corvette decal I had stashed in my desk two years ago. It struck me as strange that Stink and Will had the same favorite car. I dressed and started for the kitchen when the old ball cap perched on the shelf above my dresser snagged my eye. It was blue with a red C for Cubs, it had been Dad's. I had tried it on before, but my head had not yet grown into it. I held it by the bill and gazed at the C before putting it back in its place.

I inhaled two bowls of Lucky Charms, made my bed and headed for the garage, anxious to finish the secret surprise. The sky was clear and a rich blue, the air less humid than yesterday. I started thinking about getting up a baseball game.

Brown-winged sparrows flitted in from out of the horseweed above the tracks. I unlocked the service door and raised the overhead door. The faded orange sun had crept above the clear horizon; I flicked on the compressor and removed the tarp covering the secret surprise. I had to finish fast because the Icks would soon be gathering at the garage. Nobody except Mom knew what the secret surprise was. Since most of the work on it was done in my room, I thought it best to inform her what I was building and why I kept it a secret. She understood, but wanted it out and in the garage as soon as possible.

Texal Wonderlin and Van Gordon had helped Dad build the two and a half car garage in 1961. Mom said Dad didn't build it to park cars in, though Mom parked hers inside in the winter, he built it to follow his passion of restoring classic cars. His life was taken before he could start his first project. When my hands used Dad's tools to work on and create bikes, I felt a connection to him. The Icks' days typically started and ended at the garage. None of us wore a watch; in the summer we existed outside of time, no longer constrained by the slow ticking school clocks. Our stomachs told when it was lunch time, and parental whistles and far-reaching voices called to us if we were late for supper. Darkness usually ended our days. Icks, normally Dwight, strolled in first around nine. After him, Tex, then Stink, then Kenny; I wondered where Will would place now that he had a bike.

I had just finished the secret surprise and tossed the tarp over it when I heard the Jacksons in the alley singing *ABC*. Dwight sauntered in, turned down the radio. "My man Jack is in the garage."

"How's your mom?"

"Pretty rough today."

Light at the Rat Pond

"Sorry."

"Yeah. Me, too."

I smiled at him. "Where did you find plaid tennis shoes?"

He put the radio in his cruiser's cage. "In a store the other Icks do not shop at." He grinned, said, "It's called the style store. You dig this look?"

"All plaid is . . . is . . . you, Dwight."

"Pure quill, Jack."

I told him about the guy behind Kresge and how I didn't think it was the same guy we saw parked at Sid's. He shrugged, said, "Probably just a jerk."

"Yeah. That's what I'm thinking."

But we agreed to watch Sid's for the brown Ford.

A flash of red, a skid-stop and a trace of dust marked Tex's arrival. "Nice look, Dwight. From your cousin in St. Louis?"

"Yep. You like?"

"No."

"That hurts."

"No it doesn't."

Dwight smiled. "Square dinkham."

Tex punched my arm, then turned to Dwight. "Hey, you hear Will's a Cardinal fan?"

"Really?"

"Three to two now." They pumped their fisted right hands.

"Cubs' year this year," I said.

They laughed.

Tex headed for the tarp behind the air compressor. "We get to see the surprise today?"

"Yep."

Dwight asked, "What surprise?"

"Right here," she said, pointing at the tarp.

"Didn't know about it."

"It's his big surprise for somebody." She smiled, gave me an inscrutable look and feather-light arm punch.

We heard a tire brake on the alley, then, "Whoa!" The next thing we heard was the unmistakable sound of sneakers skidding on the alley. Then we saw Will stop via a sideways lay-down crash just outside the garage door. He missed Mom's Impala's chrome bumper by six inches.

Tex quipped, "That's some nice riding there, Will."

"Cool wreck," said Dwight. "Can't wait to see what you do at the Rat Pond."

95

Richard Newberry

Still on the ground, his face tinged red, he said, "Hey, y'all. Guess I was goin' too fast."

"Guess so," said Tex.

He stood, set the kickstand, wiped himself off.

"You okay?" I asked, eyeing the white racer.

I inspected the bike. "Not even scratched. Nice wreck."

"Thanks, Yank." He tucked his plaid button-down into his jeans and said, "Dwight, that's a cool look. Where'd you get those shoes?"

I mocked, "At the 'style store'."

"Remind me to never go there," said Tex. "And if I do, throw me in front of a fast moving train."

"It's a pure-quill look, y'all."

Dwight nodded, opened his arms to show off his unique garments. "You said it, Will. I call it the Groovy-Smooth look. Hey, I hear you're a righteous Redbird fan."

Will nodded.

"First-chop, Will," said Dwight.

Will's brown eyes turned empathetically toward me, then brightened. "I almost forgot." He pulled a baseball card from his back pocket, inspected it for post-crash damage and handed it to me. "It's not much, but thanks for building me a racer."

"Are you kidding me?" I asked.

Will frowned. "No."

"This is an Ernie Banks rookie card! Thanks, Will."

Tex eyed Will suspiciously. "Why do you have a Cub player?"

"It was mixed in with my others."

I said, "I don't have his rookie."

Will smiled.

Tex said, "Like he said, Jack, it's not much." She, like her mother, loathed anything Cubs.

Tex said to Dwight, "I told Jack last night I've been thinking about my next jump. It's going to be the coolest ever. You gonna help me again with the ramp design?"

"Just give me the details."

She looked at us all when she asked, "Think we can get some of those empty oil barrels from behind Cline's Oil and take them to the Rat Pond?"

Will looked confused.

I said, "Tex is our Evel Knievel. She does some really cool jumps."

"And this next one is going to be the best and most dangerous yet." We

Light at the Rat Pond

could see passion grow in her blue eyes as she talked about her next stunt. "Farther, higher and I've already got Jack working on the fire."

"Fire?" asked Will.

"Yes!" she said, beaming.

"What is it?" Will asked.

"That will be a surprise for as long as I can keep it," she said. Part of the allure to Tex's stunt was the secrecy.

"Man, Tex, I can't wait," said Will.

"It'll be worth it," she said.

"Speaking of surprises," I said, "I've got one for you, Will." I pointed at the tarp. "Right under there."

Tex's eyes narrowed as she fought off a frown, but there was no disguising her disgruntlement.

Dwight turned up *War* on the transistor and asked, "What is it?"

Tex, seemingly wanting to spoil the unveiling, snapped, "Is it a cruiser?"

I rolled out the secret surprise and peeled back the tarp.

They stared at the white bike, their mouths ajar with amazement.

I said, "I think it turned out pretty good."

Dwight, his eyes remaining on the cruiser, said, "Good? Might be your best yet." He looked at me. "First-chop all the way, Jack."

"If you like white," said Tex.

"That's for me?"

His wonderment became my gift. "All yours - Cardinal fan!"

"How'd you make this steering wheel?" Dwight asked, running his big fingers along the painted wood.

Will said, "Steering wheel for handlebars. That is really coo- first-chop."

Not wanting to be, Tex was impressed. "How did you figure out how to get it on there?"

"Your dad helped me."

A wince of betrayal flashed over her. "He didn't tell me."

"I asked him not to say anything to anybody."

She asked, "Won't it break easy."

"Shouldn't," I said. "I made it from white ash. That's the same hardwood they use to make bats. I think it'll handle a crash or two."

Dwight smiled at Will. "Probably find out soon enough."

We heard a skid-stop outside, then Kenny, hands stuffed in his front pockets, dawdled in. "Hey. What's go - whose is that?"

"Will's," Tex said.

"First-chop. Where'd you get it?"

Tex said, "Duh, where do you think, Kenny?"

97

Richard Newberry

"Jack made it? First-chop, Jack."

"Thanks."

"Cool steering wheel. Looks like a fancy cross."

"Good," I said. "Because that's what it's supposed to be." The crucifix necklace Will wore had inspired me. I did not, however, include crucified Jesus. "I just flared out the ends so he won't kill himself when he wrecks."

"Appreciate that, Yank."

Kenny marveled at the creation, touched the cross's smooth finish. "A custom cross steering wheel. That is pure quill."

"I've got two coats of primer and five coats of pearl white on that ash."

Said Will, "The whole bike almost glows."

"Lots of pearl-white lacquer."

Stink finally pedaled in. He set his kickstand and said, "No Cus chasing me with a switchblade - yet." A blotch of reddish-purple stain dotted his flesh just below his right nostril. "Nice cruiser. Where'd it come from?"

Tex quickly answered, "Jack made it for Will."

"I figured you had something to do with it. Cool work. Pure-quill bars, man."

"Thanks."

"You been hiding it?" he asked.

"Sort of. It stood behind the compressor for a while."

Stink noticed the decal on the neck. "Corvette. First-chop. You like 'Vettes, Will?"

"Yep."

"Me, too."

Besides the custom cross steering wheel and the custom paint job - my best yet - the old Schwinn had its original white banana seat and I added three-inch fork extensions on the front. "You guys recognize the bike?"

They didn't.

"It's Mikey's old bike."

The Icks looked at me as if they'd never heard the name, and Mikey was before the time of Will.

"The Gordons' nephew. Remember?"

"Yeah, yeah," said Dwight, and the other Icks' heads bobbed recognition.

Kenny asked, "That's Mikey's old Schwinn?"

"Yep."

Stink said, "He was pretty okay. Whatever happened to him?"

"Haven't seen him for a couple of summers," said Dwight.

Since Tex lived nearest to Van and Lilly Gordon, we looked to her. "Don't ask me. He used to stay with them for a couple of weeks in the summer, then he stopped coming."

98

Light at the Rat Pond

"I think he moved," said Kenny.

"He did?" I asked.

"I don't know."

Stink said, "What do you mean you don't know?"

"I don't know if he moved or not."

Stink rolled his small blue eyes. "Then why did you say he moved?"

"I didn't. I said I think he moved."

Dwight said, "You were just guessing he moved, right?"

"Right."

Stink briefly stared at Kenny before he asked me, "How'd you get his bike?"

"Van asked me if I wanted it. Said he needed the room in his basement."

Tex asked, "And you didn't ask him about why he was giving you Mikey's bike?"

I had to ponder the question. "You know what, I think he told me Mikey got a new bike and didn't want this old one."

Stink smirked, said, "Now are you *thinking* or *guessing* that's what happened?"

I smiled. "I know that's what he said. Anyway, it was standing behind the compressor covered up for over a year until I started working on it. You guys never noticed it?"

Nobody answered.

Tex said, "We should ask Van or Lilly what happened to Mikey."

Kenny asked, "What if he died?"

"Then I wouldn't want to be the one asking," said Dwight.

We nodded. Some things were better left to wild imaginations rather than fact.

Tex asked Stink, "You been sniffing mulberries again?"

He swiped at his nose. "They don't have a smell. But they taste good."

"Give you the squirts," said Dwight.

Kenny disagreed. "My mom says they help stop the squirts."

"Here we go again," said Tex. "The mulberry and squirts debate."

"Green apples give me the squirts," said Will. "We call 'em the green apple nasties."

The Icks nodded agreement; a debate over green apples and squirts would not be forthcoming.

Bridge Over Troubled Waters began playing on WLS, and Kenny said, "Oh, man, please turn that off, Dwight." He did.

"Well," I said, "we've all got cruisers. Let's cruise!"

Tex shouted a "wooo hooo*!*" and we hit the alley. The day's adventure was at hand. Unfortunately, Cus Lappin became a big part of it.

CHAPTER 27

How Melba did it five and sometimes six days a week Kate did not know. Fans oscillated and whirred and pushed the steamy air but did nothing to ease the oppressive heat at Son-Ray's; in the small very back room where the press machines were was the worst. Walking outside into the day's warmth was like stepping into frosty air conditioning. If it were dry heat, Kate thought, maybe working at the dry cleaners would relieve some of Melba's painful arthritis. She would call and check on her.

Kate brought some of Andrew's big handkerchiefs and wore them one at a time on her forehead bandana-style to keep the sweat out of her eyes. She slipped off the red soaked one and tied on a dry blue one. She looked at the big-faced clock, it read ten o'clock; her three bandanas might get her to quitting time. The owner let her skip lunch and breaks so she could get off early. Sometimes walking across Route 150 to have lunch at home and escape the heat for a half hour tempted her, but she'd rather stick it out and leave the oppressive conditions sooner. A radio played in vain some distance from Kate's pressing table. No matter the volume, the country singers' voices could only be heard in bits and pieces because of the fans and other machine racket. She didn't need the music's distraction anyway, for her mind stayed as busy as her hands.

Had Jack seen the vulgar man in the brown car behind Kresge yesterday? If so, he didn't mention it, and Kate wasn't going to warn Jack if she could help it. Was it the same car she suspected of following her, the same one that had pulled into her driveway yesterday morning? Why would somebody just crudely gesture at them without a motive? She knew some people didn't need anymore motivation than the vile crudeness that abided within them; those people somehow got their jollies by randomly inflicting their penchant for ugliness. Yet Kate didn't believe this act was random; it had a premeditated purpose of threat and intimidation.

Should she tell Nadine? Texal would not hesitate confronting the miscreant on Kate's behalf. But what if she was just imagining evil intentions? She had no solid proof, it could be coincidence. Maybe she was watching too much *Hawaii Five-O* and *Mannix*.

She worked the iron over a pair of black slacks. No. It wasn't her imagination. She sensed, she *knew* it was the same creep, and he had bad intentions. She

100

Light at the Rat Pond

couldn't ignore it, she had to protect Jack. Kate always had determination and a streak of independence, and after Andrew's murder, part of her getting beyond the tragic heartbreak was to become more determined, more independent. When her dad died too soon, she immediately became angry, rebellious, but eventually responded as she would later, after Andrew's murder. Part of her determination included trying to never be afraid, never allow the pain to weaken her. She had faced many trying times since Andrew's death, and had rebuked Fear and Pain's attempts to weaken her during most of those times. Yet Fear was relentless, and she felt its grip now trying to crush her spirit. At times like this, she wanted the power to will Andrew back to life, to turn back the pages of their lives so she could warn him not to go to the A & P that night. She needed Andrew at her side. Kate was afraid.

Sneaking up, it used the raucous dry cleaner, the oppressive heat and Kate's worried mind to creep into her. The formidable, vengeful enemy accosted her; the Creeping Taunt accused and mocked her. Kate rested the iron, reached for her talisman and clamped her thumb and forefinger on it. Her eyes closed, sweat seeping under the blue bandana, she said, "No. I will not listen to you today."

But Fear ignored the ring and its presumed power; it asked, *"Who is following you, Kate? Better yet, why is he following you, Kate? Hmm? Could it be your Deplorable Indiscretion? Hmm? Do you think it has to do with that night? Hmm? Maybe it's because of what you did to him."*

"No," she said, eyes still closed, thumb and finger on the ring.

Fear accused, *"Are you completely sure? I think you are very responsible for your dear husband's murder."*

The heat consumed her, her head began to swim. Kate turned and stumbled as she rushed out the cleaner's side door. The Creeping Taunt followed her out into the coolness and light. *"Are you sure, Kate? Hmm? Maybe you should ask Imagene Tucker."*

He knew that Bad was coming, almost here. He watched, waited. It had not visited him for some time, and he had not missed it - well, maybe he had. Bad confused him, for while it visited guilt upon him, it also brought pleasure. Why the conflict? He smiled at the knife, sang a snippet of a Frank Sinatra tune using different words: "Pain and pleasure, pain and pleasure . . .go together like a horse and carriage -" He laughed. Bad rhyme. Guess Bad was everywhere. When Bad stayed far away from him, for a time he thought he might never entertain it again, and would be glad for its absence in his life - maybe. Yet when Bad journeyed back his way he would welcome it, actually embrace it.

He waited. He watched.

CHAPTER 28

We could ride the alley four abreast, but the farther east we rode the more
likely our tires would find a stray, sharp cinder lurking on either side of the old
road, so we typically rode in pairs. Before the time of Will it was Tex and Stink
usually in the front, Dwight and me in the middle and Kenny blithely alone
at the back. Our new friend from Arkansas evened things, so we adopted an
unwritten shifting-partners-policy.

Will, riding at my side, asked, "Why don't we ride out on the paved road?
It'd be smoother."

"Jack calls that the 'hard road'," said Tex. "He can't ride it yet."

Stink, beside Tex in the front, said, "He's the last one. Then we'll be cruisin'
fast and smooth on the hard roads."

Will quizzed me with his brown eyes.

"Have to wait until I'm eleven."

"Two weeks from tomorrow!" exclaimed Tex.

Dwight pulled up to the other side of Will. "So we stick with Jack on this
nasty old alley until he's free at last."

We had cruised east from the garage, and that stretch of alley was much
longer than the stretch west from the garage to the railroad crossing where the
alley ended at the switchyard. From the garage headed east the alley paralleled
the tracks for over two miles and ended just inside the Doverville city limits.
Before the time of any of the Icks the old road took its travelers all the way into
Doverville. In 1970 the alley ended at a berm of earth that was protected by a
decrepit, graying wood fence. Beyond the berm feral growth took over.

Pedaling easy, I said, "I don't know what difference a few days make. I
don't think I'll be any safer or smarter in two weeks. It's Mom's stupid rule."

I slipped to the back, next to Kenny, who said, "You've never broken that
rule, have you, Jack?"

"Nope. Afraid I'll get caught and have to wait longer."

Stink smiled as he looked back. "Sounds almost sissy, Hobbs."

"Gotta have rules," said Will. "And not breakin' 'em means something –
even if it's because you're afraid you'll get caught."

Tex said, "You're sounding sissy."

Light at the Rat Pond

Will navigated well with his new cruiser and custom steering wheel. "Just think it's right to obey rules."

Stink muttered something that included cursing.

Above the tracks, spindly trees, briars, horseweed and spotty brush consumed the earth on the alley's north side. At the steepest point, we rode more than forty feet above the steel rails. The alley's north side consisted of untamed brush except for the block and a half area that was home to Cline's Oil, a small oil and fuel distribution company; the empty oil barrels Tex needed for her upcoming daredevil stunt were corralled behind the company's long, white building. Shorty Morgan had sold the property to the oil distributor, and in 1970 he still owned all the undeveloped area.

We came to the berm at the end of the alley. I pointed across the tracks, told Will, "Over there's where Cus lives."

"Hope he stays there," said Kenny.

Eyeing Will, Stink said, "It's fun to break the rules."

"Yeah," said Tex. "Jack breaks the rules - sometimes."

"You *ever* break a rule, Corben?" asked Stink.

"Goodness sakes yes." He looked around, but not for approval. "I've broken some rules, y'all. And I'm sorry I did - do."

"Holy cheese and rice," said Stink. Dwight turned down his radio, asked, "You broke them on purpose?"

"I reckon so."

"I have, too," said Kenny.

"Cabbage-gas farts," said Stink. "Is this sissy confession time?"

I tried to change the subject. "You seemed to ride okay. Did it handle good?"

Will smiled. "She's a good one, Yank."

"If you ride with us," said Stink, "sometimes we break rules."

Will didn't respond.

I said to Stink, "It's not like we're a bunch of Cus Lappins."

Tex said, "You know what he means, Jack. We do risky things. Adventure. Danger. It's fun."

"I like fun, y'all."

"Me, too," said Kenny.

Tex asked Will, "Like what kind of fun?"

"Like racin' with y'all. Cruisin' has been fun. Baseball." He shrugged. "Stuff like that."

"What about smoking cigs?" asked Stink.

We all looked at Stink, then Dwight said, "We don't smoke. None of us."

Stink squirmed on his banana seat. "I'm thinking about trying it."

103

Richard Newberry

"Go for it," said Tex.

"My mom and dad smoke," said Kenny. "But they told me if I did they'd blister my butt."

"See," said Stink. "Breaking the rules is fun and dangerous."

"It's cool," said Tex.

"I think smoking and stealing and those sorts of things are bad dangerous," said Will. "Racing and baseball and stuff like that are exciting without the bad."

"You ever see Stink try to pitch?" asked Dwight. "That's bad and dangerous."

Everybody except Stink chuckled.

"I just like good fun without breaking the rules," said Will. "It can be exciting."

Stink said, "Too sissy," and Tex nodded.

"I think Will's right," I said.

Tex muttered, "You would."

Will turned his bike to get the sun out of his eyes. "My parents have always said one thing leads to another. If you practice doing a good thing it leads to other good things, but if you practice at the bad stuff . . . it leads to more bad stuff."

Stink rolled his eyes, wagged his head. "Give me a break. All this sissy talk is going to make me puke."

"'Whatever a man sows that shall he also reap'."

We all looked at Kenny, Will was grinning ear to ear. "What?" Stink peevishly asked, "What does that mean, Hooks?"

Kenny's face and too-big forehead flushed embarrassment-red. "I'm not sure. I didn't even know I knew it. But I kinda think I know what it means."

"You know what it means, Kenny." said Dwight. He looked directly at Stink when he said, "And don't be ashamed to say it." Now looking at Kenny, Dwight said, "Because what you and Will said is right."

"Ah, c'mon, man," said Stink. "You're not going sissy too, are you?"

Dwight took his hands from the handlebars, rested them on his banana seat; his big dark eyes gathered in all the Icks. "I gotta brother in prison because one thing led to another. He ended up in prison because he robbed a gas station with a gun, but he started his trip there way before that gas station."

Although Melba believed her eldest son's cries of innocence, and that belief cost her and her family money they didn't have, Dwight knew the real story. I was, according to Dwight, the only person he ever told the truth to regarding Nicky. Brothers tend to know more about the wrongdoings of their brothers than mothers do because brothers, generally speaking, are bound to secrecy by

104

Light at the Rat Pond

some fraternal privilege. Dwight told me Nicky hadn't robbed the gas station he was convicted of, but had robbed two others in which he was never a suspect.

"My brother use to break into houses and steal stereos and TVs. Then he wanted more, so he started stealing cars and driving them to Chicago to sell. Then he decided it would be easier and faster - and more money - to use a gun to rob people. You know what he told me was the very first thing he ever stole?"

Only Will would ask, "What?"

"Cakes from the Sunbeam Bakery."

"Man," said Will.

The other Icks were quiet until Stink said, "Just gotta not get caught."

Dwight gripped his handlebars. "I'll bet every guy in prison has said that."

Stink smirked.

Dwight's story authored a serious introspective mood among us, but Kenny brought us back to an insouciant childhood existence. "Did I tell you we might be getting a dog?"

"No," said Tex.

I asked, "What kind?"

"It's either a boy or a girl."

"Oh, beans and rice, Hooks," said Stink. "Jack means what kind, like what breed."

"Oh. Oh. Like-uh-I don't know for sure, probably a mutt. Dad knows a guy who has some puppies."

Will said, "That'll be cool, Kenny. Hope you get one."

"Thanks, Will."

"We had a big old mutt back home. He died last year - older than me. Bruno was twelve years old. He was a good dog."

"We have a cat," said Tex. "It's okay. Rather have a dog."

"You guys remember our dog, Ringo?" Stink asked.

"Barely," said Dwight. "Little beagle, right?"

"Yep. He got ran over out on 150 two years ago."

"Sorry 'bout that, Stink," said Will.

Stink nodded.

"Come on," I said, "let's cruise," and we started pedaling west.

When we neared Harper's Field, Kenny asked, "We gonna get a game up today?"

"Let's do it!" said Tex. "You in, Jack?"

"When am I not?"

"Never - hey, this will be Will's first game with us. You any good?" she asked.

"I'm not terrible."

105

Richard Newberry

"That would be Terry," I said.

"Who?"

"You haven't met him yet. He lives over by Stink."

Stink said, "We call him Terrible Terry because he's lousy at baseball, but he's a live body."

On an average day we were able to round up ten players, which was okay, but twelve or more made for a good game, and we didn't have to play pitcher's hand; that's why lousy players who were at least willing to make an effort were invited. Younger siblings were almost always excluded because of our minimum age requirement of nine.

I asked, "Who we gonna get up?"

Stink could get the Birge Twins, and his cousin Kevin was visiting that afternoon, so he'd play. "I'll ask Terry and Curtis, too."

Kenny thought he could get his neighbor Donnie. Dwight counted on his fingers, said, "If everybody shows up we'll have twelve."

I asked him, "You'll be able to play?"

"Should be able. Mom's down in bed, but I'll get my chores done fast."

"Twelve would be cool," I said. "Let's meet here at two, and no matter who shows up we'll play."

Heads nodded.

We cruised back and forth on the alley long enough to see Sid's late-morning patrons start to arrive for lunch. The brown Ford Galaxie never showed.

Tex said, "Let's do some racing before lunch." Stink made a two mile round trip to get his racer. He was at the Rat Pond ready to race shortly after the other Icks exchanged our cruisers for racers.

"No sign of Cus?" asked Dwight.

"Nope," said Stink. "I was going so fast I'd just be a blur to him."

Will said to me, "Mr. Morgan sure keeps his garden neat, doesn't he?"

"I think since they never had kids the garden's been Shorty's child."

"You say he's pretty rich?"

"Mom says she wouldn't be surprised if they found out Shorty and Thelma Morgan have as much money as . . . that one guy."

Dwight looked at me. "Rockefeller?"

"Doesn't sound right."

"Howard Hughes?"

"That's it."

Will asked, "Then is that *his* old red truck parked by his house?"

"Yep," I said.

106

Light at the Rat Pond

Will said, "His house looks really nice, but that old red truck doesn't look like a rich man's truck."

"I know," I said. "Shorty's real stingy about spending his money."

"Yeah," said Dwight. "He's all about making it and keeping it."

"He looks almost like a hobo," said Tex. "His old clothes and stuff."

"If he's not one of the richest men," said Dwight, "he's at least one of the grouchiest and meanest."

Said Tex, "And you're one of the weirdest dressers."

"Square dinkham," said the Icks in unison, smiling.

"I will make plaid the style."

"Square dinkham," said Stink.

A west breeze ruffled the green leaves above us. The Rat Pond, until late June or the first of July, stayed a few degrees cooler than the outside world. By mid and late summer the heat and humidity pervaded the shade and didn't relent until mid September.

Said Kenny, "Let's do a fifteen lapper first." Thus began Will's inaugural race at the Rat Pond.

"Got us a racer!" Tex shouted as Will shot out in front. She had to catch up with him, which she did, yet the quick pace Will was setting would soon frazzle them both to back of the pack. Stink, too, did not like to eat dust, so he churned to keep up with the two leaders.

The frenzied start caught up to Dwight, Kenny and me and we found ourselves exerting way too much way too soon. It was a dusty and sweaty and heavy-breathing affair; by lap nine Stink and Tex had fallen behind everyone. To our astonishment, Will kept his torrid pace all the way to the finish. It was, and would be, the Icks' fastest fifteen lap race ever.

Dwight said to Kenny, "We got some competition in the long races."

"I know. Man, Will, good race."

"Thanks."

"Yeah, good racing," I said.

Said Tex, "That was fast. We'll see if you can keep it up in the next races."

Stink began grumbling about the performance of his bike but was interrupted by the sound of feet shuffling through dead leaves in Hoboland.

"What's that?" asked Will.

Dwight said, "Probably Hobo Hairy and Eyeballs."

CHAPTER 29

"Real hobos?" Will asked.

"Yep," said Kenny, straining to see through Hoboland's green thicket. Kenny scoffed at vampires and mummies . . . Frankenstein and the Boogey Man did not scare him. Werewolves, however, frightened him more than having to make a speech in class, and the hirsute hobo that frequented Hoboland looked like a creature who would avoid silver bullets.

Will dismounted his racer and walked to the edge of Hoboland's cover. The westward rise of the black earth set Hoboland above our track, creating a natural stage. "Wow," he whispered. Turning to us, he said, "You seen that one before?"

We all dismounted for a better look.

"Eyeballs," said Tex.

Will took a step closer to the thicket. "I'd say that's a good name."

Eyeballs looked to be in a constant state of unflinching shock; his eyes stayed so wide open that it made mine burn.

"Oh, yeah, now I see the other one. Boy, he is hairy."

"Yeah," said Tex. "He's Kenny's favorite."

Kenny quickly responded. "No he's not."

Hairy was tall and thin, and wore a scruffy brown fedora with a black band. Eyeballs, about Hairy's height, was much stockier than his companion, a big man with a big head to accommodate his bulbous, wide-open eyes. Before the time of Will, the Icks did not get close enough to the haggard looking men to socialize with them. We didn't bother them, they didn't bother us. Hairy and Eyeballs usually, yet not always, traveled together.

Stink asked, "We gonna race?"

"Is there more of 'em?" Will asked me.

"Sometimes. Mostly during the day it's just those two. But there's nights when there's more. Sometimes they have hobo parties."

Stink and Tex had lost interest and were circling the track on their racers.

Will started to step inside Hoboland. Dwight grabbed his arm, asked, "What are you doing?"

"Gonna say hi."

Kenny, as if instructing his younger brother, said, "We don't bother them."

108

Light at the Rat Pond

I said, "Kind of a Rat Pond code."

"You've never talked to them?"

Dwight, Kenny and I wagged our heads. Dwight said, "Sometimes they take a rest over by Iron Tree because it's good soft ground, but when we come down they scatter, unless they're passed out."

"Think it'll break the code to say hi?"

I looked at Dwight, who looked at me, then I said to Will, "We don't know."

"I reckon those poor souls might like a friend or two, don't you?"

I said, "Looks like they need baths more than friends right now."

"And some good clothes," said Dwight.

Will looked at him, quipped, "Not yours I hope."

Dwight smiled. "Now my clothes might just be what could get them jazzed enough to find a job and quit being bums."

Said Will, "They need a job, that's for sure. You reckon they're dangerous?"

"Maybe," said Kenny. "Especially Hairy."

"Kenny doesn't like werewolves," I said. "He thinks Hairy's one."

"He looks like one," said Kenny.

Tex hollered, "Hey! Come on you guys, let's race."

"In a minute," I said.

"You guys ever go in there?"

"Yeah," I said. "We've been in there when we're sure none of 'em are around."

"What did you see?"

Dwight said, "Bunch of whiskey and beer bottles, wooden boxes, junk."

Will clicked his tongue, slowly wagged his head. "That's sad." He leaned farther into the thicket. "I know one thing though: folks need folks, they sure do."

"They got each other," said Dwight. "That's better than nobody."

"You're right. But they need more."

Above us, a locomotive jettisoned boxcars with a rattling "boom!", causing Will to flinch when he said, "They could always use more."

"C'mon, guys!" Stink was anxious to race; so we did.

Will never won again that day. He appeared distracted. I knew his heart had left the race track for the hobos in Hoboland.

A few days from then, Will Corben would breech a long-standing Rat Pond code.

CHAPTER 30

At two p.m. that Thursday in June the sky above Harper's Field wore blue with spotted white clouds, an outfit Dwight would be proud to display. The air didn't cling with humidity, but rather soughed from the west bringing a pleasant late-spring crispness; a beautiful day for a ballgame.

For various reasons, none of the Icks played Little League baseball. The upcoming sixth grade at Kickapoo would be the boy-Icks' opportunity to play official, organized baseball. Until then, Harper's Field was the center of our baseball universe. Our games at Harper's typically turned into serious, heated affairs, where somehow, fun broke through and found its place among the disputes and weighty competitiveness. This Thursday afternoon's game, like Will's first race, would never be forgotten.

"Man!" I said, not trying to control my enthusiasm. "We've got thirteen! This is great!"

"I know," said Tex. "If we had one more it'd be almost like a real game." Her enthusiasm matched mine.

"Tell me about it!"

We had six Icks, the Birge twins, Stink's neighbors Terry and Curtis, and his cousin Kevin had a friend with him, Glen; Kenny brought Donnie.

I counted again. "Yep. Thirteen. One more would be perfect."

Names were bandied about, but each one did not meet Ick minimum age requirements. Though we were extremely tempted, we held fast to our rule - until Tex tempted me further.

"Think about it, Jack. Kenny's brother Alan is almost nine."

"Yeah," said Kenny.

We gathered near home plate, which was the farthest point at Harper's Field from the alley and Sid's parking lot. I pounded my mitt. "I don't know."

Stink said, "He's a lot closer to eight than nine."

"True. True," I said.

"C'mon, Jack," said Tex. "Make up your mind."

"Okay. Kenny, ride as fast as you can and go get -"

"Hey, y'all. Let's ask him."

Before we could stop him, Will was trotting toward a lone bike rider on the alley.

110

Light at the Rat Pond

Incredulous, Stink asked, "Does he know who that is?"

"No!" shouted Tex.

"Not a good idea, Will!" Dwight declared.

Kenny said, "No way."

"Oh, crud," was all I could say.

Will asked the rider, who, unfortunately, turned off the alley and headed our way. We had our fourteenth player.

Said Stink, "If he's playing, I'm not."

Serious grumbles of protest arose from those who knew the lone rider.

"Oh, crud," I said again.

Will, smiling victoriously, trotted alongside the rider. "Hey, y'all, Cus is gonna play. We've got fourteen!"

Glares greeted Will as he neared home plate.

"You idiot," Stink muttered. "I'm not playing."

Tex spit.

I had to salvage the game, even if having fourteen meant Cus was the fourteenth. "It'll be okay. You know he won't bother us with all the Icks here. This is our chance at a game with fourteen players, guys."

The kids who didn't know Cus were shrugging, saying it was okay with them.

"Jack's right," said Dwight. "We got the numbers. Cus isn't a fool. He knows that."

Kenny began to nod. "Yeah. Okay."

Stink said, "I'll play. But not on his team."

Cus had ridden past our games before, leering at us, and always without him being invited to join.

Tex conceded. "All right."

Cus parked his probably-stolen bike with the others behind the lone tree growing at Harper's Field, an old cottonwood that played backstop for us on the southeast corner of the grassy acres.

"This will be okay," I said, trying to reassure the doubters.

Stink said, "It better be."

A concerned murmur arose from those noticing Cus slipping the pearl-handled switchblade out of his back pocket and setting it by his bike's rear tire.

"He'll be good, y'all."

The Icks glared at Will again; his smile waned.

"Some baseball," Cus said, swiping his too-long, straight brown hair away from his eyes; in the sun of Harper's Field he had to squint, which hid his lazy left eye. "Ain't played for awhile." He pulled off decrepit dark boots, then removed his holey graying socks. I was sure they used to be white. Like the rest

111

Richard Newberry

of us, except Will with a button-down shirt and Dwight's groovy-smooth plaid outfit, Cus wore old jeans and a T-shirt. "Ready to go."

I heard Stink's cousin Kevin ask Stink, "How old is he?"

Stink shrugged, "Don't know."

"Okay," I said. "Let's go."

Tex and I were always captains and always picked sides because after our first couple of games it became obvious we were the best two players; therefore we were forbidden to play on the same team.

"Before we pick," I said, "here's a couple of rules. Any ball hit in the air that lands in Sid's parking lot is a homer, unless it's caught for an out. Same thing for the alley. Calls that are close will be decided by the pitchers. That's usually me and Dwight."

"Whatever, Hobbs," said Cus. "Let's play, man."

Cus's toxic presence had not poisoned my excitement over a baseball game with fourteen players. I started to toss the bat, reminded Tex, "No chicken claws," and let the bat go into the air above Harper's green grass.

Tex caught the bat on the part of the Louisville Slugger's handle that guaranteed she would have her thumb pressing the knob for first pick.

"Dwight," she said.

I knew it. He was as good as Tex and me, and a crafty pitcher. I eyed Kenny, who would be the logical second choice, but many unknown commodities, including Will, stood on Harper's grass that day.

"Come on, Jack," said Tex.

"Kenny," I blurted.

"Will," she said.

Crud. "Okay - uh - the Birges." You took both Birges if you took one.

"Stink and Kevin."

"Curtis," I said.

Tex eyed Cus for good reasons: the shabby appearing bully was thick and strong, could probably crush the ball. "Donnie," she said.

Cus smirked, shifted his weight, folded his muscled arms across his thick chest.

Three kids were left standing: Terrible Terry, Glen - Kevin's scrawny friend and Cus.

"Terry," I said, and Cus glared at me.

"You," said Tex, pointing at scrawny Glen. "I forgot your name."

"Glen," he said, hurrying to her side with a relieved look that stated he was use to getting picked last.

Tex, sporting a coy smile, looked at me. Cus had already started towards our team, but Ick rules said I had to say his name. "Cus."

Light at the Rat Pond

He said, "No kiddin'."

Despite Cus, everyone appeared energized and ready to play a fourteen-player game.

We weren't the first to play at Harper's Field. The Harper's four sons were in their thirties and forties by 1970, but when they were our ages they and their friends used the acreage for baseball and football games. Mr. and Mrs. Harper graciously allowed proceeding generations to use their field for pick-up games. Indelible bare spots marked the bases and base paths as evidence of the field's long history.

Our team began to pick their spots in the field. I chose to bat last since Tex got first pick. "You got first, Kenny?"

"Yep."

I asked Cus, "Where you playing?"

"Centerfield."

"Got a glove?"

He looked around; Will ran to his aid. "Here. Use mine."

Cus took the glove, said nothing.

Discord over the batting order erupted among Tex's team, which she swiftly quelled with, "If you don't like my line up, don't bat!" Grumbles gave way to silence.

The team batting supplied a catcher, who would be excoriated, and possibly kicked out of the game if nonfeasance could be proven. "Wish we had a catcher's mitt," I said.

"Ask for one for your birthday," said Tex.

"Maybe."

Dwight and I pitched for our respective teams. We threw hard enough to make hitting a challenge, while maintaining reasonable control of our pitches, which the unprotected catchers appreciated.

Kenny, pounding his glove, started the game with his traditional, "Plaaay balll!"

Thus, the most memorable game in Ick history began.

113

CHAPTER 31

I surveyed Harper's Field: Kenny at first, Brad and Bryan Birge covered the rest of the infield; Curtis stood in left, Cus in center and Terry in right. I squeezed the white, red-stitched cowhide and inhaled my glove's leather while hiding a grin behind it. This would be fun!

Tex, smiling, shouted, "You look like Stink out there! Quit smelling your glove and pitch!"

I fired a pitch toward squatting Dwight and Stink swung and missed.

"Thanks for the breeze," gibed Kenny.

Stink grounded the next pitch to Bryan Birge near second who threw to Kenny. "Out!" I exclaimed.

"No way!" Stink protested. "I was safe." He waved his arms indicating safe as he repeated, "Safe. Safe."

My fellow pitcher, Dwight, ended the protest. "You were out by a mile, Stink."

"Ah, c'mon, Dwight. I was safe," said Stink, strolling back to behind the cottonwood.

Smiling Will stepped up. "C'mon, Yank. Let me see what you got."

"You will - Will." I zipped one past his swinging bat.

"Pretty good - for a Cub fan," he said.

I got cocky and launched a curve ball that he waited for and whacked into left field over Curtis's head for a double.

Behind me, standing on second, Will teased, "Pretty good."

Tex came up and purposely drove the ball at Terry in right field, which he misplayed, and she turned what should have been a single into a triple, driving Will into home. Pumping her arms, standing on third, she shouted, "Woo hoo!"

Dwight batted fourth, clean up, he smacked a high fly to centerfield. Cus staggered back and almost missed it, but gathered it in. Tex tagged at third and dashed for home.

"Home! Home!" I shouted at Cus.

He threw a low missile that almost - intentionally, I believed - took my head off on its way to Will's glove, who was now playing catcher. The ball buried itself in Will's glove and he tagged Tex as she slid in to home.

114

Light at the Rat Pond

"Out!" I shouted, and headed for the cottonwood, happy for a double play.

Tex looked at Dwight, who had watched the play all the way. "Yep," he said, and Tex, the most competitive Ick, did not argue. She played hard, fair and square. She picked up her glove and trotted toward centerfield without a word.

Our team greeted Cus at home, congratulated him for his great throw. He appeared . . . embarrassed by the adulation. I was sure he didn't get much worthy praise during his days, and I was also sure he didn't earn it, so he seemed uncomfortable as he shrugged it off and said, "No big deal. Just a game." Yet his typically notorious hazel eyes said something different.

Newcomers watching Dwight pitch could be lured into believing the cagey eleven-year-old would be easy to hit against. Batters with such false notions would soon discover that their air of confidence had been sucked out of them as they were blown back to the cottonwood to watch the next batter try to catch up to his deception. Dwight's pitches swerved, curved and dropped, and always at different speeds.

Bryan Birge grounded out to Stink, and Brad, trying to duplicate Tex, hit the ball to Glen in right field, but it was an easy pop-up for an out. I batted third.

"Come on, Jack," said Kenny, "let's get it going."

Tex ordered her outfielders to back up.

I loved playing baseball. I was a decent pitcher, and deft at fielding, yet I did one thing better than all the Icks and most other kids my age. Once while playing the piano with her, Mom said, "You have big forearms, Jack. Must be from working with those tools all the time." And for a boy with a lean build, I had unusually thick thighs. Mom said thick thighs ran on Dad's side of the family. Both physical attributes helped me be a powerful hitter, better than most my age.

"Give her a ride, Jack," said Bryan.

Dwight smiled, tossed a lollipop curve ball, a pitch he knew I struggled to pound. I swung, fouled it back to the cottonwood. "Dare you to throw me another one."

He did.

Physical attributes, including keen eyesight, are vital to being a good hitter, or power hitter, yet without timing . . . you will create more breezes for the defense than not. But I had excellent timing.

The curving lollipop made it to the plate. Crack! The ball split Will in left and Tex in center and rolled to the white gravel of Sid's parking lot. It should've been a triple, even with my average speed, but as prolific as my hitting was, so was the rocket arm on Tex. Without a bounce Tex's throw popped into Donnie's glove at third; it took guts to field a rocket from Tex, but Donnie had done it before.

Richard Newberry

"Good throw," I said.

She flipped her blonde bangs, said, "Thanks."

From second base, I shouted, "Bring me in Kenny."

Kenny's goodly stature did not translate into being a slugger, yet he almost always made decent contact. He fouled one all the way back to the frontage road before hitting one past Stink near second; I raced to third and Kenny stopped at first.

Barefooted Cus was up. Tex had all the outfielders back up, yet none of them knew what to expect from him.

We didn't call balls and strikes, but you only got eight pitches, unless some of the eight were horrible. After seven good pitches, Dwight said, "You only get eight pitches. You're out even if you don't swing after eight." I had forgotten to announce the eight-pitch rule.

"Since when?" Cus asked.

"Always," said Dwight.

"My fault, Cus. I forgot."

"Thanks for nothing, Hobbs." To Dwight he said, "Been waitin' for a good one anyway."

"C'mon, Cus," I said, "get me home."

Dwight hurled his fastest pitch of the afternoon.

Crack! Cus hit it high and deep to leftfield, homerun distance, about to bounce onto Sid's lot - until Will flashed into the picture. His legs churned in cartoon-like, Roadrunner speed; I thought for sure they would tangle, sprawling him atop Sid's gravel. But he maintained his incredible speed and balance to make a sensational over-the-shoulder catch.

"Wholly sheep gas!" exclaimed Stink.

Tex dashed toward Will. "Woo hoo! Woo hoo! Yeah! Yeah!"

Will's habitual smile was bigger than ever as he tossed Cus his glove. Cus, robbed of a three-run homer, not smiling, snatched the glove without a word.

There are spaces of time on earth I wished would never end; earthly slices of heaven that I could live happily in forever. That June afternoon's game at Harper's Field was one such heavenly space of time; it stretched over several thrilling, ethereal innings. For over an hour nothing existed outside of that baseball game.

And for a few innings that day Cus Lappin appeared to be having fun. He was just a kid playing baseball with other kids, one of us, not a scourge of the neighborhood, but a centerfielder with a good arm and bat. I had to wonder how often Cus had pure-quill fun, if he ever had had any, or was he always a brooding threat who denied himself any happiness in his young life. Did they laugh at his house? Did his mom scoop him some vanilla ice cream and swirl

116

Light at the Rat Pond

chocolate over it before they sat down to watch TV? Did his dad take him fishing? I only knew Cus as a dangerous bully. He rode alone; Dwight said that when Cus did go to school he skulked around alone. Could a kid have no friends? A very peculiar feeling, slight as it was, introduced itself to me as I readied to pitch to Tex: sorrow, for my shabby-haired centerfielder, whispered, "Hello". Maybe Will had done the right thing by asking Cus to play. Maybe.

"Quit sniffing dandelions and get ready to run," Tex said.

Stink dropped the yellow-flowered weed and from second base watched her bat. It was the third inning; score tied one to one.

Tex again drove the ball to right field, taking advantage of Terrible Terry. He ran straight at the ball, dove, bounced his face off the ground and somehow wound up with Tex's ball in his glove. A miracle.

"Out!" I said, heading toward the cottonwood.

Tex, almost to first base, couldn't believe her eyes. "You've got to be kidding me!"

Stink was stranded at second

Extraordinary feats became routine, yet we marveled at each amazing throw, catch and hit. Stink hit his first-ever homerun, Dwight struck out six batters in a row, Tex nailed three runners at home - including a very disgruntled Cus - and she made what resides in Icks' history as "the greatest catch ever". It surpassed Will's astonishing catch, and happened to be on a ball I had hit.

The bases were loaded in the bottom of the fifth inning when I came to bat; we trailed four to two, with two outs.

"Bring 'em in, Jack, bring 'em in," said Kenny, waiting to bat after me.

Cus had made the first out, Curtis and Terry both got on base, Bryan Birge made the second out, but Brad got on to load the bases; Bryan was now catching, because Cus chose not to take his turn.

Tex waved the outfielders back.

"Come on, Jack," said Terry.

Stink, more intense than usual, encouraged Dwight. "Come on, man. Come on, Dwight. Get him out." He pounded his glove near second base where Terry stood. "Big strike out here. Big strike out."

Dwight pitched, I swung. The sweet spot of the thirty-one ounce Louisville Slugger smacked the spinning ball. Kenny shouted, "Grand slam homerun!" before the ball was even soaring over the outfielders' heads. Jogging to first, I planned to enjoy the trot around the bases as I saw Tex frantically sprinting toward Sid's parking lot. The lofty ball looked to be headed for the tavern's asphalt roof, a first for any Ick.

Tex never surrendered.

We all saw her blonde hair streaking behind her, arms and legs churning

Richard Newberry

as she raced across the gravel on a collision course with the blue and white Cub side of the tavern.

Dwight said, "She's gonna crash."

She never slowed a bit until her body slammed against the tavern. Thuwump! The impact rattled the window above her, but she bounced up, lunged left toward the concrete steps at Sid's side door. Tex flashed her glove and nabbed the ball just before it hit the side steps.

We all stared in wonder at Tex, who lay fully stretched out on the gravel with her glove resting on the concrete step. No one spoke, we were frozen by what we had just witnessed; Tex didn't move.

Somebody broke the silence: "Is she hurt?"

She twitched, then raised her head, looked our direction, then looked at her glove to see the white ball snuggled in the webbing. She muttered something, I think it was "woo hoo".

Sid and a few patrons emerged at the side door to find Tex sprawled at their feet. She waved her gloved hand at them and said something to assure them an ambulance wasn't needed. Sid and his patrons, unaware of the amazing feat that had transpired, turned back into the tavern's air-conditioned darkness.

In an earned, reverent voice, Dwight said, "That was the greatest catch ever."

"Square dinkham," said Kenny, and Will added, "Pure quill."

"Pretty good," said Cus.

Tex stood, brushed off gravel chips. Her catch earned instant veneration for the tall blonde, who hobbled our way in an air of triumphant majesty.

When her white last-year's gym shoes touched Harper's grass, the accolades poured forth.

"Best I ever saw!"

"Can you believe it? Huh? Can you?"

"First-chop, Tex."

"Better than the Cardinals."

"Better than the Cubs!"

"Better than any of 'em!"

She lost control of the smile that began with her first steps back onto Harper's Field and grew with every step thereafter. Blood trickled down her left forearm, and her left elbow was chewed up and bleeding. Players from both sides – Cus included – patted her head and back as we congratulated her.

Will asked, "You okay?"

She nodded, tried to gather in her huge smile. "Yeah."

Our games were scheduled for seven innings, yet weather or parents sometimes shortened our schedule. This amazing game was in the sixth inning,

118

Light at the Rat Pond

with nothing standing in the way of us reaching the coveted seventh, and possibly the never-before extra innings. I didn't want the heaven on earth to ever end.

No maybe about it, Will should *not* have invited Cus to play; it cost us a seventh inning, because, unlike Tex, Cus didn't make a catch.

CHAPTER 32

All game long Cus struggled to catch fly balls, and his frustration boiled into anger in the sixth inning when Will popped one to him in centerfield that should've been an easy out. Cus dropped it.

He picked up the ball and zipped it at Will, who was standing on first. Kenny couldn't catch the ill-meant throw, so Will ran to second.

"What are you doing?"

He told me, "Don't worry about it, Hobbs." His surly demeanor was back; Good Cus vanished in a blink of an eye, as if he'd never existed.

Tex batted next and Kenny made a good catch on her fly ball.

"How's it feel?" I asked her as I headed for the cottonwood. She lightly punched my arm on her way to centerfield. "Like that," she said.

We were losing by a run. Each Birge twin popped out; Dwight had settled into a pitching groove. I was our last hope in the bottom of the sixth.

Cus, comfortably back to a brooding, angry nature, warned me with spicy cursing not to make an out. He wanted to bat.

I tried to ignore him, tapped the end of my bat on the bare spot in the grass that was home plate. "Come on, Jack," said Terry. "Get a hit."

Tex, while backing up, taunted, "Easy out!"

I launched Dwight's first pitch into the Icks' Hall of Revered History. I walloped the ball so high it was hard to see, and I knew it was also hit very far. Tex, in deep center, didn't even move, for she and everybody else knew that ball was long gone. It flew over the deepest part of Harper's Field, over the alley, then disappeared as it sailed over the scrawny trees above the tracks. Weeks later we found it in the thicket just below Warren Avenue. We walked off the distance after finding the ball and Dwight said, "That's a homer at Wrigley Field."

With the ball sailing out of sight, Stink said, "Wholly sheep guts, that thing went a mile!"

"Good hit, Yank!"

"Wow!" said the Birge twins.

Dwight said as I rounded third, "Remind me not to throw you that pitch again." He turned to look where the ball disappeared in the blue sky. "Spectacular, Jack. I think that's a major league homer."

My team - except Cus - gave me a cheerful reception at home.

120

Light at the Rat Pond

"First-chop, Jack," said Kenny. "Top first-chop, man."

Caught up in the euphoria of the moment, I suddenly realized and asked, "Do we have another ball?" I did not want the game to end.

"I brought one," said Donnie.

Just after Donnie found his ball near his bike and threw it out to Dwight, our slice of heaven was consumed by hell.

Cus had dismissed the celebration and barged up to home ready to bat. "Out of the way," he growled.

Dwight intentionally held the ball.

"Come on, Flowers, pitch. It's my turn, Blackie."

Two outs, score tied, and Cus ripped Dwight's fourth pitch deep to left field; it was going to be a tie-breaking home run until Will somehow caught up to the ball and made another tremendous grab for the final out.

Cus kicked and stomped the innocent grass; spit flew from his mouth as he growled at indifferent blue sky.

Will jogged toward him, ready to toss his glove to Cus, and said, "Good hit, Cus. I got lucky on that one."

Cus pretended he was going to nab the glove but instead let it fly past him as he reared back and punched Will's stomach. We heard the air gush out of our friend; Will doubled over, gasping for air. Cus punched the side of his head and we heard a sick, bone/flesh thwack! as Cus's knuckles bore into Will's head and face, knocking our friend to the ground. It was the last punch Cus would throw that day at Harper's Field.

Tex rushed Cus from the side and slammed into him with the ferocity she had earlier applied to Sid's siding. I heard wind leave Cus. Before Cus could respond, Kenny got a long, strong arm around his neck and cinched a powerful headlock. Dwight and I jumped in next.

Seething, his face red from anger and Kenny's headlock, Cus yelled, "Let me go!" and hissed unflattering names at us. He was stone-solid and strong, but we had him subdued. He struggled mightily and sweat popped out on his unwashed forehead. Of course none of us had been that close to Cus before, and he and his clothes stunk, as we had suspected. "Let go of me!"

Tex squirmed out of the pile. "Get out of here, Lappin!"

The Icks, except Stink, had him down and restrained. I looked at crumpled Will. "Check him," I told Tex.

Kenny's headlock continued to flush Cus's face. "I'm gonna kill you, Hooks!"

Dwight, on Cus's back and constraining his right arm, said, "You'll have to go through all of us first."

121

Richard Newberry

I had his left arm and leg. The fight slowly left him, his breathing labored. I felt his muscles relax. "Let me up. I won't do anything."

Tex had Will sitting up, blood ran from his left nostril and that side of his face was already swollen and red.

"I said let me up."

Dwight warned, "You try anything and we'll knock you out, man. And I'm serious as my clothes."

"When we let you up," I said, "get on your bike and get out of here. Don't start anything." Mindful of Cus's switchblade, I told Stink, "Go get me a bat."

Bat in hand, we let him up.

His oily dark hair stood in wild tufts. He glared at us with crazy wide eyes, which made his lazy eye more pronounced. "I'll get you all!" He pulled down his blue T-shirt. "Don't think I won't!"

His eyes didn't leave us as he sidled over to his bike; he sat on the grass near the probably-stolen bike and started slipping on his nasty, graying socks. His switchblade was within easy reach. His rage had transformed into an eerie calm in a matter of seconds. He nodded as he slipped on his boots, said, "Four against one, huh? I'll get you." He spit. "Don't think I won't, 'cause I will." He picked up the pearl-handled knife, rolled it around in his hands for all to see before jabbing it in his back pocket. "All of you."

I waved the bat. "Stay on your side of the tracks."

He mounted the bike as Kenny said, "Yeah. Stay on your own side."

"I'm on your side of the tracks, Hooks, you retard."

Now I pointed the bat at him. "You know what we mean. Stay in your own neighborhood, don't come in ours."

"You guys don't own anything, Hobbs. I'll go anywhere I want."

"Stay away," Kenny warned.

"You'll be first, Retard."

Tex had helped Will up and the Icks stood in a semi-circle facing Cus while the other kids put distance between themselves and the brewing storm.

Cus pointed at Tex. "And you'll be right after Retard, Barbie. You sucker-hit me. I owe you."

"Like you didn't sucker-punch, Will? Let me tell you this, Louse. You better not let me see you coming."

"Big bad Barbie. I'm so scared." He whipped out the knife, flicked open the blade, waved it at us. "Got a special treat for Sissy Boy. He'll wish he'd never moved here."

Dwight and I stepped forward, and Dwight said, "Here's how it is, Cus. It's like you're declaring war on us. And we ain't gonna just sit around all worried about your nasty butt threatening us. So if we see even a glimpse of

Light at the Rat Pond

you in our neighborhood, we're gonna bring the war down on you hard and fast. Believe it."

"Ooooo, you scare me, big brave, Blackie." He leered directly at Dwight. "Don't forget, you live close to me. Easy –" he jabbed the knife "- sticking."

"Get out," I said.

"You won't be so tough without that bat, Hobbs." He jabbed the knife in my direction, then offered a heinous chuckle. "Stick the Icks."

Kenny stepped up to Dwight and me. "Get out now, Cus."

Cus said in an exaggerated mocking voice, "'Get out now, Cus'."

Dwight looked as fierce as I had ever seen the usually laid-back and gentle kid look. He spewed cursing and ended with, "Remember what I said."

Dwight's vehemence struck Cus with a surprise he tried to hide. "It's been fun," he said, pedaling away. "See you Icks soon."

CHAPTER 33

Stink slammed his glove down, insulted Will.

"Take it easy," I said.

"Take it easy?" Stink said. "You sticking up for him after what he caused?"

"You mean getting punched by Cus? He caused that?"

"You know what I mean, Jack." He turned to Will again. "You should've never asked that jerk to play. You're stupid, man. You and your sissy religion." He picked up his glove and slammed it down again. "Now thanks to you we got this crap hanging over us all summer. You've ruined it, Pretty Boy!"

I warned Stink, "Don't call him that again. And you know what, you didn't even help us with Cus. Where were you?"

Non-Icks, except Stink's cousin Kevin and his friend Glen, began to scatter from Harper's Field.

The scuffle had ruffled Will's usually well-groomed brown hair; his eyes had the dazed, distant look of a prizefighter coming back to consciousness after a knockout. Tex said, "It wasn't a smart thing, asking Cus to play. You doing okay?"

"Little fuzzy," he said. "My head's ringing."

Stink and his companions got on their bikes. Said Stink, "I'm the one who's got the longest ride everyday - by myself. Maybe I just need to stick around my neighborhood."

Dwight said, "He lives closest to me. I ain't gonna let that punk ruin my summer."

"You can say that 'cause you're bigger than him," said Stink. "If you haven't noticed I'm half his size. And he's already got me once." He shot an ugly glance at Will.

"He won't be back for a while," I said.

"Right," said Stink. "Says who?"

I realized I still had a vicious grip on the bat and relaxed it. "You know how Cus is. Sometimes we don't see him for months."

"Yeah," said Kenny.

Tex said, "But this is a declared war, Jack. We've never been here before. He's always been a pain in the a- applesauce, but this is different. Who knows what that creep will do?"

Light at the Rat Pond

"She's right," said Stink.

Kenny said, "He won't mess with us Icks."

Stink turned his anger on him. "You don't have to ride by yourself for twenty miles - Retard!"

Kenny withstood the few verbal assaults from the seventh and eighth graders at Kickapoo who made fun of his mental acumen, but an assault from a fellow Ick punched Kenny hard in the gut, hurt him.

"Hey, man!" Dwight said, stepping toward Stink. "You call any of us by Cus's names one more time and I'm gonna knock you out myself! You hear me?!"

It seemed the entire creation hushed at Dwight's outburst.

Stink meekly nodded.

Dwight said, "Lappin doesn't stand a chance against us. You saw what happens when he starts his ugly business with us because you just stood and watched. We're gonna take care of that cat, square dinkham, man."

"What about when it's not *us*?" Stink asked. "I tell you this, we're gonna have to worry all summer about him jumping out from somewhere and stabbing us one at a time." He pointed at Will. "Because of him."

"He's right, y'all. It is my fault all this happened."

"It's not your fault," I said.

Looking groggy, he said, "Yeah it is, Jack. I'll go see Cus and try to make things right."

"That's goofy talk," said Dwight. "You don't go anywhere near him, Will. You're smarter than that."

I said, "Dwight's right."

Dwight slipped his glove over his handlebars. "This ain't because of Will anyway."

Tex asked, "How do you figure that?"

"'Cause Cus was bad way before Will ever showed up. Will just tried to be nice to the wrong dude."

Tex nodded. "Not smart being nice to Cus."

Dwight said, "I know you're pure-quill into Jesus and the Bible, Will, but you gotta give up on Cus Lappin."

Said Kenny, "'Be wise as a serpent, gentle as a dove'."

We all looked at him; Stink said, "What?"

Kenny shrugged but Will nodded, said, "It's from the Bible. Jesus said it to his followers."

"So be wise then, Will," said Dwight, straddling his cruiser. "Stay way away from Cus."

125

Richard Newberry

"I don't care what anybody says, he made it happen," said Stink. "It's his fault."

"You know, my brother Nicky always blamed somebody else. I love my brother, square dinkham, but it's never his fault. He'd try to make you think the only reason he's in prison is because the world's out to get him. I've had good times with Nicky, but truth, he's got too much bad in him, so he does bad things. Nicky put himself in prison."

I always believed Nicky's bad was the cornerstone of Dwight choosing to serve good.

Dwight added, "Cus is bad waiting to happen."

"Just be smart about things, guys," I said. "I don't think he'll try anything in the open. He's gonna be sneaky, so that means stay off the tracks unless you're with somebody."

"And keep a weapon close," said Dwight.

Will started walking his bike as the rest of us mounted ours. Tex said, "I'm not letting that scum ruin my summer. I won't give him the satisfaction."

"Yeah," said Kenny.

Asked Stink, "What if he starts hanging around just to scare us?"

"I'm with Tex," I said. "He's not ruining my summer."

Four pairs of eyes – because Will's remained out of focus – stared at me and stated, *You have not adequately answered Stink's question.* I said, "If he tries scaring us, we'll take the fight to him and end it."

Dwight nodded as Kenny asked, "What do you mean?"

Mom had told me more than once to stand up to bullies. She said if I backed down they'd never stop pushing. "We'll ride into his neighborhood and finish it there."

"What?" said Stink. "Are you crazy?"

"We have to show him we're not afraid."

And in a way, that was how it happened.

CHAPTER 34

Kate took a sip from the sweating bottle of Pepsi, which minutes ago had been ice cold, but now barely drinkable, and decided she had worked hard enough for long enough without any breaks from the steamer that she could slip out the side door for a dose of refreshing outside air. At her current work pace she would be home by four.

The side door opened to a shaded grassy space where a redwood-stained picnic table was tucked in the southwest corner of the break area. A thin stretch of woods ran behind the dry cleaner, and the plentiful birds with their songs filled their part of the world with melodious contentment. Kate sat facing the woods, pushed back her sweaty bandana and finished the Pepsi.

The other two employees had already taken their much needed afternoon breaks, leaving Kate alone - the way she liked it. "Katherine the Great!" her father had called her, and his presence and love caused her to embrace music and life. She had never been an outgoing personality like her sister Belle, but when their father died, Kate, out of anger, started a year-long journey of defiant rebellion and became emotionally and physically reclusive. After a year passed and she started playing the piano again, her rebellion eased, but she had adopted the loner life - until Andrew. Jack now described her as a loner who liked people. Kate smiled at the words, knew what Jack said was true.

She turned to look across Route 150 at her home. Jack never knew his mother as a deeply in love young woman who had been unfettered from the gloom of a despondent recluse, rescued by the handsome and caring Andrew Hobbs. Her son never had the chance to see her as a liberated bride who rediscovered a wonderful world she thought had long since vanished from the earth; yet Andrew gave her that world. Jack had never known her as the wife/mother so in love with her family and life she thought if there were a heaven, she was there. Katherine the Great had been resurrected. But Jack had never met her.

Jack knew the loner who liked people, that was who remained after Andrew was taken too soon. Aside from Jack, Kate vowed to never again open herself to the kind of smothering hurt that made each panic-stricken breath seem like the last one she'd ever breathe. She told herself, like the birds singing in the

Richard Newberry

woods, she was content. That was a good place, right? Content being the loner who liked people.

Her mom had moved to Florida, her brother Steven left Doverville after high school and moved to Atlanta to work construction, and he now owned his own contracting business. Doverville wasn't big enough for Belle, so after college she headed for Chicago and was enjoying a successful marketing career, a hard-working husband and two children - in that order. Belle called once in awhile trying to coax Kate and Jack up to Chicago. "We'll go to Wrigley - you still like the Cardinals, right? - when St. Louis is in town, hit Rush Street and Michigan Avenue . . ."

Belle was three years older than Kate and they had very little in common, even their familial bond had been splintered after their father's death. Belle and Steven - and Irma - were at her side immediately after Andrew's murder, but those moments of trying to be a tight-knit family that they weren't presented awkwardness and Kate was relieved when it was over and they had returned to their homes.

Kate had always been fond of Andrew's family, found their hard-working yet relaxed personalities comforting. Without trying to, for they were humble people, they were a family who impressed her; not with their money - and they had earned with their hard work an impressive amount - but with their genuineness. Kate knew they went to church regularly, maybe that was the defining source for them. Andrew had been brought up in church, yet he had begun to drift from religion before they met. He and Kate went a few times a year, not missing Christmas and Easter, but it wasn't an integral part of their lives.

Something suddenly occurred to her, something poignant when it began that she now chastised herself for letting it drift from her memory. It was the evening at the funeral home, before the viewing began and it was just family. David and Evelyn Hobbs were, naturally, grieving over their son's murder; Kate through the years had observed how Andrew's parents endured hardship (none as hard as a murdered son), how they were resilient, hopeful, not angry or bitter about very trying circumstances. That evening, however, David and Evelyn's countenances were sad and empty, hope lost, and it scared Kate.

David gently took Kate by the arm and asked, "Can we speak with you for a moment, Kate?"

"Of course."

In a private room, they pulled chairs close, faced one another, and David got right to the point. "We know you and Andrew choose - chose - not to attend church, Kate. We're not here to judge you about that, not our place

Light at the Rat Pond

anyway. But there's something that's tearing us up and we're hoping you can tell us something good."

"Okay."

Evelyn held Kate's hand, said, "We know you may not . . . completely understand what we're going to ask or why, but in time we pray you will. We love you, Kate."

"I know," Kate said, and she wept. And only as David and Evelyn Hobbs could, they comforted her.

David gave her a moment before saying, "As you know Andrew grew up in church, and when he was ten he went forward at our church and surrendered his life to Jesus. Confessed he was a sinner and asked Jesus into his heart as Lord and Savior. But we know as he got older –"

"Before he met you," said Evelyn.

"Right," said David. "He began to not want to go to church. We sort of forced him for awhile, but you can't do that forever. Eventually, a person is responsible for his choices. And if Andrew was walking away, only Andrew could genuinely make the walk back."

Evelyn said, "We hoped it was just a teenage thing. We all get a little rebellious at that age."

"I'm gonna cut to the chase, Kate," David said. "The only person who really knows if a confession of saving faith is real, is genuine, is the person who makes it. The Bible tells us what to look for in a genuine believer, and we saw some of that in Andrew."

"Your son was a good person."

David said, "That's not enough, Kate."

"He was very good."

They both, sympathetically, wagged their heads. David said, "We are afraid Andrew's faith wasn't genuine, Kate. And I think you know what we believe if he didn't have a saving faith."

Appalled, Kate said, "You think Andrew went to hell?"

Evelyn said, "That's what we don't want to think, Kate. We know God's love for us is beyond our comprehension at times, and we have hope in that. But like David said, there are things to look for in a life that's been . . . transformed. That's why what we're going to ask you is so very important."

Kate could hardly take in what they were thinking, saying.

"Here's what we want – need – to know, Kate," said David. "Do you remember noticing anything Andrew might of said or done in the months or days before his death that might have indicated he was . . . rethinking or considering his . . . spiritual state?"

Kate now, sitting at the picnic table, and then, at the funeral home, recalled

Richard Newberry

Andrew's sudden rekindled interest in spiritual matters. She told them how Andrew had begun talking about getting back to church, how it would be good for them and Jack. And instead of reading his favorite magazines - *Hot Rod, Popular Mechanics* - before bed, he was occasionally getting out his old black Bible and perusing the pages.

"He started, every so often, saying a prayer at our meals." David and Evelyn's eyes and attention were riveted to Kate's words. "And you know what? One morning he got up earlier than usual and I got up a little later and saw him kneeling in front of our couch. He didn't notice me, and he stayed there praying, I guess, for another . . . half hour, probably.

"How could I forget this?" Kate said to herself and the Hobbs. "So when he comes into the kitchen, he's . . . sort of beaming, and says, 'We're going to church this Sunday,' and I said okay." Kate's eyes fell to the floor. "But we never made it to church, because the morning he prayed at the couch was the day before Floyd Lappin . . ."

David and Evelyn consoled her, but their countenance had instantly brightened. "It's going to be okay," said Evelyn, almost smiling.

David's last words in that private meeting were, "Can't pluck them out of His hand."

Kate knew what they believed Andrew's last-days' behavior meant, and she was glad for them, but it did nothing to mollify her deep visceral hurt; it did nothing to explain to her why a wonderful husband and father was taken too soon, why Jack wouldn't be allowed to know his father or her to hear his loving words and feel his caring touch. Thinking about it as she fiddled with the empty Pepsi bottle made her angry all over again - and sad. Sad for obvious reasons, but for one in particular reason she never shared with anyone. The evening of his morning prayer at the couch, Andrew and Kate had decided it was time to try to start having another baby. The love was tender and beautiful, and baby Jack cooperated as if he knew a brother or sister could result from his fuss-free, quiet night.

Kate brushed back a tear, said to the woods, "Too soon. Way too soon."

A trucker blasted his horn out on Route 150, startling her. She turned and looked in the direction of the blast. Her eyes stopped at Sunbeam Bakery across the highway. Jack had mentioned the name of a new clerk at the bakery, a name that haunted Kate: Imagene Johnson. Traffic rolled east and west as she stared at the white-blocked bakery. Kate always sensed Imagene was somehow involved in Andrew's murder, whether as a dupe or more Kate did not know, but she would bet her life there was more to the story than what Imagene told the police.

The police.

130

Light at the Rat Pond

Andrew had called from work, said he was running a little late but would still stop by the A & P for their weekly cut of rib eye, said his mouth was watering for the succulent, grilled beef, and he'd be home in a half hour. It was October, when darkness came early. She believed Floyd Lappin had waited and planned for the darkness.

Kate had been entertaining baby Jack on the carpeted living room floor where the sharp-edged table used to stand. She'd lost track of time, didn't realize Andrew should've been home. Concern had just reminded her of Andrew's tardiness when there was a knock at the door. She didn't look in the driveway because she expected Andrew, and even said to the closed door, "Why are you knocking?"

She opened the door to be greeted by two sullen-faced police officers. The taller one said, "Good evening, ma'am. Are you Katherine Hobbs?"

Instant panic.

"Is Andrew your husband?"

"Yes."

"I'm sorry to have to tell you . . ."

Kate didn't remember much after that, for she fainted, and the rest of the brutal night unfolded in a disconnected, surrealistic fog that didn't lift for days.

"What else do you know, Imagene?" Kate asked, still staring at the bakery. "You were there."

Imagene had been in the A & P parking lot, and she had been at the party in the woods the night of Kate's Deplorable Indiscretion.

CHAPTER 35

Tex, Kenny and Will pedaled away from Harper's Field and toward their homes as Stink and his companions raced east; Dwight and I stayed behind to burn boxes at Sid's. We wadded old copies of the Doverville News into loose balls and struck matches to them, then stoked the incipient fire by tearing off box flaps. Once hungry flames started licking above the rusty barrels' rims, we fed them whole boxes. It would take an hour to finish the burning inside the three barrels that lined the alley. We each earned two dollars for the job, and Sid paid cash and fast.

"You think beer smells good?"

"Not on these boxes," I said.

Dwight nodded. "Smells worse than the tavern."

"For sure."

"You ever think about tasting some?"

"Beer?"

He nodded.

"Yeah, probably."

He tore off a flap and tossed it to the flames. "I did once."

"For real? You drank beer?"

"Yep. Nicky let me try some."

"Was it good?"

"I threw up."

I laughed, he smiled.

I said, "Wonder what Will's going to tell his mom and dad about his face?"

"Knowing that cat, it'll be nothing but the truth."

I nodded.

"You think we'll really have to go settle this with Cus in his neighborhood?"

"Man, I hope not."

"Yeah" said Dwight. "I don't think it'd be a smart move on our part."

I threw in a flapless Hamms box. "I don't know why I said that. You'd have to be an idiot to ride over to Star Street and start something with the Lappins."

"Or the bravest cat on the planet."

"That's for sure. I think the Hell's Angels would think twice before taking

132

Light at the Rat Pond

on the Lappin clan." I searched Sid's parking lot, said, "No brown Galaxie today."

Dwight glanced around. "Nope."

"Thought I saw the same car parked behind Kresge yesterday. Not for sure though." A rush of flame leapt out of the middle barrel, causing me to snap back.

Dwight chuckled, said, "Careful there, Jack."

I patted my bangs. "Man, singed my hair."

He laughed a big belly laugh, and it made me smile. I asked, "What?"

"Just imagined you running down the alley with your hair on fire."

"Did you imagine yourself putting it out for me?"

"Nope. But I did imagine your mom looking out your kitchen window having to wonder, 'Is that Jack running down the alley with his hair on fire?'." He busted another big laugh.

"At least she'd put it out!"

We both laughed until our sides hurt.

A few minutes later, I said, "You know that brown car I told you about at Kresge?"

He nodded.

"The guy sitting in it gave us the finger as we drove by."

"Serious?"

"Yep."

"Your mom see it?"

"Don't think so. She didn't say anything."

"Hmmm." He looked at me, then to the parking lot where the Galaxie had been yesterday, back to me. "Same cat?"

"I don't know . . . I don't think so."

"Just some messed up dude looking to flip somebody off?"

"Probably."

"Must've been a Lappin."

"Wouldn't surprise me."

Sid paid us and we headed for the cutover.

I said, "You know how dangerous it is cutting through here now because of Cus. Take the old bat and carry it with you while you're cutting back and forth."

"Not a bad idea." He ambled toward the fruited mulberry and retrieved our hidden weapon from under the tree. Thumping the barrel of the old ash bat against his palm, Dwight said, "I'm like you and Tex though. Lappin isn't gonna ruin my summer."

I watched him trod down to the tracks and safely up the north path.

I smelled fried potatoes and onions as soon as I walked in our house. "Blue gill, too?" Our favorite meal.

133

Richard Newberry

"Yes," Mom said, busy flouring the fillets. Normally, her day attire was casual slacks or shorts and a blouse, sometimes a comfortable sundress, but now she still wore a blue bandana and jeans from work; they made her look younger. "Supper's almost ready. Wash up and set the table, please."

We had leftover cherry pie for dessert, and as I gobbled it up I told her of our greatest baseball game ever and how Cus ruined it.

Mom sipped coffee, said, "Poor Will. Are you sure he's all right?"

"He was dazed, that's for sure. But he seemed fine when he headed for home."

Mom wagged her head. A far away look briefly overcame her before she said, "Nothing but a bunch of heathens - worse than heathens, reprobates and derelicts."

This wasn't the first time Cus's actions had been the subject of our conversation, and I omitted the fact Cus now carried a switchblade.

I was somewhat surprised at the passion in Mom's next words. "If that trash is coming over here causing that kind of trouble we need to at least call the police." With her mouth and brow pinched she said, "We are not going to tolerate that riff raff getting away with - with - whatever they think they can." Her expression eased as she said, "I'm sure the police are well acquainted with that bunch on Star Street. Why do people want to live that way?"

I didn't have an answer.

"Do I need to call the police?"

"Nah, I don't think so. We can handle him."

"You know good and well that boy is dangerous, Jack."

"I don't think Cus is a boy. He looks old enough to drive, but the Icks aren't afraid. We can handle him."

She raised her brow, skewed her glance at me.

"We can. Don't worry, Mom."

"Jack, telling a mother not to worry is like the Cubs winning the World Series."

"Uh-what?"

"Ain't gonna happen." She smiled.

"That's hilarious, Mom. Really."

"I thought so."

"I can't believe my dad married a Cardinal fan."

"He married up."

"You guys ever go to a Cub/Cardinal game?"

"Yes," she said, I could see her remembering. "It was after our sophomore year at the U of I. We went to St. Louis, to the old Sportsmans Park." She focused on me. "Got to see Stan Musial play."

134

Light at the Rat Pond

"I heard he was pretty good."

"Pretty good? They don't call you The Man because you're *pretty* good."

"Did Ernie Banks play?"

"Who?"

"Ernie - ah, come on."

"Yes he did. Your dad really liked him."

"Me, too. He's Mr. Cub. Who won?"

"Sorry to say your team did that day. But you know what?"

"What?"

"I'm glad they did. You should've seen your dad. He was . . ." She gazed out the kitchen's big window, came back to me. "Very happy that day."

"Cool."

"Yeah. Cool."

I poked at the pie's crust. "This may sound weird, but I really miss him at times."

She slowly nodded, said, "I know you do, Jack. I know you do. Me, too." She reached for my free hand, briefly held it. Squeezed it. "Listen to me. I am not going to let any Lappin mess with you. Should I call the police?"

"I don't know. You've always told me to fight my own battles when I can, right?"

"I'm not sure this applies. Cus is more than a bully."

"I think I should try to handle it."

"Is that being smart?"

"I don't know. Maybe. The Icks will watch out for one another."

"He's going to be sneaky, Jack. That's how they are."

"I know. We have plans if he tries anything."

"Plans?"

"Yep."

"I don't know, Jack. I think the police need to know what that . . . trash did."

"It's okay, Mom. Really. Trust me."

"Oh, great. A ten-year-old is telling me to trust him."

"Almost eleven."

I cleared the table, she washed and I dried; we were quiet. I thought back to the snippets Mom had shared with me about Dad's murder, and they weren't much on detail. Dad had stopped by the A & P to get steaks, it was already dark, he saw a man attacking a woman at the side of the building just off the parking lot, so Dad tried to help. Floyd Lappin - Cus's uncle - killed him.

Drying a plate, I started to ask her something but stopped. Probing Mom for more details regarding Dad's murder affected her like a fork raked through

135

Richard Newberry

a raw wound. Yet tonight's passionate response to Cus and her telling me to be careful because ". . . sneaky, Jack. That's how they are . . . " provoked questions within me. What more did she know, or suspect, about Dad's murder?

"What are you thinking about?"

"Oh-uh-just that - don't forget you said Will can spend the night tomorrow."

She put the Joy dish soap under the sink. "I remember."

"And you said it would be okay to go to church with him this Sunday."

"Yes I did." Wiping the counter, she said, "Make sure Ruth calls me to square things up for tomorrow and Sunday."

It still amazed me how quickly Ruth and Louis Corben, Will's parents, had made a good impression upon Mom. But it shouldn't have amazed me, because they possessed and exuded genuineness, and like Will, after just a few moments in their company you were put at ease by their altruistic souls.

Maybe Mom was thinking how thoughtful the Corbens were when she told me, "Never mind. I'll call Ruth myself. I should ask how Will is doing anyway."

"Okay."

Plates clattered as she set them in the cabinet. "One of these days we are going to have a new kitchen."

"Can't wait."

"You are going to be impressed by what I've got planned for in here. We are going to make this kitchen into something you'd see in Better Homes and Gardens."

"Like I said, I can't wait."

"Now, for your birthday. What do you want?"

"To ride on the hard road."

She rolled her eyes. "What else?"

"A catcher's mitt."

"Catcher's mitt. Hmmm. Okay."

"Can I have a campout again with the guys?"

"I don't know. *Can -*"

"*May* I have a campout?"

"I don't see why not. Just make sure I get parents' permission."

The big kitchen window set directly above the sink. I looked out at the tall, green privet hedge that bordered our entire yard on the east. Mom and Dad had planted it before I was born to obscure the sight and sounds of Sid's place. It worked well, and it provided great cover for hide-and-seek.

"I want you to keep a safe distance from Cus Lappin."

"Okay."

"I mean it."

"Believe me, Mom, I'm not gonna be asking him to join the Icks."

136

Light at the Rat Pond

"Good idea." She put away the last glass and asked, "How about going fishing Sunday after church?"

"Sure."

"We'll get night crawlers Saturday night."

For some peculiar reason, picking worms was one of my favorite things to do with her; maybe because as we were on our hands and knees side by side at night in our yard with flashlights we related more like friends than child/parent.

With a birthday and riding on the hard road and camping and fishing in my near future I rode the giddiness to a place of confidence, where I put into motion the groundwork for more of my furtive plans. "I think Will's gonna want me to spend the night at his house again - sometime soon."

"When did you say the berries would be ready to pick?"

"Around my birthday."

She pushed shut the silverware drawer. "I thought so. That's what I mentioned to Melba."

"Did you hear what I said about spending another night at Will's?"

"Yes. Do you think Ruth would like to pick berries?"

I shrugged. "Maybe. I don't know."

"I'll ask when I call her later."

Mom's aversion of allowing me to spend the night at a friend's led to her cunningly dismissing my first appeal, which on another occasion might have stripped my confidence, bringing an end to future appeals. But this plan and its groundwork was much too important to be easily cast aside. My secret plan would not be thwarted. I had planted a seed, and a wise sower knows germination requires water, light and time.

CHAPTER 36

After supper Jack headed for the garage and Kate soaked in a hot tub while she finished *Tortilla Flats*. Afterward she slipped into her pajamas, sat in the parlor's cozy wing-backed chair, curled her legs under her and spun the phone's dial until she had completed Melba's number.

"Hello," came Melba's soft voice.

"How are you feeling, my friend?"

"Oh, Sweet Katherine, I am doing very well, thank you." Melba never hurried over or wasted her words. Her easy, soft cadence reflected the humbleness of the petite lady. And though stricken with rheumatoid arthritis, Kate never heard her complain. "Mother Flowers has been a blessing to me once again this day."

"How is she doing?"

"Like a saint." Melba's mother-in-law always and graciously helped Melba whenever needed.

"That's good to hear. I suppose the girls don't give her any trouble." The girls were Janet and Roberta, Dwight's younger sisters. Roberta had been named after their father, Robert Flowers, who was one of Vietnam's earliest causalities.

"They do not."

"I didn't think they would." Kate hesitated because of Nicky, but said what was in her heart anyway. "You're raising some wonderful children, Melba. Hope you know that."

"God is good."

"Should I plan on working for you tomorrow? It won't be a problem."

"I will be fine, Sweet Katherine. And I am so sorry I have to burden you with my work."

"You know if you don't allow me to help you're gonna be in big trouble with me, right?"

A soft, short laugh. "Yes, ma'am."

They talked about work at Son-Ray's before Kate asked, "Did Dwight tell you the berries are just about ready?"

"He did not."

"Well, according to Jack and Dwight we've got about a week."

138

Light at the Rat Pond

"I thought it should be time."

"I was thinking about inviting Ruth Corben to pick with us. What do you think?"

"I think that sounds like something Sweet would do."

Kate loathed when female clerks or waitresses called her "Honey" or "Sweetie", especially if they were her age or younger, but she cherished being "Sweet" in Melba Flowers's eyes.

"You're always thinking about others, Katherine."

"I can be pretty selfish, my friend."

"Don't try to fool your old friend, Sweet."

"I'm not."

"Be a good world if there was more Katherine Hobbs in it. You sure you don't have Jesus in your heart?"

"Pretty sure."

"That's a pure shame. But I'm praying for you."

"Thank you."

"You are welcome."

"Did Dwight tell you about their baseball game and Cus Lappin today?"

"He did not."

Kate told her Jack's story.

Melba said, "Seems my son and I have what they call these days . . . a gap of communication."

"I tell you, Melba, those people are nothing but trouble waiting to happen."

"Hard to find much of any good in them."

"I told Jack I should call the police. I'm still considering it. Who knows what nastiness that boy is capable of."

Melba knew most of the history regarding Floyd Lappin and Andrew, but not all of it. Even with Melba, who Kate shared more deeply with than anyone - including Nadine, she held back the history of the Deplorable Indiscretion.

Kate said, "I hear about so many bad things those people have done and can't help thinking their kids are growing up to be exactly like them. It worries me for our kids, Melba."

"The bad they do has hurt you deeply, Sweet. You are wise to be concerned."

"How do you not go crazy with worry living so close to them?"

"I trust in God's protection and a double-barreled ten gauge shotgun my late Mr. Flowers left behind."

Kate chuckled. "Melba, I never would have guessed you to be armed and dangerous."

"Jesus tells me I'm living amongst wolves, and there's plenty on Star Street.

Richard Newberry

So as He tells me, I hope I am gentle as a dove, but also regard His command to be wise as a serpent."

Kate wagged her head as she said, "I just can't fathom a mom - or dad - raising children in that way of life, in a way that all but promises a bad ending. Have you ever met Cus's mom, or any of the parents?"

"I have seen them here and there, but I do not know them other than by their fruit. But as I say that, I think of Nicky. What does that say about me?"

"That's not right, Melba. That's not even a fair comparison. You are raising all of your children to do right, and you know that. We've talked before that Nicky had made bad choices, but you - we - have hope for him, right?"

"That's right."

"Don't even start thinking your fruit is anything like the rotten stuff the Lappins allow to grow. Your situation is way different, Melba. Way different."

Melba was quiet for a moment, then said, "Yes, I have hope for Nicky. He knows, because he was taught the Way, the Truth and the Life."

"Yes he was. Just remember that, my friend. And I don't know a better mom than Mother Melba Flowers."

Melba softly laughed.

"I mean it."

"Sweet, I know you do."

There was another brief silence before Kate said, "I just can't help worrying."

"Something in me says you are troubled by something else that has happened, Katherine. And it is not old history, but new."

Melba had tuned-in instincts, which abetted Kate to be more open with her. "I think someone has been following me, Melba." She told her of the mysterious appearances of the brown car. "But I don't know, maybe I'm overreacting. Who knows?" "I think you should call the police tonight, Katherine."

"I don't know, Melba. I don't have any proof, and if somebody is following me they haven't done anything."

"Yet."

"Yet. Right."

"Sweet, don't mess around with this. It doesn't feel right. I have bad feelings."

"Okay." She was scaring Kate even more.

"You see that car again, you go get its license number and call the police. Promise me."

"I promise, Melba."

"Thank you. Do you want to borrow Mr. Flowers's ten gauge?"

Kate laughed. "Not yet."

Light at the Rat Pond

"This could be serious, Katherine."

"I know."

They chatted about kids and life and picking raspberries before hanging up. As soon as Kate hung up the phone it rang.

Before Kate said hello, the voice asked, "Who have you been talking to for an hour, Murphy?"

"Well, hello, Nadine."

"Oh, right, hi, Kate. Did you hear about what that Lappin kid did today?"

"Yes."

"I'm tempted to send Texal over there and just clean house. I am not going to put up with that punk coming over here causing trouble. I'll put a foot up his butt myself."

"You probably would."

"Bet your life I would. What a bunch of trash they are. That Corben kid is as nice as they come, isn't he? Figures a Lappin punk would want to beat up somebody like Will. I tell you, I might just look for Momma Lappin in town and give her a taste of the medicine she and that no good husband of hers brews."

"That would be a sweet thing to do."

Nadine laughed. "I am sweet, aren't I? They just make my blood boil - you know that."

Texal and Nadine had loved Andrew, and they hated anybody related to Floyd Lappin. Nadine's hatred debouched from the recess of her heart to the world, but Texal's simmered out of sight.

"Can't help it, Kate - hey, are you going to the races with us this Sunday? Johnny Quick will probably be there."

Kate told a slight fib. "Jack wants to go fishing. I told him I would take him."

"You can still go to the races, Murph - unless you're fishing all night."

"Jack would like that."

"When was the last time you heard a woman say, 'Let me tell you about this good lookin' man I met while I was fishing.'?"

"Yesterday."

"Cute, Murphy. Nobody has met a grade A beef the likes of Johnny Quick while fishing."

"I might."

"I give up - for now. How about next Sunday?"

"We'll see."

"Thank you, *Mom*. You know I'll never give up."

"I know, *Mom*."

Nadine laughed.

Richard Newberry

They talked briefly about Nadine's cousin's upcoming wedding and handsome TV and movie stars.

"Gotta put Cheryl to bed, Murphy. Talk to you tomorrow."

Kate set the phone's receiver in its cradle and pondered her rambunctious friend before dialing Ruth Corben's number.

"Corben residence. This is Robert."

"Hello, Robert. This is Ka– Mrs. Hobbs. Is your mom there?"

"Yes she is. I'll get her."

Robert "Bobby" Corben was the Corbens' younger son; a bit precocious, but not in a bothersome way. Kate, like she did all the other Corbens, instantly liked him.

"Hello, Kate," Ruth said in a voice that proclaimed she was genuinely glad Kate had called.

"Hi, Ruth. How are you?"

"I am doing just fine. And how are you, Kate?"

Kate enjoyed the southern parlance in Ruth's voice, and it tended to sweeten Kate's impression of this bona fide caring woman.

"Doing well, thanks. Listen, a couple of things I wanted to ask you. First, how is Will doing after today's . . .incident?"

"You know, Kate, bless his heart, he's got a little swelling and is sore, but he's the same old Will. He'll forgive and forget. Does it like nobody I've ever seen. And thank you for asking."

"It's a shame what happened, Ruth. And I am sorry."

"Thank you."

"Do you know much about the boy that attacked him, about his family?"

"Not really. Will's told me some, that the boy is in a rough way. A bit mean."

"A bit mean is a drastic understatement, Ruth."

"That doesn't surprise me, Kate. Will usually looks for some glimmer of good in a person, even with the meanest of them. He did it back home, and it didn't go well for him a few times."

"Just so you know, Cus and his entire family epitomize meanness. And I am not exaggerating."

"I believe you. You don't seem to be a soul who exaggerates. I've been wondering about trying to contact the boy's parents and talk to them about what happened. But I know from experience that sometimes trying to talk to folks like that is like trying to convince cottonmouths not to be poisonous."

"Comparing them to a nest of snakes is appropriate." Other than what little Will knew from Jack, the Corbens were unfamiliar with the Lappins' notorious

Light at the Rat Pond

history with Kate. "Take my word for it, you'd be wasting your breath. I've thought about calling the police."

"You think it's that bad?"

"I *know* they are capable of very bad."

"My goodness gracious."

"But Jack doesn't want me to interfere. He says they can handle it."

"Hmm. You think that's a good idea?"

"I know they've had their problems with him in the past, and they've stuck together and ran him off. But I don't know . . ."

"Seems like a tough spot, doesn't it?"

"Yes it does, because I've told Jack he has to stand up to bullies on his own, but this Cus is beyond your average bully."

"Sounds like it. And we've told Will the same thing about attending to his own battles, to not ignore them thinking they'll just go away, but to wisely confront the problem with an attitude of forgiveness."

"I don't think the Lappins have a concept of forgiveness."

"Probably right, Kate. Plenty of folks don't want any part of working things out in a proper way, that's for sure. But Will is a different boy, and he'll trust the Lord to show him what to do."

Kate wasn't sure how to respond to that, so she said, "He just needs to be careful with that clan, Ruth."

"I'm sure you're right, Kate. Is Jack doing okay after today's incident?"

"I think so. Like I said, he thinks the Icks can handle it on their own."

"The Icks," said Ruth, a smile in her voice. "Where in the world did they get such a name?"

"I think one of them came up with it, who knows."

"Children and their imaginations."

"Uh huh. Listen, another reason I called is because the raspberries are going to be ripe soon, in about a week. They grow wild along the railroad tracks, and Melba Flowers and I pick our fill every year, and we wondered if you would want to come pick with us?"

"You know, I've picked plenty of blackberries, Kate, but never have picked raspberries."

"Well, now's your chance. They're not red, they're black and delicious."

"Well I'd be tickled to pick with you all. Bless your hearts for asking me."

Picking plans were finalized, and before they got off their phones, Kate warned again, "Ruth, please make Will understand how dangerous Cus is."

143

CHAPTER 37

Friday morning the Icks cruised the alley; we were alert and edgy in the aftermath of Cus's attack and threats of revenge. The chance, however, of him charging out from the brushy cover wielding his switchblade was slim - as long as we rode together. Our edginess dulled quickly though because our minds became occupied with the upcoming weekend series between the Cubs and Cardinals at Wrigley Field. Outlandish predictions followed gratuitous bragging, and they both gave way to personal insults and harsh rebukes.

Sweat and thirst came early that Friday morning, for yesterday's mild air had been shoved east to make room for Doverville's more common sultry summer air. We stopped for ice cold drinks at the switchyard, and two brakemen joined our Cub/Cardinal banter. They, too, disagreed with one another on which was the better team, but they agreed Will's white cruiser was sharply unique.

"Thanks, y'all. Jack over there is the one that built it."

"Looks good," said the taller of the two brakemen. "Looks like all of you have custom bikes."

Among the nods, Kenny beamed, "We're the Icks."

The brakemen nodded and headed back to work.

After lunch we traded our cruisers for racers and raced at the Rat Pond. I expected Will to win a race, but he appeared distracted by the brush-hidden Hoboland. Before the start of our second five lapper, I told him, "They're not there today."

He coasted to the far side of the track, peered into the thicket. "Yeah. I reckon not."

"Come on!" Tex demanded. "Time to race!"

Will asked, "Does she ever get tired?"

Dwight answered, "Not even when she sleeps."

After racing we decided it was time to search the grounds above the pond's water for discarded treasure.

"Been awhile," I said. We usually scoured the hillsides' cover about once a month.

Kenny found a push mower's wheel; Tex uncovered a ragged lawn chair and Stink found some rotting plywood.

"Let's keep that," said Tex. "I can use it for my jump."

144

Light at the Rat Pond

"When's the jump?" Stink asked.

"Soon," she said, pushing back dead brown leaves with her white sneaker.

"Hey, y'all. Found some soda bottles."

"*Soda* bottles?"

Dwight told Kenny, "He means *pop* bottles."

"Oh."

Bottles were a good find. They could be cashed in for deposit money. Lesser treasures, like Kenny's lawn mower wheel, were hidden outside the south end of the race track. Valuable soda pop bottles were stashed inside Booty Tree's hollow.

"Got something good here," Stink said, wearing a crooked smile. "Come take a look, Will."

"Watcha got?" asked Dwight.

Will peeked over Stink's shoulder and snapped back like something tried to bite him.

Stink laughed and Tex asked, "What did you do?" She walked toward him.

Still chuckling, he held up a tattered magazine.

Tex stopped. "You're sick."

I asked, "What is it?"

"You know what it is," she said, walking away.

Kenny and Dwight began not-so-discreetly migrating toward what Stink held in his hands.

"That's nasty, y'all."

"Says you," said Stink.

We sometimes found nasty magazines on the Rat Pond's dense hillsides. In 1968 we laughed and giggled at the scantily clad and nude bodies, then tossed the magazines in the pond. But by 1970 those images had begun to get a strange hold on some of the Icks; a few magazines were hid outside the race track.

"Need to burn that thing."

"Shut up, goody two shoes," said Stink. Kenny and Dwight were gawking over his shoulders. "It's going in," he said.

Will looked at me. "Going in? What's it going in?" He didn't know about the secret stash place outside the track. I shrugged, pretending I didn't know. Will's subtle change in expression told me he knew I was lying.

"In Booty Tree?" he asked, seemingly offended.

"No," said Tex. "Booty Tree is only for valuable stuff, not that trash."

I felt I had to confess to Will. "There's another place we keep stuff." Pointing south, I said, "At that end of the track."

"What if a little kid found it, Jack?"

Stink said, "Quit being a baby, Corben. Nobody else is complaining."

Richard Newberry

"I do," said Tex.

"That's 'cause you're a girl."

"It's because I know trash when I see it."

"Amen, Tex," said Will.

Tex let out an "oooo yuck!" that sounded squeamish, and she was never squeamish. Bees terrified her, but she didn't react to them squeamishly, she tried to destroy them. A squeamish sound from our blonde friend captured all of our eyes.

"What?" I asked.

Stink smiled. "What is it?"

Looking at the ground, Tex carefully backed away.

"What?" I asked again.

Kenny asked, "Is it a snake?"

Safely separated from whatever the object was, Tex looked at us and said, "It's one of those stupid magazines. But it's nasty bad. Oooo." She shivered and shook her head.

Stink ran to it, Dwight and Kenny cautiously followed. They looked down at what had put the heebie-jeebies in Tex. Stink started to reach down but his hand recoiled. "That is sick," he said.

I walked to them, looked down. I didn't want to touch it, but it had to be gone. In one motion I snatched it and flung it into the murky water.

"That bad, Yank?"

"Yes."

"None of it's good," he said.

Tex said, "I'm going to have nightmares."

Still holding the first magazine, Stink looked at the water but didn't toss it in.

The snapping of brittle branches and shuffling of heavy feet through dead leaves took our attention west, toward Hoboland.

Will looked at me and I said, "Yep. That's them."

He marched directly to Booty Tree, pulled out something from the hollow, then marched into Hoboland.

Dwight asked me, "What's he doing?"

I shrugged.

But Will's sudden march to Hoboland distracted us from a very important question we should have asked: Who had recently dumped such an abhorrent magazine at the Rat Pond?

146

CHAPTER 38

Startled, Kenny said, "He's going in there with them there!"

"Them" were most likely Hairy and Eyeballs.

I called out to Will before he disappeared in the thicket. "What are you doing?"

He turned, smiled, held up his right hand. "Gonna give 'em these." He turned back to Hoboland and vanished.

Stink asked, "What are they?"

"What he took out of Booty Tree," said Dwight.

Tex said, "Looked like little books."

"They are," said Dwight.

We hurried to the race track to be nearer Hoboland. We stood not saying a word, listening for . . . shouts and screams? Gun shots? The sound of Will frantically crashing through Hoboland's thicket to escape the fiendish hobos? What we faintly heard was Will's cheerful voice saying, "Hey, y'all."

Tex whispered to Dwight, "What kind of books you think they are?"

"Bibles."

Also whispering, Stink said, "They ain't big enough to be Bibles."

"It's those little ones those guys give out at school," said Dwight.

Kenny whispered, "Gideons."

"What?" asked Stink.

"He's right," said Dwight. "They're called Gideons. Guys that came to our school and gave out little New Testament Bibles."

"And Psalms," added Kenny.

Dwight smiled at him, said, "That's right."

Stink, Tex and I nodded at the recollection.

Tex whispered, "Hear anything?"

I scanned the inscrutable mass of brush and vines and weeds and trees. "Nothing."

En masse we edged closer, moving off the track and setting our shoes on Hoboland soil. We looked and listened. A sudden "boom!" from connecting boxcars at the switchyard jarred us back from Hoboland's edge.

Kenny's green eyes were big and serious. "You think we should go in there with him, Jack?"

147

Richard Newberry

I shrugged. "I don't know. Maybe."

"He went in there on his own," said Stink. "Let him get out on his own."

None of the Icks had ever had a face-to-face with any of the hobos - until now. From a distance, we saw them jump out of boxcars and walking the tracks. We glimpsed them resting in the coolness of Booty and Iron Trees' shade, and heard them scuttling around in Hoboland; saw the smoke from their rare night fires when they got together for a hobo shindig. Yet, we had never spoken to one of them.

"Hear anything yet?" asked Tex.

Heads wagged.

"That Eyeballs is creepy, man," said Dwight.

"Square dinkham," said Stink.

"Eyeballs?" Kenny questioned. "Hairy's the creepy one. I think he's a werewolf."

"Probably is," said Stink, knowing Kenny's phobia of the beastly folklore.

Tex asked me, "We going in?"

"I don't know. I don't hear anything bad happening."

She raised her brows. "You think we'd hear it if they stuck a knife in him?"

"He'd scream or something," I said.

"Think that might be a little too late to help?"

"I guess, Tex. I don't know."

Kenny said, "One thing we know is Hairy can't turn into a werewolf until midnight."

"Need a full moon, too," said Stink.

Kenny nodded.

Tex said, "What if they covered his mouth while they stabbed him? Then we wouldn't hear anything."

We looked at her without answering.

"Waiting for a scream is probably poor timing," she said to me.

"I don't know. Give me a break."

Out on Route 150 an eighteen-wheeler whined west.

Dwight said, "Will is either the craziest or one of the most courageous cats I know. A bakery heist is one thing, but this . . . is pure-quill gutsy."

I'd never regarded the hobos as threats to our well being, especially Hairy and Eyeballs; they were just ghost-like parts of the neighborhood. Sure, Eyeballs and Hairy looked a bit menacing, but my instincts reassured me the hobos meant no harm. Now a shadow of doubt had been cast over my instincts.

Stink said, "I say we forget about him and do some more racing."

The Icks looked at him.

"What? What did I do?"

148

Light at the Rat Pond

I approached Hoboland, turned to my fellow Icks, said, "We should go –"

Leaves were crunched, twigs were snapped. Somebody was coming toward us.

I froze.

Then Will's smiling face appeared out of the thicket. "Hey, y'all." He freed himself from a tangle at his legs. "I'm gonna start a Bible study with Clarence and Arlie."

CHAPTER 39

"Clarence and Arlie?" asked Dwight.

We were standing in a deformed circle around Will on the race track. "Yep. Clarence is the tall skinny one you call Hairy, and Arlie's the one that looks like he's scared all the time, Eyeballs. I can tell Arlie's really, really nervous around new folks, but they're both okay fellas. They smell pretty bad."

The questions came fast and without pause for answers.

"Did they have knives and guns?"

"Did they try anything?"

"How come they're hobos?"

"Were they drinkin' whiskey?"

"Is Hairy a werewolf?"

"Have they killed anybody?"

"I don't know a lot yet, but they didn't try to hurt me; they were drinking something from small brown sacks, and I'm pretty sure Hair- Clarence isn't a werewolf."

While Kenny looked relieved, the other Icks quietly pondered the light shed by Will's visit to two of the heretofore mysterious inhabitants of Hoboland.

"Y'all just need to go in there with me tomorrow."

"Tomorrow?" I asked.

"Yeah. I told them I'd meet them here sometime tomorrow, maybe after we eat breakfast."

"Oh," I said.

"You guys get together for breakfast now?" asked Tex.

"He's spending the night."

I stole a look at Dwight, who almost hid his fleeting disgruntlement at that news.

"So you want to come with me here in the morning, Yank?"

"Uh - I don't know. We'll see." The idea seemed bizarre beyond anything I could've imagined myself doing on a Saturday morning - or any morning.

Kenny said, "I can't believe you went in there by yourself with them there."

"It wasn't bad at all once I got over the smell. Got to get to know folks, Kenny, before you can really know them."

Dwight fetched his radio from Booty Tree and set it in his racer's small

150

Light at the Rat Pond

cage, snapped it shut. Voices and music faded in and out until he tuned in the voice of his favorite baseball broadcaster: Jack Buck.

"Double header today, Icks," said Dwight. "Cardinals for a sweep, baby!"

"What's the score now?" asked Tex.

Mr. Buck obliged. "Three to two. Cardinals going into the top of the third . . ."

"Wooo hooo!"

"Plenty of game left," I said.

"Yeah," said Kenny.

Once again the rivalry-fueled baseball banter increased while talk of the hobos and Bible study evaporated.

A few minutes later Stink said, "Let's go get some cakes and pop."

"Sounds good," said Dwight.

I took coins from the oof tube. I assured Will this would be a legitimate trip to the bakery, no thievery. Dwight, Kenny and Will waited in the alley as Tex, Stink and I took requests and headed for the front door. The cool air washed over us and Imagene spotted me as soon as we walked in. Her plump, painted red lips creased in an easy smile as she eyed me; I nodded.

We sat on our racers and devoured the day-old sweets before riding past Shorty's neat, weed-less and emerging garden on our way to Wonderlin's Machine Shop; cold bottles of soda pop, ten cents each, waited for us there.

Like at the switchyard office, we got in and out of Texal's shop without bothering the work or workers. We guzzled and belched on our way back to the alley and our bikes.

"Mountain Dew is the best!" claimed Stink.

"Pepsi," I said.

"Squirt," said Tex, and a slight debate broke out over which soda pop really was the best; nothing was resolved. After downing our last drops from the bottles, Kenny and Will returned the empties. We then pedaled to the garage and listened to the game.

"Anything going on tonight?" asked Stink.

"I don't know about tonight," I said, "but we're going up to Grandma and Grandpa's in a little bit."

"You and Will?" asked Dwight.

"Yeah." The Icks knew I liked visiting the farm, it was a special place, and of the Icks only Dwight had been there with me once before.

I sensed an awkward tension in the garage and tried to relieve it with, "But we'll only be gone a little while."

"We're going to the drive-in tonight," said Kenny.

"Lucky dog," said Stink.

151

Richard Newberry

"Might be getting our dog tomorrow," Kenny said.

"Cool," said Dwight, parking his racer near the compressor. "We're driving to St. Louis when Mother gets off work."

"See your aunt?" I asked.

"Yep."

I said, "You gonna be gone all weekend?"

He nodded.

Tex said, "We could bust bottles on the tracks tonight."

"We'll do something," I said. "When are you going to do your next jump?"

"If you and Dwight and everybody else will help . . . should be able to do it by early next week." Tex set her red racer's kickstand. "We gotta figure out how to get six oil barrels down to the Rat Pond."

"Six?" asked Dwight.

"Yes," she said, relishing the disbelief in Dwight's voice. "Five isn't quite enough."

"With fire?" I asked.

She just smiled.

"This is gonna be first-chop, man," said Stink.

"Yes," Tex said again.

Will asked her, "You're gonna jump over six burning oil barrels?"

"They'll be on their sides," she said.

"Well I hope so, Tex. Mercy goodness. That's still dangerous." He looked at all the other Icks. "Y'all think she can do it?"

"Don't know," said Stink, oiling his blue racer's chain. "That's what makes it first-chop, man."

"She jumped over five kids on the alley last year," said Dwight.

"They were laying down though," said Kenny. "And they weren't on fire."

Will smiled, said, "I hope not. But who'd you convince to lay down while –" Four pairs of Icks' eyes looked at him. "You're kidding me? But there's only four of you."

Said Tex, "We made Kenny's little brother Alan be number five."

"Yeah," said Kenny. "She'd already jumped four. We needed Alan."

Smiling, Will said, "Y'all are crazy."

We nodded, pride on our faces.

Dwight said, "This one is gonna be pretty nasty if it doesn't go right, Tex."

"Hey, Evel has had crashes before," she said.

"Yeah," I said, "and he usually breaks a lot of bones."

She shrugged. And we knew it wasn't a pretentious shrug. Tex lived for the challenge, each one had to exceed the last, and she knew that each came with what she embraced: risk.

152

Light at the Rat Pond

"Do your folks know you do this?"

"No," snapped Tex. "And don't you say a word."

"I won't," said Will.

I said, "They know she's a daredevil. They just don't know how extreme."

"I gotta say, y'all, it's getting exciting just thinking about it."

Tex smiled at him. "You betcha."

It was quiet long enough for me to hear Jack Buck call Ron Santo's game-tying homerun.

"There you go! Yes! Way to go Santo," I said, smiling with Kenny.

Stink said, "How 'bout we try to get up a game of hide-and-seek tonight?"

Will got excited. "Really? Yeah! I love hide-and-seek."

"Let's do it," said Tex. To Stink she said, "See who you can get up."

"I'll get somebody."

I said, "Don't forget next Friday's my birthday. Get your parents to call Mom so we can campout."

"You got it," said Stink as other heads nodded. "Campout night is pure-quill action, man."

And birthday campout night's action in 1970 would never be forgotten.

CHAPTER 40

Ice cubes clinked against the empty tumbler as he plopped it atop the magazine he'd just set aside. Whiskey and water, and Sinatra spinning on the stereo: true entertainment. He was in the hidden place, hands clasped behind his head, relaxing in his comfortable leather chair. He would not contain a derisive mocking laugh at - himself! An hour earlier he again had toyed with the idea he could forever and always beat back the creeping desire to do bad. After all, he had abstained from the Bad for a few months now; that's why earlier he really thought he could deny himself . . . forever?

Another scornful laugh.

He looked at the empty glass and melting ice, decided to mix another drink.

Yes, three months had passed since he last prospected and claimed a Prize. Not a record length of time in between bad deeds, but long enough to give him the stupid notion he could overcome Desire. When in fact, deep down, he craved Desire, sought to embrace it. The latest awakening to again start prospecting for a Prize stirred when he first saw the Prize. He had to have It. Problem was, his prospecting would have to happen too close to home, and the one time he had prospected close to home he almost got caught.

He sipped the whiskey and water, grinned. Wasn't the risk part of the thrill? Absolutely. But he wanted no part of prison.

Yet he knew how clever he was, and the advantage he had. He looked at the Silencer's exposed blade, grinned again. This Prize would be worth the risk. And he'd bet all he had that this Prize was one of the Foolish Brave.

How exciting.

CHAPTER 41

The three hours we spent at the farm seemed like three minutes. After visiting briefly with Grandma and Grandpa Hobbs, Will and I scrammed for the barns and machine shed, and eventually to the small woods and creek that cut through the timber.

I said to Will, "I'd love to live here."

"For sure. It's first-chop."

After some time exploring the creek, Will said, "I noticed your grandma and grandpa are Christians."

"Yeah," I said, tossing a small branch into the clear, shallow water and watching it drift away. "They go to church."

"There's more to them than that, Jack."

I just looked at him.

"Your grandma and grandpa are . . . pure quill. I can tell."

"Yep," I said, plucking a colorful rock out of the cool creek water.

"I mean pure-quill Christians."

I shrugged. "Yeah. I guess."

"There's a difference, you know."

"There is?"

"Sure."

"Didn't know," I said, tucking the rock in my pocket.

"Jack, not everybody who goes to church are pure-quill Christians."

"Yeah? So?"

"It's important to understand that difference. Can't you see that in your grandparents?"

"They're nice - but so is my mom, and she doesn't go to church at all."

Will smiled. "You're right, Yank." And in his brown eyes and smile I could tell the lesson was over, but just for that moment.

We were on opposite sides of the creek when I stepped up to the wood's floor, took a couple of steps, then jumped for my life. "Whoa! Man!"

"What's wrong?"

"Come here! Come here!"

Will jumped the creek and joined me. "What?"

"Look!" I said, pointing to a spot ten feet away. "It's a snake!"

155

Richard Newberry

Will leaned forward. "Oh, yeah - run!" And he sprinted the opposite direction.

I started running after him. "What?"

"It's a Blue Racer!"

I quickly caught up to him and we didn't stop until we came to the edge of a recently planted cornfield. Obviously we had both been exposed to mendacious reports about the actual speed of the Blue Racer and what it would do to its fleeing victims.

We excitedly shared our snake adventure with Grandma and Grandpa and Mom before we had to head back down to Doverville. I noted none of our elders rebuked any of what would have been nonsense we believed about the snake's speed or intent, so in 1970 our fear of Blue Racers only increased. We had a story for the Icks that evening.

Mom was wiping the kitchen table after supper and said, "Don't forget I have a seven o'clock tonight." She had pushed her afternoon piano lesson to this evening.

"Got it." I dried the last plate.

"What time is Will coming over?"

"Any time now."

"What are you guys going to do?"

"Try to get up a game of hide-and-seek."

"Pee yoo! This rag stinks." She tossed it to the floor and took out another washcloth. "If for some reason you have to come in during my lesson use the backdoor."

"Right. Can we - may we stay out till ten?"

"Sure. Just stay close."

I moseyed to the garage, and five minutes later Will cruised in on his pearl-white cruiser carrying a brown paper bag from Grab-It-Here.

"That your clothes and stuff?"

"Yep."

We took them inside before Tex and Stink and the others started showing up. In my room for the first time, Will said, "Nice Cubs hat, Yank."

"Used to be my dad's."

He nodded.

The Icks were always reticent when the subject of my dad's murder cropped up.

"I'm sorry your dad was killed, Jack."

I shrugged, nodded. I could see in his caring eyes and wrinkled forehead he wanted to ask or say something else about it, yet he didn't. He would later.

156

Light at the Rat Pond

I said, "I don't really remember him anyway. Except for Old Spice aftershave. I can remember him anytime I smell it. Mom says that was his favorite."

"Your grandpa wears it."

"Yep."

Again my new friend furrowed his brow and studied the blue ball cap with the red C. He was measuring his thoughts and what words might follow them. Still, he said nothing more - yet. Frankly, I had never met anyone who exuded genuine concern for everyone he met until Will Corben. He listened, and thought far deeper and beyond himself.

"You got some really cool models, Yank."

"Thanks. I like working on them."

"It shows." He pulled out plaid pajamas from the brown bag and laid them on my bed. "I got something for you," he said, pulling out white socks and underwear.

"Gee, thanks. Just what I need."

He grinned. "Nah, them ain't it." He pulled out a model, grinned bigger.

"Where did you find that?"

"It wasn't easy. We looked all over town. Mother finally ordered it from Alexander's Hobby Shop."

Amazed, I said, "It's the '62 Mustang Prototype. Man, I can't believe you got it." I looked from the plastic wrapped box to him. "Man, thanks, Will."

Will enjoyed pleasing people, and it showed in his smile. "You can start on it tonight."

"We sure can."

He dipped into the bag one more time, pulled out a small, black, leatherbound Bible. "This is yours, too."

"Really?" I said, slowly reaching for it.

"It won't bite, Yank. Well, maybe sometimes it does."

"Thanks."

"You already got one?"

"Just that little one from - uh . . ."

"The Gideons?"

"Yeah. It's in my drawer somewhere."

"This one has Old and New Testament. It's good to have when we go to church."

"Yeah." I nodded. "Right." I'd almost forgotten about going to church Sunday with the Corbens, which meant I would soon be near Rebecca Corben. I smiled, said, "Can't wait."

"Glad you're looking forward to it, Yank."

"I am."

157

Richard Newberry

"Listen, you'll need help when you start to read the Bible. I'll be glad to read it with you, but you're gonna eventually need the True Helper before you can begin to really understand it."

"Who's the True Helper?"

"You'll see."

I hoped it was his sister Rebecca.

Will, Tex and I piddled on the tracks while we waited for Stink and whomever he was bringing for hide-and-seek. We scrounged both hillsides' thick brush for discarded bottles. Off the alley behind our house the hillsides were about twenty feet high with a fairly steep grade, providing us privacy for our track activities.

We found some bottles and I stood one on each rail; we faced toward the switchyard. "How far back are we starting?"

"You pick," said Tex.

"How 'bout ten?" I asked.

"Too easy," she said.

"Fifteen?" Will offered.

"I guess we can start there - for you boys."

I started marching out fifteen strides, but stopped after seven. I turned to Tex. "I got it."

"Got what?"

"How to get your barrels to the Rat Pond."

Tex and Will eyed me, and I said, "We'll find a spot to roll them down the hill and then roll six of 'em on the rails."

She nodded. "Should work."

Will said, "How are you gonna get them there without anybody knowing? I'm not sure the oil company wants to get rid of six of their empty barrels."

"Well, first of all we're gonna take 'em back when we're done, so they'll never miss them."

"After they've burned?" he asked.

"It'll only be the surface. They'll still be fine."

Will nodded and Tex said, "And we'll move them at night."

I said, "Have to."

"Wow," said Will. "That could be tricky."

"You betcha," said Tex, grinning.

"Okay. I'm in."

Tex patted Will's shoulder. "Good deal."

"Look at that!" I said, seeing a critter scampering over the tracks at the cutover below Sid's.

158

Light at the Rat Pond

"It's not a rat, y'all."

Tex lightly punched Will's arm - which caused me pause - and said, "We know it's a groundhog."

I returned to the bottles and started marching off fifteen strides, noticing on both hillsides that the raspberries were turning dark. Next week's picking would begin earlier than I expected. We picked up good throwing rocks and I said, "You two go first."

"You first," Tex told Will.

He zipped a rock at the bottle on the south rail, hit its side and broke it.

"Good shot," I said.

"Not bad," said Tex. She cocked her arm, threw a bullet at the other bottle; smacked it dead-center and it exploded. "That's how you do it."

She stood a bottle for me. My first rock missed. "You've got to be kidding me, Jack." I shattered it with my next throw. "Finally," she said.

We backed up fifteen more strides. "You two first this time," she said.

Will and I missed badly with our first throws. Tex stepped between us and broke both bottles with two rapid-fire shots. "Okay, I'm bored. You two are no competition."

A locomotive's horn sounded at the switchyard.

Tex asked me, "Think it's coming?"

Two more horn blasts.

"Yep," I said.

She asked Will, "Ever had a rail penny?"

"I reckon not. What is it?"

I said, "We put pennies on the tracks and they get smashed flat. Makes 'em about the size of a quarter, only real thin."

"Let's try it," he said, setting two pennies on the south rail.

I put two on the north rail. "Best to have extras. Sometimes we don't find any of them after they've been rolled over."

The Icks were smart enough not to stay down by the tracks as a train rumbled past. Before the time of Will, before any of the Icks were old enough to play on the tracks, Ick parents warned their children that if we were anywhere near one of the big black locomotive engines when it roared past, we would get sucked up into the engine like sacks of paper, and our bodies would be mangled all the way to Chicago. So fear of being mangled kept us safe during our earliest years.

But, as we aged, we had to test the "sucked up into the engine" warning, for after being warned by those same parents that if we continued to make ugly faces at inappropriate times our faces would freeze that way, Tex and Stink

Richard Newberry

committed an entire day to ugly face making, and no fixed or frozen grotesque physiognomy resulted. Therefore, one summer evening in 1968 we volunteered Kenny to discreetly stay down near the tracks while an engine rumbled by. So Kenny stood just beyond the brush, barely on the tracks' gravel as we watched from above. We crossed our fingers as the train neared our friend; Kenny covered his ears with both hands. The black engine was on top of him when we heard a familiar "pshhht"! blast of air from the engine - and Kenny was gone!

Tex and Stink gasped. Dwight and I immediately began fighting our way through the briars and brush of the hillside, down to where we last saw our friend standing. Clear of the tangles of brush we found Kenny lying face down on the gravel, his hands still at his ears.

He didn't move. Passing boxcars swayed and screeched and made a terrible racket; we could feel the earth vibrating from the heavy rolling steel, and we were scared.

I shouted at Dwight, "Is he dead?!", and in turn Dwight shouted at Kenny's prostrate body, "Are you dead?!" He still didn't move.

Tex shouted from above, "Is he dead?!"

Dwight and I looked at one another, knowing what had to be done. Dwight grabbed Kenny's torso and I grabbed his legs and we rolled him over on his back, half expecting disfigurement. His hands stayed clamped to his ears, his eyes stayed closed; he looked dead but normal.

To my surprise, Dwight smacked Kenny's face.

Kenny's green eyes opened. He looked quizzically at Dwight, shouted, "Whadya do that for?!"

Thus, Kenny survived and our respect of the tons of rolling steel was entrenched.

Now standing on the alley with Tex and me, Will appeared eager . . .almost anxious, and I didn't think it had anything to do with retrieving a train-smashed penny. The train's cars were passing with a steady ba-bump, ba-bump, ba-bump and Will looked mesmerized, like a few nights earlier when he asked about train-hopping. He fiddled with the crucifix around his neck; his face revealed a mighty, internal struggle.

Tex said, "Here comes the caboose."

We waved at the men on the faded black caboose and they waved back. We cut down to the tracks and found three of the four pennies.

Will rubbed the flattened coin. "Wow. That's cool."

We heard Stink holler, "You guys down there?!"

"Yeah!" I shouted. "We're coming up! Got anybody?!"

"Kevin and the Birges!"

Light at the Rat Pond

"That's seven," said Tex, cutting up the narrow path we had tromped into the hillside over the years.

I smiled at Will. "Hide-and-seek time."

"You know it," he said, smiling back at me.

We wouldn't be smiling when our nocturnal fun came to a premature stop. Instead, most of us would be consumed with the idea of revenge.

CHAPTER 42

By eight thirty Friday evening Kate had bathed and slipped into her favorite, mint-green, cotton pajamas. She made half a pot of coffee because she had finished *Tortilla Flats* and was going to start *East of Eden*; to her, Steinbeck's best. She had the book on the kitchen table, ran her fingers over the hard cover, remembered the day Andrew had brought it home wrapped in Christmas paper, though it was only July. She looked out the big kitchen window to the privet hedge she and Andrew had planted when it was about a foot tall. Now it was a trimmed, green wall between her property and Sid's Tavern. It was dusk, soon Jack and his friends would be tearing around the house playing hide-and-seek.

The coffee finished percolating and Kate poured a steaming cup. It didn't bother her to drink coffee late, she could drink it just before bed and easily fall asleep. She liked ice water and a cold Pepsi, but coffee was her favorite. She supposed she got that from her father. She clicked on the table lamp in the living room, set the steaming coffee on the table next to the phone, sat at the corner of the couch and curled her bare feet under her. She took a sip, closed her eyes, ready to relax with a good book.

She glanced at the beige phone, sure it would not ring again since Nadine had already called to just yack and invite her again to the Sunday night races. Irma had called when they got back from the farm, and, surprisingly, their conversation had been cordial. Melba was visiting her sister in St. Louis, and Kate had spoken to her sister Belle earlier in the week. Her brother Steven rarely called. And since they had visited David and Evelyn Hobbs earlier in the day, Kate was confident she had time to herself.

The book rested in her lap as she took another sip, recalled parts of her day. Wendy, her last piano lesson, was becoming quite accomplished. Kate had been teaching the twelve-year-old since Wendy was nine, and now Kate wondered when she would have to tell the talented musician what Kate's father had once told Kate: "You have surpassed my ability to take you further." Wendy wasn't there yet, but would be someday. Kate was a good teacher and an excellent player; Wendy would one day need an excellent teacher.

An old, familiar flutter of sadness passed through her as she remembered the day her father had said those words to her. He was right, of course, but

Light at the Rat Pond

nine-year-old Kate didn't want to hear it. She sipped the coffee, said, "Miss you, Dad."

A visit to the Hobbs' farm always stirred deep and varied emotions, most of them good, but eventually sometime after the visit she would once again viscerally revisit the pain and hurt of losing Andrew. She would never stop visiting them, and knew she should go more often. The aftermath of pain and hurt was worth it because in those moments of visiting Andrew's family, Kate felt very near to her beloved husband.

She looked around the living room. Her and Andrew's plans had been to buy this house - it was paid for - then grow the family and move to a bigger home in the country. That exact subject had been talked about over supper the night before Andrew was . . . They had decided that evening to begin trying for their next son or daughter. Three or four children had been the plan, raised in the country, with Kate training the next prodigy, having horses, raising a garden, long walks on cool summer evenings . . . vanquished plans.

Kate heard a "y'all" from outside and thought about how Will and the Hobbs had hit it off instantly. Will was not bashful about his faith, and when he asked Evelyn and David, "What do you folks think about Jesus?", well, they were right at home. Kate sometimes wished she had what Evelyn and David and Will had, it seemed real and genuine, but she knew for faith you had to believe. And, well, she didn't - couldn't. Too many bad things. Too much that made no sense to her.

She wondered at times if she was keeping Jack from discovering a real faith. She didn't oppose church, or think most people who were religious were anymore hypocritical than those who weren't religious; frankly, she didn't see much of any difference in a lot of people, religious or not - except Andrew's mom and dad - their family, really - and now Will Corben.

Kate took a bigger sip. And she couldn't forget Andrew. When they met, Andrew had that faith she saw in his parents. She couldn't deny it. She often blamed herself for causing Andrew to drift away from what he had believed, to lose - if you could - the faith he had so embraced as a boy and young adult.

Andrew had said, "Kate, look at me."

She did.

"Do not blame yourself because I don't feel like going to church anymore. That's my decision, okay? I'm responsible for that decision, not you."

She nodded, but knew her resistance to religion did not help him make an equitable decision.

"I'm the same guy with or without church, Kate. And I love you."

They embraced, and sitting on her couch in June of 1970, Kate could still feel that embrace, still smell Andrew's Old Spice aftershave. And she remembered

163

Richard Newberry

the spiritual awakening, or whatever it was, Andrew had experienced the last days of his life. She could not deny his change, and didn't want to, because it helped absolve her from the guilt she had felt about hurting her husband's faith.

Was she now being detrimental to Jack discovering for himself some kind of genuine faith? What would Andrew think? What would Andrew want? She had answered that last question when she told Jack she had no problem with him going to church with the Corbens. She would not be a hypocrite and pretend about her and religion, and Jack knew that, but she had to let Jack discover for himself.

She went to the kitchen and poured another cup of coffee. Through the kitchen window she could hear the kids out by the garage. Darkness had come, inviting the hide-and-seekers. Curled up on the couch with the book finally open, Kate started to read the opening sentence of Steinbeck's novel when the phone rang.

She thought *who in the world* . . . "Hello?"

Silence.

"Hello?"

Breathing.

"Hello? Who is this?"

"You're gonna find out," the voice whispered.

"Excuse me?"

"*Excuse me?*" the voice mocked, then, "See you soon."

"What –"

The caller hung up.

CHAPTER 43

Some of the day's heat went down with the sun, yet most of the humidity stuck around, but that never hindered any of our summer night fun, especially a good game of hide-and-seek. We were hanging out in the garage, waiting for it to get a little darker. Kevin and the Birge twins were offering to pay me to build them custom cruisers.

"You should, Yank."

I did love building bikes, it wasn't work to me, and I never shied from the opportunity to make some money. "Okay. But you guys can't get me in a hurry, okay?"

They agreed because they all had other bikes they could ride while they waited.

Tex, pacing the garage's clean concrete floor, said, "C'mon. It's dark enough now."

"I'm with Tex," said Stink.

We played in our yard and used the inside of the garage as safe base. The big backyard of Shorty Morgan's rental property between our house and the Wonderlins' property was also fair territory; none of the renters had ever complained about us using the yard for hide-and-seek.

A new renter had moved into the house in January. He was completely bald and wore a handlebar mustache; he looked to be about Mom's age, and carried his slight frame in a hurried, reticent manner. I had never exchanged words with him, he usually avoided eye contact, but a couple of times he quickly nodded my direction. He mowed his yard like he was in a race against invisible competition, with his bald head looking down at the ground. Other than mowing or slipping out his back door to take trash to his burn barrel, I hardly ever saw the guy. Nadine Wonderlin - who had her sources - said his name was Curt Lewsader. According to Nadine's sources, he had no family in Doverville and worked third shift at the GM Foundry. She called him "Creepy Dude"; he did look the part.

"Let's play, Yank."

"Fine with me. I'm easy to get along with - 'cause the Cubs beat the Cardinals today!"

Boos from everyone except Stink - who didn't care - and the Birges.

165

Richard Newberry

I turned off the garage light, left the overhead door open, said, "This is Brad and Bryan's first game with us, right?"

They said, "Yep," in unison.

"Few rules you need to know. Seeker stays inside the garage and counts - loud - to a hundred by fives. Hiders have to stay in fair territory the whole time." I pointed at and explained the boundaries.

"Hurry up, Jack," said Tex. "We could be playing."

"They gotta know the rules. Hold your horses." I showed them the cantaloupe-sized rubber ball. "If you get hit before you make it inside the garage you're it. And seekers can't hang around the garage, they have to be out chasing. That's about it. If you don't play square dinkham, you're out of the game."

Stink, looking at Kevin and the Birge twins, said, "He means play fair and by the rules."

"Exactly," said Tex, eyeing Stink.

"Why are you looking at me?"

She said, "If you get hit, admit it." If Tex hit you with a ball, the honor system wasn't necessary.

We heard Rick Spencer's car coming up behind us across the tracks. We stood at attention as the orange beast calmly roared along Warren.

"I'll be it first," I said, and started counting.

Six bodies scattered, some decrying, "Not fair!" All laughing.

Excitement tingled me as I hurried to one hundred. What was better than a good game of hide-and-seek? I couldn't think of anything. I dashed out of the garage, headed for our side yard. I could tell Sid's was already booming because cars were having to park on the alley by the burn barrels. The tavern's best night was Friday, Saturday a close second. Even crowded, Sid's rarely had a rowdy crowd. If the wind was strong out of the east I could sometimes barely hear the juke box music through my bedroom window. The only outside lighting at the tavern were two beer signs out by Bates Drive and a floodlight directly above the front entrance. So our big side yard with its privet hedge, bushes and small trees was a favorite spot for hiders.

My sudden dash to the side yard startled a body from its hiding place behind an old, sprawling lilac. I glimpsed long hair trailing a running body, heard Tex laugh as she darted out of sight around the front of our house. I'd never catch her, so I circled back to the garage, hoping to surprise her or other hiders coming from Lewsader's yard.

I made it to the west side, Lewsader's backyard, but didn't see or hear a soul. It wasn't quite dark enough yet for hiders to just plop to the ground and hide, they needed standing cover. I slowed down, stalked my prey in the shadow-less night, expecting hiders to pop out and run at anytime.

166

Light at the Rat Pond

I employed taunting to lure hiders from their cover. "I'm getting closer. I can see you. Better run. You're about to be it." I stopped, listened.

Car doors and distant voices at Sid's, tires whining on Route 150, crickets and echoing noises from the switchyard cluttered the night, but I heard nor saw any hiders. I didn't move, said, "I'm getting closer. I see you."

A noise behind me. I turned. Somebody sprinted out from behind our silver maple and dashed for the garage. It was Stink's cousin Kevin. I fired the ball and missed, it rolled to the alley. Suddenly, bodies sprung out from everywhere, thinking they could reach safe base before I reached the ball. They were whooping and laughing and taunting me.

"Wooo hooo!"

"No chance, Yank!"

"Maybe next time, Jack!"

Kevin, Stink, Tex, Will and Bryan Birge made it inside the garage, but I plunked Brad Birge on his left leg two strides shy of safety.

"You're it!"

The game went well, no complaining, lots of action and laughs.

My second time being it I ran to the side yard again, but diverted to the south side of our hedge row where three bodies were hiding. "Got you!"

The race was on. The three hiders tore through the hedge for the front yard and around the house. Tex popped up from the ground and I threw at her and missed; she laughed, slowed to a walk as I chased the errant throw.

"I'll just take my time," she said, yet gathered speed as I neared the ball at the base of the silver maple.

I snatched up the ball, started around the house, when I noticed Curt Lewsader's back porch light was on, dispelling the darkness in his backyard. Then I noticed Lewsader standing on the back stoop, moths circling above his bald head near the light. He was looking down, talking to - Will.

I stopped, tried to hear. Lewsader wasn't animated, his voice was too low to hear, but his face strained from intensity. Will's head was mostly bowed, sometimes looking up and slowly nodding. I cautiously moved toward them.

Lewsader must have seen me coming, for he looked my way before pointing his finger at Will and saying, "Now get out of here." He looked my way again before stepping inside his house, slamming the door behind him.

Will slowly walked toward me. "What's going on?" I asked.

Even in the dark I could tell Will's face was pale. He looked like I'd never seen him before: scared.

I felt my anger rise. "What did he say?"

Will looked at me. His shaken visage began to settle right before my eyes, until he almost looked like usual, easy-going Will. He looked over his shoulder

167

Richard Newberry

at Lewsader's house, said, "Reckon we shouldn't play in his yard anymore," then headed for the garage.

"Why? What'd that jerk say?"

"Nothin' really."

I caught up to him. "It wasn't nothing, Will. I saw you guys. He looked . . .ticked off."

"Yeah, he was. But it's okay."

"It is? Man, you looked pretty scared when I first saw you."

He shrugged. "I guess."

I pulled his shoulder, made him stop and look at me. Was Will near tears? I was ready to punch that bald-headed creep in the face. "What did he say to you, Will?"

He took a deep breath; tears did not come. "Look, Jack, let's just forget it, okay? It's best that way."

"I don't want to forget it. I'm ready to take my bat to that dude."

"I know you are, Jack, and that's why I want you and me to forget all about it. It's the smart thing to do. Okay?"

"No. I want to know what Lewsader said to you."

"Jack, I'm not going to tell you. Sometime - maybe. Right now I'm afraid of what you might do." He smiled. "And I don't want to ask Mother and Father if I can go visit my best friend in jail."

I had squeezed the rubber ball almost in half; I relaxed my grip. "Why not?"

"Why not ask my mom and dad about visiting you in jail?" He smiled bigger.

"No - you know what I mean. Was it that bad?"

"No, it wasn't. That's why we need to forget it. It's no big deal, Yank."

We started for the garage. "They're gonna want to know why we can't play in baldy's backyard anymore."

"I know," he said, "I'll tell them something that's the truth."

Before we made it to the alley on our way to the garage, something Will said hit me and I wondered how its reality would impact the Icks, especially Dwight. Will was quickly becoming one of my best friends. He related to me in a much different way than any of the other Icks, which made Will special. But Dwight had always been different as well, getting beyond the surface of things, and that's what made him a best friend. Could I have two best friends? I didn't think there was any law against it, other than the law of human nature.

Tex asked, "What happened to you two?"

"You're still it," said Stink.

Tex looked at Will, cocked her head at me, said, "What happened, Jack?"

"Uh . . . baldy over there said we can't play in his backyard."

168

Light at the Rat Pond

"Why not?" Stink asked.

I looked at Will; Tex looked at him and said, "I saw him talking to you. What'd he say?"

"Nothin', really. Just to keep out of his yard. Stay in our own. Stuff like that."

"Stuff like that?" Tex quizzed.

"Yes," said Will.

She was not convinced.

Stink said, "It's not even his property, man. It's Shorty's. What's his problem?"

Tex looked to Will and me, her searching blue eyes told me she suspected there was more to the story, but she said nothing.

Stink continued. "That guy can kiss my apple, man. We've always played in that yard. I say we egg him good."

"No," said Will.

Tex pushed, "What did he say to you?"

"He just . . .," Will shrugged. "He just . . . kinda acted weird and mad about us bothering him in his yard. He cussed at me and stuff. That's about it."

"That right?" Tex asked.

"I say we get him somehow," said Stink.

"We can figure out something," I said. "But not tonight. He'd know it was us."

"For sure," said Kevin.

Tex said, "I should say something to Dad. He'll straighten out Creepy Dude."

Heads nodded. Even people from outside our neighborhood knew Texal Wonderlin had the temperament of a Golden Retriever, and the strength of a Grizzly Bear. The latter, when unleashed, meant a bad day for those choosing to behave in an ugly way.

"Nah, Tex. Don't say anything. It shouldn't turn into some big thing."

"He's right," I said; then I looked right at Will, added, "But we will get revenge."

Will didn't respond, but Stink said, "Pure-quill justice, Jack."

I nodded, so did Tex.

We played more hide-and-seek, staying in our yard and having a blast, and I think we all forgot about Curt Lewsader for awhile. Well, at least until the birthday campout night.

169

CHAPTER 44

Just a stupid prank call, she kept telling herself.

"See you soon," the voice had said, not in a tone or manner of someone wanting to get together for lunch or coffee, more ominous, and not the voice of some prankish kid.

"Stupid to fret over," she muttered, tucking her feet tighter underneath her. Kate once again tried to focus on *East of Eden* and Samuel Hamilton, one of her favorite characters.

From time to time she'd hear laughter and raised voices outside as kids ran around her house, submersed in the joy of a game of hide-and-seek, not a care in the world, living for the moment. She vaguely remembered those days.

Kate tuned out of her world and joined Samuel in the Salinas Valley, until the Creeping Taunt whispered, "Deplorable Indiscretion". She squeezed her eyes shut, touched her wedding band, tried to mentally drive out the long ago wrong and all the pain she believed she had caused by her rebellious tantrum. But she couldn't force it out, it had been part of her for too long. She was sure tonight's ominous caller belonged to her haunting past indiscretion, and believed the vulgar man in the brown car behind Kresge was somehow connected to it all.

Why had she ever decided to be with *him*?

She knew why, and wouldn't lie to herself about it. It was because of her mom, and Irma's constant parade of men after Kate's dad had died. Kate wanted revenge. She wanted to shove it in Irma's face, down her throat. So she set her sights on one of the most deplorable bad boys in high school. Being with *him* made tongues wag and salivate enough to get Irma's attention.

Irma had stormed into Kate's bedroom and demanded her to, "Stop seeing that trash immediately!"

Kate looked at her, smiled, and walked away. She would extract revenge for as long as she desired, even if it meant forcing herself to be at *his* side.

The Deplorable Indiscretion reached its zenith in October of 1952. They had all gone to Parle's Woods north of Doverville after a Friday night football game. It was a frequent party spot for kids from Doverville and around the county. Beer and booze fueled the parties at Parle's Woods, and that Friday night was no different.

Light at the Rat Pond

Kate didn't drink. She'd tried it a couple of times, and each time it made her sick. She tried smoking cigarettes to fit in, but they were awful. So she entertained herself by watching how stupid drunks could be. Amusing for a brief time, intoxicated individuals' behavior soon lost their appeal, just like being with *him* had run its course. Kate was growing weary of the Revenge Game. If only it had ended one night before the Deplorable Indiscretion's consummation.

Yet, ironically, if it hadn't been for the ugly events at Parle's Woods that night, Kate might have never met Andrew Hobbs.

CHAPTER 45

Stink, Kevin and the Birges headed for home just before ten. They crossed the highway in front of Sid's and pedaled east on the south frontage road. None of us had ever seen Cus Lappin anywhere near the south frontage road, usually he skulked on the alley or tracks, so Stink and company would be safe pedaling home. I scanned Sid's parking lot for the brown Galaxie. It wasn't there.

Tex, Will and I hung out in the garage listening to WLS on Dwight's transistor until Mom called us in just after ten. After our baths she scooped extra portions of vanilla ice cream and graciously allowed us as much chocolate syrup as we desired. I felt completely comfortable in the company of my friends with Mom around. She didn't do or say embarrassing things; she knew how to have fun with kids, and how to put them at ease. Yet I noticed that night she seemed slightly distracted, and I knew something was on her mind for she, a couple of times, twirled her wedding band as she talked with us. I decided not to prod at that time, and would ask her when we were alone, but I forgot.

At the kitchen table our spoons began to clink against near-empty bowls, and she asked, "What's on tonight's agenda?"

I said, "We're gonna sneak out after you go to sleep, take your car and trade it for a Mustang, then look for somebody to race; maybe cruise Main Street, look for girls."

Will smiled sheepishly, a tinge of red on his face.

"Few problems with that plan," she said. "One, my insurance doesn't cover ten-year-olds. Two, you still have a week before you're allowed on what you call the hard road. Three, girls don't go for guys in plaid pajamas. Sorry."

"We'll just stay home then."

"Thank you."

Will said, "We're gonna work on models."

Mom nodded, and I said, "You won't believe it. Will bought me the Mustang Prototype model."

"No kidding?"

We both nodded.

"Jack's been looking forever and a day for that."

I said, "We might watch the Late Show if anything good is on."

"Fine. Have fun and keep things to a mild roar."

172

Light at the Rat Pond

"We will, Mrs. Hobbs."

Will had Mom's permission to call her Kate, but he said the one time he did he felt embarrassed.

"And thanks for letting Jack go to church with me this Sunday."

Mom set our bowls in the sink, said, "You're welcome, Will."

He asked, "You want to go with us?"

If that had been Will's first time he'd asked Mom to go to church it might have been an awkward moment, but it wasn't, and Will covered all the awkward bases when he first met Mom and asked her, "What do you think about Jesus and the Bible?"

It took Mom by surprise, and it shouldn't have caught me off guard, but it did. The last thing Will Corben would ever be was inappropriate with an adult - or anyone -, but Mom's instant facial reaction of pinched brow and tight mouth suggested he had been. She then relaxed, said, "It's nice of you to ask, Will, but I think it's kind of personal. And to be truthful, I don't know what I think or know about either one. Okay?"

"Sure," he had said. "It's just something I always ask, 'cause I think it's the most important thing in the world."

Mom frowned slightly, but nodded.

"Hope you don't think I was being rude."

"You weren't being rude, Will."

He smiled. "Good."

So when Will asked her that Friday night to go to church Sunday, she replied, "I don't think so."

"Okay, Mrs. Hobbs. Maybe next time?"

The boy was persistent. She smiled at him, said, "We'll see," which usually meant no.

"C'mon," I said, "let's go work on the models."

"Thanks for the ice cream."

"You're welcome, Will. You two have a fun night."

"We will," I said, heading for my bedroom. I always kissed her goodnight, except for sleepover nights.

"Don't you kiss your Mother goodnight, Yank?"

I stopped. "I - uh . . .well . . ."

"I always do."

I hoped humor would save me from the situation. "You always kiss my mom goodnight?"

He blushed and Mom laughed. She came to me and pecked my cheek. "All done," she said.

"Let's go," I said to Will.

173

Richard Newberry

In my room, I asked, "Why do you keep asking Mom to church? You know she doesn't want to go."

"Somebody has to ask her. You ever ask her why she doesn't want to go?"

"I've tried. She always says she doesn't want to talk about it right now."

Will considered it, said, "I'll keep after her."

"She doesn't want to go, Will. And I don't think you should bug her about it."

He frowned, thought for a moment, then said, "What if your mother didn't stay after you about doing good in school or cleaning your room, doing your chores or helping her around the house?"

"Be cool with me."

"No it wouldn't, Yank. It wouldn't be cool. 'Cause if she didn't care, you wouldn't get to go fishing and other fun stuff with her."

"What's fishing got to do with grades?"

"We don't always want to do what's best for ourselves or others, so having somebody to stay after us helps us do right. That's what good parents - and friends - do, right?"

I shrugged, said, "I guess."

"It's not easy doing what's right, Yank. It's easy to do what's easy. But that ain't helpin' nobody."

"I never thought about staying after Mom about anything - I don't think. That's what she does to me." I pondered it, said, "You know, I do have to tell her not to worry so much sometimes. And I can tell there's times when she's feeling sad, so I do what I can to make her feel better. I guess that's like staying after her."

"Yep. In a way. And why do you do it?"

"Because I care about her."

Will smiled. "You sure do. You two get along different than most children and parents."

"Different good?"

"Yep. Different cool, even."

I nodded. "Yeah, I guess we do."

"We're here to help one another, Yank. There's no age boundaries to that. But we gotta be respectful. And you know I believe the most important thing - the only real important thing - is what we do with Jesus and the Bible. Going to church is important, but not the most important thing, but it's where most people start. That's why I always *have* to ask."

I nodded, yet not fully understanding. I pulled out the old card table and metal chair from my closet. Will, pulling out the table's legs, said, "I'd say your mother's mad at God about some things, 'specially your dad getting killed."

174

Light at the Rat Pond

He was right. "Yep." We stood the table on its legs. "That's a big part of her worry and sadness."

I slid my wooden desk chair to the card table, gave it to Will, and I sat on the metal one. "She said Dad and her used to go to church some. I guess she can't understand why God would let it happen. I don't blame her for that."

"You know, Jack, there's some real head scratchers that go on that'd make anybody mad or confused, and even doubt God."

"Not you?"

"Yes, me."

"That's hard to believe."

"Believe it."

I used a razor knife to cut the plastic off of the Mustang's box. I pulled off the top and we started sorting the pieces. "How do you explain when something like my dad getting killed happens?"

"I don't. And if anybody says they can explain everything about God, or understand everything about God, well pardon me, but those people are either fools or liars - or both. Someday we'll know a whole lot more."

"I don't get it. It's confusing."

"I know."

"I don't know what to think."

He turned and stretched for my new Bible on the bed. "What we know about God and Jesus is in this book, Jack. It's a perfect, holy book. God's Word to us, His revelations of Himself to His creation. If you're as Jesus says born again or we might say saved, that's accepting Jesus into your heart and life as Savior and Lord, then you've got the Holy Spirit in you to teach you this Word."

"Holy Spirit? That's a new one."

"Well, not really." His brown eyes were intense, focused; then they relaxed, he smiled. "I hope someday this will make sense to you and all the Icks. I've been praying it will. But what I was first trying to say is God doesn't say we'll understand it all or be able to explain it all - why bad things happen to folks -, but we are told to trust Him, obey Him, even when we don't get it."

"I sort of understand that."

"Good, 'cause there's stuff that happens all the time - bad and good - that we can't explain. I'll tell you what's back of all the bad, Jack: sin. Folks don't like to think it's that simple, but it is. Now why awful things happen to those who belong to Jesus I can't explain. This here Bible says bad happens to even His children, I wish it didn't. And truthfully, what makes some folks mad is God doesn't have to explain Himself to us. He's sovereign, righteous, holy and perfect, which means He can't do wrong. It just doesn't look that way to us sometimes."

175

Richard Newberry

I thought on Will's words as I got glue, tweezers, paint and brushes from my desk. I wasn't grasping all of what he said, only some of it. "I think you're gonna be a preacher or something when you get older, Will."

"If that's what He wants."

I had to ask, "Do you think my dad's in heaven?"

CHAPTER 46

Will didn't hesitate. "Your grandmother and grandfather do. And I told you they're pure quill."

"How do you know they think he is?"

"I asked them."

"You what?"

"I asked 'em. They said with all their heart they believed their son - your dad - is in heaven right now."

A peculiar yet believing sensation overwhelmed my emotions. It was as if I had been unaware of some burden I'd been carrying, and when Will spoke his words, that burden was lifted. I had had thoughts of God and heaven and all that, whether if there was a heaven and if Dad was there, but when Will spoke regarding Grandma and Grandpa's belief that Dad indeed was in heaven, it began to become real. "When did you ask them that?"

"Just before we headed for the car."

I'd seen Will standing with them, him nodding, them smiling.

"How . . . why . . .?"

"I thought someday you'd ask me about it, so I had to find out what I could." He smiled. "The news was good."

"Yeah. Yeah." My mind was whirling in different directions. Though I still wasn't sure, I said, "That is good news." Why hadn't this ever been discussed with Mom?

"It's very good," said Will.

I nodded, still trying to believe it. Was it true? Was there really a heaven? Will certainly thought so, and so did Grandma and Grandpa Hobbs. People I trusted. Again, why nothing from Mom? I knew she had reasons, but . . .? It was too much to think about. I needed to be alone, riding my cruiser, giving time and space for all these thoughts. At that moment I sought a distraction, and turned on my clock-radio. WLS was playing *Hitching a Ride*.

I said, "Let's paint."

Will brushed blue on the engine block slow and methodically. I brushed quick strokes of the same blue onto the transmission, finished it, then chose red for the manifold, quickly finished it; my mind still on heaven and Dad.

"How can you do that so fast? And it looks better than mine."

Richard Newberry

"Done it a lot." I looked at the engine block. "You're doing good."

Will studied the models on the shelf above my desk. "You're good at fixing and building things, Yank. You never slop something together. You do it right. Just like the rest of us, Kevin and the Birges are gonna love the bikes you build 'em."

"Thanks. Mom says I got it from my dad."

"You're good with your hands. I've seen your mom play the piano. She's really good, too."

"Yeah, she is. She takes credit for my hands."

"You ever try the piano?"

"Yep."

"Any good?"

"Mom says so. But I don't like it."

"Hmm."

I finally shifted my mind from Dad to two things I wanted to ask Will about. "You gotta tell me what happened when you went into Hoboland. That was brave and crazy-dangerous at the same time."

"I don't think it was either. I just went in and asked them their names. Clarence - Hairy - is more open to talk than Arlie - Eyeballs - is. Matter of fact, he didn't say a word the whole time. Just looked around with his wide eyes, looking kind of suspicious of me. Clarence, he opened right up. Like I told you, I only got close enough to know they stink pretty bad."

"You weren't scared?"

"A little. But I reckon sometimes being scared is part of doing what's right. Fear probably keeps us from doing more that's right - and good." Will looked away, stared at nothing, began to blink more than normal (making me think of Mom when she gave me the Doofus Look), and I learned his blinking stare meant a thought was forthcoming. "This may sound weird, but I'm thinking that if folks use only their feelings when they do something, it can do more harm than good."

"How's that?"

It took him a moment to answer. "Like with the hobos, Arlie and Clarence. My feelings tell me I want to give them new clothes and food, a good home . . . all the stuff we have, Jack. Nothing wrong with that, right?"

"I guess not."

"But there sorta is. You see, just giving them stuff - which would be easy if I had it - wouldn't really help them. It'd do for a bit, but it wouldn't *really* help them. That's where my brain has to tell my feelings it takes more than just giving them stuff to really help them."

"Okay."

178

Light at the Rat Pond

"It's like homework. I'm not good at arithmetic –"

"Who is?"

He smiled. "Dwight."

"True."

"Anyway, my father's good at it, so he helps me. He's pretty busy, and it'd be easier for him to just do it for me, but he wants me to learn it, to be able someday to do it on my own. It's harder for him – and me, but he knows it's gonna take my effort, my wanting to do it, for me to ever learn arithmetic."

I nodded. "So just giving stuff to the hobos isn't as good as . . . what? Helping them get stuff on their own?"

He grinned. "That's it, Yank." His grin faded as he said, "Sad part is we know some folks don't care, don't want to help themselves."

"Then what do we do?"

He stared, blinked. "I don't know. I think our feelings would say just keep giving stuff to them, but they'd never learn. We'd have to do the right thing, like my parents have told me: there's gonna be consequences to their behavior."

"Pure quill. Mom reminds me of that one."

"What's sad and bad is if some folks are never made to face up to their bad choices. That's what Mother says, folks make choices."

"Mom says something like, 'They made their bed, now they have to sleep in it'."

Will nodded. "Yep. And I know some folks have a rougher life than others. We got it pretty good, Yank. Got family that loves us, teaches us right from wrong."

I nodded, said, "Guys like Cus Lappin."

He sighed, said, "He has it harder than us, that's for sure."

It was hard to believe that I would ever feel even a trickle of empathy for our enemy who had beaten Will and all but promised to stab each of the Icks with his switchblade. But I did.

"But, Jack, Cus has to make his choices. It's one thing to feel sorry for him, but it's gonna take him, with somebody wanting to help him help himself, to change Cus."

"I think you're talking miracle now."

He half smiled. "Maybe."

We were quiet while our tiny paint brushes smoothed paint over exhaust parts; the radio played *Spirit in the Sky.*

"Like that one," said Will.

"Yep. So does Kenny."

"Think he'll get his dog?"

"Don't know. They've talked about getting one before."

179

Richard Newberry

Will was getting faster at painting. I asked him, "Your first model?"

"Yep."

"You're doing good."

"I hope so. All your models look . . .perfect."

"They're not, but thanks." I finished with the black and set the brush in a bottle of paint thinner. "I gotta know how you got the hobos to want a Bible study."

"Asked 'em. That's all."

"They just said yes?"

"Pretty much, yep. Clarence said it'd been a long time since he'd had a Bible open and he reckoned it wouldn't hurt. Arlie watched Clarence agree so he nodded."

"I could never do that – ask them to have a Bible study."

"You gonna go with me tomorrow to the Bible study with 'em?"

"I don't know. I'm not sure. But don't say anything to Mom about it. She's not gonna think hanging around with hobos is a good idea."

"I understand." Will put his brush in the thinner. "Might seem hard to you now, but someday it might not seem that way, especially with the Holy Spirit's help."

There It was again. "I don't get this Holy Spirit stuff."

"I know it's strange to you. It's who comes to live inside you when you've accepted Jesus as your Savior."

"Really?" I asked, and I know I sounded dubious.

Will smiled, "I'm not putting you on, Jack. It's for real."

"Just never heard about him – or it – or whatever." And though Will spoke of it often, I still wasn't absolutely sold on the Jesus and Savior business.

"The Holy Spirit is sorta like another part of God, like Jesus is, but they're both their own . . . person, but still part of God."

"Gotcha," I said.

He grinned, said, "I know it seems confusing."

"It doesn't seem, it is."

"Oh, Yank, you picked a near impossible one for me to explain. Think about it this way. When somebody asks Jesus to be their Savior, the Holy Spirit comes and lives inside them; like a helper, He teaches them about the things of God, like the Bible."

"He's like a live-in tutor?"

"Yes! That's a good way to put it."

To impress Will Corben with something religious . . . well, a measure of pride eased through me.

I gave him a clean brush and opened a bottle of silver paint. I took an

180

Light at the Rat Pond

indirect route to gather vital information. "Your whole family goes to church, right?"

"Of course."

I nodded, said, "I figured."

"Why?"

"Just wondering."

Will dipped his brush into the silver paint. "She'll be there, Yank."

I attempted complete ignorance. "Who?"

"Your face is as red as that paint over there." He laughed. "C'mon, Yank. You know when you spent the night at my house you were more smitten with Rebecca than you are this Mustang."

Now despite my flushed-face reaction, I said, "You're crazy, man. You were seeing things."

He laughed again. "No, Yank, you were seeing things."

I avoided eye contact with him, kept my brush busy on the car parts.

"You always put ten coats on each part?"

"Yes."

He howled laughter. "You're killing me."

"Good."

"It's okay if you like my sister. You want me to tell her you're smitten?"

I jerked my head up. "No! What's smitten mean?"

His smile grew. "It means we could be brother-in-laws."

"Don't say anything, okay?"

"Okay, I won't. You'll just have to work it out on your own."

Time to change topics. I asked, "You ever gonna tell me what Lewsader said to you tonight?"

"Like I said, it was just a guy mad about kids being in his yard, that's all. Probably was already having a bad day and I was there to take it out on."

"You looked pretty scared when I saw you."

Will just shrugged as he put the last bit of paint on the rear axle cover.

He never said more about it, and I believed he didn't want to because the guy was our neighbor, and Will did not want to exacerbate the situation by telling me the whole truth of what Lewsader had said. I believed - no, I knew - there was more to it than Will was telling, but I let it go; later that summer I would be forced to come back to it.

"All right," I said. "But we're gonna get even for him trying to ruin our game and messing with you."

Will, surprisingly, didn't protest the idea of revenge.

"We'll come up with something and do it next Friday at our campout."

"You really think we should?"

181

"Have to, Will."

"Have to?"

"Yep."

He said no more.

We cleaned up and put away. I switched off the radio, said, "Let's go see what's on the Late Show."

From her bedroom Kate could hear Will laughing, but that wasn't what was keeping her awake. Through her screened window the night sounds, which normally helped lull her to sleep, seemed amplified, almost disturbing, but she knew that wasn't the reason sleep wouldn't come. A couple of times during *East of Eden* her eyes closed and she lingered between faint consciousness and slumber, only to become restless after she turned off the lamp and lay in the darkness.

Now, flat on her back in the dark, she stared at the ceiling, twirled her wedding band with her thumb.

"See you soon," resounded in her mind. Her attempts to convince herself it was merely a kid's prank call had failed. She knew it was a threat, and knew it was somehow connected to that Friday night so many years ago in Parle's Woods.

Her mind raced, primarily asking the same question over and over: what should she do?

She had to protect Jack and herself. She knew the police couldn't help – yet. Maybe it was time to let Texal help. But how? And wouldn't that put him in danger?

Frustrated, she punished her pillows, and flopped to her side, said, "You're imaging things, Hobbs," and tried to will sleep to come. An eternity passed before she surrendered and turned the lamp back on. She snatched her book from the table, sighed, and tried again to read herself to sleep. She could barely hear the TV in the living room. It didn't bother her; it actually comforted her knowing Jack and Will were also awake. Kate had to do something about the call, tell somebody, ask for Texal's help, something. Should she say anything to Jack? Maybe. Probably. But then how much would she have to tell him about the Deplorable Indiscretion?

She reminded herself things always seemed worse at night. With the light of day would come answers to her questions.

And for as long as it took, Kate would be carefully watching.

CHAPTER 47

The Late Show turned out to be a pretty good one: *Sherlock Holmes and the Hounds of the Baskervilles.*

We drank Pepsi, ate Milk Duds and Chuckles candy while watching the movie from our pallet on the floor in front of the television. During a commercial after a fairly spooky scene at a foggy moor, I asked Will, "You think Cus can help the way he is?"

"It's gotta be harder for him not to be mean, but yeah, if he tried he could help it. Just like Clarence and Arlie could help themselves."

Will appeared to ruminate as he slowly chewed the chocolate and caramel of a couple of Milk Duds. "You know though, Yank, folks like Cus and the hobos could sure be helped by knowing someone really cares about them."

I said, "Sorta doesn't seem fair - Cus and his family and all. I've seen his mom in town, she looks pretty mean herself. Dwight says their whole family's that way, except one of Cus's older sisters. Dwight sees her at school, says she's different; she tries to be nice. But the dad and Cus's brothers and other sister are just mean people."

"Sad, ain't it?"

"Yep. And what's weird is, now I'm starting to feel a little sorry for Cus, because it doesn't seem like he's getting a fair chance."

Will stopped chewing, through tight lips with a little chocolate seeping out, he said, "You're a good person, Yank."

"I don't know about that. Guess if anybody really thinks about it they'd feel a little sorry, too." I smiled. "Until they met him."

"True." Will swallowed, licked his lips. "It's tougher for Cus, for sure. But you know what? Sometimes the best people come from the worst places."

While I considered that, he added, "I'll bet his one sister is gonna turn out pretty good. Hope so."

I said, "It's kinda like Shorty Morgan."

"How's that?"

"Mom told me when he moved up here from Kentucky he was . . . how'd she put it? Oh, 'too poor to pay attention'. Yeah, too poor to pay attention. That made him not want to be poor anymore, so he worked hard as he could and ended up owning most of our neighborhood and being pretty rich." I tossed

183

Richard Newberry

in a couple of Milk Duds, sucked the chocolate off the caramel. "But you can't tell by looking at him he's loaded, other than his house."

"They got any kids?"

"Nope."

Will nodded, drank some Pepsi. "Yeah. Shorty's what I mean. Unless there's something really bad wrong - like being sick in the head or something - folks have choices to make. But, Yank, folks need folks, even when they think or act like they don't. Most important, everybody needs Jesus."

The commercials ended and we were quiet until the next batch came on.

I said, "Cus doesn't help himself getting friends."

"He is a mean one."

"What do you think happened to Hair- Clarence and Arlie?"

"Don't know. Reckon I might find out. I think if folks know you're being pure quill with them, they'll want to tell you their story. You gotta be sincere though. The Lord works that out. And it's important to know where folks come from, but it's more important to help show them, here and now, the way to the best life waiting up ahead for 'em. If they want it."

"How can you be so nice to people who are mean to you?"

"It ain't me, Yank. If it was me, I'd be mean right back. So I always try to let the Holy Spirit work through me. He's the one that treats folks right, not me."

"That almost sounds like *Invasion of the Body Snatchers* or something."

He smiled. "I know it's not easy to understand." He cleared his throat. "Even though God works through me by His Holy Spirit, I'm still Will Corben, not a robot. He's changing me from the inside, but I'm still the boy he created. Make sense?"

I shrugged. "I don't know. Maybe."

"My love for folks has to be sincere, Yank. And that's what the Holy Spirit helps me on. Like I said, when somebody - like Cus - knows you are pure quill, it can change them."

"I don't think Cus cares if you or anybody cares about him."

"Sometimes that's true."

The movie was coming back on when he said, "But I'm not giving up easy. I'm gonna keep trying."

Holmes and Watson's return to the screen distracted me from pursuing Will's "I'm gonna keep trying" promise.

And later that summer I was certain Will's "trying" opened the door for suffering.

CHAPTER 48

Mom, looking tired, made French toast for breakfast.

"More milk?" she asked Will.

"Yes please."

"What are you two up to today?"

Will started to say something about hobo Bible study, but stopped.

I said, "Usual stuff. Hopping trains, robbing banks, riding the hard road, playing with fire . . . usual stuff."

"You'll be playing with fire if I catch you on the hard road before next Friday."

"Come on," I pleaded. "That's only six days away. I can be just as careful today as I will be then."

"It's about rules, Jack," she said, pouring Will and me more milk. "Obeying them now gives you more freedom later."

"She's got you there, Yank."

Mom nodded.

"Oh, great," I said. "It's gang-up-on-Jack day."

"Poor baby," said Mom.

Will smiled.

"You've got syrup on your face," I told him, but he didn't.

Will took a napkin from the holder, wiped his lips.

"Still didn't get it."

He expanded his wiping.

"Still didn't."

He stopped. "Funny, Yank."

I said, "By the way, looks like the berries will be ready starting about Wednesday."

"Good." She finished her last bite. "Do you like raspberries, Will?"

"Are they like blackberries?"

"Better," she said.

"Then yes I do."

"I invited your mom, and she's going to pick with Melba Flowers and me."

"Thank you. She always liked picking blackberries."

Will and I headed for the garage right after breakfast. I had just raised the

185

Richard Newberry

overhead door when Tex slid-stopped in front of me. She dismounted, punched my arm, said, "What's going on today?"

"Hey, Tex."

"Hey, Will."

"You guys have fun last night?"

"Yep," I said.

"What did you do?"

"Worked on a model, watched The Late Show."

"Hmm," she said.

A steady north wind brought June air that was pleasantly cool and dry, and it carried with it the sweet smell of a giant sycamore that stood across the tracks just off of Warren. The rich blue sky held no clouds, only a white trail from a faraway jet.

I said, "Let's go search Sid's," so Will, Tex and I rode to Sid's parking lot and looked for dropped coins - or cash - from last night's crowd. We had found two dimes, a nickel and two pennies before Stink showed up.

"Find anything?" he asked.

"Little," I said. "Kevin go home?"

"Yeah."

We found two more nickels for the oof tube then pedaled east on the alley - alert to a surprise attack by Cus - all the way to the dead end, turned and headed back west.

Nearing Sid's, Stink said, "Rider comin'."

"Probably Kenny," I said.

The distant rider looked like a dark spot on the alley, but we could tell the dark spot's motion meant he was pedaling a bike, we stopped at the garage. Now a tall, lanky frame of a man cut across the alley, a good piece ahead of the bike rider.

"That's Shorty," said Tex. "He's probably looking at his garden."

We parked our cruisers outside the garage door, debated what our next adventure should be. I knew Will had on his mind a Bible study with the hobos.

Next thing we knew, Kenny raced in and almost wiped out doing a sudden slide-stop near our cruisers. "Hey! You guys!" The cool morning air had not thwarted the sweat beads on Kenny's big forehead. "You gotta come see what happened to Shorty's garden!"

"What happened?" I asked.

"Man, it's all tore up. Looks like a car or something drove right through it."

We mounted up and cut dirt.

Twenty yards before the start of Shorty's enormous garden, in the tall grass across the alley from the Gordons' house, was where the reckless plowing began.

Light at the Rat Pond

"Man," I said as we slowly cruised by the carnage. The driver had dug a big, deep double S that stretched into the black soil starting at the ankle-high sweet corn and ending at the peppers and potatoes at the far west end, where the driver exited back onto the alley.

"Goodness gracious," said Will.

"Probably a drunk from Sid's," Stink said.

Shorty stood near the center of his ruined garden and held his straw fedora at his right hip as his round head moved circumspectly left to right, then right to left. His brown work boots were planted near the middle of the deeply rutted S. I could not see his eyes, but the tall and lean weathered man's normally stern posture was not present that morning. It was also unusual for me to see Shorty without a hat. His hair was dark and smattered with gray, cut short, a crew cut; a distinct, white tan line showed below his scalp where the fedora usually rested.

We eventually caught Shorty's eyes as we gradually cruised past. He turned and eyed us, not accusingly, and quickly returned his gaze to the wreck of his labor. In that brief look I saw more abnormality from Shorty: bewilderment and sadness.

A silver-haired man appeared in the alley. I didn't see him much, he rented the small house next to Shorty's huge brick home. Nadine Wonderlin said he was retired from the army, an acquaintance of the Morgans, and a widower who went by the name of Dutch. He was short and stocky, and usually had a cigarette in his hand. Whether with the Icks or by myself, he would always recognize our presence with a nod or wave as he did that morning on his way to commiserate with Shorty.

Out of Shorty and Dutch's earshot, Tex said, "That's what that grouchy old fart gets."

"That ain't right to say."

"Is too, Will," she said. "You haven't been here long enough to know how grouchy and mean he is."

"She's right," said Stink. "He blames us for everything. Gives Dwight heck just because he's black."

Kenny said, "I kinda feel sorry for him."

"I do, too," said Will

"Not me," said Tex.

Stink agreed with her. "Me either. Not after all the stuff he's done to us. What about you, Jack?"

"I think he's mean and grouchy, but I know we've done stuff to him we shouldn't."

A cry of innocence in her voice, Tex asked, "Like what?"

"Using his tomatoes, his strawberries, soaping his windows -"

Richard Newberry

"That's just getting even," said Stink.

"It's not right, y'all."

"You don't know, Will," said Stink. "You ever see the way he treats Dwight?"

"Yes."

"You think that's right?"

"No. But doing wrong right back at somebody ain't no way to do it either."

Stink murmured, "Goody two shoes."

I put the thirty seven cents we found at Sid's in the oof tube. It was the first time Will's pearl-white cruiser had been at the Rat Pond. I said, "Your bike kind of glows down here."

He looked at it. "It does?"

"It does," said Kenny.

"Cool," said Will. "Did you guys get your puppy?"

"Tonight. I think." Kenny frowned, asked, "Do you think they messed up Shorty's garden on purpose?"

I said, "Shorty's been here forever; that's plenty of time to tick off lots of people. Some of 'em that used to be kids have their license now."

Stink, circling the track, said, "If it would've been bike tire tracks in his garden he probably would've shot us first, then asked questions. Good thing we're not driving yet."

Tex joined Stink on the track. "Either a drunk from Sid's or somebody getting even, Morgan asked for it."

Will frowned but didn't respond.

Stink pedaled close to Tex, sniffed. She said, "What's your problem?"

"You wearing perfume?"

"No!" She stood on her pedals and shot away from him. "Why would I be wearing perfume?"

I hadn't said anything, but I thought I had smelled perfume on her while we were at the garage. I easily dismissed it, thought my smeller was out of whack. It was easy to imagine a girl like Rebecca Corben dabbing on perfume, but Tex?

She quickly changed the subject. "What did you see at the drive-in, Kenny?"

"Uh . . . *Night of the Grizzlies.*"

"Any good?" she asked.

"Yeah. Real good." Kenny wasn't always a good storyteller, he tended to jump around in his telling, yet this excited narrative about a rampaging Grizzly Bear whetted our imaginations to the point we all agreed we wanted to see it. He finished with, "I didn't sleep a lot. I thought I kept hearing a Grizzly trying to get in my room."

188

Light at the Rat Pond

Tex had succeeded in diverting attention from her perfumed presence.

Will climbed off his cruiser and said, "I'm gonna go see if Arlie and Clarence are there."

Kenny said, "Who?"

"The hobos, Hairy and Eyeballs," I said.

"Oh, yeah."

The second time watching Will march into Hoboland's thicket wasn't as dramatic as the first, yet we all stopped and watched.

Stink asked, "He really going to have a Bible study with those guys?"

"That's his plan," I said.

We watched the thicket until Will reappeared. "They're sleeping. I'll check back after a bit." He mounted his cruiser, started his run up the hill.

I asked, "Where you going?"

At the top of the hill he answered, "Gonna help Shorty fix his garden."

"He won't want your help."

He looked down at me, smiled. "Probably not. But I'm gonna help him anyway." He then pedaled out of sight.

"Ahh, let him go, Jack," said Stink. "He's gonna have to learn the hard way."

Kenny said, "Maybe we should see if we could help."

Tex, Stink and I said, "No!"

"Okay."

Said Tex, "I'll bet you guys five bucks he'll start getting all over Will as soon as he shows up."

Nobody took the bet.

Tex asked me, "Dwight's back tomorrow, right?"

"I think so."

"Good. I think we should move the barrels tomorrow night."

"What barrels?" asked Kenny.

"For my jump."

"Oh, yeah."

I reminded her, "We don't have your ramps built yet."

"I know," she said, gazing over the track, like she was calculating the upcoming jump. "I'm only going to need a launch ramp. I don't want to try to hit a landing ramp."

Stink said, "You're just gonna land in the dirt?" He looked around, nodded, said, "Not a bad idea."

"I know. It's always the landing that gets Evel hurt."

"No kidding," I said.

She smirked at me. "Yes, Jack, no kidding." She looked back at the track.

189

Richard Newberry

"My best thing to do is land in the dirt. It's soft enough. We could make a pile near where a ramp would be. Make a softer landing."

"Might work," I said. "But we still have to build a ramp, get the gas and oil together for the fire."

A gleam was in her blue eyes. "How long to get that stuff ready?"

"I know where all the wood is, so . . . we can be ready in a couple of days."

"Good. So let's move the barrels tomorrow night."

"We need six of us, Tex," I said. "Will goes to church on Sunday nights."

She said, "He doesn't stay there all night."

"True." I thought for a moment, wondering about Will's participation, then said, "Okay. We'll do it tomorrow night."

"Right on!" she exclaimed, pumping a fist.

"This is gonna be first-chop, Tex," said Stink.

"Yeah," Kenny added.

Tex said, "Let's get our racers and do some racing!"

After she beat us in a five lapper, we climbed the hill; Kenny pedaled toward home while Stink, Tex and I pedaled the opposite direction. I said to Stink, "Why don't you start parking your racer at the garage? Save you all that riding?"

"How am I going to get back and forth? I can't walk it like Dwight does."

"I can ride you home," said Tex, "then just use your cruiser to go back and forth."

"That means I wouldn't have my racer for my neighborhood."

I asked, "You need your racer for your neighborhood?"

He shrugged. "Probably not."

Tex said, "And you won't be riding alone so much."

He nodded. "True." He looked at both of us. "Why didn't we think of this before?"

We didn't know.

Up ahead, we saw Shorty standing in his ruined garden; Dutch no longer stood with him. But there was Will, getting an earful.

CHAPTER 49

Rolling by, we heard "punks" and "no good bunch of good for nothin's" and "I don't need any help from the likes of you, I'll tell you that". Shorty's gruff, gravelly voice also issued threats to anyone involved in the destruction. Will was busy at Shorty's brown boots, pulling up ruined crops.

Tex said to me, "You owe me five bucks."

"I didn't bet."

She said, "How long before Shorty kicks Will out of his garden? Any bets?"

"About one minute," said Stink.

Van and Lilly Gordon, mowing and weeding their backyard, gave us a friendly wave; we waved back. Unlike Shorty Morgan, Van and Lilly were always nice to us.

Before the time of Will, when Dwight and I were desperate for soda pop and candy money, we searched the tracks and brushy hillsides for the prettiest rocks we could find, thinking somebody would surely pay something for pretty rocks. We solicited Van first, and sure enough, he paid us two quarters for ten of our premium rocks. Dwight and I didn't know we were at the vanguard of what would become a swift and fleeting fad, and later wanted to kick ourselves for abandoning the rock market just before Pet Rocks became a short-lived, lucrative phenomenon.

Tex inhaled deeply, said, "Love the smell of cut grass."

Up ahead Curt Lewsader stood at his burn barrel, sneaking glances at us. When we got closer to him he struck a match to the barrel's contents and refused to meet our eyes; no words or friendly wave passed between us.

Tex said, "Creep."

"We'll get even," said Stink.

At the garage, Stink parked his blue cruiser, sat his small frame between Tex's handlebars, and they were off to get his blue racer. I heard Stink say, "Watch the bumps, man," as they rode over Sid's graveled lot.

I parked my cruiser, rolled out my racer and Will's, then thought about how we were going to roll six oil barrels down the tracks without getting caught. One of our two gas cans was almost empty, so I mixed some 10W30 oil with about half a gallon of gas for the flames Tex would attempt to jump. No doubt

Richard Newberry

this would be her most dangerous and thrilling stunt to date, and I hoped it wouldn't end with a crash and burn.

Minutes later I looked up at the green and white Quaker State Oil clock and jumped on my racer. Stink and Tex would be back shortly, and I pedaled past Lewsader's burning barrel to get a look at Shorty's garden. Will was bent over working at the west end, and Shorty was busy at the other end. I saw Stink and Tex come around Sid's and met them at the garage.

Tex asked, "Will still down there?"

"Yep."

Stink said, "Can't believe Grouch Man hasn't run him off yet."

I said, "I know."

Tex took her cruiser home and came back on her racer. We saw a rider nearing the Rat Pond.

"Kenny's back," I said.

Stink said, "What takes him so long? I live twice as far away as him."

"You know Kenny," I said.

"Let's go race," said Tex, and we cut dirt.

We slowed at Shorty's garden, where Will was alone, tossing mauled plants into an old red wheelbarrow. "Hey, y'all!"

I looked around. "Where's Shorty?"

"Went to get his tiller and stuff."

Tex wagged her head. "I can't believe he's letting you help."

"He wasn't really none too excited about it at first, but he's quit griping at me - as much." Will smiled.

Stink said, "I'd never help that guy."

Will shrugged. "I just think it's the right thing to do."

"It's the suck-up thing to do - and he'd never help you."

"Maybe not, Stink. But I ain't doing it to get favors from Shorty."

Stink said, "I don't get you, man."

A tall, verdant privet hedge concealed the Morgans' enormous backyard. Shorty appeared in the hedge's arched opening, pushing a tiller. "I don't need any more of you heathens botherin' me. One's bad enough."

"Don't worry, we're not," said Stink, pedaling away.

A cigarette pinched between his lips, Shorty trundled the tiller across the alley. "Give me some room," he groused.

He could have rolled out a fleet of tillers and Tex and I wouldn't have been in his way. "You need to get off my property."

"Alley's not your property," said Tex.

He parked the tiller at the edge of the black soil, stood perfectly straight, glared at her. "You bein' a smart-mouth, Missy Wonderlin?"

192

Light at the Rat Pond

"Just stating a fact."

His gray eyes narrowed. "Let me state a fact, Missy -"

"My name's not Missy."

"Your folks raisin' you to talk to your elders like that?"

She said nothing.

Regarding Shorty, our parents basically told us, "Just don't pay much attention to him," but we were reminded to always be respectful.

"I think your daddy needs to take a switch to your hind end, I'll tell you that. And in a pig's whisper that's what I'd do if you were mine."

"Well," she said, "guess you don't have any kids to whip."

Confrontations with Shorty were usually just scraps of him griping and warning and us rolling our eyes or flicking gibes back at him, nothing prolonged. But this incident was escalating, getting uglier because of Tex's last remark. And though it was almost imperceptible, I noticed her remark stung Shorty.

"Cool it, Tex," I said.

"I'm tired of him threatening us like this."

"Get off my property. Now."

"It's not your -"

"Sandra!" I said.

She snapped a look at me. Her wide fierce eyes showed anger and surprise.

"Cool it, man," I said.

"Don't tell me what to do."

"Better listen to him - Missy."

Tex, breathing fire, started to get off her bike when Will said, "Hey, Mr. Morgan, you want to just till under what's left of this lettuce?"

Shorty's glare moved to Will. "What kind of stupid question is that? No I don't want to just till it under. You gettin' tired, boy? I can do it myself."

"Uh, no sir, I'm not getting tired at all. Just wondering."

"Well quit wonderin' and get to pullin'." He groused and insinuated again that Will was lazy.

I said, "Forget it, Tex. Cut dirt. Please." And she did, but not without blasting me with her angry face.

"What are you hangin' around for, Jack Hobbs?"

I looked at Will and he looked at me. I said to Shorty, "I'm not."

He shifted his fedora, pushed the tiller into the dirt. "Good riddance."

At the Rat Pond, Kenny, Stink and Tex were casually circling the track. I said, "You guys ready to race?"

"Let's do it," said Stink.

"I'm ready," said Kenny. "Is Will coming?"

193

Richard Newberry

Tex didn't look at me when she warned, "You ever call me Sandra again I will smash your face. That's not a threat."

"Hey, I'm sorry I –"

"You called her *that*?" said Stink.

"I just –"

Kenny said, "Why'd you call her Sandra, Jack?"

Said Tex, "Because he's a fat-faced idiot."

"I could tell she was ticked," said Stink. "Now I know why."

"I'm sorry, Tex. It just blurted out there."

She stopped circling, looked at me. "So you had no control of it?"

"That's not what I meant."

"You put me down in front of that stupid grouch."

"I did not put you down."

Stink and Kenny also stopped circling to watch the drama.

"Yes you did."

"No I didn't. I just tried to stop something bad from happening. You were really getting mad." I said, to Stink and Kenny, "I swear she was gonna get off her bike and attack Shorty."

Stink smiled. "Really?"

Tex kicked at the dirt. "He was asking for it."

"Wow," said Kenny. "Tex and Shorty in a fight – almost."

I said, "He always asks for it with us, Tex. You know that."

"And I'm sick of it."

"Yeah," said Stink.

"We all are – especially Dwight. But Dwight just ignores him the best he can. That's what we have to do."

Stink said, "You sound like Corben now."

"Maybe. But Will's the one who stopped things from getting really bad."

Kenny asked, "How'd he do that?"

"Got Shorty's attention with something else."

Kenny nodded. "Sounds like Will."

Tex started circling again. "That old fart grouch isn't going to tell me what to do or where to go, I promise you that. He tries to run everybody's life."

"Square dinkham," said Stink, joining Tex on the track.

I said, "I'm sick of it. Like you guys are. Believe me. But Shorty's not gonna change or move away. We're stuck with him."

"He might die," said Stink.

"I'm sure he will," I said. "Sooner or later."

Tex said, "I hope sooner."

We all four circled the track on our racers.

194

Light at the Rat Pond

"It's not like he's Cus," I said. "Shorty isn't out to hurt or kill us. He's just a grouchy old man who can only get to us if we let him."

Stink skid-stopped. "I say we get a little even with Morgan."

"Like what?" Tex asked.

"I'll think of something."

"You know," I said, "it's not like we're completely innocent with Shorty. How many of his tomatoes have we swiped? How much of his corn for Halloween?"

"And his strawberries," said Kenny.

"Yep," I said. "And we've soaped his windows."

"He deserves it," said Tex.

"Let's race," said Stink.

So we did, and Stink won the five lapper. We coasted around the track before starting another race.

Kenny asked, "Where's Will?"

"Who cares," said Stink. "We don't need him."

"I like Will," said Kenny.

"*I like Will*," Stink mocked. "He is a killjoy, Hooks. He's really not an Ick."

I said, "What do you mean by that?"

"Simple, Jack. Corben doesn't do adventure and danger and cool stuff like the rest of us real Icks."

I couldn't conjure an eloquent defense for Will like Dwight would. "He cruises and races."

Said Tex, "That's not what Stink's talking about. You know Will won't do anything that's the least bit dangerous or . . . breaking the rules."

"He's a goody two shoes, Jack," said Stink. "Like a Momma's boy. Almost sissy."

I stopped my racer. "Don't call him sissy. How many of us ever dared to go into Hoboland while the hobos were there?"

Kenny stopped near me. "Yeah, that was pretty brave," he said.

"To have a Bible study," said Stink. "Big whoop."

Tex stopped, said, "What about your birthday campout, Jack? You think Will's going to want to do cool stuff? I can answer that - no."

Stink pulled beside her. "He's up there right now sucking up to Shorty. Icks don't do that, man. If he's at the birthday campout he's gonna ruin it."

"No he won't," I said.

"Yes he will," said Tex.

"No he won't," I repeated. "I know Will's different. He obeys the rules and stuff like no kid I've ever seen. What's wrong with that?"

Stink said, "Makes him a killjoy."

195

Richard Newberry

"A killjoy?"

"Yes," said Tex.

"I can't believe you guys," I said. "Will's been nothing but good to all of us."

"I like Will," said Kenny.

I nodded at him.

Stink said, "So are the Icks gonna stop cornin' and tomatoin' and strawberryin' cars? Are we gonna stop doing bakery run heists and soapin' windows?"

Tex asked, "Are we gonna stop getting even - with guys like Curt Lewsader?"

I needed Dwight's wisdom. "No. No, we're not gonna stop all that stuff."

"What then, Jack?" said Tex. "What are the Icks going to do?"

CHAPTER 50

You are an accomplice in your husband's murder. Your desire for revenge and acts of deception murdered your husband. You are guilty! Guilty! Guilty!

"Stop it," she said. "Stop it now."

The Creeping Taunt had been relentless that morning. Kate fought it by scrubbing every inch of the bathroom, while the kitchen radio blared big band music, then moved to the kitchen to scrub the old linoleum. She twisted her gold wedding band for comfort, but none came. Now she had just finished vacuuming the living room carpet when she said, "Stop it. Stop it now."

Yet she knew her resolve to battle the Creeping Taunt's accusations was, at best, feckless.

Last night's ominous call warning her he would "see her soon" had punched through her wall of defense, a wall in her mind that guarded her heart against Guilt's onslaught. It was a perpetual mental exercise of metaphysical brick and mortar, and for years, although strongly tested, it held. Kate thought when night passed and morning light came the foe would be vanquished, she would be stronger. But the call's breech threatened to flood her with guilt.

She sought refuge at her piano and Mozart. She recalled a sonata and her lithe fingers deftly played the melody.

It began to work. Her mind slowly discarded the oppressive anxiety and guilt; she found herself able to slap some bricks and mortar back into the breech. The longer she played, the more relaxed she became, and she concentrated on the problem without fear's turmoil.

How many times had she determined that, yes, her desire for revenge against Irma certainly involved Kate deceiving and using *him*; she admitted to herself the deplorableness of her actions, but should she be punished forever for a bad choice when she was a teenager? Egregious actions had degrees, right? Was murder to be compared with using someone? Only if murder was the intended consequence of the using. Kate never intended to hurt anyone - except Irma.

One of the reasons Kate had picked him was because she knew he was tough and rugged; at that time he had a number of pretty girls to choose from because he was the quintessential bad boy - and very good looking. What would Kate be to him? Nothing, just another girl. But she misjudged him.

Kate glanced at the parlor clock: a student would be there in an hour.

Richard Newberry

She continued the melodic sonata, continued her trip back in time, to a place where if she could do it all over again, she would not act on revenge, not use somebody to bring it about. Corrective hindsight didn't exist; that's why she built a wall.

Kate also reminded herself that while she admitted to her past wrongs she had no proof her Deplorable Indiscretion had any part in Andrew's murder or the recent actions of the guy in the brown car or last night's caller. She assumed they were connected, but were they? Assumption procreated much illegitimate guilt. Kate had built walls before based on assumption that had no business being built. Was this such a wall? In her heart, she believed this wall needed to be built and vigorously maintained.

She decided not to approach Nadine and Texal about her possible situation. Kate didn't want to have to go back and drag out an ugly history if it was not necessary. Only her mom, brother and sister knew details about the Deplorable Indiscretion, and she would keep it that way for now. She would somehow make Jack understand he needed to be watchful, without scaring him, or having to tell him of the Deplorable Indiscretion. She would not allow her son to be hurt because of her past. Kate guarded against paranoia, but she knew the world could be evil. If anything ever happened to Jack because she didn't protect him, didn't tell him the truth . . . she would literally die.

Finishing the Mozart piece, Kate thought of a name, somebody who did know some details regarding the Deplorable Indiscretion. That somebody had been there - twice. What and how much did she know? Good questions. Kate decided a trip after lunch to Sunbeam Bakery would be necessary. If Imagene was working, Kate had some questions for her.

CHAPTER 51

"I don't know - no," I said. "We're still gonna do cool stuff. You guys know that."

"No we don't," Stink said.

"He's right," Tex added.

My eyes bounced between them. "There's stuff Will won't do. So what? We can still do them. We have been."

Stink said, "The only thing we've done so far this summer is a bakery heist."

I said, "What about racing and cruising? Or hide-and-seek? We had a pretty cool baseball game. One of the best."

"It would've been perfect," said Tex, "if Will hadn't asked Cus to play."

"Yeah," said Stink. "That was stupid."

I actually thought Cus's presence, though very ugly at the end, added greatness to the game, but I didn't even start to defend that position. "We'll still do the cool stuff we like to do, and if Will doesn't want to . . . that's what he'll do. Nothing wrong with that."

"That's right," said Kenny.

Stink picked up something off the track, sniffed it, then pitched it in the pond. "I don't know, man. I think if Will stays in the Icks he's gonna change us. We're not gonna do the dangerous stuff anymore. Maybe we'll start wanting to do sissy stuff."

I got angry, swatted viciously at gnats that had been buzzing around me. "You tell me this, both of you. What aren't we gonna get to do because Will's around? Huh? Tell me exactly."

They had no answer.

"That's right. Nothing. You just want to pick on him, get rid of him. For some reason you don't like him and he's the nicest kid I've ever met. He said he'd help us move barrels for your jump. He likes to race and cruise, play baseball and hide-and-seek. He just doesn't break rules. So for that he's a sissy? He can't be an Ick? If that's how it is, I don't want to be an Ick." (I couldn't believe I said that.)

"Cool down, Jack," said Tex.

Stink's eyes were buried in the dirt.

"I like Will," she said. "He's cool. And you're right, he's nice and pure

199

Richard Newberry

quill." She looked at Stink, who wouldn't look up, then said to me, "We're just worried he's going to change things - for the worse."

"He won't," I said.

She said, "You're going to church with him tomorrow, right?"

Stink looked up, but kept his mouth shut.

"So?" I said.

"I go to church sometimes," Kenny said.

Tex looked from Kenny to me. "Sometimes that church stuff changes kids. Makes 'em all . . . goody two shoes, you know."

I said, "No, I don't."

She said, "I had a cousin who I used to really like to go see, but when she started going to church, she got all different and stuff."

Kenny asked me, "Am I all different and stuff?"

I smiled. "Only in a good way, Kenny."

"Thanks, Jack."

I said to Tex, "I'm going to church with Will, and I'll be the same Jack after that as I was, okay? I'll still like to do the dangerous cool stuff."

Stink looked at me. "You sure?"

"Promise." He and Tex didn't appear convinced. "You think after I go to church I'm gonna try to be friends with Cus, don't you?" I smiled.

They half-smiled, and Tex said, "Okay. We'll give Church Jack a chance."

"Church Jack," Kenny repeated, admiringly.

"What can I say?"

Stink started circling the track. "I say let's race!"

So we did. Will never showed, and before we headed for lunch I heard hobos shuffling around in Hoboland.

I slowed down at Shorty's garden, Tex and Stink sped on ahead to their lunch. "Wanna get something to eat?"

Will looked to Shorty. "Go ahead," he groused.

Will mounted his cruiser. "I'll be back to help."

Shorty flicked a smoldering cigarette butt into the tilled soil. "Up to you."

Riding past the Gordons' burn barrel, I said, "The hobos are back."

"Really? Good! I'll go down there after lunch."

"Thought you're helping Shorty?"

"Yeah, that's true. I'll figure it out. You going with me?"

"To help Shorty?"

"No. The Bible study."

I hesitated, then said, "I guess."

"Good, Jack."

Mom was putting red geraniums on the front porch. "Fix yourselves some

200

Light at the Rat Pond

lunch. There's bologna and peanut butter and jelly in there. I already ate, and I have to finish these before my next lesson gets here."

"Okay," I said.

She asked, "Anything you want from the bakery? I'm going this afternoon."

"Can you get Suzie Qs?"

"Yes."

I chose bologna, Will likewise, except he added peanut butter and jelly to his.

"You're kidding me?"

"Nah, Yank. It's good."

"Your mom lets you do that?"

"She's the one who told me about it."

He offered a corner and I took a small bite. "Hmm. Not bad."

"See." Will smiled.

"We gotta tell Kenny about this. He loves bologna."

We gulped our milk and poured more. Will's usually neat hair was tussled, dirt smirched his forehead and face; his plaid button-down and jeans wore some of Shorty's garden.

"How is it working with Shorty?"

"He's a grouch."

I smiled. "Really? I didn't know."

"I think he's done it so long he wouldn't know how to stop."

"You guys talk about anything?"

"He hardly says a word - unless it's to gripe at me or somebody else."

"Why do you do it?"

Will gulped the last of his second glass of milk; a slight white mustache remained as he set down the glass. "Because Mr. Morgan is like the hobos: he needs people."

"He's never acted like it around us. He seems like he doesn't want anybody around."

"That Dutch guy is a friend of his, and he does have a wife, but I haven't met her."

"Thelma," I said. "She's not as bad as Shorty. But she's not all that friendly either."

"Hmm," said Will. "I think if you're around Shorty enough you could find some good in there. Some folks take some getting used to, gotta spend more time than usual to get to the bones of it."

"Bones of it?"

"Something my father says. It means to find out what they're really like."

Richard Newberry

"From what I know, it could take somebody two lifetimes to get to the bones of Shorty."

Will chuckled. "Well, I'm gonna try."

Yes he would.

We cleaned up our lunch area and Will said, "I'll go see Arlie and Clarence, then help Shorty for a bit more before we do the Bible study. Is that okay?"

"I'll probably be cruisin'. I'll watch for you, or find me when you're done at Shorty's."

"Good. Right."

Before the time of Will, say in January of 1970 when Curt Lewsader moved into Shorty's rental house next to us, to think that I'd be at a Bible study with hobos on a beautiful June afternoon that same year would be laughable nonsense. But that was before the time of Will.

Stink didn't come back after lunch. Tex, Kenny and I cruised the alley and goofed around on the tracks for a while before heading back to the garage. The Quaker State clock read one thirty.

"I'm gonna go see if Will's almost done at Shorty's. We're suppose to go to the Rat Pond."

"Racing?" Tex asked.

"Hobo Bible study."

Tex said, "He's really going to do - you're going with him?"

"Uh, yep."

"Can I come?" asked Kenny.

"Sure," I said, glancing at Tex.

"Don't look at me, Hobbs. No way I'm doing that."

"Okay."

"How long you guys going to be doing your Bible thing?"

I shrugged. "Don't know. Not long. Hour at the most."

"You guys are nuts. I'll see you later."

"Bye, Tex," said Kenny as she cut dirt outside the garage. She offered a meager wave.

Kenny and I pedaled to Shorty's. The grouch's old pick-up truck was parked near the garden, and Will was tossing stalks of young, green corn in the bed. We told Will we were headed to the Rat Pond, and he smiled big, said to Shorty, "Got to go do that Bible study now. I'll see you later."

Shorty, who had a wad of chewing tobacco stuffed in his right cheek, spit black ooze to the ground. "Whatever, boy."

Will told Kenny about peanut butter and jelly on bologna as we rode to the Rat Pond.

"That sounds really good. I'm gonna try it."

202

Light at the Rat Pond

At the race track, Will stood his bike on its kickstand and crossed to Booty Tree. He plucked a Bible from the hollow.

"When did you put that there?" I asked.

"The same night I came back down here and threw all those nasty magazines in the pond."

I looked at Kenny, he looked at me. We knew Stink wouldn't be happy to hear the magazines now rested at the bottom of the murky water, but that wasn't our biggest concern.

Kenny, with a solemn yet stern voice - one a parent might use on a wayward child - questioned Will, "You were here at night by yourself? At dark, alone, here at the Rat Pond?"

"Sure was."

Kenny looked at me, indicating it was my turn to continue the necessary reprimand of our friend. I said, "It's a bad idea to be here at dark, Will. Especially by yourself."

"Bad idea," said Kenny.

"Why?"

The Rat Pond, according to unwritten Ick law, belonged to us until we grew out of it and a new generation came along to assume control. Kids before us had messed around it, but never developed it like the Icks had. After arduous clearing and heavy dirt work we had a race track and a widened hill for better ingress/egress, and since no higher authority ever bothered us at the Rat Pond - even Shorty - the Icks held an osmotic deed to the land. Our property to rule over - in the light of day.

We understood we had no control over nefarious, nocturnal trespassers. The Icks decreed the area could be dangerous at night, and though we craved the excitement of certain dangers, we had no appetite for what the darkness at the Rat Pond might offer. Prudence ruled our young hearts and minds regarding this matter, and nobody was a sissy for avoiding the place at night.

Answering Will's "why", I said, "At least two reasons: hobos and Cus."

"Ahhh, those hobos won't hurt us."

Said Kenny, "Cus would."

Will nodded.

I said, "And we only kinda know about two hobos, but there's more of 'em we don't know at all. We've seen some resting in the shade along the tracks, and believe me, they don't look or act real friendly."

Kenny said, "Stink swears one chased after him on the alley last year when he was riding home."

Will looked at me. "Really?"

"That's what he told us. And I believe him because he used to take the alley

203

Richard Newberry

all the way to the oil company before cutting over to go home. Hasn't done it since. Always cuts over at Sid's."

"Hmm," said Will.

I said, "We've rode past here at night before and there's been parties going on over there in Hoboland. We've heard 'em fighting and cussing, sometimes singing, always sounding pretty drunk."

"Drunk as skunks," said Kenny.

Will tried to make light. He smiled, said, "Drunk skunks."

We'd heard Texal Wonderlin use the expression, and before he said it, none of the Icks knew skunks liked to overindulge in alcoholic beverages.

We rebuffed his smile with solemn stares. I said, "You gotta take it serious, Will. Some of the hobos could be dangerous, especially drunk."

"Don't forget Cus," said Kenny.

"That's right," I said.

"Okay, guys. I got you. I'll stay away at night."

"Promise?"

"I promise, Kenny."

I cocked my head. "You mean it?"

"I mean it, Yank."

In Hoboland, somebody was shuffling through dead leaves.

Will, raising the Bible, said, "Let's go."

Kenny and I followed Will to our first-ever hobo Bible study.

204

CHAPTER 52

We came to an opening in the thicket and saw Hobo Hairy and Eyeballs sitting on the rotting remains of a large cottonwood trunk; they were taking turns drinking from something in a small brown bag.

"Hey, y'all!"

Eyeballs about came out of his tattered shoes; Hairy paused in mid-tip; then quickly tucked the bag behind the prostrate tree trunk.

Hairy said, "Hey, hey, there . . . uh - uh . . . Will." Apparently, being able to recall Will's name took the slouch out of Hairy's posture as he sat a tad straighter when he added, "Yes, sir. Will Corben. Right?"

"Yes, sir."

Will's "sir" slightly inflated Hairy's thin chest. The lanky hobo wore much-traveled brown slip-on boots, old plaid polyester and cotton pants that were too short for his long, skinny legs, and a fairly nice purple, long-sleeved button-down shirt. A brown fedora was perched atop his long, angular head. He and Dwight had similar taste in attire; I couldn't wait to tell my friend.

Eyeballs stood, his nervous green eyes moved swiftly between Kenny, Will and me; the big man looked ready to bolt into the thicket and escape from the small intruders.

Will said to him, "These are just my friends, sir. They're okay guys, I promise."

Eyeballs, a.k.a. Arlie, didn't appear convinced. He looked to Hairy, a.k.a. Clarence.

"Ah, c'mon, Arlie." He patted the cottonwood. "Sit back down here. We can trust Will."

Arlie's shocked expression moved warily to Will. The hobo was a big man, a little taller than Clarence, who was about six foot, but where Clarence was angles and bones, Arlie was round and thick. The stitching on his ragged bibbed overalls was tested - and failed in some areas - by his bulging body.

Will said, "This here is Jack and Kenny. They're nice people." He said to us, "That's Clarence and that's Arlie."

Before the time of Will, no Ick had ever been this close to a hobo. Their fetid clothes and bodies reeked of stale and fresh booze, body odor and an accumulation of general filth, and Arlie looked bigger and scarier than ever up

205

Richard Newberry

close, and Kenny, his eyes glued to hairy Clarence, took half a step backwards. I felt as jittery as Arlie looked.

Will told us, "Say hey you guys."

Kenny and I muttered, "Hey you guys."

Said Clarence, removing his fedora and bowing, "Welcome fellers to our humble abode."

Will looked from us to the hobos, said, "Jack and Kenny want to be with us for Bible reading, if that's okay?"

Clarence set his hat back on his thick, gray matted hair. "Good company's like good hooch: the more you got, the better the party." The lanky hobo caught himself, his weathered forehead and wild, thick brow scrunched into disapproval; with downcast eyes, he said, "Hooch ain't got no place at a Bible readin'."

"Ah, don't worry about it, sir," said Will. "I know what you meant. It's okay."

Arlie, still standing, looked as if nothing would ever be okay, but Clarence's tired face looked relieved and said, "Okie dokie, then." He smiled without showing his teeth. "Be nice to have some company, won't it, Arlie?"

Arlie's nervous, all-encompassing wide eyes flashed to Clarence then back to us.

"Ah, c'mon, Arlie," said Clarence, patting the tree trunk again. "Them boys don't bring no harm. Have a sit down."

Will said, "It's okay if you stand."

That information took some pressure off of Arlie. A bit of his apprehension seemed to leave him, his eyes were less anxious.

"Fine with me," said Clarence.

The Icks had ventured into Hoboland a few times, but only when we were absolutely sure no hobos were present. The clearing could accommodate a shindig of a dozen or so hobos. They'd dug out of the black earth a small pit in the center of the clearing to have their fires. A few empty bottles and bags littered the trampled ground, and on the clearing's perimeter, where tufts of soft brush and some grass grew, impressions were left on the ground where hobo bodies took their rest. The shaded clearing allowed enough light to see clearly that the hobos' faces and necks were flushed red from years of excessive alcohol; their ages were impossible to guess because of their woebegone appearances that had accumulated after years of neglectful, transient living.

A robin fluttered noisily out of a nearby mulberry tree, startling Arlie.

"Take it easy," Clarence admonished. "You're jumpy as fleas on a hound."

Will held up his Bible. "You fellas got your Bibles?"

206

Light at the Rat Pond

Clarence looked to standing Arlie, who then wandered north into the thicket and returned with the little Bibles in his grungy, big hands.

Clarence said, "Can't leave stuff out around here."

"Okay," said Will. "You got your Bibles so let's get started." We sat on another felled tree trunk that rested at a right angle near the cottonwood. Will began flipping the thin pages of his Bible. "We're gonna start at the book of John, if that's okay?"

"Suits me," said Clarence. "Lead the way Will Corben."

Arlie just stood there, still carefully watching us.

"Uh, Will," said Clarence.

"Yes, sir?"

"Somethin' I shoulda told you before. Me and Arlie . . . well, you see - uh . . . well, we can't read a lick, not the first word."

Arlie slowly nodded his large head. "Hmm," said Will. "Okay then, how 'bout Jack and Kenny showing you fellas what we're reading, and just follow along?"

That meant sitting or standing right next to them.

"You sure, Will?" asked Kenny.

I cast a questioning look at Will, but said nothing.

"Yep," he said. "It'll work good."

Kenny looked at me, I looked at him. I knew he was still scared of Clarence, so I moved to the cottonwood next to the hairy hobo. Oh, boy, the stench.

Clarence grinned, held out the small Gideon Bible and set it between us. "Appreciate it, uh, Jack."

Oh, boy, the breath.

I nodded, glimpsing his bloodshot, blue-gray eyes. Arlie turned his big neck and his shocked, wide green eyes stared down at the boy standing next to him. For what seemed like an eternity, they just looked at one another, Kenny looking upward, mouth agape, sweat beads forming on his big forehead, his green eyes growing wide like Arlie's, and Arlie just staring.

Will said, "Okay. Good. Let's read."

Arlie pushed the small Bible at Kenny, who finally, somehow, overcame his wide-eyed fear trance and took the Bible from his giant reading companion.

Will helped us find the book of John, and he began reading chapter one. It was easy to discern Will was very acquainted with the words in the Bible. He had no trouble annunciating the antiquated King James language as he eloquently read, and elucidated somewhat, through the first three chapters.

By chapter two Arlie's earlier trepidation had been assuaged, his wide eyes quit roving fretfully to and fro and settled on the tiny words on the small pages of the Bible Kenny held in his hands. At the outset the two looked like a paired,

Richard Newberry

statue tribute to comedy, but now the statue scene of a giant man looking at the boy's book could've reflected a notion of unique profundity.

Clarence had followed my fingers across and down the pages early, yet soon closed his eyes to concentrate on Will's calming voice and drink of what Will read. Occasionally, with his eyes closed, he smiled and gently nodded.

Will quoted - didn't read - chapter three's sixteenth verse, then said, "We're gonna stop there today, fellas, but I'd like to pray before we go, if that's okay?"

"Yes, sir," said Clarence, and Arlie gave a single nod.

We all bowed and closed our eyes as Will began. "Dear Lord, please take Your Word and apply it to our hearts, and help each one of us to know . . ."

It felt like cheating, but I had to peek at the hobos during Will's prayer. Their eyes were closed, yet something I had noticed upon their countenance during Will's reading still radiated on their worn faces. I had dismissed it at first as a trick of the shade and spotty-sunlight in the clearing, but the longer I looked at them as they reverently bowed and listened to Will's prayer there was no denying what I was seeing. Their haggard and weary faces had transformed into faces that almost . . . beamed, as if they had long starved for a particular sustenance that they now had received, and it fed and nourished far beyond a typical fleshly hunger; it satiated a visceral emptiness, and I would say it filled their souls.

Will said, "Amen," and caught me with my eyes open to Arlie and Clarence, yet just smiled.

"That was good, Will Corben," said Clarence.

Arlie gave a nod to Will and to Kenny.

"You're welcome," said Kenny.

"Gotta ask you something," Will said to the hobos. "Have either one of you ever asked Jesus into your life, to be your Savior and Lord?"

Kenny looked up at Arlie, whose wide eyes deferred to Clarence.

"Well, uh, no, sir, Will. I sure haven't." He looked up at Arlie. "I can't speak for my friend -"

Arlie wagged his big head once.

Will asked, "Would you like to ask Jesus to be your Savior and Lord?"

Now Clarence looked to Arlie, who stared back at him, then Clarence looked over to Will, and began to run a shaky, dirty hand over his whiskered face. "Well, sir, you know - uh - went to Sunday School a couple of times when I was a boy, but that's about it - yes, sir. That's about it." His eyes fell from Will to the ground, and he said no more.

Will asked, "What about you, Arlie?"

A single head wag.

"Did you fellas feel *anything* when I was reading the Bible?"

Light at the Rat Pond

A single head nod from Arlie, and Clarence looked up, said, "I reckon there ain't no denyin' it. Yes, sir, I did."

"Good," said Will, smiling.

"To be honest with you Will - because you're a square-dealer - I don't reckon me and Arlie knows exactly what it means for Jesus to be our . . . Savior and Lord. But it sounds mighty awful important."

Briefly, Will explained man's built-in sinful ways and the need for Jesus - He was the only way - to save them from those sins.

Clarence nodded and said, "I 'spect He'd be saving us from, uh . . . hell?"

"Yes, sir. It would mean eternity in heaven with Him."

Clarence mulled it over, felt his whiskers; Arlie stood statue-still, looking at Clarence.

"I can't speak for my friend," said Clarence, "course he don't speak. But I gotta say for myself I don't know for sure if I'm ready to do that Will. I know the Good Book is somethin' special, might be from God Himself, and I ain't gonna sit here and tell you one thing and go do another. No, sir. Not gonna do that."

I'm sure I read disappointment on Arlie's face, but he did not respond.

"I understand," said Will. "And your honesty is a good thing, Clarence."

"Thank you, Will."

"How 'bout this?" said Will. "We'll come back tomorrow after church, sometime in the afternoon, and we'll do some more Bible reading."

Arlie, without looking at Clarence, gave a nod.

"Well - uh - maybe, we'll see. Can't say for sure we'll be around tomorrow."

For the first time, Arlie furrowed his brow and pinched his mouth at Clarence. "Okay, okay," said Clarence. "We'll be around."

"Good," said Will, standing. "We'll see you tomorrow."

We started walking away, and Arlie grabbed Will's right arm, Arlie looked to Clarence.

Clarence sighed, nodded, said, "Yep."

I didn't know what to do or think. I had grown comfortable around these smelly guys, and now things seemed to be turning ugly. Kenny stood by me, shocked surprise covering his freckled face.

Will looked up at the huge man. "What's wrong?"

Clarence, still sitting on the cottonwood, said, "There's somethin' you need to know."

209

CHAPTER 53

I was hurriedly scouring the clearing's floor for any kind of weapon to use against Arlie, knowing it would probably take a tree trunk like Clarence sat on to take down the big man. Thankfully there was no need to yank a tree out of the ground because Arlie released Will's arm.

Clarence said, "You guys need to be mindful of somethin' important."

Arlie nodded.

"What?" asked Will.

Clarence stood, straightened slowly, rubbed his back. "Boy, oh, boy, I'm gettin' old." He bent over and retrieved the paper sack he and Arlie had been tipping earlier. Clarence took a drink, offered it to Arlie, but he refused it. Clarence shrugged, took another drink.

The glow, or whatever it was, I had noticed on Clarence's face during the Bible reading and prayer had now given way to an approaching darkness.

"You boys need to keep this in mind," he said. "Ain't all of us Rail Riders what you'd call . . . friendly."

He had our attention.

"Most ain't bad fellas, but one in particular is." He glanced at Arlie, then back to us. "Don't know his real name. We call him Sticks, 'cause he carries a big ol' shiny knife and he likes to stick people with it."

"Really?" asked Kenny.

"Ain't puttin' you on, son. No, sir. You gotta be careful when Sticks is around. Mean, like a stirred up hornet."

"Wow," said Kenny.

Clarence nodded, took a drink. "He don't come around too much, but when he does, we're watchin' our backs. Me and Arlie's - mostly Arlie - had to run him off from our parties before. Tried to stick Arlie a couple of times." Clarence grinned at Arlie. "Not a good idea, huh?"

Arlie remained shock-eyed and stoic.

"Anyways, boys, you be careful around some of the Rail Riders, especially Sticks."

I asked, "What's he look like?"

"Skinny but stout fella. 'Bout my height. Favors a red handkerchief around his head, like he's some kind of Injun."

210

Light at the Rat Pond

The hobos had their own Cus Lappin.

Clarence sat down, pushed his fedora back, drank again. "Just be mindful, boys. And don't come around these parts at night. The day's pretty safe. But night's a different story."

I gave Will an "I-told-you-so" look, then thought about the stash we kept in Booty Tree, and the magazines outside the track, and how nothing - to my knowledge - had ever been bothered.

I said, "We've played and raced here a lot. Nobody's ever bothered us."

A peculiar look came over Clarence as he said, "We know. And ain't nobody gonna bother you - in the day. Night's a different story. Can't promise safety when the sun goes down."

Did we have Guardian Hobos?

"We'll remember that," said Will. "Thanks for telling us."

"Will Corben," said Clarence, "don't make the mistake of thinkin' of it as a tellin'. It's more of a warnin'."

We three nodded.

Will said, "Hope to see y'all tomorrow."

Arlie nodded, Clarence raised the brown bag.

Back at the track, an incipient maelstrom of thought began to whirl around in my mind. Bible study and hobos, Cus and Sticks, danger and Guardian Hobos flung around inside my ten-soon-to-be-eleven-year-old head. Then I remembered something that momentarily stilled the storm. "I can't be here tomorrow. I'm going fishing with Mom after church."

"Okay," said Will.

I said, "You're not coming here by yourself?"

"Yep - well maybe -" He looked at Kenny. "You can come."

"I don't know," said Kenny. "Maybe."

I said to Will, "You can't be serious about coming here alone after what they just told - no - warned us about."

"That's nighttime, Yank. I'll be here in the day."

"Still . . ."

"It'll be okay."

"Don't be a doofus, Will."

"I won't be, Kenny."

"Good."

"Kenny's right, man. But it's more like stupid doofus. Don't be that."

"I won't be. I promise."

There'd be no talking Will out of evangelizing lost souls, no matter the possible danger. We learned it was paramount in his life. Telling Will to stay

211

Richard Newberry

away from reaching the lost, no matter how insufferable the situation, was like telling a trained Beagle not to hunt rabbits.

Above us, an N & W engine revved for a slamming connect or disconnect as we mounted our cruisers. Bam! A connect.

Will asked Kenny, "You wanna go to church with us tomorrow?"

"I think we'll probably go to our church tomorrow. It's been a couple of weeks since we were there."

Will nodded. "Anytime you want to go with me just let me know."

"Okay. I will."

We rode to the switchyard for ice-cold slurps of water; somewhere in the office a radio was broadcasting the Cubs/Cardinals game. We heard Jack Brickhouse's voice give the score: three to one in the fifth inning, Cubs leading.

Kenny and I smiled, Will frowned.

Outside, pigeons flapped away from their power-line perch and up from feeding on spilled grain near the rusty-colored rails as a noisy black locomotive powered out of the yard, pulling tank, box and hopper cars behind it. We pedaled east on the alley and quickened our speed to see how long we could keep pace with the train. Racing past Sunbeam Bakery I noticed our Impala parked in the bakery's lot, and as we flew past Shorty's old truck, he stepped out from behind it and almost got ran over by three Ick cruisers. He glared and griped, but we kept racing the train with smiles on our faces.

We were losing ground; we'd fallen back one car to an open-door brown boxcar by the time we'd reached Wonderlins' burn barrels. Will, his eyes fixated on the open car, drifted into my lane, almost bumped me.

"Hey! Watch it!"

"Sorry, Yank."

Though I enjoyed racing the train, my mind wouldn't let go of Clarence's warning. Now, besides the looming of Vietnam and Cus, I had to consider the threat of a red-bandana-wearing hobo named Sticks.

We slowed down and started coasting at Sid's because the train had won, and it had all but disappeared in the verdant valley below the tracks.

Kenny said, "Did you see the look on Shorty's face?"

Will and I nodded and smiled, and I said, "That would've been some kind of wreck."

"Cool," said Kenny, slowly nodding.

"I think I'm gonna go help him some more, y'all."

I said, "You're kidding? Even after we almost flattened him?"

"He'll get over it."

"Shorty doesn't get over anything, Will."

"Square dinkham," said Kenny.

212

Light at the Rat Pond

"Ah, he ain't that bad."

"Yes he is," I said.

Will smiled. "Yep. He is."

We chuckled.

"But I'm still gonna go help him. See y'all later."

"Wait up, Will," Kenny said, standing on his pedals to catch up. "I gotta help Dad with the yard." He waved back, "See ya, Jack."

"After while crocodiles."

Alone on the alley by Sid's burn barrels, my thoughts, surprisingly, didn't return to dreadful things. Instead, I thought about Dwight being back tomorrow, and me going to church with the Corbens. My friend's return from St. Louis got shoved out of my mind by the anticipation of tomorrow morning's execution of my well conceived plan.

I smiled the gratifying smile a genius might wear after completing some inscrutable, fulfilling equation. But to my chagrin, I was about to learn a lesson in the art of planning and execution.

CHAPTER 54

After her student left, Kate, for reasons she really didn't want to contemplate, changed into a nice pair of blue slacks and a white, cotton top - a present from her sister Belle for Kate's last birthday - to go to the Sunbeam Bakery. A trip to the bakery never included a change of wardrobe, but she also felt the need to check her hair and apply a fresh coat of light red lipstick. She reminded herself the lipstick was not a big deal, for she always applied a fresh coat when going anywhere. Putting in the small, silver, looped earrings was . . . well, maybe a bit much.

While she wouldn't delve into the whys of her motive for wanting to look very presentable, she couldn't ignore the single who: Imagene Johnson, or Tucker, whatever her name had become.

Kate sat in the Impala at the bakery's parking lot, giving herself time for composure. Did she really want to do this? Not really, but recent events - the guy in the brown car and last night's ominous call - made this, in Kate's fretting mind, necessary.

She checked herself in the rearview mirror. Many women were their own severest judges of their appearance, and Kate was in that court. She tilted the mirror to get a better look. She had always worn little to no make-up; even Andrew had encouraged her not to cover "what God created beautiful", yet today she had put on more than normal. She scowled at what appeared to be incipient lines near her eyes and mouth. She'd always thought her eyes were too close together, and her mouth too small for her fat lips.

"Your lips are not fat, Kate," Andrew had said, when they were dating in college.

"You sure?" Kate had replied, running a finger over them.

"I'm sure. Take my word for it, women in the movies would love to have your lips."

"Yeah, sure."

"I'm serious. I'll bet you one day they're - if they're not already - doing things to have fuller lips." He leaned toward her, said, "And they are *very* kissable lips," and kissed her.

Kate had closed her eyes in the Impala as that memory washed over and through her, and as tender and wonderful as that kiss had been, now what

214

Light at the Rat Pond

remained of it was a twinge of heartache. She opened her eyes, and without Andrew to convince her otherwise, she decided again her lips were too big. She adjusted the mirror to driving status, gazed out the car's windshield.

How long had it been since she last saw Imagene? Had to be the trial. What did she look like now? In high school, she had been an early bloomer, easily snagging the eyes of eager high school boys with her well-placed and proportioned curves, pretty face and long dark hair. Imagene, to Kate's knowledge, had first laid eyes on Andrew Hobbs the same night Kate had, at Parle's Woods. And the flirtatious . . . witch made no secret of her yearning for Andrew. Kate and Imagene ran in different circles in high school, Imagene's much bigger, and there existed no open animosity toward one another. Yet things simmered below the surface. Kate never trusted her, and Imagene's presence at the A & P parking lot that evening in October put strong suspicion in Kate's mind. Imagene was considered only a victim in the crime, according to the police and court, and, as far as Kate knew, never suspected of any wrong doing.

But Kate had always wondered.

The Impala's front windows were down and she heard tires crunching white gravel when a car turned into the bakery outlet's parking lot.

The brown car rolled slowly by her; Kate's heart instantly increased its rhythm, but regained a normal beat as the big-haired woman inside the brown Dodge gave her a friendly wave. Barb Hooks, Kenny's mom. Kate waved back.

"Paranoid," Kate muttered.

Every time she saw Barb, the tall woman - unlike Kenny - walked fast, as if wherever she was headed an emergency awaited. This morning she had her youngest son Alan in tow. Barb smiled as she strode past, said, "Good morning, Kate," on her way to Sunbeam's front door.

"Hi, Barb." She watched the Amazon-tall red head disappear around the corner, her young son's small legs almost running to keep up.

A woman she didn't know rounded the corner carrying two brown bags full of day-old baked goods. Kate wanted to wait until she could be alone in the bakery with Imagene, and she knew Saturday afternoons were slower times at the outlet because they began to run out of product; the shelves would be full again on Monday.

She felt a little silly just sitting in her car, casing the place, and not even knowing if it was Imagene's day to work. The new employees were usually stuck with Saturday work, and usually the only clerk behind the small, Formica counter.

She began to question her decision to confront Imagene. First, could she get her alone to even ask the question, or should she invite Imagene to coffee

215

Richard Newberry

or something, then question her? And would anything helpful come from confronting her? Couldn't Imagene just lie? Yes. So why approach her? After all, she'd been deemed an innocent victim.

When Barb Hooks appeared, hurrying to her car, carrying a bag of bread and dragging Alan behind her, she gave Kate a quick smile, flashed a look that asked, "Why are you still sitting in your car?"

Kate smiled, waved, and waited to be the only car on the parking lot.

Finally alone, she opened the Impala's door and marched toward the outlet's entrance, hoping Imagene stood behind the counter, because Imagene Johnson, or Tucker, or whatever, had had a perpetual desire for Andrew, and she had been at Parle's Woods that night, and had been on A & P's parking lot that fateful October evening in 1961.

And Kate had to have the answer to at least *one* question.

CHAPTER 55

Before the time of Will, girls were nondescript creatures who were softer than boys - except Tex - and who giggled instead of laughing. It seemed their gender could easily out talk the males, whether anyone listened or not, and, generally speaking, they dressed, colored, printed and wrote neater than boys. They also had the bizarre ability to be happy in one spot, doing the things they did, without making much noise - other than their talking. Despite these oddities, they didn't strike me as far different from boys.

Until the time of Will.

My first and forever life-altering encounter with The Girl happened as I started to shove open one of our school's rear doors. I was hurrying to the brevity that was lunch recess, when, with my hand poised to thrust open the door, out of the corner of my eye I glimpsed a chestnut-haired epiphany that had the power to perform the impossible: make me forget all about recess.

She stood in the eighth-grade hall, cuddling a textbook to her bosom, and smiling. I think two other girls were talking to her, but I didn't see them. Kids trampled me as they raced out the door towards a few minutes of much needed chaotic freedom. I couldn't move, for I was mesmerized by the beauty.

She wore brown shoes, yellow knee-highs and a summer dress. Her resplendent, long, straight hair was held back by thick, yellow yarn. Above her, as I recall, a magnificent nimbus declared her being. A sense of awe overpowered me and transfixed all my senses on her presence. If she had noticed me and walked toward me, I would've died.

"Come on, Jack!" Tex punched my arm on her way out the door. "We're getting up a game."

I did not move. Beginning at the moment I glimpsed her, The Girl forever began a change in me. Seconds before the encounter my thoughts were engulfed in recess fun; then, wham! Without any warning my mind was whopped into a foreign land in a new dimension. Though the change was ultimately a gradual one, she started it with a lightning-quick smite.

"Hey, Rebecca," said Will, waving at The Girl.

The goddess returned his wave.

"What's wrong, Jack?"

"That's your sister Rebecca?"

217

"Sure is. C'mon. They're gettin' a game up."

Hence, I plotted, cajoled and did extra chores to secure an overnight at Will's.

"You know my rules," Mom had said.

Undaunted, I quickly arranged for her to meet Will and his parents at our school's Fun Night. The overnight was secured.

My yearning for Rebecca Corben somehow debilitated my ability to speak around her, and my body became Jell-O-like, almost as if I were having out-of-body experiences whenever I neared her. She was friendly, smiled a lot like Will, and was even more beautiful up close. During my overnight with Will she mostly stayed in her room. The Corbens didn't have a television, so we all played a game of Clue before bedtime. At one point in the game, Mr. Corben told a joke that made Rebecca laugh, and as she nudged me with her angelic hand, I almost fainted.

Will's seven-year-old brother Bobby said, "Jack's turnin' all white, Daddy."

I assuaged the Corbens' instant concern. "I'm okay, I'm okay." But I wasn't. The girl I was smitten with I couldn't be near without turning into a tongue tied, quivering mass of swooning Jell-O.

Now, standing confident with my black cruiser behind Sid's, deep in a river of thoughts, plans and possible scenarios, I determined that tomorrow morning I would not be swooning Jell-O; I would, instead, be something different.

And I was.

The small bell jingled when Kate opened the glass door. No customers in the bakery; behind the counter stood . . . nobody. Today's clerk must have been busy in back for the moment. She found a loaf of white sandwich bread and a box of Suzy Qs – thought about a Banana Flip – and started for the counter.

Worn, wooden swinging doors, far behind the customer counter, separated the small retail area from the rest of the outlet's warehouse and loading docks.

Kate heard somebody push through the swinging doors, and directly a dark-haired woman in a blue smock appeared at the counter. Kate stood fifteen feet from the woman, but could only see part of the clerk's profile. While pretending to be interested in day-old English muffins, she snuck enough peeks at the clerk to know for certain it was Imagene.

Kate started for the counter. Imagene, standing behind the cash register, seemed oblivious to an approaching customer; her eyes – well overdone with blue eye shadow – were fixed in a stare at the glassed front door. The attractive curves the brunette once flaunted were now filled in by flesh. Kate took no-more-than-would-be-expected pleasure from the sight of a plump Imagene.

Light at the Rat Pond

She set her bread and Suzy Qs on the counter, breaking Imagene's trance.

"Is that all for you - Katherine?" Her eyes - almost the same color as the mass of blue above them - widened and she smiled. "Katherine Hobbs. It's good to see you." (Kate hated it when Imagene called her *Katherine*.) She reached over and gently squeezed and released Kate's hand. "I just saw your son in here the other day. Jack, right?"

"Yes. He said he saw you."

"He did? Well he's a cute one. The girls are gonna be after him - if they aren't already."

"He's still more interested in bikes and baseball."

"Probably not a bad thing, huh?"

"No. It's not."

"It's good to see you, Katherine. I don't think I've seen you since . . ."

"It's been about nine years, Imagene."

"Really? Wow. That long?"

"At the trial."

She frowned, said, "That's right, the trial." Then added, "It was terrible what happened to Andrew." She gently squeezed and released Kate's hand again. "I am so sorry for you and Jack."

Kate nodded, curious if she was "so sorry" for Andrew's murder, or "so sorry" for her possible role in it, or both. When she knew Imagene in high school, Imagene wasn't known for her virtue. Rather, she had garnered a reputation as a crafty liar who could never be satisfied with what she had, and embraced coveting as a way of life, especially regarding boys. Some reputations, Kate knew, were based purely on speculation mingled with lies; others were earned. She knew Imagene's high school reputation had been honestly gained.

Imagene turned off her sorrow and brightened again, eyed Kate up and down. "You look terrific. How do you do it?"

Kate shrugged. "Umm . . . don't really know."

"I mean it, you're prettier now than you were in high school."

Kate didn't know how to take that.

Imagene, catching up to her last words, said, "That came out wrong. Let me try again. You were pretty in high school, but even prettier now. That's how I meant it."

"Thank you."

"I'm serious. You need to share your secret."

Kate didn't want to lose the alone time with her. Any second now a customer could walk in, spoiling her chance to ask The Question. After Imagene rang up the sale and bagged her items, Kate cleared her throat and asked, "Did you know?"

"Know what?" said Imagene, smiling at her.

219

Richard Newberry

Way too vague. Yet Kate knew The Question in itself would imply she suspected Imagene. Kate rarely avoided confrontation, it was best to just get things out and resolved. Still, The Question would automatically imply Kate believed Imagene, possibly, had a part in Andrew's murder.

Kate anxiously waded in with an extended version of the same question. "Did you know Floyd Lappin was planning something?"

Kate believed, before Imagene appeared offended by The Question, she first saw guilt flash over the woman's cosmetically-laden face. "With Andrew? Are you serious, Kate?"

Kate stood firm. "Yes."

"I can't believe you're thinking something like that. I wasn't even with Floyd at the time. That came out at the trial, Kate. You know that."

Kate said nothing.

Imagene's offended hurt switched to an indignation. "He attacked me. Attacked me right there on the A & P parking lot. Pulled a gun on me!"

"Why?" Kate knew what Floyd had said at the trial to answer the "why", but she was never convinced.

"Why? The creep was going to rob me, that's why. You know that. He pulled a gun on me!"

Kate just stood and stared at her, trying to read her face, hoping the silent stare would bring forth a confession.

Imagene's tone shifted again, to anger. "I don't like being accused of something I had no part in. No - part - in!"

"Somebody's following me, making threats. You know anything about that?"

"No I don't."

The door's bell jingled as a customer walked in. Imagene feigned a smile at him, then turned back to Kate, shoved the bag at her, and, in a low voice, warned, "I see your son in here again with his hooligan friends stealing stuff, tell him I'm going to call the cops."

Kate, though taken aback by Imagene's accusation of Jack and its accompanying threat, glared back at Imagene. "You were involved, I know it."

"Good luck proving it."

CHAPTER 56

Mom fussed over me Sunday morning by pushing aside my bangs and again playing with the part in my hair. She said, "I wish we had a tie for you. And those shoes . . . I don't know."

Her edgy mood from last night had evidently rolled away with the earth as it turned to greet the sun. While picking crawlers last night for the next day's fishing trip, she had nailed me with, "Are you stealing from the bakery?"

"No." I was glad it was dark.

She shined the flashlight in my face. "I'm glad you're a horrible liar."

I suddenly got very busy looking for fast and slippery worms.

She put the light back on the wetted ground. "Don't lie to me, Jack Andrew Hobbs."

I said nothing to avoid lying.

Her stare at my head bore tremendous weight.

"I have - only a couple of times." Lie.

"Two times?"

"Uh. No."

"More?"

"Yes - but I'm not anymore."

"When did you last do it?"

"'Bout a week ago, I guess."

"That was your last time."

"Yes, ma'am."

"Go to the bakery Monday morning, ask for the manager. Tell the manager what you've done, ask forgiveness and tell him you'll do whatever he wants to pay it back."

"But -"

"You heard me."

"Okay."

"Do not involve the chubby lady with the crammed on blue eye shadow."

She *had* caught us stealing! "Okay."

"All will be right then."

At that point some of her edge wore off, but something else still had her sharp. I didn't think it involved any of my misbehavior, for everything seemed

221

Richard Newberry

right between us. Mom had a way of making things right by confronting, instructing, expecting, forgiving.

"Should have taken you to the barber."

"My hair's fine, Mom."

"Step back. Let me see you."

"I'm right here."

"Jack Hobbs."

I stepped back. She looked from my black shoes to black slacks, up to my white short-sleeved shirt, and finally to my hair. She smiled, said, "You look like your dad."

"Is that good?"

"The best," she said.

"Are you done grooming me?"

"How about a little more Brylcream - I'm just kidding."

"Funny."

"I'm done," she said. "Probably a good thing you're going to church." She softly swatted my rear end. I took it as one last reminder that my limited career as a criminal had better be over.

"I'll have a lunch packed and we'll head out to the lake as soon as you get home."

I went to my room to get the Bible Will had given me. I ran my plan over and over again through my mind. The Corbens drove a Dodge station wagon; I considered the various seating arrangements that I would find upon their arrival. Bobby would most likely be in the very back seat, with Will and Rebecca in the middle seat. How would that play out? Would Will slide over, putting himself between his sister and me? Should I go directly to her side and make her scoot over? Could I bring myself to sitting right next to her without swooning? For my plan to work I had to sit next to her. I began to doubt I could successfully carry out my plan because of the Jell-O-like quivering that had previously overcome me. I went to the kitchen. I needed a drink.

Mom was at the piano, playing a mellow song I'd heard on the radio. "I'm gonna wait outside."

She smiled, pointed at her cheek, and I gave her a quick kiss before going outside.

I hadn't been in the front yard for more than thirty seconds when the Corbens' white station wagon turned into our drive. I eyed the middle seat. Will and Rebecca were there, no Bobby; I saw him in the back seat. Good, as I had imagined. The next few seconds were crucial. Will was sitting on my side, what move would he make? Should I make a preemptive move to take control of the situation?

Light at the Rat Pond

Through his open window, Will asked, "You forget something, Yank?"

"Nope." Then it occurred to me the Corbens' car had been parked for a moment and they were all looking at me as I looked at the middle seat, pondering the plan.

Will got out. "C'mon. Let's go."

Will's move indicated I would get to slide over and be right next to his sister. Perfect - except the idea of being that close to the goddess froze my feet to our lawn.

"C'mon, Yank."

"Right." I finally moved, stumbled on flat ground on my way to the open door. Not cool; I hoped Rebecca hadn't noticed my clumsiness.

Will said, smiling, "Pretty graceful. You're better on a bike." He held the door, and winked at me.

I immediately discovered Mr. Corben detested a dirty car when my awkward energy and black polyester pants met the Dodge's pristine and slick vinyl interior. I entered the car with too much sideways momentum and would've slammed squarely into Mr. and Mrs. Corben's daughter, but fortunately during my slide I turned at the last second and avoided hurting Rebecca. Instead, I toppled over and my head landed in her lap.

With the drawl of an angel from Oxley, Arkansas, she smiled down at me and said, "Well, hey there, Jack. You comfortable?"

Realizing I wasn't in heaven yet, I jolted upright, almost smashing her nose, said, "Sorry. Sorry about that."

Mr. and Mrs. Corben were turned to me and grinning, Bobby and Will were guffawing.

Still smiling, Rebecca said, "It's okay."

Mrs. Corben said to Mr. Corben, "You have got to quit making these seats so slippery when you clean." She asked me, "Are you okay?"

"I'm fine. Thanks."

We drove for five minutes before my shock and embarrassment subsided enough for me to remember my name. Will and Bobby were still talking and chuckling about my comedic ability.

Bobby leaned forward. Dark red hair, cut in a flat top, covered his round head, which sat atop his gangly, seven-year-old body. Mrs. Corben, Rebecca and Will had olive complexions, but Bobby had inherited fairer skin from his father; yet Will was the image of his dad. The Corbens were a comely family - except for Bobby. Likeable and friendly as the rest, he was yet to grow into the family's good looks. He said, "Will says you're a Cub fan. Is that true?"

"Uh, yep."

Richard Newberry

"We're all Cardinal fans - 'cept Becky. She don't care about baseball, but we like the Cardinals, right Daddy?"

"Till the end, Bobby, till the end."

Finding out Rebecca didn't like baseball did not mitigate my feelings for her one bit. At least she wasn't a Cardinal fan. Maybe, like Stink, she didn't care about teams but liked to play.

Grinning, Bobby said, "Becky's too busy thinkin' about boys."

"Please be quiet, Robert," said Rebecca. "Or I'll kiss you right in front of your friends at church."

This was too good to be true: she thought about boys and talked about kissing.

"Oooo, yuck!" Bobby replied. He turned around and looked out the back window.

Rebecca wore a red dress and a matching bow held her shoulder-length chestnut hair in place. Tan nylons ran out of her shiny black shoes and up her shapely calves, disappearing there. Her hands looked soft, delicate, perfect, and no paint covered her groomed nails. I didn't detect any perfume, but while my head had rested in her lap I noticed a pleasant, fresh smell of something akin to baby powder. Her face had perfect symmetry; golden brown eyes bejeweled that beautiful face.

"You excited about church, Yank?"

"Yes."

"I can tell." He gave me a wry grin. "'Cause you look excited."

"I am. Yep."

Nobody spoke for the next few minutes and I used the time to steal sideways glances at Goddess Rebecca. A little of the Jell-O feeling tried to distract me, but I overcame it by focusing on two small freckles on her toned and slender right arm, just above her bicep.

She looked at me, then at her arm, and asked, "Do I have something on me?"

Snapped out of my fixation, I answered, "No. You're perf- fine. Perfectly fine."

She turned and looked out her closed window.

Mr. Corben's elbow rested on his open window frame, while Mrs. Corben's window was only half way down, fresh June air circulated in the car. Bobby was quietly singing some kid song, and Will seemed interested in something outside his open window. The time had come to execute my romantic plan.

The two small freckles on Rebecca's right arm were, to my mind, a celestial sign, put there for the very purpose of showing me the way.

224

I shifted my eyes left, right, forward; heard Bobby still singing to the back window. I swallowed, made a loose fist.

Maybe a tad too hard - because it could be heard above the air blowing into the car - I punched Rebecca's freckled arm.

At least Kate didn't need to worry about Jack's behavior. He was a good - not perfect - boy, and wouldn't make trouble for the Corbens. She had been troubled by the news he'd chosen to steal cakes, yet his honesty in confessing the matter was more in line with his usual character. Only his mother could've sensed the subtle relief coming from Jack when he confessed. Dishonesty wasn't something he carried well.

Kate removed her feet from the piano's pedals, rested her hands in her lap. The possible bad behavior of last night's caller did worry her, and it had to be the same guy who had been following her. But who was he?

Kate would bet her life Imagene knew something about the stalker and his threat, and as she'd always suspected, the fat . . . witch had some involvement - other than innocent victim - in the murder of Kate's husband.

She thought back to post-trial events. After a quick trial, which included a very short jury deliberation, Floyd Lappin headed for prison and Kate remained in a gray fog of despondency, trying to feel something despite the numbness. Family tried to help, but she found the more she concentrated on baby Jack the more she got her bearings, and Jack and that concentration began to dissipate the numbness.

One of the Doverville detectives warned her to be alert to any possible retaliation from the Lappin clan, and at the first hint of any such action she was to immediately contact him. What was his name? Detective Carlton? Calton? Something like that. Anyway, there had been no subsequent harassment or threats, or anything, from anybody until now. And she was convinced the stalking caller had connections to Andrew's murder and the Deplorable Indiscretion.

Who could it be? The clan of Lappins living on Star Street were a filthy, notorious bunch, the kind that gave riff raff a bad name. But the head of the Star Street bunch, Marty Lappin - Floyd's younger brother and Cus's dad - was back in county jail, according to Nadine. Kate knew Marty had been in and out of jail and did a year or two in an upstate prison. And she also knew he had never been convicted of anything as egregious as murder. Theft, drunk and disorderly, and assaults were his majors. It was an assault that had finally landed him in prison for a while several years ago.

At some point in Lappin clan history, Floyd and Marty had had a severe

Richard Newberry

falling out, one that put them both in jail. After that, Marty and the two Lappin sisters settled west of Doverville on Star Street, while the ostracized older brother settled in parts unknown, somewhere in the woods near the Indiana border.

Kate knew the Lappin brothers and sisters from their drastically limited days at Doverville High. They were good looking kids, but mean – even the sisters. Some of Floyd's family, his mother and aunts, sat through the trial, but his siblings never showed. The guilty verdict brought no immediate or future reprisal to Kate from any of the Lappins. Had it now?

She mentally flipped through the pages of her teen and young adult life. She kept stopping at the pages of the Deplorable Indiscretion. Somebody from that period almost twenty years ago was slipping her mind; she knew because of the itch deep within her subconscious.

Who? Who was it?!

CHAPTER 57

I fixed a fawning smile on my face just before I landed the romantic punch; that stupid smile froze when she grabbed her arm and said, "Ow! Why did you do that?"

"What's going on back there?" asked Mr. Corben, averting his eyes to the rearview mirror.

Bobby had sprung up as soon as the punch sounded in the car. "I think Jack punched Becky." Teeth were missing in his smile.

Mrs. Corben turned to us. "What?"

"Jack punched Becky," he repeated.

Mrs. Corben focused her hazel eyes on me; a quizzical frown covered her pretty face.

His eyes back on the road, Mr. Corben asked, "What's wrong?"

Will was looking out his window and chuckling.

Right then I wished I were a penny that could slip down the clean, slick vinyl seat and disappear. I looked at Rebecca and said, "Sorry," then to Mrs. Corben, "I'm sorry."

Rebecca had quit rubbing her arm. "What made you do that?" Her golden brown eyes, which I had hoped would someday behold me with romantic passion, flirted with being angry. All was lost.

My pleading eyes bounced between Rebecca and Mrs. Corben. "I don't know what I was thinking." Lie. "I swear I don't know. I'm really sorry."

Mrs. Corben's perplexed frowning suddenly gave way to a knowing half-smile. I had seen the same look at times on my mom's face. "It's okay, Jack. We all do those sorts of things from time to time."

"We do?" said Rebecca.

"Yes, Rebecca, we do," she said, giving her daughter a subtle "I'll-tell-you-later" look.

Bobby piped up, "So it's okay if I punch her?"

"What?" said Mr. Corben, slightly turning his head.

Mrs. Corben rested her hand on her husband's shoulder, and that must have indicated to him that she had it handled because he turned once again to the road. She told him something I couldn't hear above the airy car, and he slowly nodded. I thought I saw his face crease in a half-smile.

227

Richard Newberry

Mrs. Corben said to Bobby, "It's never okay to punch your sister."

"But Jack –"

She held up the hand that had been resting on Mr. Corben's shoulder. "End of discussion."

Bobby shrunk into his seat.

Mrs. Corben smiled at me before she turned around.

Rebecca glanced at me, not with burgeoning anger but a degree of confusion, then set her gaze at the world passing by her window.

Mrs. Corben's smile had brought me back from under the seat, but Rebecca's demeanor crushed me like a penny under the weight of a train. I had blown it. My plan to hatch a romantic beginning with her had failed miserably, and my ten-soon-to-be-eleven-year-old heart took a dive toward brokenness. Anger at Mom flashed through me. Why had I assumed *her* advice regarding a romantic approach was wise and safe? She didn't even have a boyfriend!

I considered the punches to the arm I had taken from Tex, the ones Mom said were Tex's way of saying she liked me. Some were casual taps, others carried more force, attention getters. There were degrees to her punches, and I began to consider that there were different meanings conveyed with each punch. Maybe Mom was right, and I just hadn't executed properly. Maybe I should try again – just not immediately. My heart, while perplexed about Tex's possible intentions, began to rise from the depths of despair, riding on the hope of a second chance with Rebecca.

Pondering the resilience of the human heart, I looked at Will, who hadn't taken his eyes off the passing outside world or lost his it's-been-entertaining smile.

Sunday School was okay. The teacher, Mr. Nelson, a pleasant balding man, taught us about resisting our tendencies to do and say wrongs. Will, of all the boys in the class, was most attentive. At the end of the class, Mr. Nelson invited those that "don't know Jesus as your Savior" to go forward and ask God's Son into their hearts. I had an idea of what that meant because of Will, but I did not go forward.

Will was called upon to give the closing prayer. "Dear Lord, thank You for Your great love toward us, and thank You for Mr. Nelson's lesson. I pray that closed hearts would open today as Pastor Rogers preaches the Word this morning. In Jesus' name, amen."

A plump, gray-haired lady played a somber yet melodic arrangement on the organ while people filed into the high-ceilinged sanctuary for church. Sturdy, light oak was prominent, from the cushioned, maroon pews to the massive overhead beams, and from the pulpit to the giant cross hanging behind the choir

Light at the Rat Pond

loft behind the pulpit. I purposely avoided sitting next to Rebecca, and sat next to Will at the end of our pew.

A maroon-robed choir started to fill the loft as a younger and thinner lady played an upbeat and inviting tune on her large black piano, which had me tapping my foot on the maroon carpet.

After some congregational singing, a choir number and a soloist, a tall, lean man with black-framed glasses and wearing a black suit strode confidently to the pulpit. He had perfectly groomed and thick raven-colored hair, and his red tie stood out against his white shirt. He beamed a white smile at the congregation.

Will nudged me, whispered, "That's Pastor Rogers."

The pastor's rich, baritone voice filled the sanctuary as he opened with a prayer. He was several minutes into his sermon before I realized I hadn't taken my eyes from him or missed a word he'd preached. His rising and falling cadence, deep and authoritative, had me mesmerized. He quoted and read from the Bible, made the congregation smile and sometimes laugh, or say amen; stern one minute, not so the next. Like Ernie Banks of the Cubs, Pastor Rogers was doing what he was created to do.

With passionate eloquence he wove a Bible story around sin and redemption, hell and heaven. Sometimes the sermon produced joy within me, other times it caused me to squirm, and it always seemed the pastor was speaking directly to me. Will's furtive glances at me reinforced the idea that I was the sermon's target.

Pastor Rogers offered an invitation at the end of his message, inviting lost sinners to come to Jesus, accept by faith what the crucified and risen Savior had done for us, and allow Him to be Lord of our lives. Though our heads were bowed and our eyes were supposed to be closed, I noticed Will peeking at me.

A beckoning, invisible force seemed to be pulling me out of the pew and up toward the pastor and the redemption he said Jesus offered. Part of me knew it was the right thing to do, yet a strange struggle erupted inside me, bringing with it a dose of fear. So, I stayed in the pew.

CHAPTER 58

Mom and I only caught two fish - one each - Sunday afternoon. I was a little distracted by my earlier failed attempt to convey romantic intentions to Rebecca and forever blowing my chance with her, and the visceral battle my heart and mind endured at the end of Pastor Rogers's sermon had me off balance. But we had a good time. Whatever had set her on edge yesterday had not followed Mom to the lake.

Dwight got back from St. Louis late in the afternoon and came to the garage just before supper. I was finding wood for Tex's jump ramp.

"Do anything fun in St. Louis?"

"Not really. Kind of boring. There's no place to play there except the street."

"No bikes?"

"One."

"You're kidding me."

"Nope."

"At least the Cubs beat the Cardinals two out of three."

"They got lucky, Jack."

I looked at his attire. "Looks like you did, too." He had on a white knit pullover with horizontal blue stripes trimmed in green, and white pants with orange stripes. "You steal those?"

"You like?"

"No - well, they're you."

"Got 'em from my cousin. They're like new, man."

"Glad you're back."

"Same here. I miss anything?"

I told him about Shorty's ruined garden and Will forcing Shorty to let him help, and I told him Kenny and I helped Will with the hobo Bible study.

"Are you serious?"

"Yep."

Dwight chuckled. "Just like I told you. Will Corben can shake things up."

"I know - hey, Hairy - Clarence - told us to be careful around a hobo called Sticks."

"Sticks?"

230

Light at the Rat Pond

"Yeah. Hair- Clarence says he's mean. Got his nickname because he likes to use a knife."

"And probably not for wood carving."

"Right." I set a piece of plywood on the garage floor. "Guess he wears a red bandana all the time."

"Gotcha. Keep my eyes open." He chuckled again, and it turned into a laugh, and when Dwight laughed hard, his body laughed with him.

It made me smile; my love-lost heartache from that morning dissipated completely in the presence of my friend. I hoped Will wouldn't purvey the news of me punching his sister's arm. "What's so funny?"

"Kenny Hooks in the vicinity of Hairy having a Bible study with Eyeballs."

My smile grew. "It was somethin'."

I explained our idea of rolling the empty oil barrels down the tracks for Tex's jump.

"It could work," he said, "but it'd be tough rolling the barrels back up that steep hill at the oil company."

I visualized the brushy hillside. "You're right. It'd be almost impossible to get them back up that hill through all the stickers and weeds and stuff."

"Square dinkham."

"What if we just left them at the Rat Pond?"

"Nah. Don't want to do that. We need to take them back."

"Yeah, you're right. Plus Will wouldn't help if we didn't plan to take 'em back."

"I gave it some serious thought the last couple of days. See what you think of this plan."

So while we measured and cut two-by-fours and plywood for Tex's launch ramp, Dwight detailed his idea for moving the oil barrels.

". . . and if we do it just before dark when most everybody's in the house watching TV, nobody will say a thing."

"It's a good idea, but, man, if anybody sees us they're gonna wonder what we're doing."

"They see us doin' crazy stuff all the time anyway. Probably won't even notice."

"Uh, yeah, it'll get notice."

"Come on, Jack."

I finished the ramp's plywood top on the table saw. Dwight had already calculated angle degree, length and width for the ramp. I turned off the saw and said, "Okay. Let's try moving them your way."

"It'll work."

"It'll work - I think. I just hope we don't get busted."

231

Richard Newberry

"We won't."

"Right."

He just smiled.

The ramp was in pieces and ready; we would assemble it at the Rat Pond the day of the fiery jump.

"You got the fuel mixture ready?"

"Yep," I said. "You think it's smart she's not using a landing ramp?"

"Probably. She's just gotta stop quick - if she can - when she lands."

"Think she'll make it?"

"Six barrels. I don't know, but I hope so. If she crashes into those burning barrels she's gonna be a hurt mess."

I never seriously considered Tex might fail, and when I did, it scared me a little. "Think we got the ramp right?"

"I do. Angle's good . . . it's long enough, wide enough."

I looked at the wood pieces on the floor. "Think we should stop her?"

He chuckled. "We talkin' about Tex Wonderlin or some other Tex?"

"You're right. Couldn't if we tried."

"Square dinkham."

We set the pieces of ramp aside, and Dwight asked, "Your birthday campout still on?"

"That'd be like trying to stop Tex from jumping."

"Cool! Can't wait - hey, man! I almost forgot. Dang! How could I? Come this Friday you'll be an official hard-road rider, Jack."

I grinned. "You know it. I can hardly wait."

Sunday nights were usually slow around the garage. Most of the Icks were involved in family things on Sunday afternoons and evenings, but cruisers began to show up about seven on that Sunday night; Will was the last to arrive for barrel rolling night.

"Change of plans," I announced.

Tex froze. "What?"

Stink asked, "What kind of change?"

Kenny, still puppy-less, said, "Yeah."

Dwight explained the problem with our original plan, then described the new one.

Stink said, "This is gonna be pure quill!"

"How many wagons we need?" Tex asked.

"Four," said Dwight, and we had access to at least that many.

We went over the brief list of things we needed, then Dwight asked Kenny, "You still got that rope you lassoed the Sunbeam truck with?"

232

Light at the Rat Pond

He rolled his green eyes up toward his forehead, thought, and said, "I think so. Yes."

Tomorrow night we would attempt to carry out Dwight's plan. The excitement the Icks felt in the garage would be nothing compared to the excitement that surged through us the next night.

CHAPTER 59

First thing Monday morning I rode to the bakery. Imagene wasn't there, but the manager was, so I offered my confession and apology.

The bespectacled round man appeared perplexed about how he should treat my honesty regarding my thievery and subsequent contrition. "Your parents make you come do this?"

"My mom."

"I see. Hmm." He tapped a fat finger on his desk. "What to do? What to do?"

If he wanted me to suggest a punishment, I believed confession should've been enough.

"Tell you what, Jack," he said. "There's an area at the back of the garage where the guys wash their trucks after their runs. Come back two nights this week and help them wash, and your debt will be paid. Fair enough?"

"Yes, sir."

He tried a stern look that wasn't really all that stern as he added, "And no more stealing."

"Yes, sir."

I rode from the bakery to the cutover behind Sid's to meet Dwight. We'd planned the meet last night because the black raspberries were ripening. He was plodding up the south hill when I got there, both hands filled with the tracks' gray gravel.

"Hey, Jack."

"Rocks for Cus?"

"Just in case."

"Smart." I told him about my trip to the bakery.

"Ah, dude, busted."

"Yep. And I'm kinda glad I got caught stealing. It was beginning to bother me."

"Will," he said.

"Yeah, but even before Will."

He nodded. "'Cause you're a good cat at heart, Jack."

"I don't know."

"I do."

234

Light at the Rat Pond

We walked down to the tracks and into the lush, thorny green of the hillside. At first glance a novice picker would've seen only the exposed red berries and decided to come back another day. But we knew where the early ripe ones hid. Dwight pulled back some weeds and lifted a cane from its shade. "Oh, yeah." He looked at me. "Money time."

"Wanna pick?"

"You wanna make money?"

"Always."

Picking wasn't easy, unless you liked hot, sweaty, thorny and chigger-infested work; it took experienced pickers an hour to fill a gallon basket with the marble-sized fruit. The other Icks didn't share our proclivity to earn money no matter the difficulty, so it was just us.

We already had on our long-sleeved shirts - required picking attire, and I said, "Let's go get our buck-"

Somebody had scuffed bike brakes up on the alley. It wasn't a slide-stop, it was a furtive braking.

I looked at Dwight, wishing he hadn't dumped his rocks on the tracks. He shrugged.

We couldn't see the rider. We didn't chance moving in the clinging brush, but if Cus loomed above, we needed something to defend ourselves against his pearl-handled switchblade.

Sweat trickled down our faces as we crouched in the weedy cover; gnats, grasshoppers and other flying insects pestered us. The rider remained suspiciously quiet.

Dwight, nodding toward the tracks below us, whispered, "Rocks."

I wished for the old thirty-four ounce Louisville Slugger we had found at the Rat Pond and kept stashed under the mulberry tree, but that was futile, since the looming rider waited near the mulberry.

We quietly cleared the snagging brush and made it to the rocks, each loaded a handful, and I whispered, "Ready?"

Dwight nodded.

We were charging up the cutover, arms cocked, when we heard, "Hey, y'all. These ain't bad." He was eating ripe mulberries.

We tossed the rocks, and Dwight said, "They'll give you the runs." We didn't tell Will how he had spooked us.

"So you want to help pick?" I asked Will.

"Sure. I picked blackberries down home."

Will helped Dwight and I do our chores for Sid, but refused any money for his help.

235

Richard Newberry

"You'll need long sleeves for picking," I said, and went inside our house to get him a shirt.

Mom warned me to stay out of her and Melba's patches, and reminded me she had invited Ruth, Mrs. Corben, to pick with her and Melba.

She asked, "Should we plan on tonight?"

"Couple of days."

"You're picking."

"Trust me. In two or three days there will be a whole lot more ripe ones."

We left our bikes in the garage and strode east on the alley, purple and red-stained wooden buckets swung at our sides. Dwight had his transistor on inside his bucket.

I stopped at the mulberry and grabbed the bat. Our picking that morning would take us dangerously close to the Lappin clan.

We talked about the plan to move the barrels, St. Louis, Shorty's garden, hobo Bible study and Sticks. Will said nothing about me punching his sister's arm. In between Harper's Field and the oil company, we cut down the hill to a picking spot Dwight and I claimed for ourselves, where the raspberries ripened earlier than the rest. I set the bat in the weeds near me.

"Man," said Will. "These boogers are sure smaller than blackberries."

I said, "Takes a while to fill a bucket. But it's good money."

We had picked a few minutes when *Gimme Dat Ding* began to play on Dwight's radio, forcing us to try and dance.

At first, Will ate more raspberries than what he tossed into his bucket. "Man, these things are good. Way better than blackberries."

Dwight and I started describing all the delicious things our moms did with the berries: over vanilla ice cream, milk shakes, cobblers, pies and jam.

"Best of all," said Dwight, "is the money."

"At least five bucks a bucket," I told Will. "Sometimes people give us a dollar or two tip."

We stooped three abreast in the weeds and briars, mostly in the shade at that time of morning, and listened to the music while our fingers picked and gradually turned purplish red. A train rumbled by behind us, drawing Will's attention.

After the fellas on the caboose waved at us, Will said, "Didn't seem like it was goin' that fast, did it?"

"Faster than you think," I said.

We had worked into a quiet rhythm of picking and sweating when we heard Rick Spencer cruise past on Warren.

"Man, y'all, this is hard work."

Dwight and I nodded, then Dwight said to Will, "Can I ask you something?"

236

Light at the Rat Pond

"Sure."

"Where do you think evil comes from? I know a little about what the Bible says about the devil and all that, but where did the devil get evil? Who started it?"

Will stopped picking, wrinkled his brow and frowned. "Dad burn, Dwight, that's a tough one." He stared straight ahead for a moment before looking at us and saying, "There's things about God and His way of doin' that I can't explain or understand."

Dwight said, "Just something I've wondered about."

"Yeah," I said. "Me, too."

Will stood between us; he set his basket of berries in the weeds. "I know. So have I." He plucked a raspberry, ate it. "If I had to say where evil started, I'd say it started with freedom."

"Freedom?" asked Dwight.

"Yeah. I'd say it starts there - that's my thinking anyway."

I said, "Why's that?"

"Because God gives us the freedom to choose. In a way, that shows how much He loves us."

Dwight dropped berries into his bucket. "I don't know if that's good for us. Lots of people choose wrong stuff to do."

I nodded.

"They sure do," said Will, plucking another berry and eating it. "But let me ask you something." He looked left and right, engaging both of us. "Do your mothers love you?"

Dwight nodded; I stopped picking and said, "Yes."

"Why, Yank?"

"Why?"

"Yeah, why?"

I smiled. "'Cause I'm a great son."

Dwight quipped, "If she does, that can't be it."

Smiles all around before Will said, "Seriously, why do you think your mother loves you?"

I shrugged, started picking again and said, "It's just . . . what moms do."

"You reckon she's forced to love you?"

"In Jack's case, Will, yes."

Smiles again.

I said, "I don't think she's forced to love me. No."

"What if she was forced to love you?"

I thought about Cus's mom before I said, "It'd be weird. Different."

"Wouldn't be as good," said Dwight.

237

Richard Newberry

Will smiled. "Sure wouldn't. I think that's why God doesn't force us. He's given us the freedom to choose. In a way it's like He's showing us love by letting us choose. Kinda giving us . . . uh . . . I don't know, can't think of the right word."

Dwight turned off the radio and said, "Dignity."

Will smiled, nodded slowly. "Yeah, Dwight, that's right. Good word. God gives us dignity by allowing us to choose good or evil, or Him being our Lord or not."

"I'm not sure I get it," I said. "It doesn't make sense. If God is good and loves us, why would He let a person who chooses to do good get murdered by a guy who does evil?"

Will looked at me. "I said I don't get it all, that's for sure. But I think blaming God for the bad stuff people choose to do doesn't make sense. You think God wants Clarence and Arlie to be hobos? Or Cus to be as mean as he is?"

I didn't answer.

Will said, "And sometimes we see good come from the bad."

Nobody picked now; I asked, "How's that?"

"Just like you, Dwight."

"Yeah?"

"Think about this. Are you a better son since Nicky's been in prison?"

"Probably."

"And I think you're not ever gonna do what Nicky did. I think his choices help you make better ones. I might be wrong. But this I know, Dwight, you've made yourself smart, square dinkham, and we all know you've got a good heart."

Dwight's brown eyes were fixed on the ground. "I don't know about all that."

"I do," I said. "Even though you're the worst dresser ever."

He looked up at me, smiled. "Groovy smooth, Jack. Groovy smooth."

We got busy picking again, and Will said, "I wish there wasn't evil, but people have that choice. And it seems like everybody has bad things happen to them because of it. But it's real important how we handle the bad stuff that happens to us."

"Square dinkham," said Dwight.

"And I've come to think this, y'all. It may sound weird, but I think if we didn't have freedom to choose - good or even evil - we wouldn't know about love. I don't think love would even exist."

Will's last words ushered in a pondering quiet over us as we continued to pick and try to fill our buckets.

Light at the Rat Pond

Shortly thereafter, Dwight switched on the radio and Will said, lifting up the silver crucifix, "You know, I wear this here to remind me how much Jesus loves me, and to tell other folks about what He did for them on the cross. The Bible says He actually *became sin* for us. I can't imagine that. I know that what we were talkin' about, good and evil and all that, well, He allows it to happen, but He took every wicked thing folks have done and will do and put it smack on Himself to save us - if we'll believe. Now that's love, y'all. More than I can understand."

I sure couldn't comprehend it either, but I soon understood it was because the radio was playing and our backs were turned and we were contemplating Will's thoughts that Evil was able to sneak right up on us.

CHAPTER 60

"Sissies pickin' their little berries."

We turned together, already knowing who had spoken the mocking words.

On the dark ties between the steel rails, two sinister looking goons stood on the left and right of Cus.

"Looks like things are more even today - Icks!" He pulled the switchblade from his back pocket. "Or maybe not." The knife's shiny blade whipped out and locked into its menacing position.

Far as we knew, Cus always rode alone; to see him with two accomplices was an unpleasant surprise. They looked younger than Cus, yet brandished the same dirty-mean demeanors as Lappin did. Cus's long, dingy hair rarely saw a barber, but his thug-buddies had flat tops, which asserted their evil presence. The kid on Cus's left was lean and had a long head with a forehead that rivaled Kenny's; the other kid was short, but had the same squared head and stout body as Cus, and his ears jutted out from his head like the mirrors on a bread truck. Like Cus, they wore dingy T-shirts and grimy, tattered jeans.

Standing above them in waist-high weeds and briars holding half-full wooden buckets of raspberries, I felt very vulnerable. I expected Will to say something pleasant despite the situation, but he didn't open his mouth.

Dwight spoke first. He turned off the radio and said, "Gonna introduce us to your friends, Cus?"

"Oh, yeah. Soon as I gut Pretty Boy there you'll meet us all."

"Now why would you want to gut Will, *Custard*? Because of the baseball game? C'mon, Custard, you gotta be getting over that."

The big-eared boy asked, "Why's he callin' you *Custard*?"

"'Cause that's his name, jug ears," answered Dwight.

Jug Ears snarled, said, "That ain't my name, boy."

"Sorry, - Dumbo?"

I stared speechless at Dwight, bewildered by his eager provocation.

Through gritted teeth, Dumbo said, "It's Bart, you stupid" - and Bart called Dwight a bad name.

Cus warned, "Keep it up, Blackie, and I'll start with you."

Dwight set down his bucket, waved his hands in mock surrender as he said, "Oooo. I'm scared."

Light at the Rat Pond

Cus started up the hill but stopped when Will said, "Your fight's with me, not these guys." He set his bucket in the weeds and stepped toward the tracks.

Dwight threw out an arm, stopping Will. "Where you going? You're not a fool. Don't act like one." He looked at Cus but said to Will, "You're not gonna just surrender to this punk sissy."

Punk sissy?! I couldn't believe - or understand - what Dwight was doing.

"You hear that?" said Bart.

"Guess you want it first, huh, Blackie?"

Long Head said, "I think he wants your knife in his big black belly."

"C'mon you guys," I said. "Everybody just cool it." My words sounded noodle-limp to me.

"Don't tell me what to do, Hobbs. You're just a big sissy, out here with your little berry basket, pickin' berries for your mommy." Cus and his goons laughed.

"They're not for my mom. I sell 'em." What a stupid and useless response.

"Who cares, Hobbs?" They all laughed again.

Dwight quelled the laughter with, "What are you waiting for, Custard?"

"Quit callin' me that."

"What's wrong? Mommy and Daddy give you a sissy name? I'll bet your middle name's Pie. Custard Pie Lappin."

Cus's face flushed red; he shook from rage, growled, "I said shut up!"

I said, "Cool it, Dwight."

"Custard Pie Lappin."

Cus gripped and re-gripped the switchblade's pearl handle.

I asked Dwight, "What are you doing, man?"

"He ain't got the guts to stab anybody," said Dwight, staring down the hill at our enemy. "Do you, Custard?"

My mind raced, but not in a straight line; it was all over the place. My thumping heart seemed to increase the speed of my erratic thoughts. But the volatile situation had paralyzed my body; all I could move were my eyes.

Bart said, "Let's go cut 'em, Cus."

"Yeah," chimed Long Head.

Will, like me, appeared frozen.

Only Dwight seemed calm. He extended an arm, waved his hand, inviting Cus and the goons up the weedy and thorny hill. "Well, come on."

I told Dwight. "Stop -"

Too late.

Cus growled like an angry dog and started for the hill with the switchblade out in front. He stumbled over the rail, which made him even more furious, and his growl became a guttural scream. His hazel eyes appeared to glow red.

241

Richard Newberry

Bart and Long Head also growled and screamed as they charged the hill behind Cus.

My paralysis miraculously broke and I remembered our weapon: the old Louisville Slugger. I dropped my bucket, spilling the fruit of my arduous labor, and frantically searched for the bat.

Cus and his goons were barely slowed by the thorny hillside. They growled as they mashed through the weeds, drawing closer to us.

I spotted the bat's black-taped handle, drew the weapon and shoved Will out of the way. The railway then resounded with my own primordial scream. "Aahhhgg!"

The raised bat and my maniacal charge toward them stalled Bart and Long Head, but Cus's rage drove him up the hill. "You're dead, Flowers!" Cus seemed oblivious to my advance on him. When he reached Dwight and thrust the blade at my friend I smashed his knife-hand with a powerful, downward stroke. "Cruck!" was the sickening sound of smashed flesh and bone.

The switchblade vanished in the weeds; Cus howled with pain and fell backwards into the briars, gripping his right wrist.

I turned on the goons and charged at them. Long Head had seen enough and began a retreat, but Bart stood his ground until I whacked him in the ribs. Both goons hit the tracks running. I chased them, cursing and threatening as I waved the bat over my head. I had become a wrathful, bat-wielding boy empowered by a fury I wouldn't have believed existed within me; I wanted revenge, I wanted to inflict pain.

But as much as I wanted to inflict pain on the goons, they, even more, wanted to escape the impending pain, for they shot up through the brambles on the north hill like savvy rabbits.

I quit on them and marched back toward Cus, filled with anger and hate.

"Enough, Jack," said Will. "He's hurt bad."

Dwight stood next to our suffering enemy. "Yeah, man. It's over. You got him a good one."

Both friends warily eyed me, like I was the friendly family dog who had suddenly turned vicious.

Cus, still on his back clutching his wrist, writhed in pain. I said, "Get out of here." I pointed the bat at him, it shook from my rage. "Don't ever come here again. You hear me? Don't ever come here again!"

Cus's face displayed no menace, only agony. He stumbled down the hill and across the tracks, and managed to fight through the tangled hillside, one handed. His cohorts were long gone. He mounted his bike and pedaled away.

I wouldn't see Cus again - until August.

Still strangling the bat, I turned it toward Dwight.

242

CHAPTER 61

I had adrenaline shakes.

Will said, "What're you doin' with the bat, Yank? Like Dwight said, it's over. It's over, Yank."

"It's all good, Jack," said Dwight. "They're all gone. No more bad guys."

My fury, though not as fierce, remained. "What were you doing, Dwight? Huh? You pushed him into it!"

"No I didn't."

"Yes you did!"

"You can think what you want, Jack."

"What I'm thinking is you almost got us killed."

"No I didn't." Dwight's calm, non-contrite response inflamed my anger.

"Yes you did! You pushed him!"

"No-I-did-not."

"Y'all, please hold on a second."

I pointed the bat at Will and yelled, "And what were you doing?!"

Will looked at me, bewildered.

"You just gonna walk down there and give yourself up, get stabbed for - for - some stupid reason?"

Will said nothing.

I took a few deep breaths. "Man, Will, sometimes you gotta fight, you know? Stand up for yourself."

Dwight said, "You mean like you were doing, Jack?"

"Yeah." I lowered the bat to my side. "I fought for us."

"Before that."

"What? What do you mean?"

"Before you went all Bat Man on them, you were frozen like a statue."

"That was just at first."

"And you might've stayed Statue Man until it was too late."

"You don't know that."

"Pretty sure. That's why I started calling him Custard. Because I know you, Jack."

I said, "What's that mean?"

Richard Newberry

Will, who at first looked confused about where Dwight was going, seemed to suddenly get it.

Dwight looked away, up the tracks, then back at me. "It means I know how you are, Jack."

My grip tightened again on the bat. "How I am? You saying I'm a sissy?"

"Yank, it's not what he's -"

"Shut up, Will. You saying I'm a sissy, Dwight?"

"Not what I'm saying."

"What are you saying then?"

He sighed and frowned. "You get . . . undecided, Jack. Wishy washy, like Charlie Brown - sometimes."

"Is that right?"

"Yes, Yank."

I turned on Will, but Dwight said, "I wasn't pushing Cus when I called him Custard, Jack. I was pushing *you*."

"Me?"

"Yes, you. Like I said, sometimes you're wishy washy."

"No I'm not."

"Yeah, you are."

"Am not."

"Sometimes, Yank, you are. And there's nothing wrong with thinking about things, you know? It's smart."

"He's right, Jack. But this wasn't a time for wishy washy. We needed you to act."

"Why me?"

"Two reasons, " said Dwight. "You were closest to the bat, plus you can swing it smoother than anybody I know."

My injured pride took some comfort from Dwight's assessment of my hitting ability.

"One more thing," said Dwight. "You've been a good dude since I first met you on the alley back in second grade. You invited me to play baseball with you guys at Harper's that day; we've been pure-quill friends ever since. And I noticed something from that day on about you that I think you still don't know about yourself."

I tried to be funny. "I'm a great pitcher?"

"No," Dwight said dryly, and Will grinned.

Dwight said, "The thing you don't get is you're the leader of the Icks, and I don't think you even know it."

"I'm the leader?"

Light at the Rat Pond

"Square dinkham," said Will. "I've only been here a little while, but I noticed it right away."

It truly surprised me to be considered a leader. I wondered if the others felt the same way. A peculiar tandem of restored pride and embarrassment rose within me. Was I really the leader of the Icks?

"And the best leaders," said Will, "are like you, Yank. They're humble."

Will Corben considered me humble? Coming from the King of Humble, I now had to start guarding against extreme hubris.

"Now don't get all big head on us, Jack," said Dwight. "'Cause don't forget, you still gotta deal with your Charlie Brown."

I said, "I'd rather be Snoopy."

We gathered our buckets and spilled berries, Dwight switched on the radio and we tried to pick, but the incident with Cus had zapped our desire. We cut down to the tracks and headed for home.

Will asked Dwight, "Is his name really Custard?"

"Yep. Heard his sister call him that one day at school. Only heard him called that once, though."

"Custard," I said. "Hmm."

"You reckon he's really named after custard, y'all?"

Dwight and I shrugged.

I said, "I'm pretty sure I broke something in his hand . . . or arm."

"Don't worry about it, Jack," said Dwight. "If you wouldn't have stopped him, he'd of stabbed me for sure. You did what you had to do."

Said Will, "The way he looked, he would've stabbed us all."

"Yeah," I said. "You're probably right." But worry about the police showing up at my house began to gnaw at me.

Will stopped suddenly. "Hey. You reckon we should go back and find Cus's knife? What if a little kid would find it?"

"Or somebody like Sticks," I said.

Winter would undress much of the hillsides' concealing cover, making it easier to find the deadly weapon. We went back, found the opened knife; I was elected to keep it in a safe place.

Dwight and I ate sandwiches at my house, but Will had to check in at home. Though our berry picking had been shortened, our buckets, unlike rookie Will's, were almost full.

"Berries look good," Mom said. "You guys weren't in our patches were you?"

I finished my milk and said, "Yep. Picked 'em all."

"Well thank you," she said going for our buckets. "You just saved me a lot of hard work."

245

Richard Newberry

"We know to stay away from your turf," I said. "We got those way down the tracks." We didn't mention the latest Cus attack, and the worry over being arrested for assault hung over me while we ate. Fortunately the police didn't show up to take me in.

"Your mom doing okay today, Dwight?"

"Yes, ma'am. Seemed to be doing good this morning."

"Good," she said. "I know she's wanting to pick tonight."

"She should be able to."

We dashed out the door to go sell our berries. The Icks would be gathering at the garage shortly and we needed to be planning that night's moving of the oil barrels and setting up Tex's ramp at the Rat Pond.

We pedaled toward the Gordons', holding our buckets in our right hands and already counting the money one of our best raspberry customers would pay us.

I said, "What do you think? We've only got about a gallon and a half between us. Eight dollars?"

"Yeah," said Dwight. "That's about right."

We parked our bikes on the alley next to the Gordons' fence where the sweet smelling honeysuckle grew. We strolled to the screened back door, knocked, eager to exchange our labor for eight dollars cash.

Van answered; he always seemed glad to see us. "Well, hello, boys."

In unison, we said, "Hey, Mr. Gordon."

He opened the screen and stepped outside. "I wish you two would call me Van, but I'm not one to spoil good raising." He smiled and added, "I see the berries are ripe."

Van stood just a little taller than Dwight, and had a firm, lean build. He kept his gray hair cut short, and often in the summer wore a neatly pressed white T-shirt with casual, cotton slacks. He had been a machinist for most of his life; Van retired from GM a few years earlier, but still enjoyed helping out at Texal's shop whenever he could. Lilly Gordon was a retired school teacher; their two sons and two daughters and grandchildren were scattered throughout the Midwest.

"We've got about a gallon and a half," I said.

"Yeah, looks about right. Nice berries. But you know what? Your friend Will stopped by a little while ago and gave us some. I insisted on paying him, but he insisted they were a gift." He shrugged. "What's a fella to do? Didn't want to seem ungrateful."

We nodded, but I knew Dwight, like I, wasn't happy with our friend being altruistic with our source of income.

246

Light at the Rat Pond

"He's a good kid," said Van. "Easy to like, you know?"

We were forced to nod again.

"So what he gave us, fellas, will hold us for a few days. But you know we don't freeze them or can them, which means we'll need to buy some by the end of the week."

"Okay," I said.

Van gazed west, said, "Terrible thing that happened to Shorty's garden, huh? But I think he's about got it back in order. Bad thing when a man's hard work is destroyed like that."

"Sure is," said Dwight.

We said goodbye and headed for our bikes, still carrying our raspberries. I wanted to kick the Gordons' burn barrel, pretending it was Will. "Can you believe that?"

"Guess we forgot to tell him who our customers are."

I said, "Yeah, but he could've given them to his mom or somebody on his own side of the tracks."

"We'll straighten him out. Let's go to Sid's. He always buys some."

Much of the lunch crowd was still at the tavern when we got there.

"Boys," said Sid as we slipped in the side door of the cool, dimly lighted and smoky establishment. "Looks like you're out pedalin' berries."

"Yep," I said.

"Let's see what you got. Nice ones. How much?"

A few guys at the bar were leaning over, trying to see what we had. One asked, "Those raspberries?"

"Yep," said Dwight.

"I'd like to have me some of those. Wife makes a mean pie with 'em."

Heads nodded and other voices agreed they could use fresh-picked berries.

Sid, a big burly guy, quickly ushered us into the storage room just off the north end of the bar. "So how much for what you got?"

I said, "We figure we got a gallon and a half, and we want -"

"Twelve dollars," said Dwight.

Sid eyed him. "That's a little more than last year."

"Not much more," said Dwight.

Sid raked a thick hand through his dark, curly hair; he looked at me, then back to Dwight. "So how much we talkin' per gallon?"

Dwight and I exchanged glances. I felt a Charlie-Brown moment begin to overcome me.

Dwight said, "Seven fifty."

247

Richard Newberry

"Seven fifty a gallon?" Sid pretended to be astonished. "What did I pay last year?"

We knew Sidney Craddock knew exactly what he had paid last year. I said, "Last year the berries were smaller." I picked a plump one from my bucket. "Look at this year's."

"What did I pay last year? Four a gallon?"

"Six," said Dwight, heating up the negotiations.

"I paid five," he said.

"Taste one," I said. He did.

"Sweet, but seedy."

"They're always seedy," said Dwight. "But not always this sweet."

Sid eyed us both before saying, "Six fifty a gallon."

I said, "We know you'll at least double your money, Sid. If we get seven fifty, you can probably get fifteen."

"Seven," he offered.

We didn't budge.

"Come on, guys. We're friends here – and you work for me."

Dwight said, "It's a fair deal, Sid."

He frowned, then smiled, then chuckled. "You guys are good." He took another berry from my bucket, ate it and said, "Proud of you, even if you're robbing me."

Said Dwight, "We'll all make money."

"And that's what makes the deal work," said Sid. "Good job standing firm on your price. Just don't get carried away."

"We won't," I said.

"Okay." He said, "Seven fifty a gallon, and I can probably take about as many as you can pick."

We were gonna be rich.

Sid said, "God bless the free market."

We shook hands, and Sid added, "The way you two are goin', I'll probably work for you someday."

Outside the tavern's darkness and into the light of day, Dwight and I celebrated.

"I smell money, Jack."

"We're gonna be rich, man."

"He'll buy all we can pick."

"I know. I know."

Smiles were frozen on our faces. We were thankful for that afternoon's opportunity to learn about the financial benefits from labor, marketing, distribution and timing.

Light at the Rat Pond

Dwight said, "You know what? If Will hadn't given his berries to Van, we wouldn't be here now."

"I know. I guess we should thank him."

"Strange," said Dwight.

We hurried toward the garage because a jump ramp needed assembled and logistics and construction for Dwight's daring barrel move needed immediate attention.

CHAPTER 62

Kate had already reminded Melba about picking berries that evening, and she called Ruth Corben who said she was looking forward to joining them. She offered Ruth advice on how to dress for the prickly, chigger-infested picking; Ruth was grateful.

Kate had just enough time to mop the kitchen floor before her afternoon student arrived. She loathed the faded linoleum, and each time she had to clean it the more motivated she became to start tearing out the old kitchen. Sometimes she couldn't stop thinking about the gorgeous kitchens she saw in magazines; her mind raced with ideas of new appliances, new cabinets and countertops, and gladly ripping up the old linoleum and putting down some type of tile or even wood. She played with many new configurations for her updated kitchen. Jack did not yet know what he was in for early next year.

The phone rang as she was putting away the mop. A dose of dread ran through her because of Friday night's ominous call. She told herself the phone had rang several times since that call, and though each ring had her on edge, every caller had been family or friend.

"Quit being a sissy," she said on her way to the phone. "Hello?"

"I gotta tell you this news, Murphy," and Nadine was off and running. Kate smiled relief as her friend updated her on the latest fiasco involving her cousin's upcoming wedding.

A few minutes later the subject had changed. "Saw Johnny Quick at the races again last night. Wanna know what I talked to him about?"

"Should I want to know?"

"Probably, because we talked about you."

"What?"

"It was all good."

"Well . . . thanks, I guess."

"Relax, Murph. I just casually brought you up in our conversation. It was all on the sly. You know how I can be."

"Yes I do."

"So can I give him your phone number?"

"No."

"Come on, Murphy."

250

Light at the Rat Pond

"Tell you what, I'll give you a note to give to him."

"Sarcasm is not needed here. I'm just a devoted friend who wants to see you get together with a handsome stud."

Kate laughed. "You're too much."

"You sound like Texal."

One of Nadine's soap operas was about to start, so as abruptly as the conversation started it ended.

Kate glanced at the clock; still a few minutes until her student arrived. She hadn't invited Nadine to tonight's picking because Nadine liked the thought of gathering raspberries about as much as Kate liked going to the races. Having her there with Melba and Ruth would be an interesting mix of personalities. The thought made Kate smile.

The phone rang again.

She quickly dismissed Dread's approach.

"Hello?"

Silence.

"Hello?"

Silence.

Her heart quickened. She could hear country music playing in the background and disconnected voices, and a noise that sounded like pool balls clacking together. "Who is this?"

In a gruff whisper, the man said, "You know who this is," and hung up.

CHAPTER 63

When the Icks gathered at the garage, Will, Dwight and I treated them to the latest scary yet victorious confrontation with Cus and his goons.

"Who were the kids with him?"

"Did they all have knives?"

"Were you scared?"

"Custard?" Laughs.

"How hard did you hit him?"

"Did he cry?"

Among us, Stink was most relieved Cus wouldn't be as much of a threat for at least a little while.

"Once he heals," Dwight said, "he'll be meaner than ever. But we've got a little break."

Tex grinned. "Break. Good one, Dwight."

The buzz and fervor over Cus and his goon's plight gradually faded.

Tex said, "Let's get my ramp to the Rat Pond."

With a hammer and two screwdrivers, Dwight and I assembled the jump ramp at the base of the hill. Actual construction at the site of Tex's upcoming dangerous stunt had revved up excitement.

Kenny circled the track with Stink while they waited for the ramp to be finished. Kenny said to Stink, "Can you believe she's gonna try this?"

"It's gonna be really cool." Though Stink had a good measure of daring, it didn't match the fullness of Tex's risk taking. He, like the rest of us, was satisfied to just be part of the jump. "I'm gonna bring my camera and try to get a picture of her when she's in mid-air. It's gonna be first-chop, pure quill, man."

"Yeah," said Kenny.

Will, standing next to Tex, said, "You're gonna be flying."

Tex, who stood over Dwight and me scrutinizing our work, smiled and said, "I know."

"You scared?"

"Nah - maybe a little. But I'm more excited than anything."

"You're a pure-quill daredevil, Tex. Evel would be proud."

If I didn't know better, I would've thought Will had just spoken the perfect words if he had romantic intentions toward the tall blonde. Maybe he did, but

252

Light at the Rat Pond

I doubted it. I had noticed in school his furtive attraction to the opposite sex, but this thing with Tex was just Will being genuine Will. His words did make me wish I had used a different approach on Rebecca.

Tex turned to him. "Thank you, Will. That means a lot to me."

"You're welcome."

Tex turned back to the construction crew and again made us go through where the ramp would be exactly. Was the ramp's angle enough for her to make it over six burning barrels, was she wrong not wanting a landing ramp, and was I sure about the few adjustments I made to her racer for the jump?

After rehashing it all, she appeared ready, confident. "Now all we have to do is get the barrels here. Are you sure your idea's going to work, Dwight?"

He looked up at her, sweat streaming down his temples. "It'll work - if we don't get caught."

Will, understanding the barrels were just being borrowed, was still onboard with helping us.

Stink said, "I can't wait to move those barrels tonight. Talk about cool."

"Yeah," said Kenny.

With the ramp finished, we raced for a while. Will heard the hobos shuffling around over in Hoboland and headed their way for a quick Bible reading. When he came back we cut dirt for the switchyard and ice-cold drinks.

On the alley again, talk of the coming Friday's birthday campout sprung up.

"Wish I could sleep over with you guys," said Tex. "I don't see the big deal."

The other Icks didn't either, but involved parents seemed to have keener eyesight.

Stink, sniffing something he'd picked up at the switchyard, said, "Don't forget it's gonna be payback time for your new neighbor. For messing up our hide-and-seek."

I nodded and said, "We'll think of something."

Shorty's neighbor Dutch was sitting on his covered back stoop, reading and holding a glass of something with a cigarette in the same hand. He noticed us and waved his paperback. We returned his wave.

At Shorty's garden, Will said, "Other than new plants, you can't even tell his garden was ruined a few days ago."

"Yeah," said Stink. "It's too bad."

"I know," said Will.

Stink added, "Now we don't have any strawberries to throw at cars at Jack's campout."

"Say what?" Will asked.

"Yeah," said Kenny. "It's pretty fun. But what are we gonna do now without strawberries?"

253

Richard Newberry

We had reached the Gordons' when Will turned to me and asked, "You throw strawberries at cars?"

"Yep," I said.

"Why?"

"'Cause it's fun, man," said Stink. "It's danger fun."

We parked our racers outside the garage. Dwight turned off his radio, and said to wondering Will, "It's for the thrill of the chase."

"Really?"

"Yep," I said. "They don't damage the cars."

Tex, oiling her bike's chain, said, "We hide on the tracks up in this good spot in the grass and wait for cars to go by on Warren."

"Then, plop!" said Stink. "We smack them with strawberries, and hope they stop and chase us."

"It can be pretty exciting," I said.

"Yeah," said Kenny.

I added, "And it doesn't hurt their cars." I looked at the other Icks and said, "But it makes some of 'em pretty mad."

"They're the chasers," said Dwight.

"Good clean fun," said Tex, putting the oil can back on the shelf.

Stink said, "Strawberries in the spring, usually tomatoes in the summer and corn at Halloween."

"Ripe tomatoes," I said. "Soft ones."

"But y'all are stealin' Shorty's fruit - and vegetables."

Stink was tightening his front wheel's spokes. "So what? Who cares? He's got plenty."

"No strawberries," said Kenny.

"I'd care," said Will. "I wouldn't want somebody stealin' my stuff I'd worked hard for. It ain't right, y'all."

Stink said, "Ah, cabbage-gas farts, Will."

"Y'all could grow your own stuff and throw it if you wanted."

Dwight put a fresh battery in his transistor. "We don't have a place for a garden."

I said, "We tried dirt clods once. Some of them were pretty hard, so we quit that."

"Look," said Stink, "we're gonna have fun at Jack's campout. Don't go if you don't want to have fun."

I said, "We do other fun stuff, Will. Stuff you'll like, I promise."

"I want to come," he said. "I'll just skip the, uh . . . fruiting, or whatever it is."

Light at the Rat Pond

"It's exciting, is what it is," said Tex. "You don't know what you're going to miss."

Stink said, "You guys wanna go do a bakery run?"

"No," I said abruptly.

"Whoa, Jack," said Tex.

I told them of being ratted on by the new bakery lady, and that morning's confession to Sunbeam's manager. "I gotta help wash bread trucks two nights this week for payback."

"Wow!" said Stink. "Busted."

"Your mother pretty upset?" asked Dwight.

"Hard to say. I think she's more disappointed in me than mad at me."

Kenny looked a little scared, as if expecting to be ratted on next. Will gazed at me with what looked like reserved admiration.

"So I'm off bakery heists."

The Icks nodded.

Tex said, "So now what are we gonna throw at cars?"

Stink looked at Dwight and me. "How 'bout those raspberries you guys pick."

"No," we said together.

"There's a bunch of 'em," Stink argued.

"They're no good for throwing," I said. "Too light. Probably barely make a sound if you hit a car with two handfuls."

"Oh, okay," said Stink.

"There's mulberries," said Dwight.

"Too much like raspberries," I said.

He agreed.

Tex said, "How about the cherries in Shorty's backyard. They look ripe."

"Yeah," said Stink.

"They're light, but they have big seeds," I said. "Could work."

"Cool!" said Stink. "We get to sneak in on old gripey and swipe some cherries."

Dwight switched on WLS; *Long and Winding Road* was playing. "It's one thing to get in his garden. But to sneak in his yard? I don't know."

"Scared?" said Stink.

"Wise," answered Dwight.

I adjusted Tex's handlebars and seat for the jump. "Shorty might shoot us if he catches us in his yard."

"Square dinkham," said Dwight.

"Yeah," said Kenny.

Stink smiled mischievously. "That's what makes it great."

255

Richard Newberry

Tex said, "You guys being sissy?"

Dwight, Kenny and I said, "No."

So it was decided that that upcoming Friday night's action would include a dangerous breach into Shorty's backyard to pilfer red cherries.

"Man," said Stink. "This will be the most first-chop campout yet."

Dwight and I told them we, along with Will, had to pick raspberries with our moms that evening.

Dwight said, "We'll be done about seven thirty. Make sure you're back here by then with the stuff. Everybody cool with their wagons?"

Heads nodded.

"Good. We move the barrels tonight."

CHAPTER 64

She couldn't concentrate on the novel.

Because she didn't know if she should tell anyone, including Jack, Kate felt alone, isolated in a growing fear. Melba had said she should call the police right away. What could she tell them that would positively point to criminal intentions? She thought somebody had been following her, thought the creep behind Kresge in the brown car might be trouble. But she had not seen the guy or the brown car for a few days. They had driven to the lake to fish without a menacing stalker following them.

Prank calls. That's what the police would say they were. Just some nut getting his jollies trying to scare her. Sick and illegal, but how would they catch him?

She set down the book, replayed in her mind the last intimidating call. It sounded like he was in a bar, tavern - something like that. Possibly Sid's? The Creeping Taunt jumped on her, and she twirled the wedding band. Not much help.

"You *know* who this is," he had said.

She had to go see. She slipped on her sandals, waved at the Icks mulling around the outside of the garage, and marched toward the tall privet hedge. She rounded the hedge's south end, and began searching Sid's lot. There were only seven cars parked around the tavern; the brown Ford wasn't one of them.

Back inside the house, Kate called Nadine, told her some of what had been going on, and asked if she and Texal would keep an eye out for anything suspicious, especially an older, brown Ford.

"You know we will, Kate. I told you before we can follow you around to see if that panty-waisted coward tries anything. I know Texal could clean his clock. I don't care how big the panty-waist is."

"I don't want to put you guys in the middle of who knows what, Nadine, and cause a bunch of trouble for you."

"You know me, Murphy. I don't mind a little trouble."

"I put off saying anything more to you about it because I wasn't - and I'm still not - sure there's anything to it. Who knows? I mean other than a couple of phone calls -"

"Which sounded like threats."

Richard Newberry

"Well, yes. But nobody has tried anything. And maybe I'm just imagining somebody in a brown car following me."

"You *imagined* a creep flipping you off behind Kresge?"

"No, I guess not. But he could've just been one of this world's many creeps. Who knows? But it's started to scare me enough to involve you guys. I'm sorry."

"Sorry? Why are you sorry? Don't be sorry, Kate. We're your friends. And I'm getting pretty ticked off that this panty-waisted coward is scaring my friend."

"Melba told me to call the police when I first mentioned it to her a few days ago."

"She's probably right, but I'm not sure what they could do - yet."

"Right. I know."

"Any ideas who it could be, or why?"

She did have an idea why, but the who still puzzled her. "Not really."

"Weirdoes these days don't need a reason anyway. They just get off on being weirdoes."

"I suppose you're right. But again, it's probably nothing, just somebody being stupid. But I don't want to be wrong and end up getting Jack hurt."

"Or yourself, Murphy. Don't worry, we'll keep a good eye out and watch for anybody who might start trouble. And if they do, I hope I'm there - with Texal of course."

Kate smiled and said, "Don't say anything to anybody else though, okay? Especially not the kids. If there is anything to this - and I doubt it - I think it's aimed only at me."

"You must have some idea of who it could be."

"No, I really don't."

"And I can't imagine why anybody would, of all people, be threatening you. You're too nice, Murph. And Lord knows you aren't jilting any lovers."

Because it was ancient history, Nadine had no way of knowing Kate suspected it just might be a jilted *person* behind it all.

"But anyway, we'll watch out for you, Kate. You're not going to be alone in this."

But Nadine was wrong. That's exactly where Kate would be when it happened: alone.

CHAPTER 65

Dressed for the rigors of picking raspberries Monday evening, Dwight, Will and I, along with Mom, Melba and Ruth were filling our buckets with the fruit. Will's brother Bobby tagged along, but did not pick. Ick adventures for about two weeks would be interrupted at times by my and Dwight's zeal for the fruit of free markets and capitalism, and the other Icks were used to it.

"Berries lookin' good this year, Sweet," said Melba to my mom. "Yes indeedy."

Anyone who judged Melba Flowers by her appearance would sorely miss the mark when it came to judging the petite woman's durability and determination. The rail-thin lady, with boney hands crippled by rheumatoid arthritis, kept up with the best of us pickers. She lived, and instilled in her children, the ethics of doing right, working hard and overcoming obstacles, no matter how intimidating the obstacles.

Mom said, "We were due good ones after last year."

"You are so right. Last year was fairly pitiful."

I looked at Dwight picking next to his mom. It boggled my mind that little Melba could produce such a big boy.

Mom raised up from her spot in the weeds and briars, looked to her left. "You doing okay, Ruth?"

Ruth straightened and stretched her back. "I'm doing fine. Robert Lee Corben, get off of those railroad tracks this instant."

Bobby had been warned away from the steel rails a few minutes earlier. "Yes, ma'am."

"If I have to tell you again, all these good people are going to see your little bottom get a spanking."

Will had accustomed our ears to the Corbens' southern drawl, but I noticed subtle variances in the parlance among the family from Arkansas.

Bobby hung his head and said, "Yes, ma'am." He then busied himself with the gravel and other rocks outside the rails.

Ruth resumed picking. "That child worries me to death with these tracks. He seems to be drawn to them like a woman to a shoe sale."

Melba and Mom smiled.

"He just doesn't understand how dangerous they can be."

Richard Newberry

In an easy, quiet voice, Melba said, "Most all our children have been attracted to these rails for some reason or another, Ruth. The Lord knows I had to whip some fannies over it more than once. Yes indeedy. But Sweet here had a good idea to keep them away until they were old enough. Isn't that true, Katherine?"

"It seemed to work pretty well."

Ruth looked to Mom. "What did you do?"

Mom leaned toward her and spoke quietly to evade Bobby's ears. I knew Ruth was hearing the a-train-will-suck-you-right-up warning, the story Mom had fabricated, which other Ick parents adopted.

Ruth nodded at the idea. "I will certainly use that."

The mosquitoes were at it early that evening, and I said to Dwight and Will, "Let's go try the other side."

When we started across the tracks to the Warren Avenue side, Bobby asked, "Can I go with Will? Please?"

Ruth met eyes with Will and he said, "I'll watch him close."

"You can go with your brother."

Shortly thereafter, while everybody except Bobby was buried in briars and weeds trying to fill their buckets, a train horn blasted down the tracks. A train was headed our way.

"Bobby," said Ruth. "You need to come over here with me."

"Can I stay over here? I'll be okay. I promise. Will's watchin' me good, ain't ya, Will?"

"You get up there with your brother, and don't move from that hill until that train is gone. You understand me?"

"Yes, ma'am."

Then Ruth did not hesitate lying to her son - for safety's sake. "If you get anywhere near that train, it will suck you right up and mangle your poor little body all the way up to Chicago. And that's a long way away, Robert Lee."

"Okay, I won't," he said, inching up past us to get farther away from the tracks. "I promise."

Worked every time on the rookies.

The rumbling train eventually passed us with its familiar ba-bump, ba-bump rhythm. Bobby watched the brown and black and gray cars with the same intense interest his older brother had shown on other days. What was with the Corben brothers' infatuation with passing trains? I figured the fascination would've passed by now, since they'd been here over a month.

For some reason, I turned to watch the rolling steel, not knowing then that a train and these tracks would later haunt the Corben family.

260

Light at the Rat Pond

Kate poured raspberries into the metal colander sitting in the kitchen sink and began rinsing them. It had been a good evening of picking; lots of berries for everyone. Robins chirped and fluttered in and out of the privet hedge as dusk began to settle over the neighborhood. A rattling sound out on the alley caused her to crane a look that way.

What in the world? She stopped rinsing to watch the bewildering procession traveling on the alley. Before they pedaled out of sight, she counted four wagons being pulled by two Icks, Kenny and Dwight, while four other Icks rode as escorts.

What were they up to now?

CHAPTER 66

The ropes and tarps inside the wagons somewhat muffled the rattling, yet our plan to stealthily roll down the alley to Cline Oil Company did not come to pass. Two patrons at Sid's side entrance were drawn to the sight and sound of our passing, and such was the attention given to us that one of those patrons stumbled and almost fell on Sid's stoop.

Pedaling alongside the wagons, I said to Dwight, "I don't think this is gonna work."

"It'll work. Don't worry." He and Kenny were chosen to pull the wagons because of their bigger, stronger legs.

The last half mile to Cline's drew no more attention our way. We dismounted our bikes without setting kickstands, and quickly went about our assigned duties.

Dwight's plan had us tether four wagons together, back to back in tandem, allowing the extended handles to act as cradles for our make-shift barrel hauler. The six empty barrels would be placed in a pyramided stack, then covered with two tarps and tied with Kenny's lasso rope and one borrowed from Texal. The red wagons were united by tarp straps.

We each rolled a barrel up to the wagons, then I helped Kenny and Dwight stack while the other Icks steadied the load until it was tied.

Stink was designated lookout. "Still all clear. Nobody coming."

"Hurry up, y'all."

I said, "We are, but these are a lot heavier to lift than they were to roll."

Stink warned, "Car!"

We froze.

"It's okay. It's okay. They turned in at Sid's."

Tex asked, "You want me to help you guys?"

"We got it," said Dwight. "Just don't let them move."

With no houses near the oil company, the noise we made loading really didn't matter, which was good because the barrels produced a noticeable metal-drum percussion in the otherwise quiet night. Our biggest concern was a car showing up on the alley.

Loaded, tarped and tied, we headed west with our nine-foot tall covered wagons. Will and I used our left hands to steady the vibrating and drumming

262

Light at the Rat Pond

load on the north side; opposite us, Stink and Tex did the same. Dwight and Kenny drove us toward our destination.

"How is it?" I asked.

"It's okay," replied Dwight.

"Yeah," said Kenny.

I heard a "woo hoo!", and Stink said, loud enough to be heard above the drumming, "This is cool!"

"Not too fast," I said.

Will asked me, "What if a car comes?"

I said, "First we'll hope it's not a cop or somebody from Cline's, then we'll pull over so they can pass."

Dwight said, "It's gonna work," just before headlights hit us from behind.

"Crud," I said, turning to look. "Car."

We veered left, making room for the approaching vehicle to pass.

But it didn't pass. It stayed behind us, headlights exposing us.

Dwight said, "What's he doing?"

"I don't know," I said. "Let's just stop and let him pass."

Will looked scared. "What do you think he's doing?"

"Don't know," I said.

Once the car pulled next to us so we could see it, I said, "Oh, crud."

"What's wrong?" asked Dwight.

"Evening, boys," said the deputy sheriff. "What are you guys hauling tonight?"

Will looked as if he'd be sick.

Stupidly, I said, "Nothing."

"Nothing? Doesn't look like nothing."

None of the Icks moved or made a sound. The deputy was on the same side as Will and I.

The dark-haired deputy said, "Been a while since I've seen a covered wagon in these parts." He didn't smile when he said it, and he reached for something in the passenger seat.

Was it a good sign that he didn't turn on his emergency lights? I could read his name tag: Decker.

He turned back to us brandishing a huge, shining flashlight. He pointed the bright light on the tarps. "So what's covered up?" he asked me.

The inside of his car was dark except for tiny red and white lights; vague voices cut in and out on his police radio. I imagined six Icks, cuffed and stuffed in the backseat of the deputy's cruiser, headed for jail. Too nervous to think, and barely able to speak, I said, "I don't know."

"You don't know?" He started to get out of the car.

263

Richard Newberry

Should we run for it, or would we be shot down on the alley that had been our traveling home? My ten, soon-to-be-eleven, years flashed before me.

His radio squawked louder, which stopped his exit. He grabbed the radio's mic, identified himself and said, "Go ahead."

Suddenly he turned on his red lights and his siren wailed as he tore away from us and our covered wagons.

We gathered at the front of the wagons and nervous exultation and chatter broke out.

"Can you believe it?! Huh?!"

"Pure-apple-quill!"

"That was the scariest and coolest thing ever!"

"Can you believe it? Huh?"

"First-chop danger, man."

"Wow."

"Yeah," said Kenny, then Will puked.

"Oh, man. Oh, man," said Stink. He started to laugh.

"It's okay, Will," I said. "It's over. We're not in trouble." I shot a look at Stink, and he stopped laughing.

Will, smiling weakly, said, "That was scary, y'all."

Tex said, "Welcome to the world of Ick adventure. Hope it doesn't always make you sick."

Will smiled, so we joined him. I patted his back, said, "Macaroni and cheese for supper?"

"Yeah."

Dwight said, "We gotta get these to the Rat Pond."

The remainder of our journey rendered no surprises or attention. We unloaded the barrels and rolled them down into the darkness of the Rat Pond. A raucous train at the switchyard covered the sound of barrels banging into barrels. Hoboland was dark and quiet.

I said, "We'll get them ready tomorrow."

We took the wagons back to the garage, left them tethered for tomorrow night's return trip, and continued talking about our almost-arrests. With most things said or claimed that could be said and claimed about the night's adventure, we turned our attention to Tex.

Will asked, "You nervous?"

"Little - and that's what it's all about."

"Think you'll make it?" asked Stink.

"Don't know." Tex could be her own best promoter. "It's gonna be dangerous."

"Yeah," said Kenny. "Hope you don't catch on fire."

264

Light at the Rat Pond

Tex agreed.

We silently admired her for a moment, and she appreciated it.

Said Dwight, "You have to nail your landing."

"*If* I clear the barrels."

"The ramp's right," he said. "But your speed coming down the hill is the most important thing. Not enough, you crash and burn. Too much, you crash and hurt - very much."

"We've got a pretty good dirt landing built up," I said. "But it won't help at all if you miss it and smack into the trees."

"I know."

We all appeared calm, yet I wasn't sure any of the Icks would sleep well that night.

CHAPTER 67

When I went inside our house, Mom asked about us pulling four wagons. She must've missed our loaded return trip, so I said, "Ah, just playing."

She left it at that.

Cloudy skies and the threat of storms came with the next morning. A wet Rat Pond hill would nix Tex's jump. The stunt would have to happen earlier than planned; I hoped the other Icks sensed that.

At breakfast, Mom said, "Looks like you might get stuck inside today."

I finished the Lucky Charms, rinsed my bowl and said, "Gonna go out early in case it does rain."

"You get your hind end home before it starts storming."

"I will."

"You better."

I hurried to the garage. Tex was already waiting outside the overhead door on her adjusted red racer, looking at the dark clouds. "Can't do it if it rains. We gotta hurry."

By the time I gathered the containers of mixed fuel, all but Kenny had arrived at the garage.

Said Stink, "Mom almost didn't let me come."

"Same here," said Will.

Dwight said, "We're not waiting on Kenny. Let's go."

Just past Shorty's we saw a bike rider turning onto the alley. "Here comes Kenny," I said.

At the Rat Pond, after we lined up the barrels, Will started for Hoboland.

"Where you going?" I asked.

"Thought Clarence and Arlie might like to watch her jump if they're here."

"Good idea," said Tex. "Go see."

The first rumble of thunder sounded as Will disappeared into Hoboland. He returned a moment later with the hobos in tow. "They'd like to see it, y'all."

Kenny and I waved to Clarence and Arlie; Clarence smiled, returned the wave. He said, "Well, this is some kind of somethin', isn't it? Feels like I should buy a ticket. Course I ain't got no money." He slapped his leg and laughed, and started hacking a cough.

Clarence ventured near our race track, yet reticent Arlie remained near

266

Light at the Rat Pond

the cover of Hoboland. A murmur of thunder caused the wide-eyed hobo to look up and cringe.

This was Dwight, Tex and Stink's first up-close experience with the hobos. I wondered if Dwight noticed he and Clarence had similar tastes in clothing. Transfixed at the hobos' presence, I reminded the staring Icks, "We gotta hurry."

Tex had left her racer at the top of the hill. "It's almost time," I said. "You ready?"

"Yes," she said, nothing wavering, for she lived for the excitement.

The first flash of lightning filled the dark sky; followed by louder, sharper thunder. The wind picked up and rustled the leaves above us, the temperature was dropping.

Tex had her blonde hair tied back with a green rubber band. She marched up the hill toward her racer.

Dwight and Kenny set the ramp in place. Stink, Will and I checked the position of the barrels.

"Good to go," I said to Dwight.

"Same here," he said.

Stink checked the landing dirt, scuffed a little more onto the pile. "Looks good."

I hollered up to Tex, "You ready?"

She nodded, mounted the racer.

I poured the fuel over the barrels. "Step back," I said, and tossed a burning book of matches atop the drums.

Flames "whoofed" into existence above the barrels.

"That fire's too high," said Will.

"What she wants," I said.

We all - the Icks with Clarence and Arlie - looked up to the lone daredevil at the top of the hill. Stink readied his Kodak X-15.

"Remember," said Dwight, "your speed is most important."

She nodded.

I felt the first sprinkle of rain. The storm began to intensify. "Now!" I shouted.

Tex shot down the hill, her face and eyes fixed, determined to succeed. Was she going too fast? Who knew? The moment she would launch from the ramp we would all know.

More lightning, more thunder; flames licked at the air, wanting to taste flesh.

Tex hit the ramp.

I could not believe how high she got.

Richard Newberry

It happened so fast, but I clearly saw it all. In mid-air, standing on the pedals, she slightly tilted the handlebars back, and leaned back with them. She was three or so feet above the first three burning barrels. Dwight's trajectory calculation had been perfect.

But had she hit the ramp at the right speed?

Stink's camera flashed.

Her rear tire descended toward the flames of the last barrel.

I heard a hobo and an Ick gasp.

Tex cleared the barrels.

Relief. Then came the landing.

CHAPTER 68

The more time that passed between Prizes, the less he wrestled against his feckless adversary: Guilt. His imminent badness provoked Guilt to try again, but it didn't stand a chance. He *needed* the Prize, and the need crushed Guilt.

Long ago, at the beginning of his Prize taking, he'd had to fight an incessant war against Guilt and its mantra that bad was wrong and good was right; his conscience also joined Guilt to fight against him. Yet over the years he began to seize control over his conscience, which severely weakened Guilt. By 1970, he had so calloused his being that he barely felt Guilt's presence, and when he did feel it, Guilt had become a joke.

It puzzled him that Guilt still hung around. He had to wonder what, *or who*, gave Guilt its persistence.

The changing culture was a strong ally of his. Everyday, people were discarding their previously-cherished morals and judgmental attitudes and snatching up for themselves more of what they craved. What had been taboo a decade earlier was now accepted. Narrow roads were being ripped up and out and replaced by multiple, wide-laned highways, where behavior limits were much less restrictive. Do-your-own-thing freedom, baby.

He smiled. If they only knew how far out in front he had been of the freedom-loving culture.

He was grateful for the cultural change and its friendship, for it had assisted him in mastering Conscience and Guilt; vanquishing the two old foes to the point that they became like rubes to him. When necessary, he'd pretend to embrace their . . . attributes.

But now in June of 1970, the next coveted Prize had pricked his calloused being with pointed stupid questions and words and deeds, and it angered him.

The waiting and watching had to end. He would take the Prize before the two sneaking rubes, Conscience and Guilt, had any chance to restrain him.

He glanced at the Silencer.

Soon.

CHAPTER 69

With excitement akin to Christmas Day, I woke up early the Friday morning of my eleventh birthday. Presents and a beloved birthday campout were not the first things on my mind. Soon, very soon if I had my way, I would experience life-changing freedom. In the few seconds I stayed in my bed that morning, I garnered a better understanding and greater appreciation for what it must have felt like for the patriots of the American Revolution when they finally won their liberty.

I threw back the sheet and jumped out of bed. My clock radio read 5:40. Outside my screened window in the faint light of dawn the world was mostly quiet, save for the occasional sound of passing cars and trucks out on the highway. I slipped into jeans and a T-shirt, glued the last piece to the Mustang Will had bought me, and went to the kitchen.

I couldn't think of anything except my foray onto the hard road as I crunched Frosted Flakes. Imagining what it would be like this morning, six Icks riding on the smooth pavement with the skill and precision of our airborne compatriots, the Blue Angels, I began to also grasp a better understanding of what Mom had been saying about liberty: with it came greater responsibility.

She shuffled into the kitchen while I was rinsing my bowl. "Hard road got you up early, huh?" she said on her way to make coffee. She roused my hair as she passed.

"Yep."

The only time we met this early in the kitchen in the summer was when a fishing trip was planned.

"I know you're excited, but remember what I said."

"I do. You said I should take chances, ride careless and cut in front of cars."

She leaned against the sink, folded her arms across her pink silk robe. "Good. You were listening."

"Of course."

Unlike me, it usually took Mom a little while to hit her stride in the mornings. She yawned, then said, "You be very careful out there, Jack."

I put the milk in the frig. "I will be."

"I mean it. I want you to understand how dangerous it can be. It's different than riding on the alley. More cars - going faster, things happen faster."

270

Light at the Rat Pond

"The other Icks have been on the hard road for a while. I'll be fine."

"I know how you guys are when you're all together. Just be mindful of your new responsibilities when you ride."

"I will."

I started to leave, but she stopped me. "You're not going for a ride this early, are you?"

"No. I'm gonna wait for the Icks."

"Okay." She smiled and said, "Happy birthday."

"Thanks."

I turned again to go to my room and she said, "Jack."

"Yeah?"

She unfolded her arms, took a step toward me. "Did you happen to notice when we were leaving Kresge the other day a guy in a brown car?" She did see him. "The guy giving us the middle finger?"

"You did see him."

"Yep." I did not tell her I thought I'd seen the same car at Sid's, and whoever it was might be watching Dwight and me. We hadn't seen the car again since the day he slowly drove by us at Sid's cutover. "Why?" She hesitated, ran the fingers of her left hand through her hair, and stopped her hand at her neck. "It's probably nothing." Her hand slid to her side. "It just struck me as odd - and vulgar. Maybe you should keep an eye out for him, okay?"

Her concern for my maiden ride on the hard road had been one thing, but the concern deepened in her eyes as she spoke of the guy in the brown Ford.

"Sure. I will."

Her worry eased a little. "Thank you."

At the garage, I unlocked the service door and raised the overhead. The warm morning air began to displace the cooler feel inside the garage. I looked at Tex's red racer. I would have the rest of it fixed before the Icks showed up.

Her fiery jump had been spectacular, but the landing didn't go as planned, yet it was a spectacular crash. The bike's front tire dropped too soon and dug into the landing dirt, thrusting Tex over the handlebars. She flipped a half circle before thudding into the piled dirt; the softer landing saved her from a broken tailbone. Her racer flipped over her before she landed, and the bike slammed into Booty Tree.

After we discerned she wasn't dead, the accolades from the Icks and Clarence flooded Tex's way. She stood from the dirt pile, soiled and shaken, yet victorious. We were waiting to see if Stink had captured pieces of the spectacle on his Kodak.

Richard Newberry

I had just replaced the bent front rim on Tex's racer when the Icks began to arrive much earlier than normal.

"Woo hoo!" Tex slid-stopped outside the garage. "Your big day." She walked inside and lightly punched my arm. "You ready?"

"Born ready."

"Happy birthday."

"Thanks."

All the Icks were at the garage by seven.

Stink, smelling a dead moth he'd found on the window sill, asked, "Which way first, Birthday Boy?"

"I think down past the bakery."

"Good," said Kenny. "I've got some oof. I'll buy us some cakes."

"I'm all for that," said Stink.

"Happy birthday, Yank."

"Thanks."

Said Dwight, "Bakery's not open yet. It opens at eight."

I said to Kenny, "We'll go when we get back."

"Okay."

Dwight rolled out his orange cruiser. "Jack Hobbs is eleven today, and ready for the hard road."

I put away my wrenches. "Your racer is ready, Tex."

"Thanks. Looks good again."

Talk, some exaggerated, broke out about the fiery jump.

"Come on, y'all. Yank's ready to go. Let's cut dirt."

The Icks whooped it up as we cut across Sid's lot to get to the frontage road. Tex and Stink, leading the pack, slowed to let me pass first onto the road's hard, smooth surface.

"There he goes! Woo hoo!"

The Icks, right behind me, cheered when both my tires hit Bates Drive. I was embarrassed and exhilarated. Finally, the hard road.

Tex and Stink raced to the lead; Dwight, Will and Kenny rode beside me. I couldn't see her, but I knew Mom was watching me appreciate new freedom.

Dwight turned on his radio. "Groovy-smooth ride, huh, Jack?"

"Just like your clothes."

Tex and Stink popped wheelies and rode them briefly before setting their front tires down in front of Wonderlin's Machine Shop. "Woo hoo!"

A car came at us from the west. My brain recalled many of Mom's warnings, and I tightened my grip on the handlebars. With the Nova safely past us, I shouted at Tex and Stink, "Look out!"

They locked their brakes.

272

Light at the Rat Pond

Thelma Morgan, oblivious or on purpose, backed her behemoth Buick out of her paved drive right in front of us. We had had little contact with Shorty's gray-haired wife, so we didn't really know her personally, but that morning the Icks were shot at with a double stink eye, courtesy of Thelma.

She accelerated away, and Stink gestured with a finger.

I said, "Don't do that, man."

"Stupid hag," he said. "She almost crashed into us."

I learned quickly how important practicing alertness would be while riding the hard road.

Bates Drive curved a little south near the switchyard, leading us to the four lanes of Route 150. I got a little jittery approaching the intersection where east and west bound traffic zoomed toward their destinations. A break came in the traffic, so we raced toward the south frontage road, Kimball Avenue. Bates continued west, and at the corner of Bates and Kimball stood our two-story, brick school: Kickapoo Elementary. Starting the coming fall, I would be allowed to ride my bike to school. The coolness of that liberty had to be measured against the idea that school sometimes felt like going to prison. Of course I had no real idea what prison was like, but I thought it had to be at least related to attending school.

We cruised east, six abreast on Kimball, until traffic made us cram our bikes into one lane. Mom had said, "Walk *against* traffic, ride *with* it." I obeyed those simple rules.

Bates Drive had no sidewalks, and Kimball had random intervals of it, but we chose the road.

On the transistor, WLS played *Ride Captain Ride*, and Dwight said, "Good song."

Kimball fronted more houses than Bates did, but not many more. Goodwin, a short, dead-ended street off of Kimball, had a few houses tucked back near some woods, but in 1970, kids our age were not part of Goodwin's population.

We pedaled by Son-Ray's, then, directly south of our house, we passed a huge chunk of land that belonged to Western Brick Company. They still made bricks there in 1970, but business was dwindling. The Icks were very intrigued by what ran behind the brickyard's one hundred acres: the Tall Trees River.

Said Tex, "Can't wait until we can go behind there and play."

Heads nodded.

"What's back there, Yank?"

"River."

"Cool," said Will.

The brick company would graciously allow us to cut through their property to get to the wilds of the Tall Trees River. We had heard stories of a spooky,

273

Richard Newberry

narrow bridge that crossed over the river and debouched into a wilderness unlike anything the Icks had ever seen. Ravenous packs of wild dogs and other creatures purportedly roamed the wilderness; snakes, it was rumored, were also plentiful on both sides of the river. We had no way of knowing the danger that awaited us there.

"Yep," I said. "Fishing and exploring -"

"First-chop adventure, man," Stink said.

"Yeah," said Kenny.

And it was the dog that Kenny would finally get that started us on a very perilous journey at the Tall Trees River later that fall.

"Can't wait," I said.

CHAPTER 70

We passed Stankard's Floral and Greenhouse, and Stink's house, before turning off Kimball into the three blocks of houses that inhabited Stink's neighborhood.

"First time I've been here," said Dwight.

"Me, too," said Will.

I'd walked to Stink's house and neighborhood a couple of times, but I still felt like a pioneer seeing it for the first time on my black cruiser.

Tex and Stink led us back out onto Kimball, and we continued east toward Doverville. The next intersection marked the city limits, our parents' imposed limit for us for now, so we cut across the intersection and started back on Bates.

Stink instigated a race. After he and Tex shot out to the lead, the pack came together with each Ick leading briefly before traffic forced us into a single file in front of Cline's Oil Company. (The empty barrels - marred by flames - had been returned without incident.)

A light-hearted debate broke out about who would've won the impromptu race. We were riding six abreast again, the early morning air in our faces, traffic on Route 150 rolling by us, and my world was suddenly a bigger place.

"Looks like you're having fun, Yank."

"I am."

"Woo hoo!"

"Yeah," said Kenny.

Dwight turned up his radio.

That moment and its memory became very important to me, for our first ride all together on the hard road would be the Icks' last.

Friday evening I blew out eleven candles and Mom served each Ick a hearty piece of homemade cherry cake.

"Everyone want milk?" she asked.

Everybody did except Kenny, who asked for water. "Milk makes me far-uh . . .gives me gas." Mom joined our laughter.

"I've never heard that about milk," she said.

My presents from Mom were a model I had picked out and the usual one

Richard Newberry

hundred dollars to put toward my first car; only five more years stood between me and that car. The Icks pitched in together and bought me a catcher's mitt and five new baseballs.

We set up our old green tent in the backyard between the house and garage. Mom filled a Styrofoam cooler with ice and bottles of Pepsi; she bought two bags of barbecue potato chips and the Icks provided six Big Time candy bars and two packs of Black Jack gum.

I peeked inside the tent again. Five sleeping bags, pillows, a cooler of soda pop, chips, candy and gum - everything we needed for a great campout.

Will leaned in beside me. "Little piece of heaven."

"It's gonna be a blast."

Sundown couldn't come fast enough; that's when the exciting fun would begin. Tex had permission to stay out until 10:30.

"How about a race at the Rat Pond before it gets dark?" she asked.

"Dig it," Stink said.

Rat Pond racing always ended before twilight. "It might be too dark already," I said.

"One way to find out, y'all."

So we cut dirt and raced in the fading light; we had more wrecks than usual - and lots of fun.

Stink said afterwards, "We gotta do this more often."

The Icks agreed.

We rode past Shorty's as Stink said, "Think it's dark enough for a cherry heist?"

"Not quite," I said.

Back at the garage, Stink said, "This is gonna be super cool, sneakin' into Shorty's backyard."

We parked our bikes in the garage for the night.

I said, "As soon as it's a little darker we'll head out."

I knew Will would not be abetting us in cherry pilfering or throwing cherries at unsuspecting motorists on Warren. The knowledge stirred up a little mess of anxiety within me, because I also knew flack about Will's noncompliance would be forthcoming from Stink, and maybe Tex.

Stink wanted one more smell of the catcher's mitt before I rubbed oil into its leather. Tex and Dwight played catch with me for a bit as we worked on breaking in the glove and a new bright ball.

"Don't throw hard," I said. "I can hardly see."

Dwight asked, "How was it washing the bread trucks?"

"It wasn't easy, that's for sure."

Curt Lewsader appeared in the alley at his burn barrel. He tossed in two

276

Light at the Rat Pond

paper sacks of stuff and struck a match to it; soon, red and orange flames licked the dark above them. The bald, black-mustached man glanced our way before heading for his house.

Only so we could hear, Stink said, "Gonna get even with you tonight."

"Square dinkham," said Tex.

"What's your plan?" asked Dwight.

Stink ran to the tent. He came back smiling and holding out his hand. "Four or five of these tied to his back door."

I nodded. Of course Lewsader would have to be a moron not to figure out who booby trapped his door, but that was part of the message: mess with the Icks, we mess with you.

"First-chop, Stink," said Dwight.

Will said, "So when he pulls open his door after work - bang!"

"You got it," Stink said, admiring the pull-string poppers. "What time does he leave for work?"

"I guess about 10:30," I said.

"When's he get home?" asked Dwight.

"About . . . seven or so."

"Hope we hear it," he said.

Then Will slapped us with his comment: "I'd like to help tie them to the door."

The Icks, at first, were speechless. We looked at him as if he were a statue that had suddenly spoken.

"You?" said Kenny.

"Sure. Why not?"

"Really?"

"Really, Stink. It won't hurt him or anything."

"Steppin' up, Will," said Dwight.

Tex patted him on the back. "Well, Will Corben, welcome again to Ick danger."

Stink said, "We'll do it together."

"Okay," said Will.

I was ambivalent about the situation. I was glad to see the Icks welcoming his participation in some risky fun, but a tiny piece of me felt . . . disappointed about Will's decision; then I told myself Will was right, this prank would not hurt anyone, and Will was due a little revenge for whatever things Lewsader had said to him the night of hide-and-seek.

I said, "Mr. Dangerous."

Will smiled.

I said to Dwight, "Did you notice that you and Hair- Clarence dress alike?"

277

Richard Newberry

"He likes the groovy-smooth look."

"Uh, yeah. You two should go shopping together."

"Maybe."

We laughed.

Later, the talk came around to Cus. "So you cracked him a good one, huh, Jack?"

"He did, Stink," said Will.

"I told him he's the new Bat Man," said Dwight.

Off and on I worried the police would come to our house to arrest me for the incident. Every time I heard a siren in the neighborhood I knew my time was up. "It all happened fast," I said. "I didn't mean to break it - if I did."

Tex punched my arm. "Way to go, Bat Man. That'll teach Louse."

Kenny drained his first bottle of Pepsi, belched and said, "Lappin's really gonna be ticked off now."

I nodded.

Said Tex, "Or maybe he finally learned a lesson."

"Doubt it," said Dwight.

"I'm sick of Cus Lappin," said Stink. "Life would be groovy smooth without that jerk. Why did he have to be born?"

The Icks didn't have an answer.

I pulled the cap off of a Pepsi and took a drink of the sweet, burning cola. "He probably won't be dangerous for a while. But still be watching out."

Dwight shifted his brown eyes my way. "Show 'em what you got."

"You think?"

"Yeah."

I went to a small toolbox I kept locked, and brought out the item.

"Look what Jack's got," said Dwight.

"Cool!"

"Yeah."

"That's Cus's," said Tex, a little impressed.

"Sure is," said Will.

Stink asked, "What are you going to do with it?"

I looked at the switchblade, shrugged. "I don't know. Just keep it locked up for now."

All the Icks had to handle the knife.

Stink said, "We should carry this around, man. Nobody would mess with us."

"No," said Dwight and I together; I locked it back in the toolbox.

We finished our first soda pops and Stink said to me, "It's dark enough now."

"Yep," I said.

278

Light at the Rat Pond

Mom, startling us, popped her head inside the service door, said, "Is everybody doing okay?"

"Yep," I said.

"I'll be going to bed pretty soon, so if you need anything let me know, or help yourselves."

"We will," I said.

Ten minutes later we were ready to slink down the alley and sneak into Shorty's backyard.

"Let's go," said Stink.

I didn't know if I should credit foresight on our behalf, but we were all dressed in dark clothes, ready for nocturnal adventure.

"I'll hang out here," said Will. And part of me was glad he said it.

"C'mon with us," said Stink. "You're gonna miss some cool fun if you don't."

"Pure quill," said Kenny.

"Nah. I don't think so. I'll just wait here for y'all. I brought a book to read."

"A book?" Tex asked.

"Yep. *To Kill a Mockingbird.* Mother says it's good."

Stink wagged his head while Dwight took the radio out of his cruiser's cage and handed it to Will. "You can listen to the Cardinals. They're playin' the Dodgers tonight in St. Louis."

"Thanks, Dwight."

Stink said, "You sure you don't wanna go?"

"Yep. I'm not gonna ruin y'alls' fun."

"You don't ruin anything," I said.

He waved us off. "Go on. I'll be here when y'all get back."

I said, "I'm gonna kill the garage lights. Just use the light that's in the tent."

The Icks, minus Will, moved quietly and quickly along the dark alley; Dwight and I carried picking buckets. We huddled near Shorty's burn barrels outside of the tall privet hedge that bordered his huge backyard; across the tracks, a dog barked.

Stink crawled through the hedge's opening and reconnoitered the situation. He returned quickly, telling us, "No lights at the back of the house."

"They watch TV in their front room," I said. Will, inadvertently, had supplied valuable intelligence regarding the Morgans' nightly TV habits. "Shorty likes boxing. I think the Friday night fights are on."

"How do you know?" whispered Tex.

"Will."

"Will?"

"Yeah. He told me some stuff that he learned after helping Shorty."

279

Richard Newberry

"Makes sense," said Dwight.

"Yep." I looked through the hedge opening. "I think it's now or never."

Kenny said, "Think he'll –"

"Shhhhh!" I warned.

Kenny lowered his head and voice. "Think he'll really shoot us if he catches us?"

I said, "Nah," but it didn't even convince me.

Said Stink, "He won't catch us. We're the best."

"It might be a good idea to have Kenny be lookout while we're in there," said Tex.

I looked at him and he nodded.

"Okay," I said. "So if you see anything just give our whistle."

Kenny practiced the bob white's call.

"Shhhh!" everyone warned.

I peeked back inside the hedge.

"Car!" Dwight warned.

Headlights spotted the alley; they were coming from Sid's.

We bumped into one another as we scurried for the hedge opening. Kenny was the last one in, barely beating the car's exposing lights.

I handed Tex a bucket. She would pick with Stink while I worked with Dwight. I pointed at Kenny, then at the house. He nodded.

We crawled toward the cherry trees.

CHAPTER 71

Kate pushed back the covers and slipped under the freshly-laundered white sheet. She looked at her screened window, wished a little breeze would stir. The crickets and other creeping creatures were singing their night songs, and she wondered what mischief the Icks would be up to in that dark, outside world. She wouldn't worry. The Icks enjoyed their adventures, and they rarely brought grief to Ick parents.

She opened *East of Eden* to where she'd stopped reading, then flipped to the front where Andrew, forever ago, had inscribed a message to her on the title page. He had neat penmanship, and she read the inscription aloud.

"'To the love of my life, my wife and best friend. You are beautiful, Kate. Inside and out. Thank you for loving a boy from the farm, and blessing him with your love. Andrew.'"

She ran her slender fingers over the words, remembered how his love made her feel special, and safe. Even after they were married, he had never stopped courting her.

She thought back to a date they'd had just before the start of their sophomore year at college. They were eating spaghetti at one of their favorite little diners in Doverville.

Andrew wiped his mouth with the linen napkin, looked at her with a sincere expression, held her hand and said, "Kate, I love you, and I like you."

She started to grin, for she wasn't sure at first if it was his dry humor, but she realized quickly how sincere he was being, and it was the first time anyone had spoken those words to her. She squeezed his strong hand and said, "Thank you, Andrew."

She stared at the words Andrew had written in the book, her mind many years in the past, flooded with memories. The roar of a passing hot rod out on Route 150 snapped her out of her trance. She looked at the screen, then back to the book, and sighed.

She stuffed the pillows behind her for comfortable reading. Lost in Steinbeck's world of the messed up Adam Trask and the horrible woman Kate, real-life thoughts began to hinder her fictional getaway. The Creeping Taunt was trying to work on her with remembrances of the Deplorable Indiscretion, Parle's Woods, *him* and Imagene.

Kate fought off the Creeping Taunt's attempt to send her into a funk of despair. Some of her strength to resist came from the fact that there had not been one threatening phone call in almost a week, and no sign of a creep in a brown Ford following her.

Four silhouettes furtively plucked from the branches of the three venerable cherry trees. Like everything else he owned, the trees were well maintained; properly trimmed and pruned, and producing much fruit. The abundance of ammunition meant we wouldn't be in his backyard for long.

Dwight, staying busy, whispered to me, "Think he'll notice cherries missing?"

"Knowin' Shorty, yes."

"He'll blame us."

"Makes sense."

"He might think it was birds."

I said, "He'd still blame us."

I looked at Kenny who was squatted under the privet's arched opening. His attention was fixed on the house.

My ears tuned out the expected night sounds and tuned in to any unexpected dangerous sounds, like Shorty's back door creaking open.

Dwight said, "I think we've got enough."

I felt inside the bucket. "Yeah."

We crept over to Stink and Tex. I asked, "You guys about done?"

Stink tipped the bucket and I felt inside as I watched Kenny watching the house.

I said, "You guys are slow."

Dwight and I started helping them, but I heard something unexpected and it seized my movement. Dwight, Tex and Stink sensed my apprehension and also froze. Our backs were turned to the house. We looked at Kenny; he hadn't moved, and displayed no cause for alarm.

What was the sound I'd heard?

I started to turn to face the house when I heard the same unexpected sound. Now Dwight was turning to see. Was somebody watching us from the back door?

Kenny still showed no sign of alarm, which confused me. I could swear somebody was at the back door. I looked away from Kenny and back to the door.

The door burst outward. "You bunch of heathens!" Shorty's gravelly voice boomed in the dark. "What are you doin' in my trees?!"

Kenny whistled the bob white and ran.

Light at the Rat Pond

"Come back here you bunch of low-bellied, sneakin' thieves!"

We somehow funneled in and out of the hedge opening without crashing into a pile.

"Left! Left!" I said, trying to be heard but not recognized.

Stink and Kenny had started right, but caught themselves and ran with us toward the Rat Pond.

A rifle shot cracked the air, and a bullet zinged above our heads.

"Man!" said Dwight. "He's shootin' at us!"

I plowed into Dutch's burn barrel, but kept my feet as I led the way to the Rat Pond. "Stay off the alley!"

I saw the opening that led down to the race track and ran down into the darkness. I heard feet and heavy breathing behind me, then somebody thudded to the ground as they tried to run down the hill too fast.

"Easy! Easy!" I said.

"Kenny's down," said Tex.

"I'm okay." He'd rolled to the bottom.

We stood on the track, waiting for Shorty with his rifle. It was pitch black; the moon and stars were hidden by an overcast night sky. We must've scared the crickets and frogs and night things into silence because it was eerily quiet at the Rat Pond.

Tex whispered, "I can hardly see anything."

"Me either," said Kenny.

"We'll be able to see a little in a minute," I said. I thought I could hear all of our hearts pounding in our chests.

"You think he knows it was us?" Tex asked me.

"Dunno. Hope not."

We listened and watched.

I asked Tex, "You still got cherries in your bucket?"

"Yeah. You?"

"Plenty."

Dwight whispered, "That crazy fool shot at us!"

Stink chuckled. "That was the coolest thing ever."

"We could've been shot, man! Don't you get that, Stink!"

"Cool down, Dwight," said Stink. "We escaped, man."

"Keep your voices down," I said.

Kenny asked, "You think he'll come lookin' for us, Jack?"

"Probably not. He had his fun." My eyes were adjusting to the dark. "You guys know he said he'd shoot us if we messed with his stuff."

Dwight said, "So? What's that mean? Are we supposed to honor the man because he kept his word?"

283

Richard Newberry

"No," said Tex. "But it does mean we knew the consequences going in."

Nobody said a word.

In the silence, I thought about how darkness had made a very familiar place seem strange and spooky.

Headlights pierced the dark above us.

"Is that him?" Kenny asked.

The vehicle was coming from Shorty's direction, and moving slow on the alley.

Kenny worried, "Think that's Shorty, Jack? Huh?" "Shhh."

At the northeast corner of the Rat Pond, the vehicle stopped.

"Get off the track," I said, and we moved to deeper cover near Booty Tree.

I could finally discern the vehicle was a car; it was too dark and the growth was too thick to know the make and model. It just sat idling on the alley, then the lights went off, and the driver stepped out. Again, impossible to identify.

I whispered, "I don't think it's Shorty."

Our eyes were glued to the scene unfolding above us.

The driver stepped into the heavy brush, crunching leaves and snapping twigs.

"Does he see us?" Stink asked.

"No way," I said.

The driver stopped walking and it was quiet.

"He's lookin' for us," said Kenny.

"I don't think so," I said.

We heard something smacking into limbs and then a splash.

"He threw something in the pond," said Tex.

The driver started out of the brush when Stink sneezed.

"Man, Stink," whispered Dwight.

The driver didn't move.

We watched and waited.

"Weird time to be throwing stuff away," said Tex.

"Shhh," I warned.

The driver finally walked out of the cover, turned on his headlights and started driving away slowly.

"That was close," said Kenny.

The car stopped directly above us, near the hill's entrance. We stumbled farther into cover. Hoboland sounded vacant.

"What's he doin?" asked Kenny.

I whispered, "Dunno."

"He can't see us," said Dwight.

284

Light at the Rat Pond

"Hope not," said Kenny.

I said, "Everybody shut up." I still couldn't tell what kind of car it was.

The car just sat there, idling. The driver seemed to be staring into the darkness at us. Suddenly, a small beam of light hit our race track. The guy had a flashlight.

En masse, we scrunched deeper into the brush, snapping twigs as we did.

The searching beam stopped. The driver had heard us.

"Crud," I whispered.

"There's five of us against one," said Tex.

The driver opened his door.

Tex whispered, "I got rocks in Booty Tree," and she started slipping toward it.

"Great," said Dwight. "We've got rocks and he's got a gun."

I said, "It's not Shorty."

"He could still have a gun," said Dwight.

Tex made it to Booty Tree as the guy started down the hill.

"Hurry!" I whispered at Tex.

More headlights coming from the east on the alley.

The guy on the hill quickly slipped back into his car and rolled away, showing us square, red taillights.

I looked at Dwight, who was already looking at me. The red squares had looked like Galaxie taillights.

285

CHAPTER 72

After the second car passed, Stink said, "I'll go take a look."

Tex kept the rocks rolled up in her shirt.

Stink called from the top of the hill. "All clear!"

We gathered on the alley.

Stink said, "Wonder who that dude was?"

"Dunno," I said. "He threw something in the Rat Pond."

Dwight said to me, "I think it was a Galaxie, but I couldn't tell what color. Could you?"

"Nope."

"Think it was the same guy?"

"Who knows."

"Same guy as what?" asked Tex.

Dwight and I told them about the guy in the brown Galaxie that we thought was watching us.

Tex said, "I haven't noticed any brown car following us around."

"Yeah," said Kenny.

A train revved its engine at the switchyard.

"I know," said Dwight. "We haven't seen him lately either."

I said, "It was nothing."

Stink flung a rock into the Rat Pond's darkness. "That dude now wasn't nothing. He was looking for us, like we caught him doing something when he threw whatever it was into the pond."

Heads nodded, and Dwight said, "Whatever it was is gone now."

Tex said, "We can try to find it."

"Impossible," said Dwight.

And what happened later that night and early the next morning caused us to forget to try the impossible.

Just in case Shorty was still in the mood to shoot trespassers, we crossed the tracks at the switchyard and walked Warren until we were well clear of Shorty's. We cut down to the tracks and came up at the cutover behind Sid's. The tavern had a good Friday night crowd.

We could see the light's glow inside the tent from behind Sid's.

"He missed the best fun ever," said Stink.

286

Light at the Rat Pond

Will's brown eyes grew bigger with every forthcoming detail about our latest adventure.

Stink said, "Man, it was like a bazooka goin' off."

"It was a rifle," I said.

"Almost killed us," said Dwight.

"Y'all know he said he'd shoot us if he caught us messin' around."

I nodded.

"I guess Shorty's a man of his word, Yank."

"Pure quill."

We told him about the car and driver.

"Who you reckon was in the car?"

"Hard to say," said Dwight. "We couldn't even tell what color it was."

Tex grabbed a Pepsi from the cooler. "We're going to see if we can find what he threw in the pond tomorrow."

Dwight said, "You know what that's gonna be like? Impossible."

"Probably," she said.

We ate chips and guzzled soda pops. I looked in the garage at the Quaker State Oil clock. "It's only a little past 9:30."

"I've got to be in by 10:30 don't forget," said Tex. "Let's go do some cherrying."

Stink asked Will, "Sure you don't wanna go? Nobody gets hurt."

"I'm positive."

"Gettin' chased is a blast."

"That's okay, Stink." He held up his book. "This is pretty good."

"Okay. But me and you'll tie up the pull crackers as soon as that guy goes to work."

Will nodded.

We headed out for our spot above the tracks and my stomach began churning with excitement. Fruiting cars was one of our favorite and most exciting adventures, and though we'd never been caught, we had come close a couple of times.

The spot was a quarter of a mile east of Harper's Field, in the heart of raspberry briars. The narrow path that led up to our throwing spot was hard to see in the dark.

"There it is," I said.

Two cars traveling in opposite directions passed above us.

"Action tonight," said Stink, leading the way up the north hillside. "Cool, cool, cool."

At the top of the hill, just below Warren's pavement, the ground was soft

Richard Newberry

and grassy, protruding like a shelf on the hillside. Once we were on the shelf, our communications and movements were careful.

Tex had a bucket for her and Stink; Kenny, Dwight and I shared the other. We hunkered down for cover.

"This is gonna be fun," said Stink.

"Hope the cherries work," I said.

Tex held out her bucket. "If we get chased I'm ditching this somewhere."

"We better get chased," I said. "Just remember where you throw it so I can find it tomorrow."

I peeked up at Warren. Across the road stood a burgeoning, thirty acre cornfield; our ammunition dump for the fall, and especially Halloween.

The Icks had established rules of engagement regarding fruiting. If two cars were close together in the same lane we always threw at the last car. Hot rods were good targets because they were a guaranteed chase, but they had to be going fast enough for us to escape. We never threw when two cars were close together going the opposite direction. We never fruited the police, or never, ever Rick Spencer.

"Here comes one!" said Stink.

Hands grabbed for cherries.

"By itself?" I asked.

Stink nodded.

The car was going east, the lane nearest us, and when its headlights passed we stood and launched our cherries. They sounded like fat raindrops on metal.

Crouching out of sight, we watched.

Brake lights, then back up lights.

"Go! Go! Go!" I ordered.

We adeptly ran down the narrow path, cut across the tracks, and waited on the other side to see if our pursuer had the spunk to give chase.

The car's taillights began to flash.

"They're comin'!" Stink said excitedly.

The driver and a single passenger emerged. I heard, "Looks like cherries," and, "They're probably down on the tracks somewhere."

They started down the hill.

"Let's go," said Kenny.

I said, "Not yet. Wait."

The cursing started when our pursuers encountered the briars. We knew the path, they didn't; they'd never find it in the dark.

I heard, "You got a flashlight?", and hoped they did because that meant a chase was at hand.

"No," said the driver.

Light at the Rat Pond

Crud.

"I know you're out there punks!" said the driver. "You better not let me catch you!"

"That's the point," Tex whispered.

The Icks chuckled.

They drove away and we climbed back up to the shelf.

"Keep an eye out for that one," I said. "I think it was a Plymouth Fury."

But we didn't have to worry about that car. Big trouble came from another one.

CHAPTER 73

"Car," said Stink. "By itself. Wait. Nope. It turned."

We had to be more cautious than ever because the Plymouth might double back to catch us.

Tex said, "I'd like to get in one good chase before I have to go in."

"We will," I said. "Another one will come by pretty soon."

Unfortunately, Tex didn't have to wait.

A very familiar rumble sounded in the night. It got closer and the Icks stayed out of sight - except Kenny. To our collective shock, he raised up with a fist full of cherries and launched them at the passing Super Bee.

I prayed he would miss.

Sprinkles of fat raindrops in the form of cherries splashed against Rick Spencer's magnificent muscle car.

Stink dashed for the path.

The '68 Dodge's brakes locked and tires squealed in reverse.

The Icks were flying down the narrow, dark path. Stink, already on the tracks, was crying, "Oh, man! Oh, man! Oh, man!"

I said, "Go! Go! Go!", but it didn't need said.

Running west at the side of the steel rails, Dwight and I stopped when we heard one car door slam shut. The pursuer had a flashlight and had found our path.

Dwight said, "Is that Spen-"

The Dodge's engine revved and its tires squealed.

"There's two of 'em," I said. "Run!"

A beam of light flashed over the tracks.

Tex ran back to us. She was smiling! "Where to?"

Spencer's car had sped out of sight on Warren.

I said, "I don't know, just run!"

Running, Dwight said, "Spencer's gonna come down the alley. They're gonna box us in."

Stink and Kenny slowed to let us catch up. "C'mon!" Stink said. "We can't just stand here!"

Tex offered, "Split up?"

"No. Let's keep going." I needed time to think.

Light at the Rat Pond

We knew the tracks and how to run them, so we stayed ahead of the guy with the flashlight.

"Can't go to my house," I said.

We could escape their trap by cutting back across the tracks and running through the cornfield, but getting up the thorn-infested hill on the north side would severely slow us. I looked over my shoulder; the flashlight was closing on us.

"Go faster!" I said.

Tex and I still had our buckets of cherries. I told her, "Throw it over there. I'll get 'em later."

When we were below Harper's Field I heard Spencer's Super Bee.

"He's comin'!" said Stink.

"Which way, Jack?" Tex asked.

Kenny was breathing hard and slowing down. "He's gonna get me. Which way, Jack?"

"I don't know." Think! Think!

Said Dwight, "What about the cutover? We could hide out in my neighborhood."

I looked back again. The guy with the flashlight was relentless. I said, "No. We need cover now."

"Where then?" asked Tex.

"Sid's parking lot. We can hide under some cars."

"I'm too fat," said Dwight.

"You're not fat, just big."

"This ain't a time to worry about my feelings, Jack. I'm too fat to squeeze under a car."

"Find a truck then."

The Icks raced up the cutover. "Wait!" I said, listening to Spencer's approaching car.

Stink peeked down the alley. "He's almost to the Gordons'."

We were dead if either one of the pursuers saw us slide under a car to hide.

"Go!" I said.

The tavern's east side was darkest, so we shimmied under the vehicles parked there. The car I slid under must have just arrived because its front exhaust pipe burned my arm. We positioned ourselves to see Flashlight Guy when he came up the cutover. There was a good chance the light would spot one of us when he topped the hill.

The Super Bee's rumble neared.

I heard Stink griping at Kenny.

"Shhhh!" I warned.

291

Richard Newberry

The flashlight's beam jostled near the mulberry tree. I suddenly felt trapped under two tons of Pontiac LeMans.

Adding to the intrigue were a pair of jean-clad legs that had come from Sid's side door and were headed toward the Ford truck where Dwight lay flat on his plentiful stomach.

And then a voice in the night boomed, "Sandra! San-dra!"

Texal Wonderlin's clarion calls for his daughter could be heard all the way to downtown Doverville.

"San-dra!"

The legs walking toward the truck stopped and laughed. "Time for somebody to be in," said one of them.

Flashlight Guy made it to the alley; he hollered to the jean legs, "You see any kids around here?"

"Nope. But somebody's lookin' for Sandra."

"Yeah. I heard that."

I saw Dwight roll out from under the truck and onto Harper's grass.

Flashlight Guy started down the alley, heading toward the Super Bee and my house.

Tex, next to me under a Buick, winked and slid out, sneaked away. She would make it home safe and on time by using Bates Drive.

The truck pulled away and all I could see of Dwight laying in the grass was a dark lump.

I scooted out from under the Pontiac. The other Icks came out of hiding and we crouched near Sid's burn barrels; we could see down the alley from there. Rick Spencer's car sat idling in front of the garage.

"What are they doing?" I asked.

"Just sittin' there," said Stink. "The guy that chased us is talking to Rick."

Spencer's car suddenly stopped rumbling and its headlights went off.

Stink scampered back to the tavern's corner. "They're going into your backyard!"

"Crud. Will."

Kenny, Dwight and I stayed crouched at the barrels to see what was about to happen.

Stink, hiding against the tavern, said, "We gotta be ready to run."

I looked back at him and said, "Shhh!" I wasn't about to leave Will.

Rick Spencer, who I'd never seen outside of his car, had an average build; Flashlight Guy was shorter and stockier. They were in the alley, each holding one of Will's arms.

"Got your friend," Rick said. "Come on out." They were looking in our direction, but I didn't think we were spotted.

292

Light at the Rat Pond

"C'mon out or he pays for it."

I didn't hesitate.

"What are you doing?" said Stink.

I crouched down again. "I'm goin' down there."

"He got caught. That's his tough luck."

"He didn't do anything, Stink."

"You know what they say Spencer did to those two kids he caught cornin' his car last Halloween. You're gonna get beat up."

"Maybe I will," I said, standing again. "But it's not gonna happen to Will." I started walking toward them.

Kenny and Dwight joined me.

"I'm not going! You guys are stupid!" He glared at us. "All Will's fault."

The three of us walked side by side, like a trio of gunfighters headed directly at quicker and deadlier guns.

"Here they come, Doug," said Rick.

"Yeah, I see 'em."

I told Rick, "He didn't do anything. He wasn't there."

"I'm sorry, Jack." Will looked dejected.

"No reason to be," I said.

We stopped at an uncomfortable distance from them.

They dropped Will's arms. "I didn't think he was in on it," said Rick. His neatly trimmed sideburns followed his sharp jaw line, then jutted up to form a well-groomed, dark mustache and goatee. He looked ominous. "He was in the tent readin' a book."

Doug chuckled at the idea of reading a book.

"This all of you?" Rick asked.

"Yep," I said.

"No cowards afraid to come out?"

We didn't answer.

"Sorry," Will said again.

I said, "It's not your fault."

"Might be," said Doug. "That big light shinin' in the tent gave him away." Silence.

Rick said, "You guys are owed payback."

We wouldn't just stand there and let them beat us, but unless Kenny got riled up there wasn't a true fighter there among the Icks. Our best, Tex, was safe at home.

Rick and Doug stepped directly in front of us; their hands were free at their sides. I could smell booze on both guys.

"Hey, Icks!"

293

Richard Newberry

"What are you doing here?" I asked.

"I snuck out," said Tex. "I thought you might be glad to see me." Passing by Doug, she said, "These guys wanting to become Icks?" Tex stood beside me.

"Icks?" asked Doug. "What is an Ick?"

"We are," she said.

"Oooo. I'm really scared – Icks!" Doug laughed. "They got a girl to fight for 'em now."

Will stepped from behind Rick and Doug and joined us.

"And now a pretty boy," Doug added. He was clenching and unclenching his fists. "Or maybe you think you can whip us 'cause you got a big, fat black kid. I've beat all colors and sizes."

"What are you Doug?" Dwight asked. "About twenty? We're eleven."

"I'm twelve, Dwight," said Kenny. "Almost thirteen."

Dwight just looked at Kenny, then said to Doug, "Get your kicks beatin' up kids?"

I wanted to remind Dwight there wasn't a bat stashed nearby, and I wasn't about to get all crazy and attack barehanded.

"I'll start with you," said Doug, staring at Dwight.

Rick grabbed Doug. "Hold up, man."

Doug shook him off. "Let's take these little punks down."

"Man, I don't beat on kids."

"It's not what we heard," I said.

"That right?" Rick stepped in front of me. "What did you hear?"

"The two kids who corned your car last Halloween you beat up so bad they had to go to the hospital."

He chuckled, stepped back, said, "Man, rumors."

Kenny asked, "So it didn't really happen?"

"Two kids did corn my car, and they did get hurt pretty bad – because they panicked and ran in front of a car coming the other way."

"You're kidding," said Tex.

"No I'm not. It messed 'em up."

The Icks exchanged glances. Our rules of engagement to never throw when two cars were present had been justified and wise.

I said to Rick, "Sorry we hit your car. You're suppose to be off limits. We messed up."

"Yeah you did," he said.

"It was me," Kenny confessed. "I was the only one. Sorry."

"Sorry ain't enough – Icks. You owe me. Those stupid cherries landed in my car."

Light at the Rat Pond

"Hit me in the head," said Doug.

Tex laughed.

"It's not funny," said Doug.

I asked, "What's our payback?"

CHAPTER 74

After Rick and Doug drove away Stink emerged. "What did they say? What happened?"

"We've got payback comin'," said Dwight.

"Payback? What kind of payback?"

I said, "We've got to clean his car inside and out. He's gonna bring it here about noon tomorrow." It must've been my week to get caught and wash vehicles.

"Better than getting beat up," said Kenny.

"I'm not gonna do it," said Stink.

Dwight said, "Yes you are. You were in on it."

"But I didn't get caught."

"I have to get home before I get caught," Tex said. "See you guys tomorrow."

I said, "Thanks for backing us up." I glanced at Stink, then back to her. "It was gutsy."

She punched my arm. "You'd do the same."

We pulled the tops off of soda pops and vigorously drank.

Stink said again, "I'm not gonna clean Spencer's car. I didn't get caught."

Kenny got in his face. "Yes you are! And I mean it!"

We were stunned by his rare display of anger.

Stink gathered himself and said, "You gonna make me - Retard?"

"Cool it, Stink," said Dwight.

"I'll make you if I have to."

Stink flung his half-full bottle into the night toward the brush. We heard it shatter on the tracks.

"Hey," I said, "that was ten cents."

"I'm leavin'." Stink got his bike. Pointing at Will, he said, "It's all his fault!"

"Man, keep it down," I said.

"I'm outta here."

Dwight said, "Don't be mad at Will because you were too chicken to come out."

"I wasn't too chicken - and we wouldn't have had to come out if church boy wasn't around!" Stink glared at Will before cutting dirt into the night.

296

Light at the Rat Pond

It wasn't Stink's first temper tantrum. We'd see them once or twice a year, then he would get over it and reluctantly offer a half-hearted apology.

Said Kenny, "If he doesn't come back to help . . ."

"He will," I said. "I think he's just embarrassed." But I was wrong.

"I messed it up for y'all tonight. You look forward to this night and I got right in the way of it. I'm sorry."

"Will," I said, "any of us with a speck of brains knew you wouldn't go do stuff you thought was wrong, so cut out the sorry. Stink's the one with a problem."

We chugged down the rest of our soda pops and took turns trying to be the most prolific belcher.

"One thing about tonight," said Dwight. "We'll never forget it."

Heads nodded and I said, "It's been the best yet."

Will seemed relieved. "Really?"

"First-chop," said Kenny.

I finished a bag of chips. "Yep. We got shot at, hid at the Rat Pond -"

"That was spooky," said Kenny.

"Yep. And we saw that guy throw something into the pond, got chased twice -"

"Caught once," said Dwight.

"Yep," I said. "First time ever."

"A great campout," said Dwight.

Will smiled.

The rest of the night we joked and laughed, snacked and drank Pepsi; listened to WLS. We had a contest to see who could make the best and loudest armpit farts; Dwight won. Then one by one, the Icks finally surrendered to sleep.

I thought Stink would ride back to the campout soon after he rode away. But he never did.

I was awakened in the morning by cracking sounds that were quick, sharp and loud. I raised up from my sleeping bag wondering who was setting off firecrackers so early.

Curt Lewsader's cursing sounded prominently in the early morning quiet.

I smiled. One of the Icks had tied the string poppers to his door; probably Tex. I looked around the tent. Kenny and Dwight were on their backs, deep in sleep with their mouths lopped open.

Where was Will?

It occurred to me that he might have tied the poppers to Curt's door. I smiled again, and crawled out of the tent, expecting to find Will outside somewhere.

297

Richard Newberry

"Will?"

No answer. An overcast sky had minimized the morning's dew, and the clouds were breaking up. I yawned and stretched.

"Will."

His racer and cruiser were still in the garage. I raised the overhead door and walked to the alley. Tex was riding toward me; trains started making noise at the switchyard.

She slid-stopped in front of me. "Did you just get up?"

"Yep. You see Will?"

She frowned, wagged her head and looked around. "Are his bikes here?"

"Yep."

"Hmm."

"Weird," I said. "Hey, did you tie the poppers to Lewsader's door?"

"No, but I heard them go off."

"Had to be Will."

She said, "Wonder where he is?"

I shrugged. "I'm gonna wake up Kenny and Dwight. Maybe they know."

They didn't.

We mounted our bikes and waited on the alley. I heard a train pulling out of the switchyard.

"I guess we should go lookin' for him," I said.

Tex asked, "You think he might've just went home?"

"Not without a bike," said Dwight.

Kenny was looking toward the coming train. "Maybe he's at the Rat Pond readin' the Bible to Clarence and Arlie."

"I think he'd take his bike," I said. "But we can check there first."

The locomotive, building speed, roared by us.

Loud enough to be heard above the train, Tex said, "Rat Pond then."

I nodded, started to pedal but stopped, as did the other Icks. The passing freight cars had begun their heavy ba-bump, ba-bump, ba-bump when we noticed the twelfth car behind the black locomotive. It was an ordinary brown boxcar with its door open; nothing special - except for the smiling and waving passenger standing near the boxcar's doorway.

Will Corben had hopped a train!

We were stuck to our bikes' seats, thunderstruck by what was passing before us.

"Hey, y'all!"

We snapped out of our trances and raced to keep up with the train.

"Wooo hooo!"

"He did it!" said Dwight. "I can't believe he did it!"

Light at the Rat Pond

Kenny, behind us, shouted, "Way to go, Will! First-chop, man!"

I just smiled and wagged my head.

We were standing and pedaling, driving our legs to stay even with Will.

At Harper's Field I shouted, "Better jump!"

He looked down, then around and shook his head.

"You gotta jump now!"

Dwight said, "He's goin' too fast already, Jack."

"We'll never keep up," said Tex.

She was right; shortly thereafter we lost sight of Will and his boxcar.

We coasted to a stop, and Kenny said, "First-chop! He's the first Ick to hop a train."

"I'd never seen anybody but Nicky do it," said Dwight.

I asked, "Where'd Nicky get off?"

"I don't remember. It's been a long time ago."

"Stink will never believe it," said Tex. "He's going to be super jealous."

We waved at the guys on the caboose.

I said, "Will might be in big trouble." Joy for my friend's daring feat had been usurped by my worry for him. "Where do you think he'll be able to jump off at?"

"Don't know," said Dwight. "The train turns north pretty soon, goes to Chicago."

"Maybe it'll slow down enough when it starts to turn."

Dwight shrugged at me.

Tex said, "It would be cool if Will did ride it all the way to Chicago."

"I don't think his parents will think so," I said.

Reverently, Kenny said, "Chicago."

Will didn't make it to Chicago.

He did, however, ride the rails for sixty miles before jumping off at the Kankakee switchyard. He explained to the railroaders in Kankakee what he had done and that he fully expected them to arrest him, which, Will told them, should happen to anyone who breaks the law. He received a stern lecture regarding railroad safety and the consequences lawbreakers usually faced, yet Will suffered no arrest. He told us he thought he detected admiration from two brakemen for his daring accomplishment.

Will's parents were called, and he later told the Icks, with a wary smile, his parents did not express the slightest admiration toward his daring accomplishment, and he would have preferred the Kankakee jailhouse to the meaningful paddling he was awarded. A two-week grounding followed him home; no visitors, no phone calls.

CHAPTER 75

Because of his two-week confinement, Will couldn't help us wash Rick Spencer's Super Bee the day after the fruiting. I actually enjoyed being up close to the car we had always admired from afar; the other Icks agreed.

When Mom asked us why we were washing it, I lied. "We just wanted to."

She didn't appear to buy that answer, but also didn't press us for the real reason.

Two weeks passed slowly, and Will finally got set free; a new esteem followed our train-hopping friend once he was released. He did not fancy the exultation being cast upon him, for it reminded him of his transgression - and its consequences. The Icks, like the Kankakee brakemen, could not help admiring his outstanding achievement.

"How fast did you go?"

"What did you see?"

"See any hobos?"

"Were you scared?"

"What's Kankakee look like?"

Tex's admiration toward Will seemed tinged with jealousy, because her fiery jump had taken second place to his train hopping. "You going to do it again?"

"No I'm not, Tex."

"I'm gonna try it sometime," Kenny said.

Dwight and I said we would too, but Tex cut off the legs of our bravado with, "I'll believe it when I see it."

During Will's confinement, Stink brought a kid from his neighborhood to the garage to get Stink's racer. He was still mad, said very little, and quit coming to the garage. We paid him back with our own silent treatment.

"Where's Stink, y'all."

"Hasn't been around," I said.

Will talked us into riding to Stink's neighborhood to seek reconciliation with our old friend. Our attempt was smothered by a hostile Stink. He again called Kenny Retard - Dwight almost punched him, but most of his venom struck at Will.

"You're a pretty-boy, you sissy."

300

Light at the Rat Pond

A free-for-all almost broke out between the Icks and Stink and his new friends when Stink called all the Icks "sissies". Dwight and I could barely restrain Tex.

"Let's go," I said. "Now."

Before we left, Tex hurled some expletives at Stink and friends that were down right scary, and shocking to my ears. They even made one of the kids standing behind Stink start to cry.

We rode away, knowing Stink had renounced any affiliation with the Icks. The more we pedaled back toward the garage, the more my anger swayed into melancholy. We had never lost an Ick - until now.

Will felt worse than any of us about what happened with Stink. He blamed himself for Stink quitting the Icks. Though we tried to convince him otherwise, Will struggled to let go of the guilt.

The rest of June and most of July 1970 were good days. Dwight and I made more money than ever using Sid as a distributor of our raspberries; the Icks enjoyed plenty of baseball games at Harper's field and night-time hide-and-seek; Rat Pond races along with hard-road rides kept the fun going. We got our hands on some M-80 firecrackers to help us celebrate Independence Day. Nobody was seriously injured.

We ventured behind the brickyard to get a taste of what fun awaited us there, but when Mom found out she said, "For now, I don't want you going back there. You'll earn that privilege soon enough."

"When?"

"Pretty soon."

Vague, but promising. Our brief encounter with the Tall Trees, its spooky old dinky bridge and the mysterious land beyond the bridge had whetted our adventurous appetites; plans for our return journey there consumed a fair amount of our time during the rest of June and July.

Whenever Shorty saw us ride by he got a big kick out of pretending he was holding a rifle and shooting it over our heads.

Dwight had said, "That cat is crazy. Almost killed us and he thinks it's funny."

The brown Galaxie had been forgotten, and Cus never appeared during those days, allowing me to worry solely about Vietnam. I still yearned for Rebecca Corben.

Will, Kenny and I had three Saturday morning Bible readings with Clarence and Arlie, but Mom continued to turn a deaf ear to Will's gentle nudging about going to church with us. I had missed only one Sunday morning church service in almost two months.

The second Sunday in July I sat in the pew between Will and Bobby, and

301

Richard Newberry

listened intently to Pastor Rogers. Eloquent and passionate as always, his words that morning poured into my ears, caused me to think deeply, then traveled to my chest where the living words stirred things deep within me. For some reason, I thought back to our first hobo Bible reading, and how Clarence and Arlie's faces had glowed as Will read the Bible.

At the end of his sermon that Sunday, Pastor Rogers said, "Dear friends, if you've never accepted Jesus Christ as Lord and Savior of your life, you need to do it now. Come to Him, He loves you. He's waiting.

"Don't wait to get your life straight, or think you've got to do things right before He'll accept you. He loves you right where you are, just as you are this very moment. And if you trust Him as Lord and Savior, He'll love you so much He will not leave you the way you are, but will begin to transform you into His likeness.

"If you reject Him, His blood cannot cover your sins, and you will have chosen the road to hell. Choose God today, friend. He will forgive your sins, small and great. If you confess with your heart you are a sinner, and accept by faith what Jesus did upon Calvary and upon His resurrection from the dead, God will save you from your sins. Then - and only then - will you become a child of God, with His promise of eternal life in heaven.

"Dear friend, come."

The pulling invisible hands I had experienced before were back, tugging at me, pulling my heart toward Pastor Rogers's invitation. I looked at Will.

He said, "You need to go, Jack."

But I didn't.

Will stayed busy in June and July helping neighbors on both sides of the tracks. He offered Lewsader a free car wash to help patch things up, but the creep just said, "Stay off my property."

Tex told him, "It's not your property," and matched the bald guy's glaring stare until he walked off mumbling.

Will seemed to eventually give up his guilt over the Stink incident; mainly because, by himself, he rode to Stink's neighborhood to try and convince him to come back. Will was met by the same attitude from Stink we had witnessed on our first trip to reconcile.

One hot July morning, Will didn't come to the garage. We waited for him, but he never showed.

Kenny said, "Maybe he hopped this train that's coming, and he'll wave at us as he goes by."

"He didn't hop the train," said Tex.

But we did watch the entire train pass before heading out on our morning adventures.

Light at the Rat Pond

I said, "Probably just got stuck doing something at home. He'll be here later."

Kenny's neighbor Donnie had started part-time riding with us in June. He was only nine and a half, but showed promise of having the ingredients necessary to become an Ick. He asked, "Will really hopped a train?"

"Yep," I said.

"Cool," he said.

"Yep."

Will rode in that afternoon, looking and acting distant or bothered - something, certainly not the usual Will.

Tex asked, "Where you been?"

"Just had stuff to do."

"Stuff at home?" I asked.

"Yeah, kinda." Will didn't know how to hide a lie, but we probed no further.

Later that day as we cruised the alley, I fell to the back of the pack to ride alongside him. "I can tell something's bothering you. Heck, all of us can."

He spoke so only I could hear. "Yeah, sorry. Got something I gotta work out, Jack."

"Can I help?"

"No. Not really. I gotta figure it out first."

"Is it bad?"

"It's not good."

"Man, Will. Let us help."

He looked at me, said firmly, "No."

"Okay. I'll give you space, man. It's not about Stink is it?"

"No."

"Is it your family?"

He wagged his head.

"Is somebody bother -"

"Jack. Drop it. Please."

Maybe he was bummed because I hadn't went forward to accept Jesus. But as he clearly wanted, I dropped it.

Over the next few days Will gradually returned to his normal self - almost; something lingered. And the time came when I wished I had pushed him and not dropped it.

But before that time came, August arrived, bringing rare storms; Mom was taken right in the middle of one.

303

CHAPTER 76

It was pouring rain. August had started unusually wet, driving Kate inside to start chores planned for fall. She listened to the classical music station on the kitchen radio as she papered the pantry's shelves.

She smiled at the thought of Will having hopped a train and riding it to Kankakee. Of course if it had been Jack, he would still be grounded.

"Shoot," she said when she realized there wasn't enough paper to finish the job. Raining or not, she was going to Kresge to get more paper; the shelves would be finished tonight.

She called Nadine. "It's me."

"Hey, Murph. You decide to come over and play Monopoly with the Icks?"

Kate looked at the kitchen clock: ten till seven. "They're still playing?"

"You know Monopoly can be a marathon."

The game had started at three that afternoon, and at about five Nadine started calling parents to see if their kids could stay for supper; she was making pizza.

"You hungry, Murph? There's a little pizza left."

"I'm fine, but thanks. Is Jack behaving himself?"

"No."

"Okay, good. Listen, I have to run to town for a minute. Is it okay if Jack stays there until I get back?"

"You know we'd adopt him if you'd let us."

"You'd have to pay for college."

"Hurry back, Murph."

Kate looked out the kitchen window, saw that the rain had slacked and decided against an umbrella. She had to wash her hair later anyway.

She climbed into the Impala, switched on the wipers and lights, checked her mirrors and backed out onto the alley. There had been no sign of the brown car or anyone following her the past several weeks, and the ominous phone calls had also stopped. She sighed relief, thinking whoever it was had exhausted their demented fun with her, and had moved on to something or somebody else. She had quit thinking the strange events had anything to do with her past.

Just inside Doverville's city limits, she switched the wipers to low, but noticed dark, threatening clouds in her rearview mirror that were coming from

304

Light at the Rat Pond

the west. A bigger storm was imminent, she hoped she wouldn't regret leaving her umbrella at the house. A parking spot was available near Kresge's back door, and she swooped in and took it.

She hurried out of her car. The temperature had dropped and the wind was ferocious. She looked to the sky, saw the storm clouds racing at her; lightning flashed, followed quickly by a boom of thunder. Kate rushed to the back doors.

Almost running into an exiting customer, she said, "Sorry," and stepped inside ahead of the storm.

She went right to the paper she needed and found an empty check-out lane. She strode to the rear glassed-doors and could see only sprinkles of fat raindrops hitting the parked cars and lot.

"Gonna make it," she said.

She pushed open a door, checked the alley in both directions before heading to the Impala. The storm brought a darkness that made it seem much later than it was. The wind had lost its ferocity, but still gusted. A flash of lightning and boom of thunder startled her, but she would make it to the car before -

Kate let out an "oomph!" and dropped the bag of paper as the stout man slammed against her side. His strong right arm wrapped around her, and he was in control, steering her away from the safety of her car.

"Kate Murphy," he said. "Been a while."

Overcoming the sudden shock, she jerked and tried to wrench free from his powerful right arm.

"Settle down," he said, still steering her on the wet parking lot. The long-haired man pulled a gun from his brown leather jacket. "You keep it up and I'll shoot you right here. Understand?"

There was a smattering of vehicles parked behind the store, but not a soul to help. Kate quit struggling.

"Good girl."

The fat sprinkles turned to heavy rain, and he hustled them to a car not far from Kate's: a brown Ford.

He forced her inside from the driver's side and shoved her across the vinyl seat. She screamed, "Help!" and reached for the door lock but her trembling fingers weren't fast enough. He thumped her skull with the gun and her head bounced off the passenger window; she cried out and he warned, through gritted teeth, "Shut up! Shut-up-now!"

He looked around as he settled into his seat. Nobody had heard. Pointing the gun at Kate, he said, "Do not make a sound. If you scream again I will shoot you. Do not doubt me."

Kate, struck with fear, looked into the man's wild, hazel eyes, and his anger seemed to shift to demented enjoyment.

Richard Newberry

"So far so good, Kate." He reached under the driver's seat and pulled out a thick roll of gray tape. "Give me your hands."

Kate's heart pounded. "Who are you? What do you want with me?"

He held up the roll of tape and smiled. "I want your hands."

"No."

"Ah, Kate. Don't be like that." He thumped her head again with the gun.

"Ow!" She reached for the side of her head; blood smeared her fingers.

He grinned and said, "Hurts, don't it?"

She winced.

He snapped, "Now give me your hands!"

Tears welled in her eyes. "What are you going to do to me?"

"You'll see. Now give me your hands."

"No."

He raised the gun to hit her again, but stopped and sighed. "You know, you're just gonna make it worse for you - and bad for your son."

"Jack?"

"That's him."

"What about him?" Her fear shifted to anger. "Don't you touch him! Don't you dare touch him!"

The pouring rain pounded the car and washed over the windows, creating a concealing veil around the Ford. He pulled a hunting knife from under his seat, set it next to him. The shiny blade seemed to sneer at Kate. He was eerily calm. "You gotta understand here, you don't tell me what to do." Then he shouted, "Now give me your hands!"

She gave up her hands. He tightly wrapped the wide tape around her wrists, immediately slowing the flow of blood to her pulsing fingers. Lightning flashed and thunder clapped. He grinned at her, said, "Think it'll rain?"

He picked up the wood-handled knife and the blade cut through the tape like a razor. He admired the knife before saying, "My weapon of choice," then locked the seatbelt across her lap.

"Please don't hurt my son."

"That's up to you."

Bewildered and panicked, Kate asked, "Why are you doing this? What have I done to you? Who are you?"

"I'll give you the scoop as we head north."

"Where are we going?"

He brandished the knife, growled, "Shut up!"

She turned and faced forward.

"See. You can do what you're told." He patted her leg. "Good girl," he said, like speaking to a dog.

306

Light at the Rat Pond

The car reeked of stale cigarette smoke and alcohol. She noticed a half-smoked joint stuffed in the overflowing ashtray. The guy wasn't quite six feet, but had the form of a bodybuilder. His eyes and whiskered face showed signs of premature aging, probably from years of rough living. He looked familiar, but she could not place him. "Do I know you?"

He started the car, wiped his side of the windshield with the back of his hand. "Remember this," and in a gruff whisper he said, "See you soon." He laughed.

Kate tried to keep her terror under some kind of control, otherwise she wouldn't be able to think clearly at all. "I don't know who you are."

"You know, it kinda hurts that you don't remember me. I know I've put on a little weight since high school, but I made use of it with the weights in the joint. Got myself in pretty good shape, don't you think?"

She still couldn't remember him.

"Hate it when pretty women don't remember me. Take a better look and I'll give you a hint: Floyd Lappin."

She recognized him instantly, and mentally chastised herself for not doing so earlier, when they were right here behind Kresge and he flipped his middle finger at her and Jack. He was part of the past she couldn't bring to mind when she knew there was someone or something she was forgetting.

"You're Mickey Cook."

CHAPTER 77

"Finally," he said, putting the car in gear. "Not the skinny kid you remember, huh?" He pulled out of the parking spot. "Gave you and your kid the finger from right about this same spot the other day. I knew you didn't know who I was."

Kate wished now she hadn't been so distracted by the storm when she got out of her car; she might've noticed the brown Ford and avoided this trouble. He turned right onto the street and headed north. Despite the heavy rain, he kept the wipers on low to maintain a wet cover. "Now you need to pay attention to what I'm gonna tell you."

Kate looked at him.

"You listening good?"

She nodded.

"Good." He patted her jeans up near her thigh, left his hand there. She jerked her leg away. "Ah, ah, ah. Here's what you need to understand." He grabbed her thigh, held on. "First, I don't want *any* sudden moves from you. None. Got that?"

Kate loathed having Mickey's hand on her, and his strength scared her.

"Two. Keep-your-hands-down. Don't even think about tryin' to show somebody our little bondage thing we got goin'."

She needed to stay focused, but her frantic mind insisted on pulling her back to the night long ago at Parle's Woods.

"Three - you listening?"

She nodded.

"Three." He pointed to a small CB radio mounted under the dash near him. "If you scream or try gettin' attention your way, it'll just take one click on that mic to tell my buddy to take care of Jack when he leaves your neighbor's house. Got it?"

Her mind raced back to the present. "Don't you dare hurt Jack."

"Whoa, Kate, pretty feisty there. I like it. Kinda sexy." He rubbed her thigh. "You've changed since high school, haven't you? You use to be just a sweet cute thing. But I gotta tell ya, and don't take it wrong, you're a whole lot prettier now than you were then. Fine lookin' woman."

Kate remembered Mickey was a talkative kid in high school, which was

308

Light at the Rat Pond

unlike the rough crowd he hung around. She hardly knew him, but never saw him as a threat. She glanced at the knife sitting at his side.

"Oh no you don't. Best to get that thing out of your pretty head – how is your head by the way? Little sore?" He chuckled, then said, "Number four is if you try anything at all to escape, I'll slit your throat right here, right now. Like I said, don't doubt me."

She didn't. His unpredictable moods frightened her.

"My times of threats and just scaring you are long gone." He turned left at a stop light.

"Don't hurt Jack, please."

He patted her leg. "You behave and you won't have to worry about Jack." His hand stayed on her leg.

Repulsed, Kate closed her eyes, tried to block all thoughts.

"You enjoying this?"

She wanted to say, but didn't, that she felt like puking.

He slid his hand down to the knife.

Kate opened her eyes. "What is this all about? Why are you doing this to me?"

He made a turn. "You gotta have some idea. I don't remember you bein' stupid, and I remember you liked usin' people. Are you still that way, Kate?"

"Using people? What are you talking about?" But she knew what he meant.

"Ah, c'mon, don't act all innocent. You're not good at lyin', I tell you that." The light turned red and he had to stop. The only cars near them waited across the intersection. Mickey checked all directions as he waited.

Did she dare jeopardize Jack by screaming and pounding on the window, hoping someone would rescue her? Mickey Cook wasn't the same glib, innocuous kid she remembered from high school. He was now a very scary man. She would not risk Jack getting hurt.

"You used him and you know it. We've all done it. But yours is backfirin' big time. He just can't get over it – or you."

Kate's haunting history had come, as she worried it might, to the present. "It's about Floyd, isn't it?"

"You think?"

"That was a long time ago, Mickey."

"Can't argue that. You'd think he'd moved on, wouldn't you? That guy always had plenty of girls and women." He wagged his head. "But you . . . he can't get out of his stupid head."

"We were just kids."

"Yep. But you knew what you were doin', and Floyd didn't – or didn't want to believe it. You probably didn't expect Floyd to go nuts for you. He ain't one

309

Richard Newberry

to show or tell you much about how he's really feelin', never was. But he fell hard for you."

They turned north onto Route 3, a four-lane artery through Doverville that would eventually dwindle to two outside the city limits. Traffic was most prevalent on Route 3; it would be Kate's best opportunity to somehow try to escape. But what would be the cost?

"If you're thinkin' what I think you're thinkin', best to stop it now." Before she knew it, he picked up the knife, made a swift, two-inch long slit on her forearm. She didn't feel the razor-sharp incision at first, but winced when she saw blood flow out of her. "Next time it'll be your throat."

Her skin began to sting from the cut, and the side of her head throbbed. "What are you going to do to me?"

"You'll see soon enough."

Mickey seemed to idolize Floyd in high school, but never had the genuine bad-boy swagger Floyd had. She didn't think Mickey had the pure viciousness of his idol. Maybe she'd been wrong.

"If you're going to kill me anyway, why shouldn't I start screaming right now?"

He looked at her. "Because of Jack." He looked back to the wet road and said, "Who said I'm going to kill you?"

"I know you. I can identify you. You won't want a witness."

He smiled. "Let me guess, you like those cop shows on TV, right?" He laughed. "How do you know I'm not just gonna do my thing and then head for Mexico? I'm sick of this town anyway. So you'll find out soon enough what you got comin'."

Somehow she had to protect Jack. He was innocent. She wasn't sure she could draw attention because of the rain's cover and drivers paying close attention to the road. She would have to roll down her window, but Mickey would probably kill her before her screams attracted anyone. And if somehow she did alert anyone to her impending murder, would she, even if she gave her life, be able to save Jack? Would the Wonderlins be warned in time to protect him?

"Where are we going?"

"Remember Parle's Woods?"

CHAPTER 78

The rain slowed to light and steady. Mickey snarled at all the red lights he was catching and the pick-up truck stuck to his bumper; he rolled down his window and flipped a finger at the truck behind them, and the driver backed off when the light changed green.

"Better back off," he said, ready to brandish the gun. He said to Kate, "Drivers, huh?"

They drove the speed limit on Route 3. A car like Kate's stayed up with them in the right lane for a block. Kate shifted her eyes toward the Impala's driver; the lighter rain had improved visibility. *Please look, please look, please look.*

Mickey raised the knife, slit her forearm again. "What did I tell you?" He sped past the Impala and settled in the right lane about two car lengths ahead of it. "And don't get blood all over my car."

Kate looked at her wounded. Two tears streaked her face, but she fought back the others. "Why Parle's Woods?"

"It was the beginning of the end there. He thought it'd be the right place to do it."

"Do what? What are you going to do?"

He ignored her, and instead said, "I tried to warn Floyd back then that you were up to somethin'. Told him you were playin' him for some reason. He punched me right in the head as soon as I'd said it. I made sure I had some distance whenever I warned him again."

He lit a cigarette. "Yep. Tried to tell him." He blew smoke in her face. "You were from a better part of town than us, so I couldn't figure out why you'd be all hot and bothered for a boy from the poor side of things. And we were a rough bunch, not what you were used to. He was a good lookin' kid, I'll give you that. Still has some of that left. But I *knew* you was up to somethin'."

The four lanes of traffic began to funnel into two on the outskirts of town. Kate wouldn't give up, but the hope of escape or somebody rescuing her began to fade with the narrowing road.

"I didn't think you was one of those chicks who had the hots for the bad boys, like old - uh, what's her name . . . Imagene. Yeah, Imagene. Remember her?"

"Yes."

Richard Newberry

"That broad was hot for Floyd, I'll tell you that. Man, what a lucky dog. Mickey chuckled and said, "Course I got lucky with Imagene myself."

Kate wasn't surprised.

"But you weren't like her. I knew it. There was somethin' classy about you. Maybe that's what he got all bent out of shape about. He'd never had a classy girl. What were you up to back then?"

"I guess you've been in prison with him."

"Did some time," he said, sounding proud of it.

"So now he's sent you out to do his dirty work, is that it?"

Mickey smiled at her with his yellowing teeth. "Nothing he'd like better than to be here in person. Trust me. But he's gonna be gone a while yet." He returned his attention to the road.

"So like I said, he's making you do his dirty work."

Her choice of words angered him. Through gritted teeth he said, "Nobody *makes* me do anything. Get that straight right now." His hands relaxed on the steering wheel. "Let's just say I owe him big time. He took care of me on the inside."

"Just like high school then."

"How's that?"

"You're his chattel."

She chose that word hoping it would produce the exact response it did.

He looked perplexed, not knowing if he'd been complimented or mocked. "What's chattel?"

She didn't know why she chose to provoke him; maybe to just get even, maybe to get him distracted, giving her a chance for escape. She did take a small amount of pleasure using her next words. "You know, like slave or stooge or peon -"

He punched her hard and square on the temple. She instantly saw twinkling lights, felt dizzy and started to swoon, but somehow willed herself out of the fading light and back to throbbing consciousness.

"I ain't - nobody's - peon! Got that!" He floored the gas pedal, left the closest headlights far behind them. "You better shut your face!"

He eased off the gas, collected himself. It was his turn to get even for her words. "You and Floyd ever get intimate?"

Kate didn't answer.

"He said you did. Said you really liked it." He snapped, "What's wrong?! All out of smart words, Kate?"

She looked out her window at the darkness, knowing that beyond the glass corn and soybean fields stood in the night, and some of the fields belonged to the Hobbs' family, and Andrew had worked those fields. She found no

312

Light at the Rat Pond

encouragement in her thoughts, only despair. The lights of Doverville were long gone; all that remained were the distant headlights of a vehicle far behind them.

When Mickey said, "I think he still loves you," Kate first thought he meant Andrew. "I mean he thought you two were true love, man." His laugh was scornful. "Floyd was blind."

Fifteen minutes to Parle's Woods.

Mickey raised the knife. "You're gonna tell me what you were up to back then. And you're gonna tell me now."

Kate didn't speak.

He cut her again.

"Stop it!"

"Tell me."

The last cut was deeper. Warm blood streamed down her arm and mingled with the blood from the other cuts.

He wagged the knife. "Told you I prefer this. Now tell me."

She knew Irma suspected why Kate had started the Deplorable Indiscretion, but her mom never confronted her with her suspicions, for to do so would've meant Irma having to explain her penchant for "entertaining" a variety of men - right after her husband's death. And in 1970, Irma still indulged in copious lovers.

Steve and Belle, who also had gotten the connection between Irma's trysts and Kate's rebellion, never spoke about either to Kate. The Deplorable Indiscretion was a taboo topic in the Murphy home.

"It was because I hated my mom."

He lowered the knife. "Your mom?"

"Yes." And to her surprise, a sense of relief began to overtake her. Starting to finally confess it felt good, even if the confession would be heard by a gun-toting, knife-wielding ex-con. "She was acting like a hussy after my dad died."

"Your dad died - yeah, I remember hearin' about that. Had a music store or somethin', right?"

"Yes."

"How old were you?"

"Thirteen."

He nodded, frowned, said, "I tell ya, family can mess you up."

Kate dismissed the idea of giving a lecture on personal responsibility to Mickey Cook, knowing it would fall on deaf and dumb ears. "I was a kid, but still shouldn't have done it. There was no excuse for it, but I was angry, very angry. Hateful. Sick to death of the constant parade of men in and out of our house - her bedroom - where my dad had been only a few weeks earlier."

313

Richard Newberry

He shrugged. "Maybe it's the only way she knew how to handle . . . you know . . . things."

Mickey Cook for the defense.

Kate rolled her eyes, then looked at him. "Really?"

"I don't know, I'm just sayin'."

"Right. You're just saying."

"Don't get snotty about it."

Kate shut her eyes, thought back. "So my junior year I chose to use Floyd to get back at her." She opened her eyes, looked straight ahead. "I shouldn't have, but I did."

"I knew it. I knew it. I knew it."

"I pretended to like him. Brought him around to the house so my mom could get a good look. She already knew his reputation, which helped. I wanted her to think things with him were serious. She did, and I guess so did Floyd."

"Yeah, I remember you guys had just started hangin' out and he was already actin' like he was gonna marry you."

She continued confessing, "I didn't set out to hurt him. Like you said, he was good looking and had girls to choose from. And I knew he was tough and mean, so another reason I picked him was because I didn't think I would mean much to him; that he'd get over me quickly."

Mickey thumped his chest twice with his right hand. "Man, you can't go around messin' with a guy's heart. You messed him up good, Murphy."

Great advice on how to treat people from a guy who had kidnapped her at gun point, taped her hands, hit her with a gun, cut and punched her.

"You gave him the bad news that night after the football game, up here at Parle's."

"I did."

Not at all regretfully, but more with pleasure, he said, "You know you got Andy Hobbs killed, don't you?"

CHAPTER 79

Kate's carefully constructed and fervently maintained mental wall, which for the most part had held back shame and guilt for years, collapsed. She squeezed shut her eyes; warm tears traced her face.

"Not good news, huh?"

She raised her taped hands, swiped away the tears; wanted to stab Mickey in the heart.

"Keep your hands down."

She glared at him.

"Was that the first time you met the Hobbs kid?"

Right then, Kate decided she would determine her fate, not this pile of trash next to her. She would provoke him, causing him to accelerate the car; she would lunge at him and send the Ford hurtling off the road and into the dark. He wasn't wearing his seatbelt, so she stood a better chance of surviving the crash. She strained to see beyond the car's lights as she watched for a tree near the road.

"Was it?"

"Was it what?"

"The first night you met Hobbs?"

"Yes."

"He sure sucker punched Floyd."

"No he didn't. Andrew had warned him before it started."

"Not how I remember it."

"Choose to remember your way. I'll choose the truth."

"There goes that smart mouth again." He back handed her. "Watch your tongue, woman."

Kate's bottom lip started bleeding and swelled. She looked in the rearview mirror and noticed the headlights that had been far behind them on the straight, flat road had closed the distance.

"I don't blame Floyd for slappin' you around that night. Sounds like you had more than that comin'. But I gotta say, I don't think that farm boy stood a chance against him. Floyd's one bad dude. But I thought wrong that night."

Andrew Hobbs had noticed her being manhandled outside the bonfire, near

Richard Newberry

the dark of the woods. He approached them, said, "Hey. Hey. Settle down. No need for that. She's a girl."

Floyd glared at him, said, "None of your business - farmer."

"If you don't stop I'm gonna make it my business."

"That so?"

"I don't want trouble -"

"You've stepped right in it," said Mickey.

Andrew said to Floyd, "I just want you to calm down and to quit hurting her."

Floyd shoved Kate toward Mickey and charged Andrew. The kid from the farm didn't look tough, but come to find out, his muscles were hardened by years of farm work, and it quickly became clear Andrew Hobbs knew how to box. Floyd never landed any of his wild punches. Andrew connected with precision, twice, and the fight was over, leaving Floyd crumpled atop scattered leaves.

Mickey released Kate, disappeared.

"You okay?" the dark-haired boy asked her.

Kate nodded.

"You need me to take you somewhere?"

Then she said something very stupid. "No, I'll be okay."

"You sure?"

She wasn't. "Yes."

"Okay," he said, and left in a pick-up truck.

She foolishly left the party with drunk and mean Floyd. It was horribly ugly in his car driving back to Doverville. He was driving erratically and too fast off of the gravel road and onto Route 3's pavement. He lost control and rolled the car. Neither were hurt, and they both went to jail; only Floyd was locked up. Irma came and got Kate.

Mickey was eyeing the headlights approaching them from behind. "Idiot's got his brights on."

Kate, sick from guilt, delayed the plan to provoke him. She had to ask, "What do you know about the night Floyd murdered Andrew?"

Mickey, eyes in the mirror and getting angrier every second at the brights-driver behind him, said, "Like I said he never got over you - or that night at Parle's." The vehicle behind them backed off, dimmed his lights.

"More like it you stupid idiot." Mickey relaxed a little. "So - uh - yeah, Floyd started watchin' you two when you got back from college and got married. I tell ya, he was - like - uh . . ."

"Obsessed."

316

Light at the Rat Pond

"Yeah. Obsessed. And then he made a plan to set up Andy that night at the A & P. Worked good."

She envisioned stabbing Mickey with his hunting knife. "Did you know it was going to happen?"

"Nah. Floyd told me all about it in the joint."

"Was Imagene in on it?"

He crammed the cigarette butt into the overflowing ashtray. "I dunno."

"You don't know?"

"Nope. He never said."

A train horn sounded. Lights began flashing red at the unguarded crossing up ahead. "Can you believe this? I'm gonna make it." He stomped the gas, the car's rear-end swished sideways, then corrected.

"You can't beat that train!"

"Watch me." The speedometer showed eighty five and climbing.

When she'd planned to crash them into a tree Kate thought there would be an outside chance she might survive the impact. They stood no chance against a train, and a survival instinct overcame her. She pounded the dash with her bound hands. "You're going to kill us!"

He bared and gritted his yellowing teeth.

The fast moving train blasted warnings as it neared the crossing.

She considered trying to unlock her door, opening it and hurling herself out into the darkness and any mercy that might be there for her. "Mickey!"

He slammed on the brakes, putting the car into a sideways skid toward the other lane. He somehow corrected the slide and skidded to a stop on the wet pavement before ramming into the speeding train. The crossing bells clanged as the red lights flashed in the dark.

He laughed maniacally. "That was somethin', man!" He pounded his palms on the steering wheel, screamed, "Yeah!"

Kate wondered how much more she could take. "You're an idiot."

He just smiled as he straightened the car. "You know Dillinger said he never tried to rob a bank in Doverville because of all the trains? Figured he'd get hung up by one."

Kate didn't care. She just wanted Mickey dead.

"Man, that was close."

A vehicle pulled right up behind them, put on its brights.

"What the -? This idiot needs to turn off - What's he doin'?"

She glimpsed in Mickey's side mirror a tall, lean man getting out of an old pick-up truck. The man started for the Ford's driver's door.

Mickey brought out the gun, looked at Kate. "You say anything, you're both dead."

317

Richard Newberry

Kate saw the man's torso disappear in the mirror, then there was a knock at Mickey's rain splotched window.

Keeping it concealed, Mickey moved the gun up toward the door as he slowly rolled the window halfway down. He cocked a look out the window. "What's goin' on, old time-"

Reminiscent of the punches Andrew threw that night at Parle's Woods, a single, accurate punch from a large, boney fist knocked out Mickey Cook.

CHAPTER 80

With red lights flashing, signals clanging and the train still rolling, he peered in through the half-open window. "Kate?"

She felt like crying, but held it back.

"You okay?"

"I'm fine."

"You're bleedin' like a stuck pig. Don't give me that bag of moonshine."

The sound of his gruff and gravelly deep voice was music to her ears. Kate looked at her blood-streaked left arm; she smiled at him and said, "Just flesh wounds, Ambrose."

He opened the door and Mickey's upper body slumped out and his head thudded against the wet pavement. With the dome light on now, he pushed back his fedora and got a better look at Kate. "Lord have mercy. We gotta get you to the hospital." A red flush of anger filled his round face. "He hit you?"

She touched her fat lip. "A couple of times. But I'm okay."

"I'll come over there and get you out of that tape. Hold on."

Ambrose "Shorty" Morgan lifted Mickey's head to see if he was still out of it, then dropped his head back to the pavement.

He took a worn but sharp pocketknife from his bibbed overalls and started cutting her free. "I knew he was up to some no good. I can't see none to well, but it didn't look right back there at Kresge. Can you stand up?"

Kate did, and hugged him tight. "Thank you, Ambrose. Thank you." She again fought back tears.

His lean body was rigid, like he didn't have much practice at consoling, but he did pat her back as they stood together in the rain.

She looked up at him. "I think you saved my life."

"Glad I could help, Kate. I'm just lucky my old eyes saw that gun in time."

"Jack," she said suddenly.

"What about him?"

"I've got to call him. He might be in trouble."

"There's a pay phone back at the Sinclair. I'll get you there quicker than greased lightnin'."

He escorted her to his truck where Thelma waited. She gasped when she saw Kate up close, and Thelma was much better at consoling than her husband.

319

Shorty hurried and hog-tied Mickey with the gray tape, then wrapped it around his head twice to cover his mouth. He tossed Mickey over the side of the bed and his restrained body jounced the truck when it landed among all the garden tools in the bed. Shorty turned on the Ford's flashers and jumped into the truck, did a u-turn and raced south.

"Don't get us in a wreck, Ambrose."

"Kate said Jack might be in trouble. Gotta get to a phone."

Thelma looked at Kate. "What's happened to Jack?'

"Nothing - I hope."

Shorty explained how he'd been waiting on Thelma, who'd run into Scott's - a store right next to Kresge, when he saw the long-haired man come up on Kate. "Can't see all that good anyway, and with the rain -"

"I told you to start wearing those glasses we got for you."

"So I told Thelma when she got to the truck we was gonna follow that brown Ford. 'Cause I thought he'd grabbed you."

"I'm very glad you did." Kate worried for Jack, and wouldn't fully appreciate her rescue until she knew if Jack was safe.

Shorty whipped the truck into the Sinclair lot, right by the pay phone, and Thelma handed Kate a coin.

She called Nadine.

Even as a kid he'd liked rainy days, rainy nights. A good storm never scared him, it excited him. He liked the dark that came with storms. It felt . . . cozy. What was that television show about the family with Frankenstein and Dracula . . . oh, *The Munsters*. Yes. They also liked stormy days and nights. He would've fit in with them. They had a blonde niece who was all-American normal, but the rest of the Munster family thought she was the strange looking one.

He was in his secret place, handling the razor-edged Enforcer. He almost got the chance to use it the other day, which made him happy and a little frustrated, because *almost* was never good enough. The Prize had been so close. He closed his eyes to envision It. Yes, he would soon have It.

He opened his eyes when the thunder shook the house above him. He smiled, tried to remember the pretty girl's name from *The Munsters*. Mary? No. Martha? No - Marilyn! That was it. They couldn't see she was the normal one of the family. And because he had mastered deception, nobody could see that he was the monster.

CHAPTER 81

Mickey Cook said he made up the story of having a partner watching me in case things went wrong; it was an effective trick to keep Mom subdued. No evidence turned up pointing to an accomplice, and he never named Floyd Lappin once. Mom told me Floyd and the clan on Star Street, while closely related, were otherwise estranged, and not a threat to us - at least not regarding this incident. Mickey was headed back to prison, and Mom wondered how proud he'd be of his second stint; a much, much longer stay.

I said, "Proud?"

"I'll explain sometime."

Her swollen lip had healed and the knot on the side of her head was gone. The bandages on her arm would be off soon, but tiny scars would remain there. She put up a bold front for me, and I told her to quit trying to pretend being kidnapped, stabbed and beaten was just part of life.

"You're not in the Hell's Angels, Mom."

That brought her first genuine smile since the horrible ordeal. "Can I at least join the Icks?"

I smiled back. "You're way too tough for us."

And she was tough, yet she needed to allow herself time to be scared, sort it all out, talk it out. She lamented her new state of hyper-apprehension and being what she called "overly skittish".

"I'm almost afraid to drive anywhere, or be alone."

"Give yourself a break, Mom. It was a scary thing that happened to you."

I stayed close to home for a while, and she didn't say it - for to do so would've belied her bold front, but I knew she was thankful. A big step on the path back to normalcy for her was when, one evening after supper, she told me why Mickey Cook had done what he did.

I listened and watched as she explained what she called her Deplorable Indiscretion, and I heard and saw the emotional agony she endured while confessing it to me. Grandma Murphy's role was mitigated by Mom's sense of personal responsibility and to protect my feelings toward Grandma. My perception of Mom changed that evening. I finally started seeing Katherine Murphy not only as the correcting, loving mother she was, but also as a kid, like me, capable of making bad choices.

"Jack I need you to say you forgive me – and mean it."

I wondered how she could've secretly carried, for all those years, the heavy burden of self-imposed guilt. I never imagined my mom capable of manipulation and deception. I thought about the pictures of her in the old photo albums, when she was in high school. Now that girl became real to me, and though I felt I deserved the right to be judgmental toward her, I couldn't be.

"Don't blame yourself, Mom."

"But I do, Jack, because it's my fault your dad's not here."

A very small part of me, the indignant part, wanted to say, "You're darn right," but instead, I thought of Will's responses to Cus and Shorty and Stink. "You've always taught me I'm responsible for my choices. So is Floyd Lappin excused from his mean choices because of what you did?"

"I think this is different."

"No it's not. Bad stuff happens to all kinds of people all the time. Bad and good people. So people make good choices, even when the bad comes, right? I love you Mom. And there's nothing to forgive, but if you want to hear me say it, I pure-quill forgive you."

She looked at me for a moment, then smiled and said, "When did my son get so old, and how did he get so wise?"

"I have a good mother – and a good friend from Arkansas."

When Will came to the garage a little later that same evening he again appeared troubled by something.

All the Icks were there, cleaning or fixing racers and cruisers. I cornered Will back by the air compressor. "What's eatin' you, man? I can tell you're not right."

He looked away, bit his bottom lip. When he looked back at me all he said was, "Somethin' I gotta work out on my own, Jack."

"You said that before. I'm your friend, Will."

"And a good one."

"So tell me. Let me" – I pointed at the other busy Icks – "us help."

"I will. I promise. Just give me a little more time to figure it out, okay?" He put on a happier face that made me think of Mom's pretentious boldness of the last few days. "You're not fooling me."

"I know. Just give me time."

I later regretted not pushing him for answers. "Okay. Whatever you want."

"Thanks," and he acted more carefree for the time he was there.

A few minutes later he said, "I gotta go home early."

"What's up?" Tex asked.

Light at the Rat Pond

"Mother's birthday is Saturday, and I'm trying to finish a birdhouse I'm building her."

Kenny, wiping his front wheel's spokes, said, "Won't be dark for a while."

"Yeah, but I need some daylight to see good in our old shed."

I said, "Should of brought it here."

"I thought about it." He loosened a nut to adjust his cruiser's seat. "But I was afraid she'd see me carrying it out. It's almost done."

Dwight worked his radio's dial to get a better reception from WLS. "So how's it looking?"

Will said, "Not bad."

"Let us see it when you're done," said Tex.

"I will."

I joked, "Yes you are."

The Icks got it and laughed.

Kenny said, "Jesus was a carpenter."

Will climbed on his blue racer. He smiled at Kenny and said, "He sure was."

Kenny added, "Wonder if He ever built a birdhouse for His mom?"

"Don't know. Maybe. See y'all tomorrow."

323

CHAPTER 82

The rest of the Icks headed for home a couple hours after Will left. I took a quick shower and Mom scooped ice cream for us. I was rinsing my bowl when the phone rang. I looked at the kitchen clock: one minute till ten. Our phone never rang that late, unless –

"Hello?" Mom answered the phone in the living room.

The late-hour call had my interest, so I was on my way to Mom when she said, "Let me ask Jack, Ruth. Hold on just a moment." She covered the phone's mouthpiece, asked me, "Did Will just leave before you came in?"

"No. He left early."

"How long ago?"

"Couple of hours, maybe."

Instant concern on her face. "You sure?"

I nodded.

Mom looked at the phone in her hand, hesitated, closed her eyes, opened them. She tried to disguise her concern when she said, "Ruth? Sorry it took so long. Jack says he left a couple of hours ago." Mom winced, not wanting to give that news to Ruth.

Mom listened. Her eyes raced with Mother's Worry. She'd nod, say "yes" and "mhm" before looking at me again and saying to Ruth, "Let me ask him." She covered the phone again. "You sure it was that long ago?"

"Positive. He was headed home to work on – something."

"He was?"

"Yes. It's a surprise for her birthday, but tell her to look in their shed."

"Jack said he left early to work on something and he might be in your shed. You already did? Oh."

I asked, "He's not there?"

She waved me off, and said to Ruth, "I see. I see."

I raised my voice. "Will didn't make it home?"

Mom wagged her head.

"They looked everywhere?"

Trying to listen to Ruth, she still managed to nod at me.

I raced to my bedroom, changed into play clothes and headed for the door.

324

Light at the Rat Pond

"Hold on, just a second, Ruth." She cupped the phone and asked, "Where do you think you're going?"

"To find Will."

"You don't –" she caught herself. "Go see if you can find him. But be very careful, Jack."

I hopped on my racer and pedaled toward the Rat Pond, calling Will's name along the way. A locomotive idled near the Gordons' house, waiting to pull the attached cars to their destiny. I saw an open boxcar but knew Will wasn't foolish enough to do that again. I carefully watched both sides of the alley as I hurried to the only place I could think of he might be. He had been foolish enough to go to the Rat Pond at night before by himself, but I thought our warnings and the hobos' tale of Sticks would have been enough to warn him away. Still, it was the only place I knew to look. Maybe he'd lost track of time reading the Bible to Clarence and Arlie.

I slid-stopped at the hill's entrance, dropped my bike. "Will!"

The moon's light illumined only the tops of the trees above the Rat Pond. I cautiously took a step toward the hill. "Will!"

Nothing. No sound from the dark region below me, including the hidden Hoboland.

I took another step. I stood where the hill started its descent. I listened. The night creatures made no sound; the darkness and eerie silence spooked me, but I took another step. "Will!"

If it had been the day, I'd have had a clear view of our race track. As it was, my eyes couldn't penetrate the dark abyss. I took another step, slipped, caught myself.

Suddenly, I thought I could see something below where the track was; something that . . . glowed. My eyes began to adjust, I took another step down the hill. A noise behind me caused me to whip around. Nothing there. I turned back to the Rat Pond, focused on what appeared to be a faintly glowing object.

A strong foreboding menaced from the blackness, warning me not to take one more step. My already thumping heart accelerated. I stood on the hill trying to discern what the glowing object was.

My eyes adapted to the dark enough so that my brain finally recognized what I was looking at. Dread and sickness fell upon me.

At the bottom of the hill, emanating out of the dark, lay a glowing, pearl-white cruiser, and there was no sign of Will.

I raced home. Mom asked if I was sure it was his bike, then made a call she hated to make.

I hurried back to the Rat Pond, despite Mom's protest, to make sure my eyes weren't being tricked. The glow was still there.

Richard Newberry

Headlights from both directions appeared on the alley. Mom pulled up about the same time the Corbens arrived.

"Show me, Jack," said Louis Corben.

Mom stuck close to Ruth; they stayed back from the hill's entrance.

I pointed, said, "There."

Louis had trouble spotting it at first.

I could hear sirens. And before Louis could start down the hill, police cars, with whirling red lights were on the scene. Probing spotlights and flashlights instantly dispelled parts of the darkness below us.

I recognized one of the sheriff's deputies from our barrel-moving night: Officer Decker. I don't think he remembered me. He asked Louis and me, "That the bike?"

"Yes," we said together.

Suddenly there was commotion in Hoboland. Decker shouted to the two other deputies, "Got runners!"

Chaos ensued. Branches snapped and cracked as bodies crashed through the dark thicket in Hoboland. The deputies hurried down the hill; beams from their flashlights bounced all over the race track and toward Hoboland. There was no way of knowing how many hobos were scrambling to escape.

I heard Decker shout, "They're gettin' out the south side! Anybody over there?!"

No.

More crashing bodies and wild lights, then shouting.

"There's one! Stop!"

"I see him! Stop! Stop right there!"

"I ain't done nothin'! I ain't done nothin'! No, sir!"

They'd caught Clarence.

We could hear him protesting behind the jostling lights that were coming up the hill. I heard Decker say, "We'll never catch the other ones."

"I ain't done nothin'!" Clarence was brought up the hill in handcuffs, without his fedora, with a deputy on each side. He saw me on the alley. "Jack! Jack! Tell 'em I ain't done nothin' to nobody." His old eyes were wide and scared, like Arlie's. Where was Arlie? He must have been one of them that got away.

I weakly raised my hand at the tall, skinny hobo.

Mom, startled, said, "You know him?"

"Yes."

While they were stuffing him in the back of Decker's car, Clarence pleaded, "Tell 'em, Jack. I don't hurt nobody." The door was slammed shut; Clarence's eyes begged me to do something to help him.

326

Light at the Rat Pond

A plain sedan with a swirling light on its dash raced toward us from the switchyard. A man, broad-shouldered and slim-waisted with short, wavy dark hair, got out of the car. He strode toward Decker and the others with the confident gait of a man who knew his purpose.

Mom had temporarily forgotten about my acquaintance with Clarence, and fixed her eyes on the good-looking six-footer.

After some hushed discussion with the deputies, the man, dressed in dark slacks and a dark pullover, turned and walked toward us. He nodded and said, "Folks, I'm Detective Gus Calton." His firm approach was mitigated when he saw Mom. "Kate - Katherine? Katherine Hobbs?"

"Yes."

"How have you been?"

"Okay, I guess."

"I heard about that mess with Mickey Cook. Glad you're okay."

"Thank you."

"Is that - are you, Jack?"

"Yes, sir."

Mom explained later that Gus Calton had come to the house the night Dad was murdered.

He broke from familiarity and returned to keen professionalism. "Are you Mr. and Mrs. Corben?"

He took Louis and Ruth aside and questioned them, making notes on each answer. Finished with the Corbens, he came back to Mom and me.

"You found the bike, Jack?"

"Yes, sir."

"Call me Gus."

I was nervous and scared. "Yes, sir."

"Will was with you and your friends until when?"

"About seven thirty. I guess."

"He left earlier than usual?"

"Yes."

"Do you know why?"

I looked to Ruth. Earlier she and Louis had prayed as they stood on the alley among the commotion of flashing lights, questions and squawking radios. She seemed to be aging before my eyes. "He's building a birdhouse for his mom's birthday. He had to finish because her birthday's tomorrow."

Mom winced.

Gus nodded, made more notes, then asked me, "And you know the vagrant who's in the deputy's car?"

"That's Hair- Clarence."

Richard Newberry

"Do you know his last name?"

"No, sir."

"How do you know him?"

"He's always been around, but never bothered us. Will started having Bible readings with him and Eye- Arlie, so Kenny -"

"Who's Arlie?"

"Clarence's friend - and he never bothered us either."

More notes, and then, "You were saying something about reading the Bible."

"Yeah. So Kenny and I helped Will with Bible readings a few times."

"Jack?" Mom said.

"They never bothered us. Ever. And they liked the Bible readings."

Gus continued to question me about our contact with the hobos. Did any of them ever bother us? Did we hang around the area at night? Had I noticed any new or strange vagrants in the area?

I told Gus what we'd heard about one called Sticks. "But we've never seen him."

He seemed interested in Sticks, and made me repeat what I'd told him.

I didn't mention that Will had been noticeably bothered by something lately because I didn't know what it was. I wondered if Louis and Ruth had noticed their son's unusual demeanor.

"Okay, Jack," said Gus. "You've been helpful. Thanks."

I nodded.

"I want you and your friends to be careful around here until we figure this out. Okay?"

"We will."

Mom said, "I'll make sure of it."

He nodded and walked to the deputy's car where fidgeting Clarence waited.

I had one big question. Where was Will?

CHAPTER 83

At daybreak the Rat Pond area was thoroughly searched again. The Icks stood and watched the activity from the alley outside the garage. Police, some with dogs, and neighbors scoured the hillsides on both sides of the tracks. Busybodies slowing for a look on Warren were quickly ordered to move on.

Dwight didn't turn on his radio that morning. The Icks were lost in a strange land, not knowing where to go or what to do. Like Ruth Corben the night before, we had aged overnight.

I said, "I knew he wasn't at the Rat Pond as soon as I could tell it was his cruiser."

Tex asked, "How'd you know that?"

"It wasn't on its kickstand. Will always uses his kickstand."

Dwight's hands were jammed in his back pockets. "Where could he be?"

"Could be bad," said Kenny.

We looked at him.

"Sorry."

"It's okay, man," said Dwight. "You just said what we're all thinking."

Mom came out to check on us. "You all stay close."

"We will," I said.

"I'm going to be with Ruth. Call there if you need me." She reminded me, "And don't you go anywhere."

To think something bad might have happened to Will made me sick. I was in a fog, detached, unable to think clearly. I got on my cruiser and turned small circles on the alley.

Kenny said, "Maybe he hopped a train again."

"No way," said Tex.

"Yeah," said Kenny, drooping his head. "I wish he was here."

We all did.

Kenny and Tex got their cruisers and circled with me. Dwight stood on the alley, watching the searchers. I knew his impressive mind was at work.

"What are you thinking?"

"I don't know, Jack."

"You're thinking something."

329

Richard Newberry

He scratched at his burgeoning afro. "I'm trying not to think what I'm thinking 'cause it isn't good."

I didn't want more bad thoughts than I already had, so I left it alone.

Some searchers had made it to the hillsides behind our house. We saw Louis and Shorty and Van among them.

I said, "I don't think it was a hobo."

The Icks agreed, but Dwight added, "What about that one - Sticks?"

"Maybe," I said. "I told Detective Calton about him. But we've never seen him around."

"Doesn't mean he didn't do something," said Tex.

"Yep, I know." I stopped circling. "Here's the thing. I don't think Will was at the Rat Pond. I think his bike was pushed down the hill."

Dwight asked, "So what are you sayin'?"

"I'm not sure."

Tex said, "Could've been Cus."

"He hates Will," said Kenny.

No doubt Cus stood atop the list of suspects.

Tex said, "There's somebody else we should think about."

We looked at her. "Stink."

"Stink?" I said.

She nodded.

Dwight said, "He's sneaky and a rat, but he's a chicken rat. I don't think he'd do anything like this."

"Maybe," she said. "But don't bet against it."

In the silence that followed I noticed while most of our world was focused on finding Will, others carried on with their routine, oblivious to the travail in our hearts and minds. Customers pulled in and out of Sid's, the switchyard clanged and banged, traffic rolled on Route 150, and the birds and insects went about their business. It somehow didn't seem right to me.

I just blurted it out. "You think he's dead?"

More silence.

The next morning we knew.

CHAPTER 84

The morning came hot and sunny, and I was doing something I never did on summer Saturday mornings unless rain forced me inside: watching reruns of cartoons. Yet I really didn't pay attention to what was happening on the screen.

Mom was playing Chopin's melancholy *Raindrops* in the parlor when the phone rang; she hurried to the living room, answered on the second ring. "Hello?"

Seconds later the blood drained from her face. She looked at me and listened to the caller. Her moist, green eyes let loose with tears that streaked her pale skin.

I turned off the TV. I knew without hearing it that my friend Will was gone forever. Mom nodded and spoke softly into the phone. I went to my room and cried.

Railroaders near Chicago had discovered Will's body inside an empty boxcar. The boxcar was part of a train that had pulled out of our switchyard; the train that sat idling on the tracks the night I was calling out for Will.

I had heard of death. Young and old were dying in Vietnam, students were killed at Kent State, Mom spoke of relatives I'd never met who'd died and Dad was murdered. I didn't *know* any of those people. I therefore did not have an opportunity to love them. The blatant ugliness of death had suddenly and crudely invaded my life. I was not prepared for it. We had lost another Ick - forever.

Parents tried to shield the Icks from the details of the gruesome acts inflicted upon Will, but we found out anyway. And what we found shattered our already broken hearts. We were introduced to an evil that sickened us. Will had been molested, strangled and stabbed.

The Icks were banished from hard-road riding, exploring and the Rat Pond. Kenny could only ride to the garage if he had a friend along. Melba insisted Dwight carry, at all times, our old Louisville Slugger for protection while coming to the garage. I would meet him on the tracks below Sid's carrying my own bat. After supper, the Icks were confined to our yards. Night-time excursions were prohibited. The knowledge of lurking danger paralyzed our neighborhood; the heinous crime had ended our liberty and Will's life.

Richard Newberry

The first day at the garage after we learned of the atrocity perpetrated against Will, Kenny said, "I want to kill whoever did it."

"Get in line," said Tex.

Dwight asked, "Who could do something that sick?"

"I don't know," was all I could say. "I don't think even Cus has that in him."

"Had to be that Sticks cat," said Dwight.

Tex, sitting on her racer, said, "It's pretty creepy knowing some sick freak came around here and did this. I want revenge."

"Yeah," said Kenny.

Dwight said, "I guess they've still got Hairy locked up."

"Yep," I said. "It's in the paper. But there's no way he did it. No way."

Tex said, "What about Eyeballs?"

"Arlie?" I questioned. "Nah, I don't think so. He never bothered us either."

"Yeah," said Kenny.

"They're gonna put it on Hair- Clarence if they don't come up with somebody else," said Dwight. "You watch."

"It can't be him," I said. "And I don't think it was a hobo that did it."

"Why not?" asked Tex.

I didn't have an answer - yet.

We were allowed to ride the alley between our house and the bakery, so we pedaled toward the bakery. Looking at his garden as we rode past, Shorty suddenly appeared at his burn barrels. He raised a hand to stop us.

His saving Mom had changed our - even Dwight's - view of the curmudgeon. He still had a crustiness toward us, but it was far less combative. We stopped in front of him.

Below his straw fedora, Shorty squinted his gray eyes, took a deep drag from a cigarette before crushing the butt with his brown boot. He tipped back the fedora, exposing the distinct line between weathered, dark skin and the start of white scalp. He hooked his long thumbs into the straps of his overalls, cast his eyes downward, then up to us.

"Sorry for your loss," he said. "Will was a good boy, meant well for everybody. Never met a soul like him. It's a shame what happened to him." His deep, gravelly voice was breaking, but he caught himself. "Terrible shame."

He started for the garden, but stopped. "I reckon whoever done such a thing to Will better pray the police catch him before I do. And that ain't no bag of moonshine."

CHAPTER 85

It was the night of Will's visitation.

The shock and heartache that had oppressed me the days immediately after Will's murder now had to contend with a growing anger that I aimed at people and God and . . . Will. My dead friend's idea about good coming from bad, that the ugliness in life was sometimes necessary to open our eyes to unforeseen beauty, had become, to me, absolute nonsense.

I wanted revenge. I wanted the murderer to pay with his life, and I would gladly exact payment from the beast. Anger drove me to a relentless pursuit to find Will's killer. The police were convinced Clarence had done it, but I knew they were wrong. I accused Curt Lewsader with a glare each time I saw him. I waited for Cus to show his ugly face in our neighborhood again; when he did, I'd go after him. The mysterious Sticks no longer frightened me. If I ever saw the red-bandana-wearing hobo I would beat him with my Louisville Slugger, then question him.

But anger was a heavy thing to carry around, and by the night of the visitation, I had become weary from the weight and lack of sleep, and frustrated by not knowing the truth.

Mom sat next to me on the couch. She wore an ankle-length, dark dress, which made her look modest and elegant at the same time. "Are you about ready?"

"I guess." I had on the same clothes I wore the first time I went to church with the Corbens. That morning, when I flopped into Rebecca's lap, seemed so long ago.

She hugged me, as she often did lately.

"Mom?"

"Yes?"

"Will's in heaven, right?"

Because she had her own issues with God, the legitimacy of her answer was in question. "He was a good boy. I'm sure that's where he is."

I didn't have the energy to tell her that Will said just being good wasn't good enough. "He really believed in heaven."

"I know he did."

I looked at her. "I know how you feel now."

333

"What do you mean?"

"I'm mad at God like you are."

"Jack, I never said –"

"It's okay. I get it. I hope someday you'll quit blaming yourself for what happened to Dad. Wasn't your fault. But I guess we expect more from God."

She traced her fingers over my back, didn't say anything for a moment, then said, "Don't be mad at God, Jack. It's no way to live."

"You are."

"Maybe not so much anymore."

"Really? Why?"

Any doubt I had regarding Mom's earlier answer about heaven would not accompany her next answer. "I don't know if it's any one thing. It's hard to explain, Jack. But I'm beginning to think I've been wrong . . . about different things."

"Like being mad at God?"

She shrugged. "I don't know. Maybe."

I thought back to how often Will spoke to Mom about Jesus and God and Bible things, and how whenever he spoke about Them to anyone, there was never a shadow of doubt in him or his telling. Will Corben was pure quill, and Dwight was right: our friend from Oxley changed things.

Mom asked, "You ready?"

I couldn't stay mad at Will. In a sometimes uncertain, dark and scary world, he always brought goodness, even now. "I'm ready."

Mom said, "Look at all the cars."

The Corbens had moved north a little more than three months ago, yet the funeral home's parking lot was full.

"Think they're all here for Will?"

She said, "I wouldn't be surprised."

We parked, and I noticed a bike leaning against the building's white brick. Mom asked again, "You ready for this?"

"Yes."

There were two visitation rooms; we walked through a smattering of people outside the first one, but people were crammed into the hall outside the second room. We stood in line several minutes to reach the guest book. After Mom signed our names, we proceeded slowly toward the doorway that led to Will's body.

The configuration of the large room combined with the long line prevented me from getting an overview of everyone there. I wouldn't glimpse the casket

Light at the Rat Pond

for several minutes, but I did see people from Will's church that I recognized. I didn't see any of the Icks or Ick parents, but I did notice, ahead of us, an older kid that looked out of place among the well-dressed visitors in his scruffy jeans and white shirt. I did not recognize him from behind, and assumed it was one of Rebecca's friends.

"Hey, Kate." We turned to see Nadine and Texal Wonderlin.

Mom squeezed hands with Nadine as Texal said, "Hello, Katherine. Jack."

Next to Texal stood Tex; she had on a dark blue dress. I tried not to stare, and nodded her way. "Hey."

"Hey back," she said. Tex wore the vacant, uncertain look that all the Icks had worn from time to time the last several days. And I knew, like me, it felt uncomfortable and surreal for her to be standing in a funeral home, waiting to see the body of a friend.

Mom asked, "Where's Cheryl?"

"Babysitter," said Nadine. I wondered if she would be her usual buoyant, talkative self, but she wasn't. And her restrained decorum, while appropriate, caught my attention like her daughter's dress had.

Mom visited quietly with the Wonderlins as the line moved. Pretty soon we were through the doorway and the sweet aroma of a room full of beautiful bouquets greeted my nose. I was sure Stankard's Florist had been used for many of the flowers; I wondered if Stink and his parents would come.

I could now see a little more than before. The large, main room with the casket was painted white and had dark maple trim. Flowers were everywhere. The chairs were full in the small enclave just off the main room, where people chatted; sometimes I heard a laugh, and there were more smiles than I expected. I saw kids from school with their parents, and the Gordons were in line talking to Thelma and Shorty. I got a better look at the back of the older kid I didn't recognize, and felt sorry for him because of the butchered haircut somebody had given him for the occasion. The long line looped left and then passed in front of the polished, light gray casket. The casket was open, but I still couldn't see Will.

Mom said to me, "The Hooks are here."

I turned and waved at Kenny. His dread of crowds was acting up, he could barely raise his arm to wave back for fear he'd draw attention to himself.

I asked Mom, "Have you seen Dwight yet?"

"Not yet. But they'll be here."

Most of the folding chairs in the main room were occupied. A few of the women dabbed white handkerchiefs and tissues at the corners of their red eyes, some folks sat quietly watching other folks, but the majority of the people were engaged in lively conversation. The mood of the place wasn't what I had imagined. I looked toward the casket, and saw what was defining the mood.

335

Richard Newberry

At the head of the casket stood the Corben family, greeting folks with their genuine, warm smiles. Bobby fidgeted a little, and Rebecca, beautiful as ever in a black and white dress, looked a little overwhelmed. Louis and Ruth embraced and shook the hands of friends, family, acquaintances and strangers. I had watched Ruth age on the alley the night we found Will's cruiser at the Rat Pond. Now, with the body of her oldest son next to her, in a casket, she was vibrant and beautiful again. The Corben parents had a right to look a little worn, and they did, but from what I could see from my place in line, they were comforting those who had come to comfort them. I knew that the Corbens' poised and benevolent presence was pure quill; that was what they were, because what they possessed was pure quill.

We made it through the line's loop and were moments from seeing Will. The kid with the bad haircut must have been alone, for he was sandwiched between two well-dressed men. The kid was four people from the Corbens. I stepped out of line to get a better look at him.

No way. It couldn't be.

I took a step forward.

Mom whispered, "What are you doing?"

I took two more steps.

"Jack, get back in line."

I had to see. I took several steps until I was standing next to the kid. "Cus?"

"Hey, Hobbs."

CHAPTER 86

I was stunned.

Cus stood at the foot of Will's casket; I stood next to Cus, staring at him with my mouth open, and not knowing what to say. With a good bath, bad haircut and an attempt to be presentable, he didn't look the same. The lazy eye was the same, more noticeable without long bangs draped down his forehead and face, but I could see where Cus, in this groomed condition, would have no trouble attracting girls.

"Take a picture, Hobbs. It lasts longer."

"What are you doing here?"

"Free country."

I lowered my voice. "You hated him. What are you up to?"

"None of your business, that's what."

I noticed he was squeezing something in his right hand. "What's that?"

"Like I said, none of your business."

"You try anything in here and you'll be dead."

He looked around, then back at me and said, "Guess I'm in the right place."

I didn't want any ugliness to break out, so I tempered my voice. "C'mon, man. What are you going to do?"

"I owe him."

"Not here, Cus."

"You don't know what you're talkin' about, Hobbs."

The line moved, and I said to the man behind Cus, "I'm sorry. I'm not cutting in line. I just wanted to talk to him."

The man said, "It's okay. You can get in front of me and talk to your friend if you want."

Friend? I said, "Thank you," and got behind Cus, worried about what he was about to do.

My preoccupation with Lappin had so distracted me that when I looked ahead and saw Will in the casket it startled me. Twice in two minutes I had been surprised by transformed appearances. Will didn't look like my magnanimous friend from Oxley; death had made the boy in the casket look . . . fake, like a wax figure of the real Will.

337

Richard Newberry

I started to feel light headed, but gathered myself when I remembered something Will had said to me.

"We're just hangin' out in these bodies, Yank. You know that?"

"I did not."

"Yep. It may not seem like it to you, but just like me you're dyin'."

"That's really good news, Will."

He smiled. "It's the truth. Square dinkham. But I don't worry at all about it. Know why?"

"Nope."

"'Cause someday I'll have a body that's forever. And that body will be better than Superman's."

Now looking at the pasty vessel that had been Will, I preferred to imagine him in his new, supernatural body, gracing the heavenlies with the same friendliness and love I had known on earth.

Cus raised his hand to the light gray casket.

"What are you do-?"

He ignored me as he gently placed the object atop the casket.

I looked from the object to him, then looked back at the object before asking him, "You make that?"

"Yep."

It was a small, neatly carved cross; lashed together by thin strips of brown leather.

Before I could comment on the excellent carving, Cus nodded at the Corbens, and they smiled back. He left without saying a word to them. He turned back to me and mouthed, "Meet me outside."

I nodded.

I was next in line. I stared at the cross, wondering what in the world?

Ruth said, "That's very nice, isn't it, Jack?"

"Yes. He made it."

Louis said, "Well, he's done some carving before, that's for sure."

Rebecca asked, "Who is he?"

All the Corbens, including Bobby, were surprised when I told them it was Cus Lappin.

Ruth and Louis turned for another look, but he was gone. Ruth said, "So that was Cus?"

"Yes."

Will's parents' look of surprise slowly shifted to questioning frowns before settling into faces of knowing as they smiled at Will. Louis said to Ruth, "He never stopped, did he?"

338

Light at the Rat Pond

It looked as though Ruth would cry, which made me well up and cry. She pulled me to her, hugged me. I said, "I miss him so much."

I heard her sniff. "So do we, Jack."

Rebecca said, "You were his best friend, Jack."

That didn't help me to stop crying.

Louis put his hand on my back and said, "He loved you like a brother."

That didn't help either.

Mom came to my side, held my hand and said, "It's okay. It's okay."

It took a moment to compose myself. Ruth handed me tissues from a nearby box, and Bobby said, "Hey, Jack."

I wiped my nose and eyes. "Hey, Bobby."

I looked again at Will, then my eyes traveled to Cus's cross. What had happened between the two of them? I looked one more time at my friend -.

"Where is it?" I asked.

Ruth said, "Where's what, Jack?"

I pointed to Will's neck. "The crucifix he always wore."

Louis looked to Ruth and said to me, "It was gone when he . . . came home."

Cus.

I went to find him.

339

CHAPTER 87

The August night was warm and muggy; Cus sat on the bike with his arms folded across his chest.

I got right to what I was thinking. "Did you take his cross?"

"What?"

"The crucifix he always wore. Did you take it off of him?"

"When would I do - you're thinkin' I did it? I killed Corben?"

"Everybody knows you hated him. They heard the threats. I was there when you ran up the hill to stab Dwight, but you were there to kill Will." It hit me I was accusing him of murder and didn't have a bat or rocks or any weapons of defense, and he might've been carrying another knife. But my sense of vulnerability was overcome by my outrage. "Why are you here? What's with that cross you made?" I stepped closer.

He didn't flinch, and said, "Back off, Hobbs. You're an idiot if you think I killed him."

"You were out to get him, Lappin. Don't act all innocent."

He unfolded his arms and grasped the black handlebar grips. He looked away from me and seemed to be watching the one-way traffic passing in front of the funeral home. "I didn't touch him."

"You're a liar."

I expected venom as he turned back to me, but he just plainly said, "No I'm not. I'm not a liar. I'm a lot of things, Hobbs, but I don't lie on purpose."

I frankly didn't know what to say to that.

"I know who I am, and it ain't good sometimes, but it's what I know. Here's what you need to know before you go blamin' me for what happened to Corben."

He folded his arms again. "Remember the first time I saw him at that little race track of yours?"

I nodded.

"I thought he was a sissy or somethin' like that. I wanted to pound his face in. Then at the baseball game he just got under my skin, and I wanted to beat on him so bad."

Will obviously struck something visceral within Cus, something that stirred up instant hatred for the new kid.

340

Light at the Rat Pond

He dropped his hands to his lap. "I get that way. Can't help it. So after you guys ganged up on me, I really wanted to hurt all you guys - bad, especially Corben. I kept watchin' and waitin'. Bet you didn't even know I was around."

"Nope."

He nodded, seemed proud of his sneaking ability. "I was gonna cut him up when I saw you guys on the tracks, I'll admit that. I wouldn't kill him, just wanted to mess him up, scare him bad. You saved his and Dwight's butts."

I glanced at his wrist.

He raised his right arm, rubbed his wrist. "You didn't break it. But you hurt it good." He put his hands back on the handlebars. "I owe you payback for that one, Hobbs."

"It was your own fault."

"Maybe. Maybe not."

I was glad I didn't understand how his mind worked.

He asked, "You got my knife?"

"Yep."

"Figured. Keep it - for now."

"Really?"

"Yep. So then one night before dark, guess who comes ridin' down my street?"

"Hell's Angels?"

"You're funny, Hobbs." He wagged his head, as if still not believing who was riding toward him. "Here he came on that white bike with the wooden cross steering wheel. I couldn't believe he was there. I'm thinkin' he's either lost or an idiot, but for sure he's gonna wish he'd never ended up on my street."

"Are you serious? He rode to your house alone?"

"Uh huh."

"What happened?"

"He rides up to me, says he's sorry for all the - what'd he call it? 'Ugly business.' Yeah. Says he'd like to try to be my friend."

"You're kidding me?"

"Told you I'm not a liar, Hobbs."

"What did you say?"

"Started cussin' at him, told him not to ever come around my neighborhood with his sissy talk. I picked up some rocks and started throwin' 'em at him; told him I didn't want to ever be his friend, and if he ever came back I'd kill him."

The Morgans came out of the funeral home and headed toward Thelma's big Buick. Shorty spotted us, said something to his wife and she walked on to the car as he peeled away and strode toward us. He wore a brown suit with a brown fedora. He eyed Cus and asked me, "Everything okay here?"

341

Richard Newberry

"Yeah," I said. "It's good."

"You sure?"

"Yep."

"Better be." He nodded once and walked away.

Cus said, "Heard he saved your mom from some kidnapper. That had to be wild."

"He did and it was." I left it at that. I wanted to know about Will. "So what did Will do?"

"He left. But he was back in two days."

Will had said nothing to me about dropping in on Cus. "He was?"

"Yeah. He was."

"What did he want?"

Cus looked off, like he was trying to recreate the scene in his mind. "I was on my bike this time, and he comes ridin' down the street, wearin' that stupid smile. Before I can even start cussin' him, he tells me how he's been prayin' for me, and starts goin' on about Jesus and Bible stuff. I start headin' right for him, pedalin' as fast as I can, plannin' on rammin' right into him."

In the shadow of the funeral home where we stood, Cus looked at me and I could see his demeanor soften. "I couldn't figure him out. But I began to quit thinkin' he was retarded or stupid. I'm ready to slam into him and beat him to death, and he's just sittin' in the middle of the street on his bike, smilin' and talkin' about Jesus and wantin' to be friends with me." He wagged his head, still not believing Will's actions.

"What did you do?"

"Ran him off again."

"Will was pure quill, Cus."

"Pure quill? What's that?"

"The real deal. Genuine. Not fake."

"Yeah. I guess he was. And I decided he was one of the bravest people I ever met. I take that back. He was *the* bravest person I've met."

Cus hung his head, spoke quietly when he said, "That kid seemed to really care about me. It wasn't about him wanting to suck up and not have to worry about me comin' after him." He looked up at me. "You know?"

The vulnerability coming from the voice of the meanest kid I knew stunned me. I could have never imagined the kid I dreaded, the kid who beat Will with his fists, had in his soul any room for compassion.

I just listened.

"Probably not much of a thing for you, Hobbs," he said softly. "But I ain't had a lot of the carin' kind in my life. There ain't been nobody treat me like Will Corben did." He gazed toward the street again. "After I chased him away

Light at the Rat Pond

the second time I couldn't stop thinkin' about what he did. Why would anybody come back to try to be my friend after I promised to beat him good?"

I said, "I don't know," but I thought I knew.

Staring straight ahead he said, "There ain't never been anybody treat me like Will Corben did. And I ain't feelin' sorry for myself, just sayin' what's real. But it was like he . . . cared about me. Somehow he believed I was worth him gettin' his head beat in again. That's what I ended up thinkin'. He thought I was worth somethin'." He looked at me. "Can you believe that?"

Chopped hair, white button-down shirt and all, Cus seemed a different boy in that moment. "Yeah, I can. He was special, Cus."

"Yeah, he was." Suddenly, the softness in his voice and face were gone; replaced by a hardness and edge I expected from him. "It ain't right what happened to him. And you need to know somethin'."

"What?"

"There's some dude out there in your neighborhood ain't who they're pretendin' to be. You got a real rat close by. A bad one."

CHAPTER 88

"Who is it?"

"Don't know."

"How do you know about him then?"

"Juvie."

I saw the Flowers' Pontiac pull in off the street. "You heard about him in juvie?"

"Yeah. Said the guy likes to do nasty stuff to kids, like what happened to Will."

"Who said it?"

Cus shrugged. "Just some kid. I didn't know him."

"How do you know he's not making it up?"

"'Cause the kid was scared, Hobbs. And what he said that dude did to him ain't somethin' you go around braggin' about."

"So why'd he tell you?"

"Got me. Like I cared. But this kid . . . I don't know. Like I said, he was scared, man. He said the dude said he would kill his family first and then torture him if he said one word about what he'd done to him. Kid said the guy had a scary lookin' knife, kept actin' like he was gonna cut him up."

"Will was cut up."

Cus nodded.

I met Dwight's eyes as he walked toward the funeral home with his family, I nodded his way. My big friend fixed his eyes on the kid on the bike, and Dwight looked puzzled.

Cus said, "I'd heard stuff in juvie before about some guy around Doverville havin' it for kids."

"How did that kid know where the guy lives?"

"Said he was in the car with his mom on 150 headed for town, and saw the rat mowin' his yard."

My mind was whirling. "Where? Which yard? Which side of 150?"

"I don't know, Hobbs. He said all he could remember was it was past the school somewhere."

"Did he say what he looked like?"

"Nope. And I didn't ask."

344

Light at the Rat Pond

"He didn't tell his mom?"

"Guess not. Like I said, he was scared bad tellin' me. But it seemed like him tellin' me made him feel better. I don't know, and I really didn't care. But I didn't forget it."

Van and Lilly Gordon were walking to their car, and Van gave me a quick wave; I returned it.

"I know the cops think some bums did it to Will," said Cus. "But I ain't sure."

"I don't think so either. But there's this one they call Sticks, and he's suppose to be a mean one. Likes to cut people."

"That right?"

"That's what they say." But I had doubts about Sticks's involvement, especially now that I had Cus's scary story, reliable or not; I felt anxiety building in me. I said more to myself than Cus, "Somebody in the neighborhood." The name that came to me was Curt Lewsader.

"Just tellin' you what I heard in juvie. And the thing is, Bad is usually the first to know what other Bad is up to."

Kenny and Tex came around the corner of the building.

Cus spotted them. "Looks like Retard and Barbie are lookin' for you." He said, "Keep your eyes open, Hobbs," and pedaled away.

When Kenny got to me he asked, "Was that Cus?"

"Yep."

"Thought so," said Tex. "What was he doing here? What were you guys talking about?"

I said, "You're not going to believe it."

Frank Kiss, owner of Kiss Disposal and our neighborhood's garbage man, had an eighty-five-year old uncle who had never tried water skiing, and he decided it was never too late to try. His lethal heart attack on Doverville Lake was the reason Frank was a day late emptying the burn barrels along our alley. And Frank's delay led to the evidence we found, which gave credence to Cus's story.

Two evenings after Will's burial, Tex, Dwight and I - Kenny was on vacation in Florida with his family - were cruising the short strip of the alley we were allowed to ride on, when the roar of revving car engines grabbed our attention.

"Look," said Tex, pointing across the tracks.

We stopped and watched an unfamiliar blue SS Chevelle running alongside

Richard Newberry

Spencer's orange Super Bee on Warren. Both drivers took turns goosing their powerful motors.

"Gonna be a race," I said.

"I'd pay to see it," said Dwight.

The cars headed west and out of sight, to a strip of road north of us.

Tex said, "Think Rick will win?"

"Probably," I said.

Dwight turned on his radio, and turned it up when he heard Stevie Wonder's voice. "Man, it's hot. Wish we could go to the switchyard for a cold one."

I checked my pockets. "I got money for a pop. We'll split it."

"Sounds good," said Tex.

Stuffing the dime back in my pocket, I noticed something through the bottom breathing holes of the burn barrel we were parked near. I got off of my bike for a better look at the partially-burned picture. I bent down, peered in, jumped up. I looked at the house.

Tex asked, "What's in there?"

Still eyeing the house, I said, "Look in there."

They climbed off their bikes, peeked in.

"Oh, man," said Dwight, now also looking at the house.

Tex said, "It's one of those nasty pictures like we saw at the Rat Pond."

After I told the Icks Cus's juvie story, we had focused on Curt Lewsader as the likely guy. Now we stood shocked, staring at the house before us.

CHAPTER 89

At the garage, I said, "Should we tell somebody what's in there? It'll probably be emptied tomorrow."

Dwight said, "Even if we tell somebody, what are they going to do with burnt pages from a nasty magazine? It's no proof of anything."

"It's the same kind of picture we found in that really nasty magazine at the Rat Pond," said Tex. "People shouldn't look at that stuff."

"But they do," said Dwight.

With a look of disgust, she said, "Sickos."

I asked, "Are those kinds of pictures against the law?"

Dwight shrugged. "I don't know."

"Should be," said Tex.

Dwight's radio was off. The abundant cicadas' chant filled the August evening's air. I said, "Somebody else might've dumped that magazine in his barrel."

"Not impossible," said Dwight.

None of us could believe whose burn barrel we found it in.

"And like I said, it doesn't prove anything."

Tex and I agreed, but considering Cus's story . . . we now had to be wary of a new suspect.

"Wait a minute," I said.

They looked at me; Dwight asked, "What?"

"Doesn't he drive a Torino?"

"Yep," said Dwight.

I said, "It has square taillights."

"You're right."

"So?" said Tex. "A lot of cars do."

I looked at her. "Remember the car that sat on the alley above the Rat Pond on our campout night?"

"Yeah - it had square taillights. And he threw something in the Rat Pond."

"Yep," I said.

Dwight said, "Still not enough proof, Jack."

"It starts to add up, Dwight. I can't believe it might be him either, but we can't ignore what we know."

347

Richard Newberry

Tex asked, "What can we do about it?"

They looked at me. "I don't know. But we gotta try something."

Then I remembered. "Will's crucifix."

"What about it?" said Tex.

"I noticed Will didn't have it on at the funeral home. His mom and dad don't know where it is. They said it wasn't on him when they first saw his body."

Dwight said, "Could've been lost somewhere during the . . .you know."

"Maybe," I said. "But I'll bet whoever killed Will has it, like a souvenir or something. I've read about stuff like that."

Tex said, "Like the Zodiac Killer?"

"Maybe. I don't know."

Dwight said, "You're right though, Jack. We gotta do something. They've got Clarence locked up and he didn't do it."

I nodded.

"I might have an idea," said Tex.

We listened.

"I noticed his car is always gone by eight o'clock on Saturday nights this time of year. I think it's bowling night or something."

"Yeah," I said. "You're right. I've seen him carrying bowling bags to the car on Saturday nights."

She said, "I don't know when he gets back, but I know it's after ten. I noticed that when we used to get to stay out later. So we could sneak in the house sometime after eight this Saturday and look for Will's crucifix."

"Yeah," I said, feeling like we were finally getting somewhere. "And the house would be empty."

"Let me get this straight," said Dwight. "You two wanna go live with Nicky in prison by breaking into a house, to try and find a little crucifix that might not be there. Is that it?"

Tex was smiling. The very idea of a daring break-in had her excited. "We won't get caught."

"I've told you before that's what all the guys in prison have said."

"I know it's risky," I said. "But like you just said, we've got to do something."

"I wasn't thinkin' about a felony, Jack."

"I don't think it's a felony, is it?"

"Does it matter? We could go to jail."

"Probably just juvie," said Tex.

"I don't want no part of any of it: juvie, jail, prison . . . none of it. 'Cause if it didn't kill my mother, me gettin' locked up, she'd kill me when I got out."

I said, "You got another way, Dwight?"

"I don't know. Not right now."

348

Light at the Rat Pond

A sheriff's car cruised toward us on the alley. Every evening since Will's body was found, deputies had made at least two slow passes back and forth, about an hour apart. The car stopped at the garage; it was Officer Decker.

He rolled down his window and we walked to the car. "How you guys doing?"

We told him okay.

"Good. Need to ask you something. You guys ever see or hear about a transient called Sticks? They say he's always wearing a red bandana."

We told him what we had heard but that we had never seen Sticks. "I told Detective Calton about him the night we found Will's bike."

"Who told you about him?"

Dwight and Tex eyed me; I said, "Clarence."

He nodded. "Well keep your eyes open for him, but don't approach him, okay?"

We said we would, and he started to pull away but stopped. "What did you guys do with those oil barrels anyway?"

We told him about Tex's fiery jump, and that we returned them to Cline's afterward.

"How many barrels?"

"Six," Tex said proudly.

"Not bad," he said, and continued his patrol.

"Sticks didn't do it," I said to Tex and Dwight. "Should've I said something about what we know?"

"No," said Dwight. "We don't have enough yet."

Tex said, "That's why we have to check in his house, Dwight. Jack and I will do it. You won't have to."

"Yeah," I said, nodding at Tex, then looking at Dwight. "You're right about not doing that to your mom. If something would happen and you'd get caught, it'd be bad for her."

"I'm not scared to do it," he said.

"We know," said Tex.

"You're smart," I said. "Thinking about your mom is right."

He said, "It ain't gonna be like heisting cakes at the bakery."

"I know," I said. "But you know the cops aren't going to listen to us and go after him. Like you said, we don't really have anything yet. And they've got Clarence."

Tex told him, "We can do it without getting caught."

He looked at us, his expression even more serious than before. "You better not get caught. This cat won't mess around. If he catches you, he'll kill you."

CHAPTER 90

Mom was ironing in the kitchen. "You're in a little earlier than usual," she said. "It's not even dark yet."

"I know."

"You hungry?"

"Nope."

I sat at the kitchen table and stared out the window.

She set the iron upright on the board. "You okay?"

Besides fretting over a killer in our neighborhood, she worried about how I would respond to what happened to Will. She didn't push me, yet stayed very aware of my moods and actions. We had talked several times about how I felt and what I was thinking, and it was good to share what I could with her. Sitting at the kitchen table that evening, however, I didn't think I should share what was consuming my thoughts, since they involved me committing a crime, felony or otherwise.

I looked at her. "Yeah. I'm okay."

She picked up the iron, started pressing her white blouse, the one she had on the night of the Mickey Cook incident. One thing about the horrific act perpetrated upon Will, it distracted Mom from the horror she had recently lived through.

She had not yet shared the ordeal with her family for reasons of having to relive bad history. She would tell them someday. Yet she had faced the Hobbs family with the truth of her Deplorable Indiscretion, and asked for forgiveness. Grandma and Grandpa told her it was nonsense to blame herself for any of what happened, and they loved and hugged her until she understood they meant what they said.

Still, Mickey Cook and Will's murder brought new energy to the innate, Mother's Worry. She wasn't a frightened mess by any means, just finely tuned to everything happening around us.

"Someday this will all be over, Jack. Then things will get back to normal, or close as they can."

"Yeah."

"I know you hate early curfew and not being able to ride and play like you did before. But you will again, just give it time."

350

Light at the Rat Pond

"Just started on the hard road."

"I know."

"I guess going to bed early is helping me get ready for school when it starts. Hooray."

She smiled.

Actually, I was going to use going to bed early to facilitate the break-in plan hatching in my brain.

The phone rang, so Mom rested the iron and answered it. "Hello? Yes he is. Just a moment please." She pointed the phone at me and mouthed. "Louis Corben."

"Hello?"

"Hi, Jack, it's Louis Corben." The sound of a southern drawl had been in my ear almost everyday since May, though it had been absent the last several days. Now it was back. "Hi, Mr. Corben."

"You doing okay, Jack?"

"Yeah, sort of."

"I understand. Listen, we were wondering if you'd like to go with us to church this Sunday? We'd sure love to have you with us."

Like son, like father. I didn't have the heart to tell him, like mom, like son, I had begun to harbor a slight grudge against God. "Sure, okay. I'll go."

"Terrific, Jack." A subtle joy resided in his voice, something unexpected from a father who had just lost a son. "We'll pick you up at the same time as usual, okay?"

"Yes, sir."

It was hot in the house; I couldn't sleep. I would come up with a good break-in plan, discover a fault, then start over again. Anxiety about the coming Saturday night's crime began to cling to me like the humidity. Finally, at ten till two that morning, I had a solid, but not perfect, plan. No matter what, there was risk, and if Tex came up with a better plan, I would follow it. I rehearsed the unlawful act in my mind one more time before putting it aside.

I still couldn't sleep.

So I did something I'd never done before: I got up, knelt beside my bed and prayed.

"Dear, God. This is Jack Hobbs - but you already know that, I guess. Will said You know everything. So I guess You know I'm - uh - sorta . . . mad at You. That's probably not a right way to start things, but . . . I can't lie, can I? You'd know if I was lying, right? Will said You know everything from the beginning to the end, and more. I gotta say, I don't get that, but

Richard Newberry

if Will was right, You already knew I didn't get it. This is confusing to me. How the heck - oops, sorry. Is heck a cuss word? Shouldn't cuss while I'm praying. What I was gonna say was how in the world do people talk to You, since You already know everything? Seems kinda . . . I don't know, weird, maybe. And I'm not sure if me being a little mad at You is good for me. You probably don't usually have people tell You they're mad at You. Maybe You do. Who knows - besides You? I sound like an idiot, don't I? Sorry about that. I'm new - but You already . . . ah, forget it.

"I'm mad because of what happened to Will. I know he said good stuff can come from bad stuff, but he was such a good kid, God. Why did You let this happen? Why not do something to this creep, or Cus or some other bad person?

"He really loved You, as You know. I guess he's there with You right now, right? I hope so. He sure believed it. But You have a bunch of good people with you already. Doesn't seem fair to me. But I know Will wanted to please You more than anyone. He said he was just passin' through here, doing what he thought You wanted. Man, he really believed. Oh - sorry - I wasn't calling You man, it just . . . well You know.

"So I had to tell You - even though You already knew - I'm confused and mad and I want revenge. Will told me it's Your place to get revenge. But crud, I don't want - ah, man - I mean - is crud bad? I don't think so, but I won't say it again here. I promise. But I don't want to wait for Your revenge, 'cause Will said You're loving and good and forgiving and have a lot of that grace - I'm not sure I understand that yet - but I don't want You forgiving the guy that killed Will. He doesn't deserve it."

When those last words came out of my mouth, I suddenly remembered the words from the Bible, in John, that we had read to the hobos. And I remembered other things Will had told me about Jesus and His sacrifice for all mankind; that's why Will wore the crucifix, to remind him of the sin debt that Jesus paid on the cross, for all that would believe.

"If we got what we deserve, Yank, we'd all end up in hell. Just remember John 3:16, okay? He loves you, Yank. He loves you."

My attitude became contrite as God's Word and Will's life resonated within me. "I'm sorry. I'm wrong. I know that."

I thought back to the times at church with Will and his family as Pastor Rogers preached and I felt a strange, loving pull on my heart, yet I remained in my seat. "I've said no to You a couple of times, haven't I?"

I half-expected a booming "Yes!" to fill my room, but it was silent.

"Don't give up on me, please."

Light at the Rat Pond

Will said He wouldn't.

"One more thing, God. You know what I'm planning. And in a way it's wrong, but I'm trying to do what's right by doing it. I don't know how You feel about it, but if You're on my side, would You please help me find Will's crucifix if it's in there? And if it's in there, please get Your revenge."

CHAPTER 91

Saturday evening in the garage, Dwight said, "If you do find the crucifix in there you can't take it. You have to leave it for the cops to find somehow."

Tex and I nodded.

"Man, I still can't believe it might be him. What if somebody else threw that magazine in his garbage can?"

Tex said, "If somebody did, Dwight, then the crucifix won't be in his house and if we get caught we won't get killed."

"I can't believe it could be him either," I said. "But you and Will both said people aren't always who they pretend to be."

He nodded. "True. But keep in mind who got us thinkin' it might be somebody around here. I still don't trust Cus."

Early Thursday morning, the morning I prayed, a raucous storm blew through Doverville and shoved the heat and humidity east, leaving behind a fall-like coolness. People who had air conditioning turned it off and opened their windows to welcome in fresh, crisp air. That made our Saturday night task a little easier.

Tex and I met in the alley behind her house at nine thirty. We were in bed by nine the previous two nights to aid our nine thirty escape.

"Scared?" she asked, keeping her voice low.

"Nah - yeah, I am."

"Should be. But it's exciting, isn't it?"

"Scary exciting."

She smiled. "Let's go."

In jeans and dark T-shirts, we swiftly snuck along the alley to our destination. The house was dark; no car in the driveway. We moved quickly to the side of the house. A dog across the tracks barked. We watched and listened. We were sure the people in the house next to us would not hear us. We covered the lenses and checked our flashlights.

I looked up at the small window where we would sneak in; a screen was in it. I whispered, "We only have about a half hour."

Light at the Rat Pond

"I know."

We had decided to narrow our search to bedrooms and the basement; Tex had the bedrooms, I would look in the basement.

Crouching against the house in the dark, I looked at her. She had her blonde hair tied back with a rubber band. Her face showed no sign of fear; it was alive with anticipation, excitement. Maybe for the first time, I realized Sandra "Tex" Wonderlin was a pretty girl. Very pretty.

She whispered, "Why are you staring at me?"

"I wasn't. I - uh - just started wondering if I should do this alone. I don't want anything to happen to you."

"Don't worry about me. I'll probably have to save your butt."

"Hope not."

A car appeared in the alley. We dropped to the ground as the car rolled west.

"We gotta do this now," she said.

"Right."

I looked up at the screened window. My heart sank and I said, "Oh, crud."

"What's wrong?"

"Something I didn't think about."

"What?"

"If I boost you up to the window, how do I get in?"

She looked up, then at me. "You're right. But I can let you in the back door."

"Don't want to take that chance."

"Nobody will see."

"Oh, crud," I said and pushed her down with me to the cool grass.

"What are you doing?"

I whispered, "Somebody's in the alley. And they're looking right at us."

We hugged the ground, didn't move. My heart thumped in my chest.

Tex raised up, then waved the person our way.

"What are you doing?!"

"It's Dwight, doofus."

Our big friend slipped into the backyard and joined us at the side of the house. He whispered, "I got to thinking you'd need help getting up to that window."

Tex, looking at me, said to Dwight, "Glad *you* were thinking."

Dwight got on his hands and knees and made a platform with his back. I pushed up the window, took out the screen and slid it to the bathtub below. I shimmied in head first, then turned to land on my feet. Tex did the same. A fast exit would be near impossible.

355

Richard Newberry

Dwight lumbered away; he would be waiting for us in the brush above the tracks.

We switched on our lights.

"Ready?" I asked.

"Born ready, Jack."

Tex headed for the bedrooms and I looked for the basement door. If we had time, we would check closets outside of the bedrooms last. I glanced at my watch: we maybe had twenty minutes.

I found the basement's entrance, and pointed my light at the thick gray, wooden steps; they made no sound as I walked down them. I could hear Tex's hurried steps above me.

I scanned my light over the wide-open space. I saw a washer and dryer, furnace, hot water heater, Ping-Pong table and an old leather chair. A workbench, tidy like the rest of the basement, stood against the wall next to a large, drawer-filled toolbox. Two metal cabinets stood against the wall opposite the workbench. I started with the cabinets.

The shelves were neat and organized; easy to search. Nothing.

Tex was busy upstairs. I chose the drawers of the toolbox next. He kept his tools clean and orderly. I imagined he never had to dig around for the tool he needed; it would be exactly where it was suppose to be. The toolbox took longer to search than the cabinets, and I didn't find the crucifix. I hoped that very soon I'd hear Tex exclaim she'd found it. I shined the light on my old Timex. It was five minutes until ten.

"Crud."

I looked through every jar of nuts and bolts and connectors sitting on the long, wood shelf above the workbench. Nothing.

Ten o'clock.

I told myself not to worry about getting trapped in the basement. I had to be fast but thorough. I found nothing in the old leather chair or around the furnace. There wasn't really anything else to look through in the uncluttered basement. I decided to run the light over the large room one more time before going up to help Tex.

The only part of the basement with any finish work was the wall where the workbench and toolbox were. Somebody had framed a narrow wall out from the concrete and covered it with dark paneling all the way up to the exposed floor joists. They'd done a good job, but in my heightened state of suspicion, I wondered if it was there to cover something.

I shined the light at the big casters on the toolbox. Maybe?

I unlocked the casters and started rolling the heavy box away from the wall at an angle. I needed just enough room to look behind it. I fixed the light on

356

Light at the Rat Pond

the now exposed paneling; I moved the light up and down, back and forth – then stopped. I felt the cool board where the light stopped. There was a seam. I traced it until I could no longer reach it. A hidden door.

A mélange of excitement, fear and anxiety coalesced into robust energy as I frantically searched for a way to open the concealed door. No latch, no knob, no nothing.

"Crud!"

Then I pushed on it, and it opened outward. "What the –?"

It was a small window-less room, about the size of a big walk-in closet, one Mom would love. Maybe a sealed off coal room. I moved the light around. There was a tan, wing-backed chair, a record player with Frank Sinatra records near it on a small, round table; a lamp and clear glass ashtray sat on the table. The confined room smelled of cigarettes and alcohol.

I shouted, "Tex!"

On each side, there were two, wide, plywood shelves, about six feet long. Cardboard boxes filled the four shelves. I switched on the lamp.

I shouted, "Tex!" again before realizing the confined space smothered my voice.

I pulled a box from a bottom shelf. Magazines. Nasty ones like we had found at the Rat Pond. I pulled out another box. More of the same. The next box held a film projector, and the two boxes next to it had reels of film. I pulled a box from the other side. Inside it was a dark wooden box with a howling wolf engraved in its top. I lifted the hinged lid.

The large knife was in a black leather sheath.

I turned, thought I heard Tex's voice, and stepped toward the door. "Tex?" No answer. Hearing things.

I set the cardboard box on the table and took the knife from its red velvet bed. The slightly curved handle was made from some kind of ridged bone. I pulled it out of the sheath. Just the sight of the eight-inch blade scared me; it made Cus's switchblade look innocent.

The top edge of the blade had serrated, menacing teeth; the bottom edge was razor-sharp. The weapon was what the kid had called *The Enforcer*. I quickly put it away.

I turned again, thought I heard Tex. I wasn't mistaken this time. From the top of the basement steps, she shouted, "Go! Go! Car's here! Go, Jack!"

"Just a second!"

"No. Now!"

I pulled another box. More magazines.

"Jack! Now!"

357

Richard Newberry

The next box had boys' and girls' underwear in it, and beneath them was a cigar box.

"Hobbs! Get out now! I'm gone!"

The cigar box held various items: marbles, a pink metal barrette, a bracelet, Bazooka Bubblegum . . . and Will's crucifix.

I wanted to take it to show the world this guy killed Will, but knew I couldn't. I hurriedly put things back, clicked off the light. Rolling the huge toolbox back in place, I heard a car door shut. No time to lock the casters. I raced for the steps.

Just as I got out of the basement, porch light poured into the living room as the door was opened. Lights came on. I couldn't make it to the bathroom to escape. I scrambled to the closest closet and stuffed myself inside.

CHAPTER 92

I tried to contain the fear rattling me; I had to think. I was stuffed in a coat closet near the basement entrance. The bathroom we'd used to come into the house was off the dining room. How in the world could I make it across the room and into and out of the bathroom without getting caught?

Impossible.

The spooky knife hidden in the basement scared me. Would it be used on me? Suddenly, I felt as if I were suffocating in the dark closet.

Fight the fear! Concentrate. Think about what happened to Will. Put this creep in jail!

I could breathe again.

She said, "I'm going to bed and read."

He said, "Be right there. Gotta hit the bathroom first."

Not good. There was no way Tex could've put the screen back in the window, and she would've left it out for me. He was going to find it, and know, and start looking. Panic and fear tried to beat my heart out of my chest.

But his steps didn't go the way I expected. There was another bathroom!

I heard him come out, then the dining room light vanished from underneath the closet door. He headed in the direction of the bedroom, but his steps ceased as he muttered something about bowling balls.

The closet's wood floor was empty. Were they stored where I hid?

His steps said he was coming to the closet.

No! No! No!

I gripped the door knob, leaned back with all my weight; too scared to cry. I began to worry about Mom. What would happen to her with me dead?

I heard a slight thump as he set the balls on the carpet outside the door.

Doorbell.

He muttered, "What the -?"

Doorbell again, then pounding on the entrance door.

He walked away, saying, "Hold your horses."

I cracked open the door. The dining room was dark; I saw him turn the corner to answer the door.

My chance - and I took it.

I bolted from the closet, tripped over a bowling bag, but stumbled on

359

Richard Newberry

toward the bathroom and the open window to make my escape. I surprised myself with the swiftness and agility that accompanied my acrobatic exit. I landed hands first on the cool grass and tumbled safely into the neighbor's hedge. Exhilarated, I got to my feet and dashed to where I hoped Tex and Dwight were waiting.

It hit me as I ran for the tracks, had ding-dong-ditch saved my life?

I spotted them near the brush off the south rail. In a hushed voice, Tex said, "Jack! Over here."

I was so glad to see them that when I got to them I wanted to give big hugs.

Tex said, "You're an idiot. You know that, Jack? Huh? I said go and you didn't. And I know you heard me. You are a stupid, stupid idiot."

Still shaking from what just happened, I took the scolding, understanding my friend had been frightened for me, and that she cared deeply. "I should punch your face." More deep care.

"I'm sorry. I really am. But I needed a few more seconds."

"That was more than seconds, Hobbs," she said, cooling down a bit.

"I found it."

Dwight said, "You did? You found Will's crucifix?"

I nodded toward the house we stood below. "It's in there."

Tex said, "That sicko."

I told them about the hidden room and its contents.

"Sick freak," said Tex.

Dwight wagged his head. "Man, you just never know."

A car blaring rock music cruised by behind us up on Warren.

He asked, "You think she knows?"

Tex said, "How can she not?"

Dwight and I shrugged.

Dwight said, "Now we gotta figure out how to get the cops in there."

"I know," I said.

"Any ideas?" asked Tex.

We had none.

I said, "Who did ding-dong-ditch?"

"Me," said Tex. "Told you I'd have to save your butt, buddy boy."

"You sure did. Thanks."

"You're welcome."

They wanted details on my escape. I stopped in the middle of my telling, dread filling me. "Oh, crud."

"What?" asked Dwight.

"The bathroom screen. I didn't even think about trying to put it back in.

360

Light at the Rat Pond

He's gonna know somebody's been in there. Plus I didn't get to lock the wheels on the toolbox"

We looked up at the house.

I said, "Let's move down," and we ran to a spot below the garage.

"If you would've come out when I told you to we could have put the screen back."

"I couldn't, Tex. I just started finding stuff. I told you that. Maybe he'll think the wind blew the screen out of the window."

"Not a chance," she said.

"Cat would be suspicious even if the wind did do it," said Dwight. "He's livin' in secrets, man."

Tex, looking a different kind of scared than if a bee was after her, said, "We're gonna have a sicko murderer after us."

I said, "How's he gonna know it was us?"

"I don't know. Fingerprints or something." Tex being scared increased my fear.

Dwight said, "He's not gonna have stuff to check for fingerprints. So don't worry about him thinking it was us. There are real burglars around, you know."

"He's right," I said.

Tex said, "You're the one who said he'd be suspicious."

"He will be. That means we have to figure out something really fast, 'cause he might start ditchin' evidence."

Justice suddenly seemed imperiled.

An idling train at the switchyard sounded its horn and its bright white light started our way.

An encouraging thought came to me. "Listen. He's probably not gonna notice the screen being out tonight. He already used another bathroom and was going to bed. We've got a little time."

I saw Tex get an idea. "Hey! I got it! We set his house on fire, then the firemen, and probably the police, would go in and find the evidence. It could work."

"I don't know," I said.

"Might burn up the evidence," said Dwight.

"I didn't say burn the house down. Just start a small fire, big enough to get the cops and firemen there."

Doubting our skills as pinpoint arsonists, I said, "Which one of us is good enough to do that?"

She said, "You know how to mix fuel for a good fire."

"Yeah, but . . ."

361

Richard Newberry

Dwight said, "Let's save that idea in case we can't come up with anything else."

Tex said, "One night to figure out how to get the cops in there."

"Yeah, but it's better than no time."

Dwight agreed. "We need to get out of here and go home. Think of everything you can and we'll meet at the garage early tomorrow."

I had forgotten about going with the Corbens. "Right after lunch."

They nodded, and Tex said, "Still got my fire idea."

"Maybe. We'll figure out something," I said. "We're the Icks, and it's for Will."

And as I crawled through my bedroom window I decided to do what Will would have done.

CHAPTER 93

I knew better than even attempt sleeping. It was as far from me as the moon. I laid in bed, under the covers because of the cool night air. Every so often I could hear some noise from Sid's, but most of the tavern's Saturday night sound was blown away by the strong northwest breeze.

Like Will would have done, before I got in bed I prayed, asked God to help us figure out a way to nail the murderer, and also thanked Him for my escape.

Will had been in my life for only about three months, yet he left an indelible impact on me, the Icks and Mom, and I was sure on anybody who got to know him at all - including Cus. So many lives were lived in a self-centered bubble, lives that spanned several decades would end without a vestige of an altruistic existence. During Will's brief adventure in our world, he had sown seeds that would produce an abundant harvest for many years. I still questioned God for His motives in allowing Will's death, and wondered how much more he would have done given more time. Yet, in my bed that night, I started to get an inkling of what and why God had allowed what He did.

My mind drifted to the first time I met Will at school, his foreign southern drawl, the first race he won at the Rat Pond, the great game at Harper's Field, trying to bond with Shorty and his daring attempts at befriending Cus. The Bible studies with the hobos, and the morning we saw him waving and smiling at us from the passing boxcar . . . I smiled and wiped the tears from my face.

I heard a noise right outside my window, turned to see a giant head with bulging, wide eyes staring at me. I gasped in fear until I realized who it was. "Arlie?"

In a quiet voice with rapid words, the wide-eyed hobo said, "Hi, Jack. Clarence didn't do it so you gotta help him because I saw who did and wasn't Clarence killed Will. You gotta help, Jack. Please."

Stunned at his presence and the fact that I'd never heard him speak before, it took me a second to comprehend what he'd said. "What - you saw?" I went to the window.

"Yes I saw. I did. I saw Clarence didn't do it and I know who did so you gotta help him. I saw who did put Will on the train, Jack. Not Clarence. I want to show you."

363

Richard Newberry

Arlie carried his usual bodily stench, but I smelled no alcohol on his breath. "You saw who did it? You know where he is?"

"Yes. Yes. I saw who it is. It's not Clarence, Jack. Let me show you, okay? Please?"

"You can show me now?"

"Please? Now. Okay?"

Months earlier I would have never crawled out of my window in the middle of the night to go looking for a killer with the huge, smelly hobo. But I had, thanks to Will, gotten to know Arlie. I got dressed, and, with anxiety but no fear, crawled out of my window. "Show me."

He started lumbering west on the alley, and I knew exactly where he was taking me. I said, "Let's cut down to the tracks and sneak in."

"Good idea, Jack, gotta be quiet so can be sneakin'." He ran off the alley and into the thick, thorny brush, not hindered by the lack of a path; I followed in his wake.

We stopped running below the house Tex and I had broken into earlier. Now Arlie's words were slower, more deliberate. "It's him. He done it. I saw him push the pretty bike down the hill. I saw him put Will on the train." Tears flowed out of his wide eyes and streaked his stubbled face.

"It's okay, Arlie. We're gonna get him. You saw."

His eyes narrowed. "It's not okay, Jack. Clarence is in jail. Will is dead."

"I know, but you and me are going to tell the police, okay? We're gonna get him."

He stared at the house. "I will kill him."

"No, no, no. Not that. You'll just get in trouble." I hoped like crazy he wasn't dead set upon revenge, because me trying to prevent it would be like a flea trying to stop a charging rhino. "We're gonna get him. We're gonna call the police and you're going to tell them what you saw. Okay? My mom will help."

His hands were squeezed into big fists.

"We'll get Clarence out of jail, Arlie. We will. I promise. And that guy will go to jail. But we have to do it right. We have to go call the police."

"The police took Clarence. They think he did it."

"That's right, but now you'll save him, Arlie. You'll tell the truth to the police and you'll get Clarence out of jail and they'll put Will's real killer in jail."

"Will they believe me?"

"Yes they will. And I'm going to help them believe you. I promise."

He said, looking at the house, "I want to kill him," yet now he seemed less determined.

I didn't tell him I felt like helping him do just that. "Come on. Let's go tell my mom."

"Okay."

Before we ran to Mom, I looked at the dark house where I had enjoyed the smell of honeysuckle, and where Dwight and I had sold our raspberries and even some colorful rocks. I thought about the smiles and waves and kind words that came so many times from that inviting backyard. And as I looked, much of my youthful innocence was forever lost; stolen by a man in a mask.

Mom's eyes grew to the size of Arlie's when I shook her out of her sleep and she saw the big man standing in her bedroom. "Jack? What's going - who is that?"

Arlie turned his large head away and looked at the floor.

"It's okay," I said. "This is Arlie. He's Clarence's friend."

She sat up and pulled the covers to her neck. "Who is - oh, yes."

I nodded.

"So what's wrong?"

I started with the story Cus told me at the funeral home. She listened, but her eyes moved between mine and Arlie's, who had stuck himself in a corner. When I got to the part about finding the magazine in the burn barrel and what we decided to do she no longer cared about Arlie's large, but timid presence.

"You broke into their house?! What were you thinking, Jack?"

"I had to, Mom."

I then told her what I had found in the basement. Now her eyes drifted to focus on something invisible as she slowly wagged her head, disbelieving and stunned. She looked back at me and said, "I have to get dressed. You two get out and I'll hear the rest of this in the kitchen."

She started a pot of coffee, muttering, "This can't be. This can't be."

Arlie refused to sit; he stood again in a corner. I said, "Tell Mom what you saw."

She looked at him and he got the same wide-eyed nervous look he had the day Kenny and I first met him with Will, at the Bible reading.

"It's okay, Arlie. Just tell her what you saw. Tell her, and talk slow."

He looked like an enormous kid who'd been sent to the corner and now had to confess his bad deed. He looked up at Mom, but quickly tossed his eyes back to the linoleum.

She said, "It's okay, Arlie. You can tell me."

His head still lowered, he rolled his eyes to see her and she smiled at him. He slowly raised his head, started telling what he'd seen. His voice was low and his words too fast.

"Slower, Arlie," I said. "Okay? Like before."

Richard Newberry

"Okay, Jack," and he told Mom what he'd witnessed.

"It's just so hard to believe," she said, pouring more coffee.

"But it's all true, Mom. We have to call the police."

She did, and asked if they would contact Detective Gus Calton.

An hour later, Detective Calton sat in our kitchen while two police officers waited outside.

He smiled at Mom as she poured him a cup of coffee; she returned the smile. Just what were my eyes seeing between them?

"Okay, Jack . . . and Arlie. Tell me what you know."

CHAPTER 94

He made several notes during our tellings, and when we finished, he said to me, "I'm going to pretend I know nothing about your reconnaissance mission."

Detective Calton had a search warrant in less than two hours. The next morning, the detective returned to our kitchen and told Mom and I what had happened after he left last night.

Shortly after he and the police knocked on their door and began their search, Lilly Gordon broke under the pressure despite Van screaming at her to, "Shut your mouth!" She confessed what she knew and suspected about her husband's despicable and disgusting crimes. She didn't, however, think he was capable of murder, but Will's crucifix proved otherwise.

At the police station, Lilly told Detective Calton what she knew about the night Will Corben's bike was found at the Rat Pond. A few days before that night she had come home from grocery shopping and found Van and Will in the kitchen drinking lemonade. Will had been helping Van with some yard work, but she noticed right away that Will looked uncomfortable, or out of sorts. She wondered then what Van had said or done to the boy, but she said and did nothing about it; like always, she pretended nothing was wrong.

The night of his murder, Will had knocked on their back door and asked for Mr. Gordon. She could tell Will was agitated by something, but she didn't ask. She heard them exchange heated words on the back porch; she didn't want to know, and hid in the bedroom. She later heard strange sounds in the basement, but chose again to ignore whatever was going on. Lilly served a short sentence in a prison south of Doverville.

We learned from the newspaper and Nadine that no other murders were linked to Van Gordon's insidious behavior; only Will's.

"Bad thing is," Dwight said, "the things he did to all those other kids, in a way probably killed them."

The Icks felt sorry for another victim we'd known: Van's own nephew, Mikey.

Van denied everything. He died in prison. A vengeful inmate stabbed him thirty times.

367

CHAPTER 95

I knew, on this earth, it was the most important thing I would ever do.

Was it because He called me? Was it because of Will Corben's life? His death?

Yes.

Mom, sitting next to Ruth Corben, watched me slip out of the cushioned pew and go forward.

School started, and the neighborhood began to settle into an after-the-time-of-Will routine. The Icks were set free to ride again and race at the Rat Pond; Clarence and Arlie eventually came back to Hoboland.

Kenny's neighbor Donnie was still in the candidacy stage of becoming an Ick. One day in the garage he noticed a bike in the corner, suspended from the rafters. "Is that Will's cruiser?"

Kenny said, "Yep," and added, "'For the tree is known by its fruit'."

And after a Rat Pond race one late evening, Donnie pointed to a place just above the murky water. "Look! Man! It's a big rat!"

Dwight said, "Isn't what you think."

"It's a possum," said Tex.

"For real?"

We nodded.

The Icks' appetite for danger and adventure would be satiated in the coming months. Sticks made his presence felt, Shorty vanished and had we known what awaited us on some of our trips to the Tall Trees River . . . we might have stayed home.

Mom informed me of the upcoming kitchen remodeling on our way to Kickapoo's open house. She also informed me on our way back from the open house that she wasn't blind and could see what I was trying to do with her and my new sixth grade teacher, Mr. Gritton.

"What?" I said, and she gave me the doofus look.

Funny how Mom would go from no men in her life to two; that's a story for another time.

Light at the Rat Pond

As for me, I had begun the journey of a new life. Will had brought a bright light to our world, and it was my turn to be one of the bearers of that light. I hoped I could follow his example.

A test of the genuineness of my new life came the first Saturday morning after school started, while we were racing at the Rat Pond. And I did what I told Mom months earlier I wouldn't do.

A lone rider stopped on the alley above the track and tried to stay hidden behind the horse weed and brush. He waited and watched.

I knew who it was, and shouted, "Hey! You wanna come down and race with us?"

He hesitated.

"Come on! You're not sissy are you?"

That made him move. And my amazed friends watched as the invited, lone rider raced down the hill and joined the Icks.

Not yet the end.

CPSIA information can be obtained at www.ICGtesting.com
Printed in the USA
LVOW07s1814050515

437311LV00003B/694/P